Static... barely audible began to make itself heard through the noise.

"... dark ... so cold ... going to hurt me ..."

"Who is this?" she asked.

"Alice," the child's voice said. "Don't want to go back."

"Alice, can you tell me where you are?"

"Help me ..."

"I want to ..."

"Da hurt ... Da hurt ... Da kill!"

The static was getting louder now.

"Da come! Oh, no!"

The terror in her voice shook up everyone in the studio.

Through the static Rena hears a door slamming, footsteps, furniture overturning and Alice screaming....

THE VIOLET CLOSET

Gary Gottesfeld

FAWCETT GOLD MEDAL · NEW YORK

A Fawcett Gold Medal Book
Published by Ballantine Books
Copyright © 1989 by Gary Gottesfeld

All rights reserved under International and Pan-American Copyright Conventions. Published in the United States by Ballantine Books, a division of Random House, Inc., New York, and simultaneously in Canada by Random House of Canada Limited, Toronto.

Library of Congress Catalog Card Number: 89-91306

ISBN 0-449-14570-0

Manufactured in the United States of America

First Edition: November 1989

In memory of Adele Malkin

My thanks to psychologists James A. Lough, Ph.D., Judith Todd, Ph.D., Lea Witemberg Engle, M.A., and especially Steven Franklin for his expertise and assistance.

Book I

May 28–29

Prologue

Monday, 4:35 A.M.

The hot sun felt good beating down on Rena's city white skin. So did the cool plastic raft that gently swayed under her tired body. Her fingers hung over the sides and lazily floated over the top of the turquoise water.

She lifted her head and tried to make out the shoreline, but the glare of the sun bleached everything beyond recognition. The sky was linen white and without clouds.

Putting her hand up to her forehead to block out the glare, she looked for boats on the horizon. There were none, nor were there ernes or any other seabirds that normally hugged the coastal waters. She then listened for human voices. Again nothing, only the rhythmic sound of the tide splashing on the raft.

The nothingness was more peaceful than anything she had ever experienced before. She lay her head back down and let the serenity of this deserted place envelop her in a white shroud.

A gentle breeze started blowing, sending a tingling sensation up her calf. The feeling then began working its way up her inner thigh.

Slowly, as if in a trance, she looked up. A young man, probably just out of his teens, was quietly lifting himself out of the water and onto the raft. He sat down next to her, making slow circular motions down her arm with his fingers. The water from his hard, wet body dripped on her stomach, causing spasms to shoot through her groin.

She felt no fear of this boy. She wanted to say something to him, but he leaned over her—his body blocking out the sun like a solar eclipse—and gently put his hand on her mouth. When she tried to move away, he bent down and kissed her, his tongue tracing her top inner lip. This time she offered no resistance.

With the self-assurance of a man twice his age, the boy quickly removed the bottom half of her bikini and tossed it in the water. He then used his knee to spread her legs apart. Again, there was no resistance.

Rena moaned as he entered her. He made no thrusting motions, letting the waves under the raft do the work for them. She dug her nails into his muscular back, never believing this kind of completeness could exist with any man, let alone a stranger. They were like Fred Astaire and Ginger Rogers—never a false step, every move in perfect rhythm like synchronized swimmers.

The sky darkened, the wind picked up, and the waves began to strike the raft harder. Rena locked her legs around the boy, grabbing him by his thick curly hair and biting into his shoulder. He cried out with a mixture of pain and pleasure. The rain came, gently at first, then in a violent downpour, causing a newer, more euphoric sensation.

Nothing in her life had prepared her for these feelings; neither her sexual relationship with Terry nor her liaisons with other men.

She felt they were like two comets fused together, orbiting the envelope of space for eternity.

The sound of ringing in the distance.

Go away, go away!

It became louder, more persistent.

The boy's body began to dissolve.

No, no, no! Come back!

She tried holding him tighter, but he was breaking up and blowing away like cigarette smoke in the wind.

Wait! Please! It's been so long!

The sea began fading, then the shoreline.

There was no going back. Rena gave in, opened her eyes and picked up the phone. "Hello," she said, clearing the sleep from her throat. With her other hand she turned on the night-light next to her bed. The sun would not come up for at least another hour.

"Woke you, huh?" It was Stacey, Rena's assistant.

"Boy, does your timing suck."

"You with a guy?"

"Better than that."

"One of *those* dreams, huh? Sorry. They sure can be better than the real thing sometimes, can't they? You did ask me to make sure you're awake."

"I know, thanks," Rena said, pushing the covers off and sitting up. "Let's hope our little friend doesn't oversleep."

"I doubt it. She's been on time every night this week. Honestly, Ree, I don't know why you just don't call the police. There are too many idiots floating around out there, and they're drawn to high-profile personalities. You know that. I mean you should, you're a shrink. Look what happened to Indira Ghandi." Stacey, working on her degree in psychology at UCLA, had a tendency to mother her.

"Where's Ben?" Rena asked, wanting to change the subject.

"Asleep, where all sane people are at four-thirty in the morning. Do me a favor, call me when you hear from her, okay?"

After hanging up, Rena went to the bathroom, quietly, so as not to wake her daughter, Cathy, and doused her face with cold water. She then went into the kitchen and perked extra-strong coffee, staring at the wall clock every few seconds.

Two more minutes. Rena knew the phone would ring on time. Her mouth was dry from nervousness.

When the coffee finished brewing, she poured herself a mug, took it into the bedroom, and sat down on the sofa to wait.

At exactly 4:50 the phone rang.

Rena went over to the desk and turned on a Sony phone recorder that she had borrowed from an engineer at the radio station.

As she picked up the receiver, she thought, All right my little darling, this time I'm ready for you. Talk to me.

Rena knew there would be no surprises. The dialogue would be the same as it had been for the past five nights, with few variations. If Rena pushed too hard, the girl would hang up.

"Yes," Rena said, steadying her voice. "It's you, isn't it, Alice?" There was static on the line, just as there was the times before.

"Yes," a shy little girl's voice answered after a few seconds.

"Is your daddy not there?"

"Da not here. Help me." The slow staccato voice was still there.

"And your name?" Rena knew it was Alice from past conversations, but the script had to be followed.

"Alice. Dark . . . so cold. Da hurt me."

"I won't let your daddy hurt you, I promise. Just tell me where you live and I'll come get you."

"Hobby . . . hobby," she said, after a pause.

That's not in the scenario, something's changing, Rena thought, not letting her hopes get too high. "What's a hobby, Alice?"

"No go back. No more wally! Wally hurt! Da hurt!"

She's starting to panic, something she never did before. "Do you know your address, phone number? Alice, please give me something to help you. Do you know your last name?"

She was now hysterical. "No kill, Da! Please, no kill! I go now," she said, breathing hard.

"Will you call me again?" Rena asked.

"Yes," Alice said.

"Alice, please listen to me. Try to find out your address."

The line went dead.

Different this time. She never used the word "kill" before. And what's hobby? Rena thought as she dialed Stacey's number. The pattern was changing, getting more intense.

"Well?" Stacey said.

"Well, I think you're right. I'm calling the police," Rena said as she unplugged the recording device from the receiver.

"Good for you. What we don't need is one more nut case running around L.A."

"Except I'm not reporting it as a crank call. I'm telling them that there's a strong possibility that a young child is out there and in extreme danger."

"How would she get your home number? You're not listed," Stacey said, stifling a yawn.

"I don't know. Her voice . . . the hyperventilation . . . it's just too sophisticated for a little girl to invent."

They would see each other at work and talk more. Right now Rena wanted to do some work on today's show and upcoming lecture before going to the station. She would wait until later to call the police and give them the tape. Wait until a decent hour so they wouldn't think she was a crank caller.

There was something more than professionalism making her get up before five in the morning to talk to this child. The terror and helplessness in her voice disturbed her; it pushed buttons that connected deep within her own childhood. Wisps of memories, like pale gray shadows began to filter through her consciousness.

"Please, Mommy. I don't want to go back to that school. They hate me there. The kids tease me and do terrible things to me," Rena said, crying, clutching Elaina Halbrook's white chiffon cocktail dress. She was ten years old then and they were standing next to the electric gates outside the mansion.

"Stop that. You're making a spectacle of yourself," Elaina said crossly. She pushed Rena away and looked toward her guests, who were drinking champagne and orange juice on the veranda, embarrassed that some of them may have been watching. "Look at that, you've ruined my dress." She furiously scrubbed at the dark spots of tears and mucus on her dress with a small lace hankie. "Halbrooks don't act like this. You know better."

"Mommy, it's so far . . . thousands of miles away. Let me go to school here." She was trembling. Her stomach was cramping and she felt the need to go to the bathroom.

Elaina bent down to Rena's level. She could sense her daughter about to grab on to her again, and she put her hands on her small shoulders to keep her at a distance. "It's a wonderful school, Rena. Most children would give their eyeteeth to go there. I went there, your grandmother went there, and her mother before that. That's where you're going to learn the social amenities to get you through life."

Guests standing on the veranda, dressed in white trousers and blue blazers, were waving their hands, motioning for Elaina to join them.

"I have to go, darling. Things will get better at school, I promise you. Anna will accompany you to the airport." Elaina made kissing sounds next to both sides of Rena's face without her lips touching her cheeks, then got up and walked quickly over to her guests.

She watched her mother grab a champagne glass from a tray

and, without once looking back at Rena, usher the people into the house for Sunday brunch.

Tears began to stream uncontrollably down her cheeks, and her body ached from the feelings of rejection and loneliness. Anna, Rena's nanny and confidante, put her arm around her shoulders and gently steered her toward the waiting limousine. Before they got in, Anna straightened out the collar of Rena's school jacket with the gold emblem next to the heart, brushed at her plaid, pleated skirt and wiped the dust off her black patent leather shoes.

As the limo pulled away, Rena looked out the back window and watched her house getting smaller and smaller, until it finally disappeared under a barrage of elm and oak trees.

Rena shook her head, trying to erase the humiliation and fear of so long ago. "Child abuse comes in many forms," she murmured, "and not all of them are physical."

She played Alice's tape. The part about "Da kill" she replayed twice. Then one more time.

"Da kill," Rena said to herself, leaning back in her chair. "Hmm . . . now just who did Daddy kill?"

Chapter 1

Monday, 8:35 A.M.

Rena had just gotten off the phone with the police and the conversation had not gone as she had hoped. She talked to a Detective Gerald W. Jaffe, who suggested, after listening to the tape over the telephone, that it sounded like a child with a sleeping disorder having some fun at her expense. He then asked if she had any children, and how old. When she told him that Cathy would soon be nine, he started chuckling. "Probably one of her schoolmates who might be jealous of her. Happens all the time. If it continues, change your number."

Possible, Rena thought. Except she was so damn believable. Yet what he said made sense. She took her glasses off and rubbed her eyes. Getting up before five the last few nights was beginning to get to her. She could hear Cathy shuffling around in the kitchen getting ready for school. Rena put her notes for her lecture into her briefcase and went into the kitchen.

"Hi, sweetheart," she said to Cathy, who was standing at the counter pouring Cheerios into a bowl.

"Hi, Mom." Cathy turned and gave her a hug. "I'm gonna be late for school, again."

"You're always late for school."

"Be nice to me, Mother. There's a lot of pressure on me now that I'm about to begin my torturous journey into womanhood. I'm going to have to cope with boobs and confused sexual identities." She brought her bowl to the table and sat down.

"You sound prepared," Rena said as she sat next to her.

"Yeah, well, I read your paper on abnormal adolescent behavior, the one you wrote for *Psychology Today*. Terrific stuff,

Ma. Now I know all about what makes me tick," she said with a mouthful of Cheerios. "By the way, when do I get my present to make the trek easier?"

"Not until your birthday, you know that," Rena said, grinning, as she took an apple from the fruit bowl.

Cathy wiped away the milk that was dribbling down her chin. "You going to tell me what it is, or what?"

"Not a shot." She bit into the fruit.

"Aw, come on."

"Your birthday's not for two more weeks. You'll like it, I promise."

"It isn't clothes, is it? I mean, it's not fair getting clothes on an important occasion like this. I'd get that stuff regardless." Concerned, Cathy put her hands on her chin and leaned on the table. "Please just tell me it isn't clothes. I won't ask anything else."

"It isn't clothes. Now can we drop it?"

Cathy let out an audible sigh of relief. "Thank you, Mom, thank you. Dad is still coming to my party, isn't he?" She looked worried.

"He said he was," Rena said, trying not to sound bitter. Terry had broken promises to Cathy in the past. "I'm sure he'll be coming. He's taking you back to Carmel with him the next day."

"Oh God, I can't wait!" she squealed, pulling her hair. "Daddy told me I can ride Silver Dollar. I'm old enough now, you know."

Rena started laughing and shook her head. "Absolutely amazing," she said.

"What is?" Cathy asked seriously.

"One minute you're discussing adolescent theory with me like a doctoral candidate, the next you're carrying on like the little girl that you are."

"I'm allowed," Cathy said defiantly. "I'm going to be nine."

"Yes, you are," Rena said, holding Cathy's face in both hands and kissing her on the cheek. "Now get going or you'll really be late."

"It's okay, Mom," Cathy said as she pushed her cereal bowl aside and grabbed her books. "Everyone's late during the last two weeks of school. There's nothing to do except study for finals. During the study period, all the girls get together and confess about which guys they'd do it with if they were old enough."

"You never told me about any of this," Rena said. "Who's the guy?"

"Oh, yeah." Cathy shrugged nonchalantly. "His name's Roger Harris. He's sort of a nerd. Thick glasses that keep falling down his nose. You know the kind I mean?"

"They're the best kind," Rena said.

"Anyway, he's real cute though, you know. 'Cept the other boys in school tease him 'cause he'd rather cut open frogs than play soccer. Anyway, I got to go."

As Cathy raced to the back door with her books Rena said, "Cathy, I need to ask you something."

"What, Mom?" Cathy asked impatiently.

"Have you given out my private number to anyone?"

"Why would I do that?"

"Just asking. Are any of your girlfriends upset because you like Roger Harris? Jeannie Applebaum, for instance? She was always jealous of you because she had kinky hair and you didn't."

"Give me a break, Ma," Cathy moaned, rolling her eyes. "Ask me that after you see him. I mean Rob Lowe's got nothing to worry about. I gotta go. Good-bye." She rushed out the door hoping she hadn't missed the bus.

The rest of the morning was spent writing the theme for today's talk show. Rena wanted her program to have a different theme each day, and callers would phone in their problems relating to it. Yesterday's was a good one: sexual harassment in the office. The phones rang off the hook.

Today would be child abuse. It was a topic she normally stayed away from; the sponsors didn't like it. Cream rinse is a hard sell when you've spent several minutes talking to someone who was molested as a child. Obviously, this girl Alice, whether she was indulging in a prank or not, had rekindled her interest in the subject.

No, it couldn't possibly have been one of Cathy's friends, Rena concluded. Her telephone number was private, and Cathy understood not to give it out to anyone. If some of her callers got hold of it, it would be an around-the-clock nightmare.

She had to admit that she loved the notoriety and attention

the job offered, but she had to be careful. Many of her callers had deep-seated problems and were fastidiously screened before they were allowed on the air. During the three years she had worked as a talk-show psychologist, she had received numerous threats. Some of the crazies were tracked down by the police and arrested—most weren't, however.

Remember Indira Ghandi, Stacey had told her.

Rena then blocked out everything, including Alice, and concentrated on today's program. It wasn't until an hour before her show, while she was in the shower, that she allowed herself the luxury to dwell upon something other than her work. She closed her eyes and cleared her mind, waiting to see what would evolve. This was a game she played with herself every day at this time. If Rena was anything, she was a creature of habit. Terry's face took shape in her head and her eyes bolted open.

Terry, of all the men in this world. What self-destructive crack in my cast-iron psyche made me fall so completely in love with you?

Emotional pain is strongest in children. And in order to survive, they cope with it in one of three ways: they hate, they withdraw, or they use it as a catalyst for becoming overachievers. Rena fell into that third category.

The house she grew up in was not made for children. Monets, Van Goghs and Rubens' clung to every inch of wall space. Priceless "things" from all over the world that Elaina collected were precisely placed in each room. Couches and chairs from the era of the Sun King were ribboned off and were not allowed to be sat upon except on special occasions. To Rena, it was a museum, not a house. Simon, her father, who was not a fancier of "things," put up with them because of Elaina. It was only the paintings he cared about. Besides, his work kept him away most of the time and he was too involved in building an empire to notice the underlying sadness in his daughter.

Rena was elated to be sent away to private school when she was ten years old. At least there were other children to play with and furniture to sit on and not revere. But that happiness was short-lived; her shyness and plain looks didn't help make her many friends. She was laughed at and shunned openly by her schoolmates. Rena blocked them out and focused on her studies, using the hurt as a stimulant to achieve better marks. She graduated high school as valedictorian.

Four years later she graduated from Stanford, *summa cum laude*. She majored in psychology and planned to go on to Columbia for her masters and doctorate.

She was no longer that shy little girl cowering in the hallways of that big house, afraid of touching anything in case it might break and bring on Elaina's fury. Her successes at school gave her confidence; she developed wit and an outspoken personality.

Her awkward, undeveloped body blossomed into full womanhood by the time she reached eighteen. Men began noticing her and she reacted by taking care of her physical appearance and watching how she dressed. There were a couple of affairs, but her passion was restricted to her work. To be a psychologist, to help ease the pain in others, that was what she wanted more than anything. She was the heir to Simon's millions and she could afford the luxury of altruism.

Simon offered her a vacation in Europe as a reward for her scholastic excellence and she decided upon the Cyclades Islands in Greece. Her intellectual reasoning for choosing the Aegean was the thrill of seeing Delos—the home of Apollo and Artemis—and walking along the steep, volcanic hills of Santorini. But the real reason, the one that her subconscious would not admit to, was that the Cyclades represented a freedom that she only fantasized about in her remotest dreams. It was there that her generation, freed from the restrictive chains of European and American conventionalism, allowed themselves a summer of uninhibited glory.

The most notorious of the islands was Mykonos, and that's where Rena chose to spend the last three weeks of her vacation. And it was there that she met Terry.

It was a hot July day and Paradise Beach was crowded with nude sunbathers. Rena was lying on the rocky sand by herself, reading. A thirty-six-foot sailboat was quietly anchoring near the shore and she put her book down to watch. A lone sailor, tall and slim, with long tanned legs, was pulling in the spinnaker.

How beautiful he is, she thought.

After he neatly folded the sail, he jumped into the Aegean and waded ashore. He was wearing a French bikini that barely covered his middle. As he passed her going to the taverna at the top of the beach, he glanced her way and smiled. By the time her clinical mind weighed the alternatives and decided to return the smile, he was looking in another direction. Sighing, she returned to her book.

That night, as she ate alone at Katerini's restaurant overlooking the sea, the waiter brought an ouzo and water over to her table. She waved her hand and said there must be some mistake. Then she saw the sailor from this morning sitting at the bar smiling at her. He was the one who had bought her the drink. Her heart jumped. He came over to her table and introduced himself, asking if he could join her. She nodded yes.

"Thanks for the drink. I hope you don't mind, but I don't like ouzo."

"Neither do I. It was just a way of getting a reaction from you. I couldn't get one this morning."

"You remembered me?" She was shocked. There were hundreds of women on the beach, many of them prettier than she.

"Sure. You were the only one wearing a bathing suit. If you want to stand out in Mykonos, that's the way to do it."

They laughed.

They talked until two in the morning, drinking retsina and Turkish coffee. He told little about himself, only that he had graduated from a small college north of San Francisco and that he was trying to find a business to get into, preferably something to do with boats. But he was a good listener and he hung on to every word she said. His experienced green eyes studied her face, drawing out her life story. By the time he brought her to his boat that night and made love to her, he knew everything, including the fact that she was the daughter of Simon Halbrook.

They were together constantly for the rest of her vacation. She stayed with Terry on his boat, sailing to the islands of Delos, Syros, and Tinos, walking hand in hand through the ruins.

When it was time to go, they drove in silence to the airport. She stared directly ahead in the jeep, not daring to look at him, afraid that if she did she would break out in tears. Nothing in her short life had ever come close to the happiness of these past two weeks. Nothing.

He held her and kissed her as the small plane was filling up with passengers going to Athens. He said that he would be returning to the States in a month and then they would be together.

"Why not come back now?" she asked.

"Because I want to sail to Turkey. I promised myself that."

Rena nodded sadly. He would not be coming back. At least not for her. Yesterday, while cashing a traveler's check at the American Express, she saw him through the window sitting at a taverna talking with a Dutch girl, their eyes locked together in anticipation.

She was wrong.

Two weeks before she was scheduled to move to New York to attend Columbia, Terry showed up at her door. He looked disheveled and windblown, but he was tanner than when she had last seen him and his green eyes were even more alluring. She leaped up, wrapped her legs around his waist, and kissed him. Laughing, they danced and twirled themselves about the lawn.

Simon watched them from the window upstairs. Seeing Rena happy like this made his heart soar, but there was something about this man he didn't like. Simon had an instinct for picking winners and this young man wasn't one of them.

Instead of going to New York, she moved up to San Francisco with Terry and enrolled at Berkeley. Three months later she became pregnant.

When she told Simon the news over the phone, he wanted to know what their plans were concerning marriage.

"Terry's not ready for that kind of commitment, yet," she said, hesitating. "He thinks I should get an abortion." She tried covering up the hurt but he could hear it in her voice.

"That son of a bitch!" Simon bellowed under his breath. He flew to San Francisco the next day, unannounced, and went to where Terry worked—a custom-sailboat shop in Tiburon.

Terry was slapping the last coat of varnish on the hull when he looked up and saw Simon's large body standing over him. His mouth went dry; he was afraid of this big man. He started to stand up but Simon waved him down.

"This will only take a second," Simon said disdainfully. "What would it take to open up your own business?"

"Uh?"

"That's not an answer."

"You mean a boatmaking shop?"

"Whatever the hell it's called, yes."

Terry brushed his hair back with his fingers, thinking. "I don't know. Maybe a hundred thousand, maybe a little more. Why?"

"Find out precisely. I'll send you a check. Meanwhile, you're going to marry my daughter. Arrangements are already being made in Los Angeles." Simon started to leave.

"Excuse me, sir." Terry said, standing up.

"What is it?" He didn't bother to hide the disgust in his voice.

"Uh . . . this is kind of fast. I mean, marriage is a little rough for me to handle right now. What happens if you give me the money and I get cold feet and back out?"

Simon didn't say anything. He glared at him for a second, then walked out. Terry froze. The look on Simon's face more than answered his question.

They were married at the end of the month on the lawn of Simon's estate. It was a small affair, attended by some close friends and his next-door neighbor, the mayor of Los Angeles.

Six months later Cathy was born.

Rena dropped out of school to become a full-time mother. Her studies would wait. She remembered the loneliness of her own childhood and vowed it would be different for Cathy.

Terry, to Simon's surprise, had a head for business and his catamaran company started to grow. He was away most of the time selling his boats in Hawaii and the Caribbean.

Rena was happy.

Simon waited.

The marriage soon began to fall apart. There were rumors of other women. Terry was coming home less often and, when he did, smelled of sex and alcohol. His excuses for staying out were lame and contradicted each other. If Rena questioned him too much, he would get gruff and tell her to mind her own business. She could feel him slipping away.

When she found him in bed with a friend of hers, she knew it was over. Humiliated, hurt, she took Cathy and moved back to Los Angeles.

She enrolled at USC and threw herself completely into her studies. Books became her friends again, barricading her from the hurt of a failed marriage. Two years later she received her Ph.D. in Clinical Psychology.

She delved into her new profession with a passion, and within a year she had more patients than she could handle. She was thinking about hiring an associate when Simon called and said that Bud Masterly wanted to talk to her. She had known Bud for years. He was the owner of several radio stations and a good friend of her father. Over dinner at Jimmy's, Masterly offered her a job as host of her own talk show.

She laughed. "Come on. I'm a psychologist, not Johnny Carson."

"I'm looking for a psychologist. A lot of people are hurting these days. There's an untapped market for that kind of thing out there."

"Curing neurosis in people can't be achieved in three-minute spots over the radio."

"No, but it could be a start on the right track for many of them. It certainly can't hurt."

The idea was tempting. "Why me?"

"You're good at what you do. Plus, you're beautiful. How many doctors can you say that about?"

"They won't be able to see what I look like over the radio."

"They can hear you, can't they? You have a terrific personality. You should share it with more people. And if it works the way I think it could, then we're all that much better for it."

"You mean richer."

"Same thing."

He was right. Within two years, her program became the top-rated radio talk show in Los Angeles. A best-selling book on self-improvement followed, with another one on the way. As her success grew, the passion for Terry and the pain that came from it faded. Only sometimes, when she allowed herself to be gripped by a sadness buried deep within her, did those feelings rear their ugly heads again.

By the time she finished dressing, she realized it was later than usual. She raced to her Jag and peeled down San Vincente, trying to make up the time. Lateness was something she never tolerated in herself; a little anal-compulsive residue from the past. I owe you for that one Elaina, she thought.

She put a Mozart concerto in the tape deck to calm her nerves and help her concentrate on today's program. But Alice kept popping up inside her head.

Who is she?

"Okay," Rena said out loud, turning up the music, "if this is no ruse, then I have to ask the ol' question again. Who did Daddy kill?"

Chapter 2

Monday, 10:30 A.M.

Charlie opened his eyelids to the roar of a B-52 trapped inside his head.

Gonna be a real bad one. Worse than last week's, his instincts told him.

The bright morning sun hurt his eyes and he closed them, not daring to move, hoping the pain would subside.

It got stronger instead.

Charlie thought about a shoe salesman he had met last week at Peppy's Bar on Wilshire, a tiny guy, with greased hair and long, nicotine-stained fingers. While downing a boilermaker, he told Charlie that the best way to get rid of the pain was to close your eyes and think of it as a small dot. "Now, when you see the dot, then picture it exiting through the holes in your ears. It's mind over matter. Since I've been doing it, I've never had to look at the inside of another Excedrin bottle," he said, winking at Charlie.

Gritting his teeth in agony, Charlie tried it. The dot, instead of coming out his ear, turned into a furry creature with sharp pointed teeth that slowly began to gnaw its way through his cranium.

He opened his eyes again and tried concentrating on the floral pattern on the dirty yellow wallpaper, wishing the animal would finish eating what was still left of his brain and leave. The pain began to drop a couple of decibels and the alcoholic fog started to burn away. He swallowed a few times, letting the saliva eat through the thick coating of last night's J&B that still clung to his throat.

The more he stared at the yellow wallpaper, the more he realized something wasn't right. It's the wallpaper. I don't have wallpaper in my bedroom, he realized. Jesus! Where the hell am I?

He closed his eyes one more time and tried thinking about last night: a few drinks on the plane from New York . . . picking up his car and driving to Peppy's . . . more drinks. Vague memories of telling Peppy some Quayle jokes . . . loud laughter from the regulars, especially from a woman sitting a couple of stools down. That's all.

Being a veteran of lost nights, Charlie knew that this wasn't his room. He began to wonder if whoever lived here was also in the bed with him. Charlie knew better than to make a quick movement with his head to find out. It would restart the creature's appetite. Instead, he inched his hand toward the middle of the mattress, half praying he would find nothing but empty space. A silent "damn" escaped from his mouth when his fingers scraped against naked, beefy buttocks.

Slowly, as if pushing through Jell-O, Charlie moved his head toward the person. She was completely covered, except for a small tuft of orange hair on the pillow. Charlie didn't fail to notice the black and gray roots.

Dear God, please don't embarrass me like the other times! he thought.

He had an urge to peek under the covers. Maybe his luck had changed and Bo Derek was lying next to him. Looking at the orange hair again, he decided: More like Hermione Gingold. Let this one remain a mystery. The main thing now was to untangle himself from the covers, find his clothes, figure out where he was, and get the hell out before she awoke.

Inch by inch he moved his body away from the bed until his right foot felt the edge of the mattress. When he lowered his leg to the floor, a shudder went through him from the cold linoleum.

As he stood up a wave of nausea engulfed him. He grabbed the night table, fighting down the vomit that was climbing its way up his throat. Wiping away the cold sweat on his brow, he thought, Don't blow it now. You almost have it made. A few deep breaths and the sickness started to fade.

Charlie looked around for his clothes. One sock and inside out undershorts were all he could find in the bedroom.

After ten minutes in the living room, searching on his hands and knees, including wading through thick dust under the couch, he found his shoes, shirt, and pants. The other sock was a lost cause.

He quickly dressed in the bathroom. Charlie knew it was the wrong day to be hung over, and he cursed himself for doing it as he splashed water on his face from the stained sink. He had an 8:45 meeting with Bitterman and, after glancing at his watch, knew he was going to be real late. No time to go home, wherever that was from here, and change.

This has to be on the top of your all-time self-destruction list, shithead, he thought to himself as he brushed his teeth with his fingers. Bitterman hated lateness. Besides, it was a bad sign when the publisher, not the editor, called you in for a meeting the first thing in the morning. He had an idea what it was about, and his aching, dehydrated body was not up for a confrontation.

Charlie took a look at himself in the cracked mirror of the medicine cabinet. He had a good body, and most people, especially women, found him attactive. Their opinion would probably swing the other way if they could see me now, he groaned to himself. His eyes, surrounded by large dark rings, were sunken into his skull, and the red capillaries running through his nose resembled streams in search of the mother river. His skin was the color of Cream of Wheat, and his reddish blond hair, normally thick and wavy, was matted and dull.

A burning sensation, starting in the pit of his stomach, began working its way up his body, leaving a trail of molten lava. He dropped to his knees, put his arms around the piss-covered rim of the toilet bowl, and started retching.

He stayed in that position for a couple of minutes, his head submerged in the bowl, until the sickness passed. You just might make it, ol' chap. One more time you just might make it, he thought as he wiped his face with toilet paper. He wasn't a kid anymore and he knew he didn't have many "one more times" left.

With a shoe under each arm, he quietly tiptoed out of the bathroom and headed toward the front door, silently praying that his find from last night wouldn't wake up.

The answer to where he was hit him as soon as he smelled the salt air outside.

Santa fucking Monica! He moaned.

It was a clear day and he could see the tip of the Venice Pier winding its way into the Pacific. Jesus Christ, I was supposed to be downtown two hours ago! he thought.

His mood worsened when he put his hands in his pockets and discovered his car keys weren't there. Peppy must have taken them from him; he always did when Charlie got this blitzed. Whoever the girl was upstairs must have driven last night, he realized.

The ground felt like it was moving under his feet, and he held onto the lamppost until the sensation stopped. He looked around trying to get his bearings. Wilshire was about a mile north of here. With luck, he could grab a bus and be only three hours late for his appointment. That wasn't too bad; he'd kept Bitterman waiting longer than that.

"Oo-la-la Charlie, but you do look like shit this morning," Bitterman's secretary, Tanya, said through a crack in her tight lips. It was her lunch break and she was at her desk cutting out the Ralphs coupons from the *L.A. Times*.

"How you gonna find a husband with a mouth like that, Tanya?" Charlie said, picking up a "fifty cents off" coupon from a box of Tampons.

"My, we are in a nasty mood today aren't we, Charlie?" she said, grabbing the coupon out of his hand.

She was a middle-aged spinster who seemed to have an endless supply of lace blouses that she wore buttoned up to her chin. Charlie felt that any man inventive enough to get her as far as her bedroom would find wall-to-wall stuffed Snoopys.

"You'd best go in. Mr. Bitterman's been waiting for you all morning. In fact, he's been going over your expense account since seven."

"He's in a pissed mood, huh?"

Tanya smiled. "Pissed is much too mild. Think of something more along the lines of X-rated. Oo-la-la!"

"Look," he said, leaning over her desk. "What's my chances of you becoming human for a minute and giving me a couple of aspirins? It was a rough night."

"Your chances don't seem to be too good, Charlie. Unlike you, I don't need aspirins. Nothing stronger than Evian passes these lips." Moving away from him, she picked up the Calender section from the *L.A. Times* to fan away the stale odor of alcohol that hung in the air.

"Oo-la-la," he said to her as he opened Bitterman's door.

Bitterman was leaning back in his chair with his hands folded behind his neck talking into a phone cradled under his chin. Frowning when he saw Charlie, he motioned for him to sit in the leather chair next to his smoked-glass Italian desk.

"I don't care if Howard Hughes kept a concubine at the Sands," Bitterman said into the phone. "Nobody gives a diddly shit about him anymore. He's dead. I told you to stick with Madonna and that little guy she's with. . . . What's his name? . . . Yeah, that's the one. If you got to give me dead, give me Presley. At least he still sells papers." He hung up, stretched, and cracked his knuckles above his head. "Bunch of kids," he said to Charlie, shaking his head. "They all think they're a day away from winning the Pulitzer."

"Not like the old days, right, Mr. B.?" Charlie's spirits brightened. Maybe this wasn't going to be so bad. He hoped, however, it was going to be short. The office had that southwest look, the same as those trendy restaurants on Melrose, and the peachy pink walls did not help his hangover.

Bitterman didn't say anything. He just stared at Charlie and clucked his tongue against the roof of his mouth.

Sighing, Charlie turned his eyes to a William Buffett lithograph on the wall.

"Charlie, Charlie, Charlie," Bitterman said as he put the tips of his fingers together and looked up at the ceiling. "What are we going to do with you?"

Suppressing a deep urge to return, Bitterman, Bitterman, Bitterman, he innocently said, "Gee, what are *we* talking about, Mr. B.?"

"I don't even know where to begin, Charlie, there's so much," he said softly.

Charlie had worked for this balding, little man for too many years to be drawn in by his smooth manner. Ralph Bitterman was like a skilled boxer throwing light jabs for ten rounds, waiting patiently for an opening. Once he saw one, he turned into Two-Ton Tony Galento. Bitterman was only thirty, but to Charlie he seemed a lot older. He was the kind of guy who always looked middle-aged, even in kindergarten.

His father, Barney Bitterman, had started the *Tattler* over fifty years ago with three hundred dollars he borrowed (or stole, depending on who told the story) from his brother, Max. His idea was to print sensationalism, not current events, and to sell the papers to the women of America. The best place for that, he discovered after following his wife around for two weeks, was at the checkout line at the supermarket. He'd spend hours crouched behind the cereal section, watching housewives sifting through magazines while waiting for the women in front to finish counting out coupons or to cease searching in the bottom of bags for the correct change.

The idea took off. When Barney retired after a triple bypass, handing the controls of his business over to his son, Ralph, the newspaper had a nationwide circulation of over three million.

"What seems to be the problem?" Charlie asked Bitterman as he shifted uncomfortably in the expensive, Italian leather chair. He wished he had downed a beer before he got here to take the edge off his hangover.

"Getting into the Venice Beach life-style, hey, Charlie?" Bitterman said, staring at Charlie's sockless feet.

"It's a long story."

"They all are with you, Charlie." He didn't grin back and Charlie knew he was in deep shit. Bitterman tore a long piece of tape from the calculator on his desk and tsked, tsked while scanning it. "You work for a family-owned newspaper, not an oil cartel," he said, staring at Charlie. "The way to make a profit is to stick to a budget. It's a sound philosophy that works for IBM as well as mama-and-papa operations."

"And it's a good philosophy, too, sir."

"Were you aware of the amount of per diem that was allocated to you?"

"Did I overstep myself in the financial end, Mr. B.?"

"Overstepping would be a gross understatement."

"You have to understand, she was a hard nut to crack."

"Hard? How so?" Bitterman leaned into his desk, trying to get his face closer to Charlie's. "Perhaps you could enlighten me. When last we talked, I was under the illusion that all you were going to do was take the red-eye to New York and get a wham-bam interview with the girl that gave Whitey McLeary the overdose. Find out what his last hours on earth were like . . . his last words. All you had to do was talk to her for an hour or so, spend the night at the airport Holiday Inn, then back to L.A. in the morning. It was all so simple. Where did it go wrong?"

Charlie took a pack of Camels out of his pocket, remembered Ralph was a weekend 10K freak, and put it back. "Wrong is not the right word, sir. 'Long' would be more like it. It just took longer. When I first got there, she was so scared she wouldn't talk to anyone, not even to her lawyer. She didn't even want the ten grand we offered her for the story. I mean the girl's no Phi Beta Kappa. She was just a groupie who followed McLeary around. The most she ever hoped for was a ten-minute rumble in the sheets with him. When he asked her back to his hotel, she had no idea she'd be giving the guy his last speedball, let alone be charged with murder one an hour later. It took a little longer than we had originally planned to get her to loosen up."

The veins on Bitterman's temple started throbbing. "Five days is more than a little longer!"

"I felt it would pay for itself. It was an exclusive. The *Trib* or the *Times* would have given up their firstborn for it. A rock superstar found dead from drugs . . . A strange girl in his room . . . A grieving wife and child left behind. The little people out there love shit like that." Charlie fingered the Camels again.

"Nobody's bitching about your work. It was good copy. The problem is the goddamn expenditures." He put his bifocals on and looked at the printout. "Here's a beauty. You ran up a six-hundred-and-thirty-five-dollar bar bill at the Oak Room at the Plaza."

"That place is way overpriced. You know what they charge for one ginger ale?"

"What the hell were you doing there? You were supposed to be at the airport Holiday Inn!"

"She said she needed a place with ambience to help her remember the events of that night." Aw, the hell with it! He popped a Camel from the pack and lit it. If Bitterman didn't want ashes all over his Navajo rug, he'd better produce an ashtray.

Reluctantly, Bitterman took one out of his desk drawer and

passed it to Charlie. "It didn't mean you had to sleep there, too. The bill for the Plaza—a suite overlooking the park—came out to one thousand two hundred and fifty-three thirty-seven!" His face was beginning to turn bright pink, and there was a twitch at the corner of his mouth.

"The cabbies were on strike. Ever try riding the subways at night? There's a war going on right under the streets of New York. I wonder if Congress knows about it." He realized he hadn't eaten anything today when he took a deep drag off the cigarette and felt light-headed.

"Let's try this one. It keeps getting better." Bitterman's throat muscles were constricting and his voice began to break. "Here's a two-thousand-seventy-one-dollars-twenty-six-cent bill for a mirror."

"I think it was an antique. At least, that's what they told me."

"Why is there a mirror on the bill, Charlie?"

His head was throbbing, and he could really use a scotch about now. Barney Bitterman would have had one for him. Sure, he would also rant and rave over the bill, basically because he was a cheap bastard. But he also knew what kind of revenues a top story like this would bring in. Eventually he'd calm down, break open a bottle of single malt he kept in his desk, and they'd hoist a couple. The old man would slap him on the back, tell him to get back to work, and that would be the end of it. "Look, one of Whitey's fans recognized her and tried punching her out," Charlie said wearily. "I grabbed a wrought-iron candle holder on the table and swung at him. I completely missed but did manage to hit something, namely the mirror."

"You're one hell of a white knight. I also see here one table and two chairs .. total seven hundred and twenty dollars. You want to run that one by me?"

"He wasn't easy to bring down."

"His attorney called Friday. He wants twelve grand for medical bills or he'll bring suit against the paper."

"That's kind of high for just twelve stitches. I'd ask to see those bills if I were you."

Bitterman let out a deep sigh and ran his fingers through his thinning hair. "Charlie, I don't mind you trying to destroy yourself, it's your right. I'm an ardent supporter of the Hemlock

Society. But why are you trying to take this paper down with you? Maybe you're really secretly working for our rivals."

"I wouldn't do that. I've been true blue to this paper for twelve years." Charlie was about to ask Bitterman if there was a beer in the fridge next to the empty bar but thought better of it.

"We also received complaints from the Plaza that you and that whore were drunk, dancing nude in their fish pond."

"Hold on, Mr. B., the girl might be a murderer, but she's not a whore. Anyway, she never charged me."

The deep pink of Bitterman's face had now turned into deep purple. He went over to the door and opened it. "You're fired," he said. "Go create havoc on someone else's newspaper."

A surge of relief swept through Charlie as he took his last hit off the cigarette. If it was true, and he was trying to destroy himself, he didn't need to depress himself further by looking at Bitterman's face every morning.

Smirking, Bitterman said to Charlie as he got up, "Now you'll see what the real world's all about. It's not an eighty-six-proof fish pond out there."

As he went out the door Charlie put his finger on Bitterman's nose, tapping it as he said, "I'd tell you to go fuck yourself except I hear your father beat me to it the moment your little ass scooted down the birth canal."

Walking out of the office, Charlie heard "oo-la-la" coming from the reception area.

Wilshire and Western was jammed with lunch crowds, and Charlie had to elbow his way across the intersection to get to the bus stop.

His mood was sour as he dropped his quarters into the slot of the change box and edged his way to the back of the crowded bus. The only vacant seat was next to a bag lady who looked as if she hadn't taken a bath since there was a Catholic in the White House. Reluctantly, he sat down. He knew he'd better think about regrouping, except he wasn't sure about his options. First off he had to get his car keys back, then start contemplating his life. Preferably he'd do the latter in a dark, cool place, and that fit the description of Peppy's on Wilshire.

"Charlie, my main man!" Peppy said as Charlie walked inside the dark bar, temporarily blinded from the bright sun outside. Peppy was at the far end of the counter tossing a big bucket of ice into the freezer, getting ready for the happy-hour crowd. The air-conditioning was off, and the heat made his white shirt stick to his muscular frame.

Charlie sat down on a bar stool, rubbing his eyes, trying to get used to the darkness. He liked Peppy's Bar because there was nothing faddish about it. Except for a couple coats of paint and new seat covers for the stools, it looked the same as it had fifty years ago. It had an art deco feel to it: chrome light fixtures and frosted glass with figures of women holding bubbles etched in them.

The bar was empty now except for a Mr. Slick in a three-piece suit sitting at a corner table holding hands with a dark-haired beauty half his age. He was wearing a wedding ring, and the glow in her face as she clung to every word he said told Charlie he was married—but not to her.

"You're a real asshole, you know that?" Charlie said to Peppy in disgust as he grabbed the draft Peppy poured for him. He quickly swigged it down, trying to stop his hand from shaking by holding it steady with the other hand.

"What'd I do, babe?" Peppy asked, his chipped front teeth glistening as he grinned. Charlie finished off the mug in a couple of gulps and Peppy slid another one down to him.

"You promised me you wouldn't let me out the door with anyone unless she was from my own species," Charlie said. He took two deep swallows, wiping the foam from his mouth with his hand, the edge inside him beginning to blunt.

"You talking about that bozo from last night?"

"Unless she was a princess who turned into a fucking frog this morning, I guess that's who I'm talking about."

"There was no stoppin' you. I tried. Honest to God, I did."

"Couldn't have been too hard."

"You want to know how hard I tried? I'll tell ya. When she went to the bathroom, I grabbed you like this." He clutched Charlie by the lapels of his shirt, pulling him up from the seat, their noses almost touching. "I said, 'Charlie, what the fuck you doing? You go home with this beauty and you might as well blow your brains out, 'cause no one's gonna let you live this one down.' You don't remember any of this, do you?"

Charlie shook his head, trying to break Peppy's strong grip. He released him and Charlie fell back onto the stool.

"Know what you said to me after that?" Peppy was really getting into it, trying to hold his laughter.

"It's not important," Charlie said, starting to cringe.

"You put your arm around me and said,"—Peppy put his hands to his heart and blinked his eyes like a silent-movie star— " 'I'm in love for the first time in my life.' You said she looked just like a young Rita Hayworth."

"Peppy, you got to stop."

"Nope," he said. "You got to hear this. This is the best part! It's when you gave her a quarter for the jukebox."

"Oh, no! Spare me, will you!" Charlie put his hands to his ears, closing his eyes.

Peppy easily pried his hands loose from his ears and forced them down on the counter. "She played 'Twilight Time' and started doing a slow bump and grind to it. You said"—not letting go of Charlie's hands—" 'Peppy, look at that beautiful red hair. The way she's movin' her body, she looks just like Rita Hayworth dancin' with all those veils in *Salome*.' I said to you, 'Charlie, you're fucking crazy! Her hair ain't red, it's orange. And she don't look like Rita Hayworth, she looks like Clarabel!' "

"You're really getting off on this one, aren't you?"

"The regulars were fallin' off their stools, they was laughing so hard. Let me tell you one more thing and I promise to shut up."

"Come on, Peppy." He tried to get up from the stool but Peppy grabbed him by the shoulder and held him down.

"Listen to this! At one point, while holding her hand, you looked her in the eye like a lovesick dog and sang all the words to 'Love Me Tender' in her ear. I swear, it made me want to cry."

"Fuck you, Peppy." He pushed his arm away and got up. "Give me my keys."

Peppy opened the register, grabbed a set of keys from the change box, and tossed them over to him. "Come on, Charlie, I'm only razzin' you. You were always a good sport about things like that . . . hey, hey, hey." Winking, he tapped him on the arm with his chunky fist.

"I got fired today, and my financial statement is on par with the street people."

"Hey, sorry to hear that. I guess that means you ain't paying for these drinks, right?"

"You were always a good sport about things like that . . . hey, hey, hey. Be seeing you, Peppy," he said, heading toward the door.

The girl with Mr. Slick in the corner was now crying, and he was trying to wipe away the mascara running down her face with his monogrammed handkerchief. He kept looking over his shoulder, red-faced, hoping no one noticed.

Charlie noticed. Nope, he thought, she definitely wasn't married to that dumb shit, and I bet she just realized it, too.

His '76 red Mustang, parked across the street, had a twenty-eight-dollar parking ticket stuck under the window blade. Charlie dumped it into the glove compartment along with the rest of the unpaid tickets.

He drove up Wilshire toward his duplex on Sycamore. The traffic, which seemed to double every year in L.A., was at a near standstill. The queasiness had gone away with the beers, but he couldn't shake the depression that seemed to be digging its way into his soul, staking out a permanent home for itself. Feeling claustrophobic, he opened the window, but quickly shut it again when the exhaust fumes from the bus in front of him made him light-headed. He made a detour south on La Brea, then east on Olympic, hoping the traffic would be lighter. It wasn't.

He turned the radio on, hoping to hear the Dodger game. They were playing the Cubs at Wrigley Field, and if he was lucky he still might be able to catch the last couple of innings. If anything could take Charlie out of his depression, it was a game between those two clubs. What he heard instead was Vince Scully talking about flood warnings that were in effect in Chicago. The city was under six inches of rain and was being battered by eighty-mile-an-hour winds. No breaks today, Charlie, my boy.

He pushed a couple of more buttons on the Motorola, scanning the stations, then stopped when he heard a woman's rich, deep voice. It was that psychologist, but he couldn't remember her name. She was talking to a stressed-out person over the phone, giving advice on child abuse. Charlie had listened to her a couple of times before when he was stuck in traffic. Settling in for a bumper-to-bumper ride, he turned the volume up.

Chapter 3

Monday, 1:47 P.M.

Stacey was standing next to Rena's space in the station's parking lot, arms folded and shaking her head as she watched her drive up. "Cutting it pretty thin, aren't we?"

"Sorry. Couldn't get anything together, today," Rena said, slamming the door of her Jaguar convertible and racing up the stairs with Stacey into the back entrance of the station. "What time is it?"

"You're on in ten minutes," Stacey said, trying to keep up with her.

"Shit."

"Fart face was licking his chops, hoping you wouldn't make it."

"I bet." She stopped short in the hall. "Damn! I left my briefcase in the car."

"Get going. You'll be late. I'll get it." Stacey raced down the corridor, her long black hair, almost Asian in texture, flying in every direction. She was wearing faded 501s with rips in the knees and an old "Bruce Springsteen—Live In Concert" T-shirt.

Stacey had applied for the job as Rena's assistant several months ago. Fred Lovell, who worked for Rena as a call screener, knew Stacey from the university and had told her about the possible job opening. Rena met with her and liked her immediately. She was bright, attractive, and strangely elusive. And it was this ambiguous quality, Rena noticed with amusement, that turned every man's head at the station. The smell of aftershave lotion seemed to permeate the air whenever she was on

32

her shift. After work she'd occasionally get together with some of the crew and have a couple of beers at the Columbia Bar and Grill across the street. Once, on her way to a date, Rena passed by the saloon and saw her with the guys inside. Stacey was sitting slouched in a chair, one foot across the table, the other in the lap of the chief engineer, dangling a Corona by the neck. The Rams game was on the big screen at the bar, and they were boisterous, having a good time, screaming for Frontierre to find a real quarterback. She was so relaxed, so much one of the boys, that some of the secretaries that worked at the station who were sitting at a table by themselves, all decked out in May Company's finest and sipping piña coladas with little umbrellas, could only glare at her, wondering where they had gone wrong. Rena could have told them in one word: illusionary. Her nickname for Stacey was "the cotton-candy kid"—the minute you think you have her, she dissolves, leaving only a memory of what could have been.

Rena got to the booth just as Murray Spahn, the restaurant critic, whom Stacey liked to call fart face, was signing off his show with his usual ". . . and have a gastronomical day, folks." When he saw Rena standing outside, he shook his head, pointed to his watch, and silently mouthed, "You're late." Giving him her sweetest smile, she mouthed back, "I know." He was wearing a bright red, Armani sweater, and with his huge belly and earphones covering most of his small head, he reminded Rena of a character out of one of those Japanese-made Saturday-morning cartoons.

The red light in the booth went off, meaning a commercial was on, and Rena went in.

Murray stood up and pulled down his sweater, which had risen up over his stomach, exposing a patch of white skin with matted black hair. Removing his earphones and handing them to Rena, he said, "Another day late. I wonder what some of your colleagues would have to say about that."

"Good question. I'll have to ask them one of these years," Rena said, taking the earphones and putting them on the desk.

"I almost gave away one of my favorite soufflé recipes to those housewives out there, trying to stall for time because of you," he said, shaking a finger at her.

"I guess God must be on the side of your audience today, Murray."

"I suppose that's meant to be sarcastic. That's not very funny, Rena. I take pride in what I do." He moved closer to her, the sweater pulling up over his stomach again. Being only five-foot-three, he had to arch his neck to look up at her.

"Oh, lighten up, will you, Murray. It's just a soufflé. It was the same one you made for the Christmas party, right?"

"Yes, it was," he said, sounding a little indignant.

"Well, then," she said, smiling as she sat down.

"Well, then . . . Well, then, what?"

"I think she means it sucked, Murray," Stacey said, coming into the booth and handing Rena her briefcase. "Anyway, I hate to break this up but we got a show to do, old sport." She put her hand on his back and maneuvered him toward the door.

Holding on to the doorknob, he turned to Stacey and said with a nervous whisper, "Will you let me know about Friday?"

"No can do this week, sorry. Great color for you, Mur." She pointed to his red sweater. "Makes you look like Captain Kirk. Beam me up, Scottie," she said while closing the door on him. Murray smiled at her through the glass partition, and gave her a wink, then left.

"What's this Friday stuff?" Rena said, wiping Murray's hair tonic off the head phones with a tissue. The hourly newsbreak was coming from the other booth and she still had a couple of minutes before she went on.

"Oh, fart face wants to take me to an opening of some new restaurant on Beverly. Cajun food, I think. I hate that stuff. It's so damn hot. The people from Louisiana must be walking around with holes in their stomachs as big as manhole covers."

"Doesn't he know you're living with someone?"

"Yeah, he doesn't care. He's not looking to get laid, at least I don't think he is. He's looking for your basic restaurant arm prop, one that won't embarrass him by ordering a glass of rosé and a well-done steak." She was glancing at another glass booth, at the director inside, waiting for the signal. "Did you call the police?"

"Yep."

"What did they say?"

"Probably a prank."

"That's all?"

"That's all," Rena said, shrugging. "For all I know they may be right. Anyway, they're not going to do anything about it. They said it's probably one of Cathy's friends who's responsible."

"Civil servants . . . they're all a bunch of assholes. All they care about is their pension and an early retirement. Maybe I should do my thesis on the bureaucratic mentality," Stacey said, shaking her head in disgust.

The director gave the nod and cued up the show's music.

Both women said together, as they always did, "It's showtime, folks!" Stacey then left the booth and joined Fred in the room next door to help screen the calls.

Rena looked down at her phone lines on her desk and saw they were not lit up, not yet, but would be as soon as she introduced today's topic. Her director was now counting down with his fingers: five . . . four . . . three. At one he pointed to Rena. She was on.

"Hello, this is KROS and I'm Rena Halbrook. For the next three hours I'll be on the air talking with you. The subject I would like to discuss today is one that I haven't touched upon yet, at least not on the radio, but it's an important one . . . and unfortunately as common as the cold. I'm talking about child abuse. If you've *ever* experienced it, or you *are* experiencing it now . . . or perhaps you're someone who *is* abusing a child—I would like to hear from you." Hear that, Alice, she thought. "Our phone number is eight-four-six-three-thousand. We'll be right back to talk more about it after this message."

"Double your pleasure, double your fun . . ." cued up, and Rena felt a pang of embarrassment; the issue was too sensitive to be marketed with commercials like this and she should have known better. Especially when she remembered how enraged she was at the network who aired a movie about the Holocaust: one second she was seeing thousands of Jews going to their deaths . . . the next she was bombarded by Ronald McDonald and his Big fucking Macs.

Insensitivity of the eighties . . . a topic for another show, she thought.

One more thirty-second spot and she was back on. All the lines were lit up, and she was somewhat surprised by the quick response. Maybe that's what the program needed—more controversial topics. We'll see.

The next three hours went quickly for Rena. The callers were more interesting than usual, coming from more diverse backgrounds, and their stories were riveting: one man told about how, when he was a boy, his father would punish him by first beating him, then taking him to San Pedro and forcing him to be tattooed. By the time he was fifteen, and the authorities stepped in, his chest and arms were covered with slogans and pictures of wild animals; and there were other tales . . . depictions of beatings, rapes, disfigurements. The sponsors might not like it, but damn, this was a good show today, and she was getting a rush from it, the first one in a long time.

The last hour was almost over. One more call and that's it. She moved into the microphone and said, "We'll be winding up our final hour." She pressed the button for the caller. "Hello, you're on the air."

"Yes, hello. My name is Harriet. I was physically abused by my father and I'm afraid I'm going to do the same thing to my son," she said quickly, her voice high-pitched and nervous.

"That's not an uncommon thing, Harriet. Most abused children become abusers themselves in later life. It's a terrible legacy that's handed down from generation to generation. How old is your son?"

"Three."

"You said you were afraid of abusing him. Do you mean you haven't as yet hurt him . . . that you just have fantasies of doing so?"

"That's correct."

"Okay, Harriet, let me explain why you have these feelings. But first I want to hear more about your father. It's important to know—"

Loud static blasted through her headset, hurting her ears.

"I think we're experiencing some technical difficulties," she said into the microphone while looking at the director. He shook his head, shrugging, then fiddled with some switches.

"I'm sorry, Harriet. Are you still there?"

The static remained. A barely audible voice began to make itself heard through the noise.

". . . dark . . . so cold . . ."

A shiver shot through Rena's spine. This isn't happening, she thought. "Who is this?" she asked, her voice trembling. She already knew the answer.

". . . going to hurt me . . ."

"Who? Who's going to hurt you?" she said, glancing around the booth. The workers were beginning to come out of their offices, standing near the glass partition, staring in.

"Alice," the child's voice said.

"Alice. That's your name. . . ."

"Hobby . . . hobby . . ."

"It's hard to hear you. Can you speak louder? How did you break through to me?"

The director gestured to Rena, asking if she wanted to go off the air by making a slit across his neck with his finger. Rena waved her hand, no.

"Hobby . . . don't want to go back."

"Go back to where? Listen, can you tell me where you are?"

". . . help me . . ."

"I want to . . ."

". . . Da hurt, Da hurt . . ."

"No one's going to hurt you. I won't let them. Just tell—"

"Da kill!" Her breathing was getting heavier. She was beginning to panic.

"Alice, listen to—"

"No more wally! No more!"

"Give me your address, Alice."

The static was getting louder now and it was hard to make out all the words.

"Wally hurt . . . oh, wally hurt."

"Do you know where you live?"

"Da come! Oh, no!"

The terror in her voice shook up everyone in the studio.

Through the static, a door slamming, then footsteps, a piece of furniture overturning. Alice screaming: "No Da . . . please no! No kill . . . please!" The awful sound of a body hitting something hard . . . moans . . . bones snapping, a long, horrifying shriek.

Then silence. Only the steady hum of a free telephone line.

"Alice, are you still there?" Rena said weakly. Her mouth was dry and she could feel the blood pumping in and out of her heart. She looked up and saw the pale faces of the employees, their hands pressed against the glass, watching her. One of them was Murray, his face a sickly white.

Her head began to spin. From somewhere far off she heard the director groan, "Jeeesus!" She could feel Fred's arm going around her for support and heard the sound of Stacey's voice talking to the police over the phone. She wanted to say something to her audience, but what? What could she possibly say that would smooth over the trauma of hearing a child being brutalized or maybe even murdered.

She didn't have to say anything. The station manager took care of it by cutting to a commercial. "Please don't squeeze the Charmin," blared from the studio speakers.

Chapter 4

Monday, 4:32 P.M.

Mrs. Markowitz was putting out the garbage on the front lawn with the help of her two sons as Charlie turned into the driveway. The boys' heads were closely cropped, and long black curls ran down the sides of their ears. Her three younger children were playing on the grass, screaming, while the toddler held on to her long skirts, sucking her thumb. Mrs. Markowitz, wearing a kerchief over her head, glanced at Charlie and nodded stiffly. She and her family shared the duplex with him. In the five years he had lived here, separated from them by only a dividing wall two inches thick, they had never talked except to mumble a few niceties about the weather. Her husband, a Hasidic rabbi, always smiled politely at Charlie, scratching his straggly red beard and tipping the brim of his black felt hat as he rushed off to his congregation—but that was all. Their isolation from him was so complete that it might as well have been an ocean and not a plaster wall that separated them.

Sometimes at night, while lying in bed, Charlie would listen to them from behind his side of the plaster wall. He could hear them whispering to each other in Yiddish, crying out each other's name as they made love. He'd close his eyes and imagine her velvety white skin that the sun never touched, plus those thick, hard hips and solid calves that rippled when she walked.

Charlie gave Mrs. Markowitz's legs one last look as he hit the remote control that opened his garage door. He drove inside and sat there, leaving the radio on and the motor running. A wave of exhaustion washed over him. He didn't feel like getting out, not just yet. He reached in the back and grabbed a paper bag on the floor with a pint of J&B inside. He swallowed half the scotch, trying to push away the feeling of desolation that stubbornly clung on. It didn't work. It rarely did anymore.

Jaimie breezed into his head.

Oh, God, Jaimie!

That beautiful blond hair with large curls that turned almost white in the sun. Giggling, beckoning him to catch her as she ran away from him on those little two-year-old bandy legs in Brooklyn's Brighton Beach.

Charlie took a large swig, trying to remember her face. Sometimes, if he didn't try too hard, he could catch it just right: blue eyes, a swirl of freckles running along the bridge of her peeling, sunburned nose. There was more, but time was beginning to put a haze on it.

And then there was Rosie.

Oh, Jesus!

She'd be sitting under an umbrella in her two-piece, trying to protect her delicate skin from the sun, watching them as they romped in the cold Atlantic or built sand castles with moats. Her lips would be clamped together and her chin moving forward, then sideways, as she ground her teeth, watching . . . always thinking. It was the thinking that bothered him the most. He never asked her what was going on inside her head, because whatever it was, he knew, wouldn't be any good—not anymore.

Two more hits on the bottle. His mind was so filled with old memories, he didn't hear the garage door close on it's automatic timer.

Good old Rosie.

They met during the march on Washington in '67.

Charlie Halleran, age twenty, was considered the brightest journalism major to graduate Brooklyn College in the last decade. He was immediately scooped up by the *New York Post* and offered a job as a correspondent on the city-hall beat. The Washington bureau, aware of his talents as an interviewer, sent for him to talk with the leaders of the march.

Charlie flew into Washington on October 21 and headed toward the Capitol building. Thousands of people jammed the streets. He had just finished talking with Dr. Benjamin Spock on the lawn near the Lincoln Monument when he felt a surge from the crowd pushing him toward the Pentagon. There was electricity in the air and Charlie could feel something big was happening.

People, as far as the eye could see, were running up the steps, screaming, demanding an end to the war. Charlie was caught in the middle; there was no way to stop and turn around without being crushed. Every nerve ending in his body seemed alive; history was being made today and he was part of it. Next to him, also racing up the steps, was a pretty girl with olive skin and long, straight black hair. She had her fists raised in the air, shouting that all troops should get out of Vietnam.

Charlie wondered what would happen once they reached the thick steel doors of the Pentagon. He soon found out. The doors opened, and soldiers, dressed in battle gear and carrying M-16s, ran out. They swooped down on the crowd, smashing heads and bodies with the butts of their rifles. Charlie hit the ground, putting his arms over his head to protect it. The others did the same. A few minutes later, Charlie looked up and saw the soldiers dragging away some of the bloodied, dazed protesters and pushing them inside the building.

Next to him, the pretty girl with the dark hair suddenly stood up and began calling the soldiers "motherfucking fascists!" They turned in her direction and Charlie groaned. She was the only one standing and she made an easy target.

One of the soldiers, a young kid with acne scars on the back of his neck and a red pug nose, pushed past his comrades, trying to get at her as he held the stock of the M-16 out in front of him. The girl stared at him, not moving. Her large, black eyes, filled with defiance, dared the soldier to do something. She was frail looking, and the oversized, red-checkered lumber jacket she was wearing made her seem smaller than she was.

Charlie didn't know if she had a death wish or was just plain naive, but he couldn't let what was about to happen, happen. He grabbed the back of her coat and threw her down on the ground just as the rifle stock came crashing down. He covered her body with his and took the blow between the shoulder blades. The pain was sharp, taking away his breath. As he gasped for air he caught a glimpse of her beautiful face under his, and he knew, even though he was writhing in agony, that he could fall in love with her.

"You okay?" he said as soon as he could breathe again. The soldier had backed off and joined the others in blockading the doors.

"Yeah, fine," she said, running her fingers over his brow. "You?"

"I am now," he said, grinning. "What's your name?"

"Rosie." She looked up at the soldier with the acne scars. "I'd like to kill that pig!" she hissed.

The hate in her face was strong and Charlie believed her. She began to grind her teeth as she glared at the boy with the M-16. Because of his attraction to her, Charlie took that look of intensity to mean depth, something he found lacking in the women he dated. It wasn't until years later, during a meeting with her psychiatrist, that he discovered that the look wasn't profundity but hostility, which was only one symptom of her deepening psychosis.

At one in the morning, they took the bus back to New York. The coach was almost empty, just a few late stragglers from the march, most of them sleeping. Rosie and Charlie sat in the back, whispering. She said she was a writer, but made her living as a waitress. Putting her hand on his thigh, she talked passionately about the French existentialists: Camus, Sartre, Genet. He could see her intelligent eyes sparkling in the darkness, and her hand was beginning to burn a hole in his leg. Charlie's spirit soared heavenward. No, she was nothing like the other girls he knew, and he felt that a soul mate had been delivered to him.

By the time the conversation turned to the poetry of T. S. Eliot, Rosie had her hand on Charlie's crotch and was unbuckling his jeans. Pushing his bell bottoms down over his knees, she knelt between the seats, and while reciting from "The Love Song of J. Alfred Prufrock," went down on him.

Two hours later the bus pulled into the Port Authority and Charlie was madly in love.

They went back to her place. She lived on the top floor of a five-story walkup on Hudson Street. The apartment was a mess; dirty dishes were piled up everywhere, and black grime was permanently embedded in the walls and ceilings. She didn't apologize for the condition and Charlie liked that.

He also liked the little dark hairs on her arms and the fact that she didn't shave under her armpits.

Rosie took him into her living room, where the walls were covered with bookshelves. The floor was strewn with records and overflowing ashtrays containing cigarette butts and pot seeds. He sat down on a couch that was covered over with a batik spread. They shut the shades to block out the early-morning sun, lit some candles, smoked a joint, did a ten-minute rap on the relevance of Godard's *Alphaville* compared with his more experimental film *Made in the USA*, and then got it on right on the Pakistani straw mat on the floor.

The next morning he went back to the house where he lived with his deeply religious aunt, packed his bags, and moved in with Rosie.

She had eggplant parmigiana waiting for him. Growing up on boiled, overcooked Irish food, Charlie ate like it was his last meal. Between sips of Chianti, they had a disagreement on whether or not Bob Dylan's "Ballad of a Thin Man" was really about a closet queen, then hugged, kissed, smoked some more grass, made love again, this time on the batik, and discussed new plans.

One of their plans included marriage. Months later, the day after Johnson told a TV audience with his hangdog look that he would not seek another term, Rosie and Charlie tied the knot in city hall. For the next two years, until he was drafted, Charlie forced himself to believe their union was solid. He was too young to remember his parents, had been raised by a spinster aunt who never embraced anything to her breasts except King James's New Testament, and so the idea of marriage meant everything to him.

Rosie's brooding began to disappear after they were married. She no longer stayed up nights chainsmoking in bed, seeing the Vietnam War and other atrocities as a forerunner of the Apocalypse. She took a job as an editor with a children's-book publishing house. Her appearance also began to change: denim and faded workshirts were replaced with more colorfully matched outfits. She had her hair cut short, more in style with the uptown look. Single friends, unless they were in the creative field or gay, were replaced with couples, preferably married. She also became a fanatic about keeping the apartment clean. One time Charlie came home and found her standing on a ladder washing down the fourteen-foot ceiling with soap and water.

Charlie was moving up fast in the journalistic world. He was beginning to be highly respected as a political writer and was making connections in important places. CBS's affiliate station in New York approached him and asked if he would consider being the political analyst on the six o'clock news. With his looks and delivery, he'd be a natural, they told him. Charlie laughed, thinking that he was too green to give Cronkite a run for his money just yet. Maybe in a couple of years when he had a little more experience under his belt. Meanwhile the *Post*, feeling pressure from rival newspapers, offered him a daily column as an incentive to stay with them.

Everything was on an upswing for Charlie and Rosie. They were the darlings of the West Village, with interesting friends and a social calendar that was always well booked three months in advance. People scrambled all over the city to be invited to one of their famous Sunday brunches.

Then one day Rosie started laughing and everything began to slide downhill.

It wasn't a hysterical form of laughter; instead, it was the kind that stayed in the throat, sounding like phlegm rattling around—heh . . . heh . . . heh.

Anything would start it going: the Sunday funnies, the way Charlie's hair looked in the morning when he first woke up, even Nixon's presidential swearing-in ceremony on television. Sometimes she would sit in her bedroom alone, stare at herself in the mirror, and break out laughing. Friends were beginning to be uncomfortable around her and started staying away.

Charlie didn't know what to make of it. He began to grow concerned, especially the time they went to a showing of an antiwar documentary at the Bleecker Street Cinema. It was Saturday night, the house was packed, and it happened during the scene where a grieving Vietnamese woman was trying to crawl into the grave with her dead child, a casualty of an American air strike. The voice-over was spoken by a United States Army general who said that gooks don't have the capacity to cry for their dead. The silence in the theater was shattered by Rosie's throaty chortle. Once started, it couldn't stop, getting more and more manic. The audience was outraged, shouting at her and threatening, telling her to shut up and leave. Charlie managed to get her out of the theater. All the way home she couldn't stop laughing, the tears rolling down her face.

"Didn't you see it?" she said, finally calming down to where she could talk.

"See what?" he said, not understanding.

"Her tooth. The tooth of the woman who was crying for her child," she said. "Her gums were all black, the same color as the inside of her mouth, and she only had one tooth left in her mouth."

She didn't say anything else, and by the time they reached Sheridan Square and went into Smiler's to buy a quart of milk, his curiosity was at its peak. "For God's sakes, Rosie, what about her fucking tooth?"

Rosie's lips began to spread, and the heh-hehs started again. Finally, after taking a deep breath and controlling herself for a second, she said, "My God, it was so obvious, Charles. I don't understand why you don't see things when they're right in front of you. How could you possibly be a writer? With the woman's mouth open like that, everything was dark inside except for that one tooth. She reminded me of those old Felix the Cat cartoons we watched on TV when we were kids. Remember when Felix would run toward the camera with his mouth open, until the whole screen became the inside of his mouth, black, except for the one white tooth." She started to laugh all over again.

"And that's it?" he said, after a pause, when she didn't say anything else.

"That's it. Dammit! I feel so alone living with you. You never seem to understand me," she said irritably. She remained silent the rest of the way home, except her eyes were glazed, as if she were in some other place.

That night, thinking she was on drugs, possibly mescaline, he searched the apartment. When he didn't find any, he really became uneasy and called a friend who was interning at Bellevue.

The friend told Charlie he didn't like what he was hearing and that he'd see her if she was willing, but not to push it if she didn't want to come. When Charlie brought up the possibility of her going into therapy over a dinner of linguini and clams, she threw a tantrum, cursed him, and flung her plate across the room, hitting the wall. She ran into the bedroom and locked the door, not coming out or eating for two days. When she did emerge from the room, she looked pale and tired. She made herself a peanut butter and jelly sandwich and sat at the table, eating it slowly, not looking up at Charlie. For the next two weeks, she never once laughed, cracked a smile, or said a word to him. He knew better than to bring up her seeing a doctor again, at least not until things were patched up between them.

Soon after, he was drafted. The night before he was scheduled to leave for Fort Dix, he awoke to the wet feel of Rosie's mouth on his penis. She looked up and said, "I'll miss you, Charlie."

A rush of love for her swept over him. It reminded him of that night in the bus coming back from Washington.

They made love for half the night. Afterward, lying on her back in the dark bedroom, the sweat rolling down her breasts, she lit a cigarette and told him she would go see his friend the psychiatrist, if that's what he wanted. She just wanted to please him. Smiling, Charlie put his arm around her and kissed her gently on the forehead. He said, yes, that's what he wanted.

Enough!

His eyes were tired and he wanted to close them. It was hot in the garage, and the air was thick and smelled funny. The empty scotch bottle slid from his hand and onto the seat. As an icy sleep descended upon him he heard a child's voice on the car radio. The alcohol and the carbon monoxide in the closed garage clouded his brain, and the words he heard were disjointed. Something about her name being Alice . . . needs help . . . closet . . . Daddy kills . . . lots of terrible screaming. Then another voice, an older woman's . . . says she wants an address.

He tried opening his eyes but they wouldn't go past the slits. Charlie grinned as he thought, Gee, Alice, I remember you. What are you doing on the radio? You're supposed to be . . .

Be what? He was much too tired to think about what she was

supposed to be. Another time, maybe. It was getting hard to breathe. As he closed his eyes once again he remembered something. He remembered that he had forgotten to turn off the car motor. "Dumb shit," he muttered as his body floated into darkness.

Chapter 5

Monday, 5:46 P.M.

Sergeant Gerald W. Jaffe sat in his brown Ford Fairlane, wiped the tobacco juice off his close-cropped, blond mustache with his finger, and stared up at the radio station. Next to him, on the seat, under crunched-up Bazooka bubble-gum wrappers and a tin of Red Man, was his police pad with Rena Halbrook's name scribbled in pencil.

He was in no hurry to meet the famous psychologist. He wanted to sit here for a while, chew his wad of bubble gum and tobacco, and think about how that bitch had taken his life and flushed it down the sewer. Sometimes the hate he had for her would get so bad that he'd go into his apartment and hit the pillow with his sap until he'd roll over on the bed from exhaustion, gasping for air. Other times, he'd take a drive into the barrio and beat up on transvestites, the nickel-and-dimers, even the whores.

Yet, six months ago he had never even heard of Rena Halbrook. Six months ago he was happily married to Mary, a good, Catholic girl. He had two well-behaved, God-fearing boys and a three-bedroom tract home in Northridge. Today, because of this doctor, he was living alone in a one-room apartment on top of an appliance store in a white-trash neighborhood of North Hollywood.

Six months ago Mary was a real good kid: never gave him any lip, watched her figure, kept within the household budget, and made sure the boys got to Little League on time. She never seemed to mind when he went out with the guys, had a few drinks, and came home a little snookered. Sure, he might have lost it a couple of times: got too drunk and slapped her around. Those things happen. It didn't mean he didn't love her. Besides, she never complained much about it.

Those years with her and the boys were the best in his life: the picnics in Griffith Park with the men and their wives from the station house; the beer parties; tossing around the football with his sons. He even built a brick patio in the backyard with his own hands so they could have more room for their Sunday barbecues. All gone now.

Six months ago Mary called this Halbrook cunt and told her how he beat her up, how he terrorized the kids, how they were scared to death of him, how she wanted to leave him but was afraid, how she met a nice guy, a schoolteacher, and they were having an affair. . . . Told her all this on the air with a couple of million people listening in, including the wives of some of his best friends. The good doctor told his beloved Mary that he was a sick man, that she should take the kids and leave him, that she knew of a good psychologist that could help her.

It was six months ago, almost to the day, that Mary had the locks changed while he was at work and signed a restraining order barring him from the house. He was handed the papers by one of his own men during roll call, in front of the whole station. As he read the order, his face flushed with anger, and he could hear the snickering in back of the room from some of the rookies as they stood at attention.

Today, Mary was working in the cosmetic department at Robinson's, attending night classes at L.A. City College, and—this was the part that killed him—had that sissy schoolteacher living with her, sleeping in *his* bed and cooking steaks on *his* patio.

When Lieutenant Margolis handed him the case early this morning, he took the assignment himself rather than give it to one of his underlings. Some of the men at the station were a little surprised at this move. They knew Jaffe didn't like working the streets if he didn't have to, that he was just cruising now, doing time for a couple of years until he retired at forty-five.

Jaffe got out of the car, into the hot evening air, and spat the wad of tobacco and gum into the gutter. Mustn't make a bad impression on the dyke, he thought. The only thing she probably chews is muff.

In the elevator, he picked pieces of lint off his C&R checkered jacket and straightened his tie, thinking that the gods realized their mistake when they screwed up his life and decided to make it up to him. This was his chance and he wasn't going to rush it. He'd take it step-by-step, look at all the options, and then when he was ready, nail her to the fucking wall.

When he reached the fifth floor, a page pointed Rena out. She looked irreproachable to him standing there in the hallway. She was holding several folders under her arm, dressed in a stylish, gray cotton suit, giving orders to several people, one of them a real looker with long black hair. Everything about this Halbrook bitch was perfect, not even a hair out of place. He had an urge to carry her screaming into a cow pasture loaded with dung and rape the shit out of her. He wondered how godlike she'd look then.

Watching her, he felt his anger coming back and that suited him just fine. She was the kind of woman he had desired his whole life but was always put down by: the rich-bitch type that talked nice, wore pretty clothes, and knew how to order from a French menu. The kind like those cunty public defenders who looked so beautiful in the courtroom cross-examining him on the stand, staring at him unafraid, smiling as they easily cut him to ribbons with their big words. He needed the anger. Without his family, without his self-respect, anger was the only thing that kept him from chewing on his beretta.

They had stopped talking and were looking his way now. He hoped his feelings hadn't shown through; sometimes they had a tendency to do so. Wiping his mustache with his handkerchief, making sure there were no tobacco stains on it, he coughed nervously and walked over to them. He unbuttoned his jacket and tucked the back of his shirt into his pants so they could see the gold badge on his belt.

As he got nearer he saw she was smiling at him, not condescending like he was some kind of a field hand, but warm, sincere, and this threw him a little. But the other one, the one with the green eyes and black hair, there was nothing warm about the way she was looking at him. And the jerky-looking guy next to her, the nerd with the sour puss, there was nothing too friendly about him either.

"Hi, I'm Rena Halbrook," she said to him, extending her hand.

"Sergeant Jaffe, ma'am," he said, touching the tips of her fingers lightly. He felt stupid saying "ma'am," sounding like fucking Joe Friday. The rich ones always made him feel stupid, and say dumb things.

"Didn't I talk to you this morning?"

"Yes, I think it was me, ma'am." *Shit*.

"You guys always this prompt?" Stacey said sardonically. "I called two hours ago."

A young bitch in training, he thought to himself, looking at Stacey. "Sorry about that," he said, forcing a grin. "I wanted to check with the phone company first, see if they knew how this call might have been pulled off." To Rena, he said, "I'd like to hear the recording of your conversation with this girl, if you don't mind."

"Of course. Let's go into the studio." She told Stacey and Fred she'd see them tomorrow, then turned and walked down the hall at a fast clip, not waiting for Jaffe.

As he followed her, his elbow casually rubbed against Stacey's breasts when he squeezed his body between the people clustered around the hallway. "Excuse me," he said, grinning into those cold green eyes.

Rena, who was several feet in front of him, didn't bother looking back to see if he was behind her. He felt like a coolie. Those rich bitches wait for no one, he thought to himself, trying to keep up.

With the studio monitors pumped up, the screams unnerved Rena even more than the first time. When it was over, finally, she took the tape out of the machine.

"Well, what do you think?" she said uneasily. During the playback, she felt his eyes on her, as if he were more interested in her than in the fate of this girl.

"Pretty gruesome stuff, huh?" he said casually as he unwrapped the L'il Joe cartoon off a piece of Bazooka and popped the pink gum in his mouth.

"You don't sound very concerned, Sergeant Jaffe. Don't tell me you're *still* under the impression that this is a prank conceived by a nine-year-old."

"Well, they *are* a hell of a lot more sophisticated today then when we were kids, wouldn't you say?" he said, grinning, as he straddled the only chair in the booth. As soon as he sat down he realized his mistake. Talking to her meant he would now have to look up at her, and her down at him, a position he didn't want to be in.

"Not necessarily. At least not—"

"No . . . What about sex?" he said, standing up again. "In my day kids went just so far and that's it. Parents would kick your teeth in for just *thinking* about going further. Today, kids—"

"I'm sorry the sexual revolution had such an adverse effect on you," she said a little pungently, folding her arms. She was beginning to be irritated by him.

"Look at the kind of violence they're displaying today. You want to know something . . . I'd rather be robbed by a serial killer than a punk teenager. Know why? I'd have a better chance of surviving. And I'm not blowing air . . . that's statistics," he said, pointing a finger at her. "Anyway, we're not going to discount the idea that this is a practical joke being played on you by a kid. We also have another theory we're working on. We've been pretty busy the last couple of hours, contrary to the belief of that cutie," he said somewhat offended.

"Who are we talking about?"

"The one that was standing next to that sulky guy with the glasses in the hall."

"Her name is Stacey Miller, and she is *not* a cutie, she's my assistant."

"And the one with the droopy nose—what's his problem?"

"I'm afraid you'll have to ask him yourself." It wasn't just his attitude, it was his whole manner that bothered her: his checkered sport coat, the smell of his hair tonic, the Police Special sideburns . . . even his tie clip made into a dollar sign.

"You said you had another theory. What is it?" she asked curtly.

"I hope you're not going to take this personally. It's just that we have to look at all the angles," he said, taking out a pad from the pocket of his jacket and flipping over several pages.

"Take what personally?"

He blew a bubble and sucked it back into his mouth, leaving a small trace of pink substance on his mustache. "First, let me preface this by telling you that this idea was brought up only after a thorough investigation on whether someone could actually break into the phone lines here. See, we've been busy little bees . . . not playing around."

Fragile ego on this one, she thought. "What did you come up with?"

"Well," he said, making tiny popping sounds with his gum, "You see, I had the phone company check out your lines . . . wanted to see if there was a possible cross-connect problem along the way. You know, like getting a different party on the line while talking to someone else."

"That's ludicrous," she said, getting angry. "How in God's name can someone call me in the morning, then accidentally break into my line and talk to me again in the afternoon?"

"Hey," he said, throwing up his hands, "just checking all corners. That's my job. Anyway, the answer is no, everything is A-okay with your system."

"What about an emergency break-in with the assistance of an operator. That's possible, isn't it?"

"In *your* own home, yes . . . but not here," he said, shaking his head. "Just can't happen. You see, you have a special over-the-air number and it's not set up for that sort of thing. But if by a million-to-one shot it did happen that way," he said, again throwing up his hands in the air, "then I'd better have checked into that, too, wouldn't you say?"

He actually was waiting for an answer. "I would say," she finally said.

"And that's what I did. I found out Ma Bell keeps a log containing all emergency break-ins they make." He patted his stomach, looking confident. "And there doesn't seem to be a record of your phone number at this station on it." Again he blew a bubble, this time a big one.

She felt her mouth go dry. "What about human error? Isn't it possible that an operator neglected to log the call?"

"Uh-uh. They're not the swiftest breed in the world. Christ, I dated enough of them to know that. So it's left up to the computers to do it."

"This is ridiculous," she said as she poured herself a cup of water from the cooler. Jaffe declined one for himself even though she didn't offer him any. "Then how could she have broken into my call?"

"Ah, that's where our other theory comes in," he said, cracking a smile.

She was starting to feel uncomfortable. This man was too smug, too sure of himself. "Sergeant, I have a strong sense that you're leading me down a country road that, at least from your perspective, is a four-lane highway. Do you want to tell me what this is all about?"

"Miss Halbrook . . . Gee, I'm sorry, maybe you prefer being called doctor."

"I don't give a damn. Will you please go on."

"Sure thing." He sat on the end of the console, stretched out his legs, crossed them, and folded his arms. "You've employed a PR firm . . . Stern and Harvey, is that right?"

"Yes, what about it?" She was surprised he knew that.

"They've got one heck of a reputation."

"I'm afraid I don't see—"

Bingo! She finally did see.

"Wait a minute! Are you implying that I set this whole thing up as a publicity stunt?" she said, glaring at him in disbelief.

"No, ma'am, I'm not implying anything," he said, putting up his hands again. "I told you before, I have to look into every corner."

"They're a respectable firm that's been around for years. I'm simply using them to publicize a book I've written. Do you people actually believe I'd do something as underhanded as this?" she asked incredulously. "Do you understand what moral turpitude is in my profession?"

"Wait a minute, hold on there now. You remember that late-night talk-show host a few years back—what's his name? Yeah, Randy Jones, that's it," he said, snapping his fingers. "I think the show was taped out of Cleveland."

"No, I don't."

"Real late at night . . . On one of those cable stations. His show was a real stinker and he was on the verge of being tossed off the air. A couple of days before his last show, he disappears . . . mysterious like. The media starts picking up on it . . . not heavy, mind you, but they're starting to sniff around. A week later . . . *Boom!* Ransom demands on audio cassettes are dropped off at every radio station in Cleveland. They're asking a million dollars for this character. Little Randy Jones, a guy who couldn't get arrested a few weeks before, now gets the attention of every newspaper, radio, and TV station across the country. The night Ted Koppel is supposed to do a five-minute segment on him . . . guess what? Our superhero magically returns. Claims he escaped by beating up three of his kidnappers and gets to stay on Koppel's show for the whole half hour. You got to understand, this is a puny, one-hundred-thirty-pound dude, and if you sneezed too loudly he'd probably wet in his pants. He somehow beats the crap out of three bad guys, somewhere he says in southern Pennsylvania, and finds his way back to a TV station in Cleveland. Just in time to talk to Koppel through one of those hookups. Are you with me so far?"

"I'm sure you're heading back to the barn with your point."

"You better believe it. Twenty police officers working full-time . . . over a thousand man-hours combined trying to find this bum. Cleveland shelled out a quarter of a million dollars in expenses trying to locate him. Guess where he was all that time? Bermuda. They got a trace on him through the airlines. He was soaking up rays all that time at some posh resort. But by then it was too late. He made 'Night Line' and became a national celebrity, even if it *was* for a couple of weeks. Now this is the point: Right before he disappeared, he hired the firm of Stern and Harvey to represent him."

"So did many other people."

"The account representative at the firm admitted to the hoax and got sixty days in minimum security picking up tin cans on highways."

"Hold on . . ."

"I can give you other examples of scams that this company was involved in."

"I don't need—"

"All I'm trying to tell you is that this is just another angle we have to look into."

Her upper lip had beads of sweat on it. Jaffe liked that. Miss Perfect was beginning to melt.

"Look," she said finally, fighting to regain some control, "there's a good possibility that there is a child somewhere out there who is either hurt or dead. What do the police intend to do about it?"

"Out where, Miss Halbrook? San Diego . . . L.A. . . . the San Gabriel Valley. Where?"

"I don't know," she said, her lips trembling.

"Well, neither do we. You're on a pretty powerful transmitter. Covers half the state. Now, there's nothing we can really do unless she calls again. We're putting a tracer on your phone here at the station," he said, pointing to the one on her desk.

"She won't be calling again," Rena said softly.

"Oh . . . you know that for a fact, do you?" Jaffe said, lifting his eyebrows.

"I didn't mean that I have control over the situation. I meant that she won't call again because she's probably dead," she said harshly.

"You're being much too sensitive," he said, cracking another bubble. He wanted to grab her by the top part of her throat, gently hold it and while stroking her hair, explain to her what she did to his life and to the lives of other guys like him. Not now. That would come in time, he believed.

When he was gone, Rena picked up the phone to call Cathy, thought better of it, and placed the receiver back on the cradle. A slight irritation over a few phone calls had turned into an all-out nightmare, with implications, now, that could discredit her career. And it was only happening to her and no one else. Why?

Television crews from the late-evening news programs were milling about the lobby as Jaffe emerged from the elevator. They rushed over to him, thrusting microphones into his face.

Jaffe took the gum from his mouth and tossed it in the ash tray next to the elevator. He patted down his hair and buttoned his jacket. The TV lights came on and warmed his face. He put on his professional smile. He was ready for them.

"Who is this Alice?" said a pretty face he recognized from TV news.

"We don't know. We're still checking all the possibilities," he said with his monotone police voice.

"What kind of possibilities?" yelled another reporter, a Mexican guy.

"Missing persons, similar complaints of battered children, and"—he took a long pause to achieve the right affect—"central casting."

They jumped all over this remark, jockeying for position to talk to him. Questions, all overlapping each other, were tossed out, wanting him to explain what he meant. Jaffe shook his head and muttered something about refusing to make any more statements until all the facts were in.

"Hopefully, I'll have something for you very shortly," he said, smiling, as he threaded his way past the mass of newspeople. Are you watching, Mary? he thought. Eat your heart out, 'cause you'll never see that faggot you're living with on TV.

Jaffe felt good. He had handled the great doctor a lot easier than he thought possible. Something, however, was nagging at him as he got into his car and turned down Santa Monica Boulevard. He first felt it when he was listening to the tape in the radio booth. It had to do with this kid, Alice. There was something vaguely familiar about all this, but he couldn't put his finger on it. He soon put it out of his mind when he reached Hollywood Boulevard and Gower.

He parked the car, turned off the headlights, and sat there in the dark watching the hookers dressed in hot shorts selling their wares at the curb. He'd be patient and wait. One of them, he knew, would see him and walk over, showing him her tits, squirming against the car door trying to get him horny. He'd smile at her, hold up a twenty, then as she reached in to take it, show her the badge. She'd drop the bullshit act and get into the car because she knew she had no choice. He'd take her to a deserted area near Las Palmas, where he always went, and she'd give him head and she'd be good at it, convince him that he was the best, because she knew the score.

He saw one approaching the car from the passenger side. She stuck her head in the open window and smiled, exposing a gold tooth. Her skin was dark, black as midnight, and even though she wore heavy makeup, he knew she was no older than sixteen. Jaffe liked that. Near the corner of her left eye was the tattoo of a teardrop, which meant she had done time in the slammer. He liked that, too. As he held out the twenty to her he could feel his other hand clenching into a fist. Oh, he was going to have a *real* good time tonight.

Chapter 6

Monday, 5:55 P.M.

"A real schmendrick," said Rabbi Markowitz, looking down at Charlie lying spread-eagled on the lawn.

"Let him be, Yussel. I'm sure it was an accident," said Mrs. Markowitz, sitting on the grass next to Charlie. She took his head in her arms and cuddled it to her large breasts.

"Shikker. He's lucky to be alive," said the rabbi, shaking his head.

"He smells, Mama," said the oldest boy.

"That's not nice. Go inside and finish your homework," she said, scolding him.

Charlie looked up for the first time and saw the entire Markowitz family peering down at him, their heads blocking out the sun. He took a few deep breaths. The burning in his lungs eased up and his head started to clear. He could have gotten up but he wanted to stay where he was for a while, enjoying the feeling of Mrs. Markowitz's breasts, never expecting to see her clear white skin this close up.

"Do you mind if I ask what I'm doing on the ground?" Charlie said, nestling his head a little deeper into her bosom.

"I bet he goes around asking for spare change," said the younger Markowitz, playing with the tzitzit sticking out from the bottom of his shirt.

"Be quiet," the rabbi said, slapping the boy lightly on the side of the head. He turned back to Charlie. "You want to know why you're lying here, my friend? I'll tell you. You're lying here because it's a much better place to be lying than in there." He pointed to the garage. "In there you would now be a dead man.

And men who die in garages tend to lower the price of real estate."

"Did you pull me out?"

"Look at me. Do you think I'm Lou Ferrigno?" He spread his arms showing a small, wiry frame that topped out at maybe 135 pounds. "It was my wife who smelled the fumes and pulled you out of the car. You're a lucky man. Thank her. And the next time you try to kill yourself, do it someplace else. With the schvartzes moving in right next door, who needs *this*!"

"Do you think you can get up, Mr. Halleran, or do you want the paramedics?" Mrs. Markowitz asked him.

"No, I think I'll be all right. Thanks for what you did," he said, nuzzling his head into her chest one last time. Actually, he would have liked to stay down there awhile longer, but something was gnawing at him, something he heard on the radio before he passed out, something about a girl named Alice . . . except that couldn't be. He moved his head away from her breasts and leaned up on one elbow. Mrs. Markowitz stood up, grabbed him under one arm with her big hand, and easily helped him to his feet.

"I really wasn't trying to kill myself, you know," he said, feeling a little woozy.

"Sure . . . until the next time. Just not in the garage, okay?" the rabbi said, patting him on the shoulder.

Charlie stayed in the hot shower for a long time, trying to wash away the booze and dirt of the last couple of days. He thought about Alice. Whatever happened on the radio had to have been a hallucination. Probably the carbon monoxide; he knew what those fumes could do to your head. Except . . . No, he didn't want to think about it any longer; thinking about Alice also meant thinking about Jaimie—they were interchangeable, and the pain was as fresh as yesterday.

When he couldn't stand the hot water any longer, he got out and looked for a towel. Remembering that he hadn't done his laundry in weeks, he searched through the hamper until he found one that was soiled but usable. He grabbed a pair of old jeans and a Brooklyn College sweatshirt from the closet, dressed, shaved, brushed back his wet curly hair, then went into the kitchen. He took a coffee cup off a stack of dirty dishes in the sink, rinsed it out, tossed in a couple of tablespoons of Maxim freeze-dried and filled it with lukewarm water from the tap. In three quick gulps the cup was empty. He grimaced from the taste, but the caffeine did the job; it cleared his head.

He was hungry. The last time he had put anything in his stomach was on the plane to L.A. The flight attendant said it was pepper steak, except it tasted like cardboard. There wasn't much in the fridge that resembled its original color, so he settled on a can of Dinty Moore stashed in the back of the empty pantry.

He brought the stew and a couple of bottles of Miller into the living room, placed them on the cluttered coffee table, and threw the old newspapers on the floor to make room. He turned on the TV, flipped through the channels, stopping when he saw a hyped-up sportscaster giving the baseball scores. Maybe things were going to look up: the storm was over in Chicago and the Dodgers were going to play a doubleheader with the Cubbies the next day.

The local news came on, and he leaned back on the couch with his bare feet propped up against the coffee table. It felt good to relax. He decided he wouldn't do anything for a couple of days, then maybe call some of the newspapers in town for a job. The Valley had a couple of decent ones. Perhaps he'd try the *Enquirer*. Why not? As long as they paid weekly, that's what counted. He was too broke to give a shit about what he wrote anymore. Maybe he'd try his luck in New York again. He would handle it this time.

Yep, things could only get better, he thought as he unscrewed the top from another Miller.

Then he heard Alice's voice again. This time it came from the television set.

An anchorman in one half of a split screen, with perfect blue-white hair, was sitting behind one of those prop desks, listening to a tape from the phone conversation between Alice and Rena. On the other half of the screen was a printout of that conversation.

Charlie slowly put the beer on the table and dropped to his knees on the carpet in front of the TV. He sat in that position, not moving, muttering, "JesusJesusdearsweetfuckingJesus!" He stayed that way until the segment was over and the weather report came on.

It wasn't a hallucination, it was a fucking nightmare. Either that or he was going crazy.

He felt an ache in his stomach, like someone squeezing his intestines, as the picture of Jaimie's face popped into his head again. He shut his eyes, trying to push the pain back into the darkness. Dammit! Every time he thought he had a handle on it, that feeling came back, jumping up like a jack-in-the-box out of nowhere, laughing as it stuck its tongue out at him.

Those curls . . . Dear God . . . that golden hair!

And Alice . . . Again Alice.

An idea began to take shape in his head—an idea that even a jerk like Bitterman would go crazy over. Except Charlie would never sell it to him . . . unless, of course, the money was right.

He put a call in to the *New York Post*, asking for the Metro section. He said he wanted to talk to an old friend who was editor in chief there, named Tom Winston. Charlie was told by some guy, probably a reporter, that Tom retired six years ago. Lived somewhere in Baja, and spent most of his time fishing. Charlie then asked if he could switch him to the archives and if he had a name of someone who worked in that department who could help him. The man said sure, anything for a buddy of old Tom.

Old Tom . . . Christ! When Charlie knew him he was just-turning-middle-aged Tom.

Yup, things just might begin to turn around now, Charlie thought. Maybe now he could take all that pain and use it to his benefit. Jaimie would understand; she'd want him to be happy.

"This is Brenda, can I help you?" a cheery voice on the phone said.

"Hope so," said Charlie. "You come highly recommended."

"I'm not going to touch that line."

"Smart girl. Look, I need a favor."

"Yeah?"

"I need something in your back files that happened in the Bronx a while ago."

"How far back?"

"Eighteen years."

"Oh, brother, do you know what time it is? Are we giving or

taking a couple of years? Tell me you know exactly so I can go home before the muggers come out."

"I know exactly. Eighteen years." He gave her the year, month, and day of what he was looking for.

"You're lucky we're computerized. Give me a couple of minutes, okay?"

"Sure," Charlie said, his jaw beginning to clench. He remembered the date as if it were yesterday. How could he forget? It happened a couple of months before . . .

Charlie rubbed his eyes, trying to shake the pictures loose from the walls of his head, but they stubbornly clung on, refusing to go away.

Those curls . . . those freckles!

Rosie kissed Charlie good-bye in the Port Authority bus terminal the next morning. An hour later he was on a long line waiting for his induction physical at Fort Dix.

The *Post*, before he left, offered him a proposition: volunteer for 'Nam, do a year as a grunt, and keep a daily journal. It would be called *A Soldier's Diary* and printed every day under a pseudonym of Charlie's choosing; the army and the public would never know it was he until after his tour of duty. With the Pulitzer looming in his mind, Charlie took them up on the offer.

Three months later, just before he was scheduled to ship out of San Diego on a transport boat to Southeast Asia, he received a letter from Rosie saying that she was pregnant. He ran to the nearest pay phone and called her. Laughing, he told her how much he loved her, and that he'd be back in a year. "Jesus," he said, jumping up and down in the phone booth with happiness, "pregnant, and I have to go to war. This is straight out of *Thirty Seconds over Tokyo*!"

Charlie came back in one year as he had promised, but most of the time was spent not in 'Nam, but in an army hospital in Thailand.

When he had gotten to Saigon, a major in charge of a supply depot noticed how fast he could type and assigned him the job of being his secretary. Charlie protested, telling the major his talent would be wasted, that he was really trained to go into the bush and off little guys in black pajamas.

"You some kind of fucking asshole or what?" the major said,

squinting at him behind sunglasses. "Every man out in the bush would give their left nut to be in your place right now. You're white, you're educated, and you can type. That means you're now my woman. The only thing I don't like about you is the fact that you don't wear a dress . . . and that better change. Now get the fuck out of here!"

Charlie kissed his byline good-bye that night and got drunk for the first time in his life. For the next couple of months he worked behind a desk typing out a general inventory of bathroom supplies for the entire United States Army stationed in Saigon.

One hot morning, during a heavy monsoon rain, Charlie walked into his office and found a requisition on his desk for five hundred cases of toilet paper to be delivered to Delta Company in Chantrea. The requisition was marked "Immediate Response" in red letters—which meant "Top Priority"—and signed by his superior, the major. Two things bothered Charlie about this order: First, D Company was supposed to be on an operation in the Plain of Reeds in the Mekong delta; and second, he had never heard of Chantrea. He went over to the map of Vietnam on the bulletin board and scanned it area by area; Chantrea wasn't there. This didn't make any sense. He then went over to the hangars where the transport choppers, the UHI Hueys, were kept and asked the ground sergeant if he could take a peak at some aerial reconnaissance maps.

Sticking the maps under his slicker so they wouldn't get wet from the rain, he went into an outhouse next to the airstrip, locked the door, and painstakingly inched his way through them. It didn't take long before Charlie found what he was looking for, and it made lots of sense.

Smiling, Charlie went back to his office and wired the *Post* in New York, hinting lightly at what he suspected and saying he would wire again if his suspicion was confirmed. He then ran across the compound in the downpour to the major's office.

"Gee, sir," Charlie said as innocently as he could, wiping the mud off his boots on the mat outside the office. "I think there must be some mistake." He explained to the major about the purchase order for the toilet paper for Chantrea. "Except Chantrea," he said, "is not in 'Nam."

The major lit a cigar and said nothing, never taking his eyes off Charlie.

"It's a small village deep in Cambodia, sir. Now that's got to be a mistake, sir, because the president told the nation only last week that he'd never let the war spill over into that country. I guess when you signed the requisition, sir, it was only for toilet paper and you weren't paying much attention to where it was going."

The major slowly puffed on his cigar, not saying anything for several seconds, then asked softly, "What's your assessment of the situation, Private?"

Charlie sat down without permission and said, "Well, sir, I see it as an either/or situation. Either we're giving a seminar in Cambodia showing the natives how Western civilization toilet-trains itself . . . or maybe some of our boys are illegally stationed over there and running around with dirty assholes."

The major sighed long and deep while rolling the cigar around in his fingers, then said finally, "That's pure speculation and, if spread around, could cause our government—which is going through a lot of shit right now back home—a great deal of embarrassment. I'm sure you probably have one or two suggestions on how to help nip this rumor in the bud before it gets out."

Charlie took a cigar from the major's humidor, leaned back on it, and lit it. He knew he was right about everything and home free. He said, yes, he did have a suggestion, and that was for the major to find himself another girl Friday. If this one request could be granted, then Charlie would give his word as a soldier in the United States Army that he would keep his mouth shut for the good of his country.

Two days later Charlie got his orders to join a search and destroy unit of the Fifth Infantry Division in Thua Thien province. Before leaving, he sent a wire to his editor at the *Post*:
HOPE YOU KEPT PAGE ONE WARM STOP SUGGEST YOU INVEST IN SCOTT PAPER PRODUCTS STOP OUR BOYS WHO ARE DOING SOME R&R IN THE LAND OF THE KHMER ROUGE SAY IT'S THE LATEST RAGE EVEN PREFERRED OVER GOOD OLD THAI STICK STOP

The bush was wet and humid, and for the next several weeks Charlie learned how to live on his stomach. He wrote every moment he wasn't carrying his M-16, or didn't have to dig holes in the ground to hide from enemy shells, or scurry out of the way from the miscalculations of U.S. F-4 Phantoms raining napalm down on him. He wrote about the closeness of the men in his unit, the rice farmers that lived in the delta, and always about death. For three short weeks Charlie had his byline on page three of the *Post* . . . until one hot July night when it all came to an end.

He was sitting on the ground leaning against the remains of a fallen tree, wrapped in a blanket to keep out the insects, and drinking some kind of native hooch made of fermented rice and berries. A young grunt, who had just arrived a couple of days before, got up and walked into the woods to take a leak. The kid wandered into a restricted area looking for privacy and triggered a claymore no more than twenty feet from where Charlie was sitting. The explosion blew the boy to bits. It also blasted apart the tree Charlie was leaning against, sending hundreds of wood particles, some as big as steak knives, into his body.

He was airlifted to Saigon, then to Bangkok for further surgery. After nine months of hospitalization, he was on his way back to the States with a Purple Heart but no byline.

Rosie was waiting for him at the docks in San Francisco, clutching three-month-old Jaimie in her arms as he disembarked from the ship. When he tried putting his arms around Rosie, she moved away and stiffly offered her cheek to be kissed. Charlie could see the coldness in her eyes and hoped the only reason for it was because he was away for a year. But when he picked up his child and saw how she was covered with filth and excrement, Charlie knew things had gotten worse with Rosie.

Back home, he spent every minute he could with his infant daughter, getting to know her. Rosie, during the first weeks, stayed mostly in the bedroom with the TV on, staring out at Charlie as he played with Jaimie on the floor. She was put out by it, his laughter and Jaimie's squeals of delight an intrusion on her private world.

Charlie went back to work for the *Post* and became their inside man at Gracie Mansion. The mayor, who didn't have any children of his own, treated Charlie like a son and wanted him as his personal aide-de-camp. Other job inducements came pouring in: the *New York Times* offered him a position with their Washington Bureau, and he was again approached by CBS, this time by the network. They were all high-profile jobs that Rosie's deteriorating condition prevented him from taking. By this time, Rosie was spending hours sitting at the kitchen table with a faraway look, smoking cigarettes, staring into space, grinding her teeth. Eventually she was unable to take care of Jaimie and Charlie had to hire a live-in. When she did not snap back in time, he decided it would be in the best interest of everyone, especially hers, that she be committed to an institution upstate.

Charlie knew the marriage, now, was not a workable situation. The months she was hospitalized gave him a freedom he grasped with his whole being. He began spending his nights away from home, hanging out with the top political guns of New York, and meeting women who were constantly making headlines in the society pages of his paper.

When Rosie returned, Charlie's heart sank. At first he was angry because it meant curtailing his new life-style, but that soon turned to guilt and self-reproach when he saw how fragile and helpless she had become. The passion he once had for her was gone, but he couldn't leave her, not right now, not until she was better. This was a decision he would later regret.

Charlie came home one night, having worked late on a story for the morning edition. He heard the TV in the bedroom, the voice of Little Joe talking to Hoss. He didn't see Jaimie and figured she was in the bedroom with Rosie watching the show. Charlie made himself a sandwich from leftover meat loaf and opened a can of Schlitz. When he finished, he went into the bedroom, saw both of them asleep under the covers, and turned off the set. Normally he didn't like Jaimie sleeping in bed with them, but in the darkness she looked so peaceful, and he was too tired to get her up. After he undressed, he got under the sheets, nudging Jaimie, hoping she'd move so he'd have more room. She wouldn't budge and Charlie decided to make the best of it by sleeping on his side. His hands felt wet and sticky from touching her, and the sheets were damp. It wasn't warm enough in the room for this kind of perspiration, and he assumed Jaimie had wet the bed. Except there was a smell to it, a familiar smell, one he had encountered in Nam too many times. The smell of blood! As he bolted up he heard Rosie's dreadful laughter.

Heh, heh, heh.

She was on the other side of Jaimie, sitting up, with something dark in her hand. Charlie grabbed Jaimie and lifted her in his arms. Her body was limp, her arms and legs dangling lifelessly in his grip. He turned his head toward Rosie, mouth open, wanting to say something, but the dark thing she was holding was now in the air and he knew in that split second there was nothing he could say that would change anything. A patch of light from the street lamp outside reflected off the object, and Charlie saw that it was a large kitchen knife. As it plunged deep into his left lung, he got a momentary rush of déjà vu: the flash of wooden slivers exploding inside him in Nam.

"Hey, you still there?" Brenda said.
"Still here," Charlie said, his mind coming back to the present. Sweat was trickling down his armpits.
"I found what you were looking for. This is pretty grizzly stuff."
"No shit," Charlie muttered.

Chapter 7

Tuesday, 7:51 P.M.

The air conditioning in the Hyatt was a welcome relief to Charlie from the hot muggy air outside. Funds were low right now, and he had parked several blocks away and walked to the hotel rather than give the valet three bucks.

The collar of his broadcloth shirt was tight and the heat was chafing his neck. He loosened the button and pulled down his tie while scanning the festivity marquee in the lobby. There it was: DR. RENA HALBROOK, TONIGHT AT 8:00 . . . IN THE ORANGE BALLROOM.

Charlie removed his jacket, draped it over his arm, and followed the trail of ballroom fruits: Pear, apple, tangerine, until he got to the one with a picture of an orange over the front door.

Inside, almost all the seats were taken by women, with a smattering of men—people who had time to listen to daytime talk shows. Charlie could see it was mostly an older, middle-class group: pastel polyester suits for the women and short-sleeve white shirts with pen cases in the pockets for the men.

There was a vacant chair in the middle of the back row and Charlie squeezed his body down the aisle trying to get to it. The woman next to the seat let out a squeal as he stepped on her toe. He mumbled an apology and sat down.

"That's all right. I'm used to it. I have such big feet," she said.

Charlie smiled.

"I noticed you standing at the door and I said to myself, 'Boy, does he look familiar, but I don't know from where.' "

He turned around and looked at her. She was wearing gobs

of turquoise jewelry around her neck and thick, wire-rimmed glasses that were scanning him like security cameras. Her hair was long and parted in the middle with strands of gray.

And yes . . . she also looked familiar.

"Didn't you belong to Elysium Fields?" she said, smiling at him, her knee touching his.

"I don't think so. What's that, a country club?"

"No, it's a nudist colony. I'm sure it's you. You have a scar on your chest, right?" she said, tracing it lightly with her finger on his shirt.

Now he did remember. Except it wasn't at a nudist colony, it was at Peppy's . . . maybe two years ago. Third bar stool from the right. They went back to her place afterward. She lit incense that smoked up the room and played an album of Gregorian chants. He remembered lying in the bed later on, her sleeping body on top of his, and the incense burning into his lungs. There was something about that night; maybe it was the cheerless medieval music still playing in the other room, or the way she screwed with her eyes open, but in the darkness he had a vision of Rosie lying in that bed—heh-hehing—and his heart started pounding. He wouldn't close his eyes. He waited until he could hear this woman's deep rhythmic breathing, then pried his numb arm away from under her neck, dressed in the hallway, and left. His car was at Peppy's, and it took him most of the night to walk back to his place.

"I don't go to nudist colonies. I'm a Baptist fundamentalist," he said, avoiding her fishlike eyes.

"I could swear. . . ." She put her hand up to her chin, thinking. "Did you ever take a course in the postmodern literature of Indochina?" she asked finally, her knee, again, pressing against his.

Before he could answer her the lights faded and Rena walked over to the podium from behind the curtain. The audience applauded, some fervently, with their eyes misting over. They had that same pastoral look Jennifer Jones had had whenever she talked to the white lady in *The Song of Bernadette*.

Charlie knew she was fairly young but had no inkling she would be this pretty. Listening to her compelling, rational voice over the radio, he assumed she'd be more of the professorial type, the kind you wished had a body to go with that mind.

Brenda, the girl who worked in the archives at the *Post*, said she'd like to get together with him whenever he was in New York. Charlie told her he'd take her up on it, trying to remember if he had ever met a good-looking Brenda. He didn't think so. Seeing he was on a roll, he asked her for more information—anything she had in her files on Rena Halbrook. Brenda had obliged. When he hung up, he glanced through his notepad and was a little surprised at what he discovered. Rena Halbrook's father was one of the richest men in the country. He owned Morgan Labs, a pharmaceutical company, plus a real estate empire that included many of the luxury hotels in the Hawaiian Islands and Caribbean. As a hobby, to get away from the everyday grind, he'd bought the Blues, a Los Angeles baseball franchise, a couple of years back and was currently in negotiations to purchase the city's basketball team.

"The guy acquires possessions like the world was a Monopoly board," Brenda had said to him. She also told him that his wife had died many years ago and that Rena and her daughter, Cathy, were his only living relatives.

Charlie leaned forward in his chair, watching Rena as she casually conversed with her audience. He wondered what it would be like to be married to the sole inheritor of a fortune, probably in the ballpark of almost a billion dollars. Bet'cha Peppy'd even extend me credit, he thought.

For the next two hours, Rena talked about relationships, love and anger, and how to overcome neurotic handicaps and become independent, healthy individuals.

He noticed the smooth way she carried herself, definitely self-assured and charismatic. The audience seemed drawn in by the softness of her voice, even by the way she stressed certain words. Their heads, acting like magnets, followed her every movement. Her thoughts were clear and spontaneous; nothing felt rehearsed. Charlie looked at the people and saw them nodding and agreeing with her, many of them clutching Rena's latest book to their breasts as they listened, cradling it as if it were the Holy Scriptures.

She sure knows how to work a house, Charlie thought.

The two hours went by quickly. Afterward, she walked among the audience answering questions and autographing her book. Charlie stayed in the back and watched.

"Don't you want to meet her?" the woman from Peppy's asked as she got up. She was holding a blank piece of paper for Rena to sign.

"Another time," Charlie said.

As Rena walked by, the woman handed her the paper. Rena signed it, smiled at her, and then moved to the other side of the room.

"She's wonderful," the woman said as she placed the signed paper carefully in her purse.

"The best," Charlie said, standing up.

"Going?"

"Yep."

"Too bad. I thought if you weren't doing anything, maybe we could go for a drink. I know this place on Wilshire . . . ouch!"

Charlie stepped on her foot again as he slid past her down the aisle.

He caught up with her in the parking lot of the hotel as she was about to enter her Jag.

"Dr. Halbrook," he said pleasantly, staying several feet in back of her so she wouldn't be frightened.

"Yes?" she said wearily as she put her briefcase in the trunk of the car.

"My name's Charles Halleran, and I'm a reporter for the *L.A. Tribune*." He held up his old press ID from the *Tattler* for her to see, covering up the name of the paper with his thumb. "Can I talk to you for a sec."

"About what?"

"About Alice."

"There's not much to talk about," she said, getting into the car.

"I think you're wrong."

"Sorry, but I'm late for an appointment."

Charlie waited until she started her engine. "Her name's Alice Mendoza," he said, raising his voice over the sound of the motor.

"What?"

"Mendoza. That's Alice's last name . . . in case you didn't know."

She turned off the motor. "How do you know that?" she said cautiously.

He took out a legal-size envelope from his jacket pocket. "Everything you want to know is in here. If you like, we could go for a quick drink and you can look through this. I think you'll be just as amazed as I was."

"Have you spoken to the police about this?"

"I wanted to talk to you first."

"They're the ones I think you should consult, not me, Mr. . . . ?"

"Halleran. I'm afraid they won't find her, Dr. Halbrook," he shouted again over the engine.

"Why not?" she asked as she backed the car out of the space.

"Because she's been dead for the last eighteen years."

Chapter 8

Tuesday, 10:43 P.M.

They sat in the back of the Hyatt bar to be away from the piano player who was plunking out a tired version of "New York, New York." The place was jammed, mainly with out-of-town businessmen. At the bar a hooker was sipping a wine spritzer and waiting for the shy John sitting next to her to get drunk enough to make a move.

Rena opened the envelope Charlie had given her, courtesy of Brenda and Federal Express, and took out photocopies of old clippings from several New York newspapers. They were all dated eighteen years ago. As she laid them out on the table she noticed that the more sensational the tabloid, the more shocking the headline. She saw Charlie's byline on the article from the *Post*.

He flagged down the waitress and asked Rena if she wanted a drink. She shook her head no, not looking up from the clippings. He ordered a double J&B for himself.

"I don't think we're going to be here that long," she said, frowning.

"I drink fast."

She put on her reading glasses and scanned the articles.

The glasses sitting on the tip of her nose made her even more sensual than she already was. No, you don't meet women like this at Peppy's, he sighed to himself.

"I was working as a reporter with the *Post* in New York when this happened," he said to her.

"What's this all about?" Rena said, looking pale and shaken.

74

The clipping described the brutal torture and murder of a seven-year-old Puerto Rican girl named Alice Mendoza.

"Let me start from the beginning," Charlie said, licking his dry mouth. He looked over to the bar, where the waitress was laughing at a dirty joke one of the customers was telling, and wished she'd hurry up with the drink. "I was interviewing the captain of the Twelfth Precinct in the Bronx eighteen years ago, something to do with allegations that some of his men were on the take, when in walks this guy reeking of Old Spice. He confesses to the desk sergeant that he just killed his daughter. He did not look like your average, everyday murderer. This character was maybe five-foot-three and dressed to the hilt—a frayed suit neatly pressed, white shirt, tie, worn shoes nicely polished. He said to the sergeant that after he killed her, he took a shower to wash away the mess and dressed neatly so the police wouldn't think he was a bum. He said it was important what they thought of him."

The drink came. Charlie quickly gulped down half of it. "There was a possibility of him being a crazy . . . that the whole thing was nothing but a fantasy in his burnt-out mind. That's what everybody at the station thought. A couple of uniforms were sent to check his story out and I got permission to tag along. The address he'd given was a condemned tenement in the South Bronx. The door was locked. We broke it in without too much trouble." Charlie paused, letting the scene pass through his head, then finished off his drink. "We found her. It wasn't hard to do. Her body was scattered everywhere in the room. I was a political reporter for the paper at that time, and the most blood I ever saw on the job before that was when a city councilman, looking for votes in Prospect Park, got hit in the face with a baseball from a Sunday Little League game. But this was something else. One hell of a mess. Parts of her were everywhere. If it weren't for that long red hair, you'd never know it was a girl."

"That was a long time ago. What does this—"

"I'm coming to it," Charlie said. The alcohol kicked in, helping him talk about it. "The mother of Alice ran off to Vegas with a guy a couple of years before, abandoning the poor kid. The father went crazy—locked Alice in a closet, beat her, sexually abused her, practically starved her to death. There was no family, no friends, no one to check up on her. She spent something like four years of her life locked in a damn closet."

"I still don't see—"

"I promise you *will* see. Since I was the first to break the story, my editor felt that I should stay with it, even though it wasn't within my field of expertise. I flew to Vegas to locate the mother. I found her. She was renting a third-rate motel room off the strip, using it to turn tricks. I couldn't find her home address. The interesting part about her was that she wasn't a PR."

"What?"

"Puerto Rican. She wasn't Puerto Rican. She was fair-skinned with bright red hair, maybe of Irish descent. That answered my first question concerning the color of Alice's hair. The father was dark . . . lots of African blood in him, and I originally thought the mother would be the same."

"Did she know what happened to her daughter?"

"No. She was frightened of her husband and never left a forwarding address. I tracked her down through the DMV."

"Why didn't the police try to find her? It was *her* child."

"She wasn't the daughter of Donald Trump, you understand. Just the offspring of a hooker and an unemployed Puerto Rican. It would have cost the city twenty cents in phone calls and maybe five minutes of someone's time to try and locate her. I guess they figured they had more important things to do." Charlie caught the waitress's eye and pointed to his empty glass.

"How long is this story going to take, Mr. Halleran?" Rena asked impatiently.

"I'm turning the corner," he said, smiling at her. "After I tell the Mendoza woman what happened, she goes into a five-minute act—beats her breasts, cries—tells me that she should never have left her baby with that maniac. She told me that he also beat her when she lived with him. Now get this! Then she goes to the mirror, fixes her hair, puts on some makeup, then excuses herself because there's a guy waiting for her at the Sands."

Rena squirmed in her chair. She was thinking of her own daughter.

"A real mother of the year," he said.

"Okay, so both girls had the same first name. So do Ronald Reagan and Ronald McDonald . . . so what?"

"Both of them were kept in a closet."

"And both Ronalds are clowns. It's nothing but a coincidence. You also mentioned that Alice has the same last name as this murdered girl. You want to tell me about this one?" she said skeptically.

"I'm coming to that. First, let me give you another similarity." She's not going to be easy, Charlie thought. "She kept saying the word 'hoppy.' "

"Hobby," she corrected him.

"Okay, hobby. What she was really trying to say was Holmby. That's the name of the street she was living on. You asked for her address, remember? Alice . . . *my* Alice lived at one-thirty-two Holmby."

The waitress leaned over Charlie, smiling at him as she let her ample breasts rest on his shoulder while putting his drink on the table. Rena looked away from this obvious display and glanced at the Schlitz clock on the wall. Cathy expected her home a half hour ago. She knew she should leave, but there was something about this man—maybe it was his desperation as he awkwardly tried stringing both girls together. No, it was something else. Probably those intelligent blue eyes staring into her, causing a fluttering sensation in her stomach. Whatever it was, she didn't want to get up, not yet.

"What does an eighteen-year-old murder have to do with yesterday's phone call?" she asked.

Charlie took a deep breath; it was now or never. "I know this might sound a little crazy, and believe me, there's no one more cynical than I am, but I honestly believe that *your* Alice and *my* Alice are one and the *same* Alice."

"My God," Rena said, closing her eyes and nodding. "I should have known."

"Think I'm crazy, don't you?"

She just stared at him, not answering.

"I guess that means you do. Okay, I can understand that."

"Perhaps you have an unusual religious affiliation, Mr. Halleran, that makes you think the things you do. Whatever it is, let's just say I don't share your point of view." She took her glasses off and tossed them into her purse. "If you'll excuse me, I'm rather late."

"Isn't it possible?" Charlie asked, touching her arm to stop her from leaving.

"What's possible? That this child is a—what? A poltergeist? Casper the friendly ghost? What kind of bullshit are you trying to hand me?" she said, pulling her arm away.

"Okay, answer me one question then. How did Alice break into your phone lines?"

She didn't say anything, but the anger began to subside and Charlie knew he was back on the right track.

"There's no way anyone could have hooked into your line. I'm right, aren't I?" he said, seeing it in her face.

"I guess I'd have to say you're right, at least about that. How do you know?"

He shrugged. "I called the phone company. They told me nothing could have gotten past your line. At least nothing living." Actually he had called a friend of his at the station this morning who told him what Jaffe and Rena had talked about. It seems that Jaffe was bragging to everyone who would listen about how he made mincemeat out of the "bitch."

"I'm a psychologist, Mr. Halleran, and the only ghosts I'm interested in are old neuroses that pop back into our lives to haunt us. By the way, I didn't know that the *L.A. Tribune* went in for this kind of reporting," she said, more than a little suspicious.

Charlie could feel this thing starting to turn around on him. "The article I'm planning to write wouldn't be for the *Times*," he said, clearing his throat. "I was thinking of going national with it . . . more along the lines of *People* or *Life*."

"I see. Like moonlighting."

"Right."

"The *Tribune* doesn't mind this?"

"Who's to know?" he said sheepishly.

"And why do you need my stamp of approval for this?" she said as she picked up the plastic stirrer and toyed with it between her lips.

Damn! She even looks good doing that, he thought. "Because the story would be nothing more than conjecture without it."

"And my okaying this would give it the necessary validity?" she said with a disbelieving smirk.

"Let's just say it would help." He felt it going awry again.

"Good money in it, huh?"

"Not bad. It could be good money for both of us." He knew it was the wrong thing to say as soon as he said it.

"Ah, I see." She was beginning to see, but first she needed to make a phone call to be sure. She excused herself and went toward the rest rooms.

He watched her slim body walk across the lounge, as did the guy sitting at the bar talking to the prostitute. Charlie groaned and massaged his temples, wondering what had possessed him to think she'd buy into his craziness. Maybe he'd try a new angle, explain to her how many of her colleagues were now doing extensive research in the field of parapsychology. Maybe he should just stop thinking and get the fuck out of here while she was in the bathroom.

The first call she made was to Cathy to apologize for being late. She endured a few "aw Moms," then told her to stick a frozen pizza in the oven and that she'd be home in twenty minutes.

The next one was to an old friend of the family, Theodore von Rosmond, the publisher of the *Tribune*. Von Rosmond was the kind of man who wore a Harvard tie, even on Sundays, had tea and scones every day at three, and was on a first-name basis with the president of the United States, who occasionally spent weekends with him at his home in Palm Springs. He was also the kind of man who knew the name of every employee who worked on his paper, including the trainee who made the Dunkin' Donuts run for the staff. The name of Charlie Halleran was not one of them. That's not to say, however, he didn't know of him by reputation. He told Rena what he knew about Charlie: at one time he was a top, well-respected New York journalist who, for some reason unknown to him, had hit bottom.

Rena arrived back at the table. Charlie made a motion to stand but a flick of her hand told him not to bother.

"Now, where were we, Mr. Halleran?" she said, sitting down and leaning into him. "Oh, yes, we were in the midst of discussing an article about an eighteen-year-old ghost who comes back to re-create the scene of the crime. Why do you suppose she wants to do that? Do you think her killer is still at large?"

"No, I don't think so," he said, running his finger around

the rim of the glass. He could see by her attitude that it was a lost cause. What the hell . . . *Go for it*. "As a doctor in the field of psychology, you're aware that parapsychology is a respected branch of your profession." He hoped his voice didn't betray the stupidity of that statement.

"I don't know how respected it is but I do know it exists. Except that the studies are done in a controlled environment, such as a laboratory . . . not in a free-form theatrical setting of a dingy closet somewhere in the South Bronx. Seems the only thing missing in this scenario is Ebenezer, Tiny Tim, and a partridge in a pear tree. But then we'd be getting very gothic, and that wouldn't work in LaLa land, now, would it?" she said, smiling.

Charlie let out a long sigh, like a slow leak in a tire.

"Too bad you weren't writing this for a newspaper like the *Tattler*. It would make a hell of a story."

"Oh, God," Charlie groaned.

"Did you actually think I'd lend my name to a cheap scam so that rag of yours could sell more newspapers? What a desperate man you must be, Mr. Halleran," she said, shaking her head.

Desperate was the key word and it stuck in his stomach like barbed wire. He could tell her that he no longer worked for the *Tattler*, that he was going to free-lance it to a bigger paper. Except that it wouldn't matter, because it would still be a rag, only bigger. All he wanted right now was to end this evening and tap-dance out of here as gracefully as possible. "Well . . . it *was* a long shot," he said, his face a bright red.

"Yes, it certainly was," she said, getting up. "And a cheap one."

Good exit line, he thought as she turned to leave.

As she got into her car, Rena had a strong desire to go back into the lounge and ask him what happened to make him blow such a bright future. According to von Rosmond, Halleran could have been another Brokaw or Donaldson. He wasn't exaggerating; she had seen firsthand his personality and charm. Instead, she opted to go back home to spend time with her daughter. There weren't enough hours in her life to deal with everyone's problems, especially someone who just tried to hustle her.

Hopefully he'd find a good therapist to help him get his life back in order.

Charlie jiggled the ice in his empty glass, thinking he'd go it alone. It would be a harder sell, maybe even a lawsuit, but that had never stopped him before. Christ! He even had the headline picked out: GHOST OF MURDERED CHILD HOUNDS FAMOUS RADIO PERSONALITY. Good title. It would sell a lot of newspapers.

Except he wasn't feeling as good as he normally did when he was onto a sure thing. Maybe it was her adverse reaction to him, or that he was trying to make a buck on the tragedy of this girl, or even the fact that his own daughter had been brutally murdered by a parent. No, he just didn't feel good about any of this and he didn't know why.

Except he did know why.

There was a story here, a real one, and instead of chasing it down—following leads, spending hours in libraries going over microfilm, talking to people who remembered, who saw—he elected the easy route: sensationalism. Facts only got in the way of this kind of reporting; they clouded the headline, made it smaller. He remembered a time, though, when following a story and not the headline was the real thrill. He liked his work then.

He had a daughter then.

Two girls with the same first name, both locked in a closet, both tortured, abused, maybe the same street address, maybe both murdered . . . and eighteen years apart. Even a jerk, like himself, would eventually see that it had to be more than a coincidence. That's the *real* story. Not this bullshit about ghosts and radio shrinks. A younger Charlie would have seen it and gone after it.

He loved then.

The waitress came over to the table with a fresh drink. "On the house," she said, putting the glass on a new cocktail napkin. This time she leaned over in front of Charlie, giving him a good look at her deep, freckled cleavage. "What happened to your girlfriend? You guys have a fight or something?"

Charlie looked up at her and saw her tired smile and the thick pancake makeup covering the dark circles around her eyes. After looking at Rena, there was no comparison. He pushed the drink away and asked for the check.

Shrugging, the waitress handed it to him and drifted off to another table.

Outside, in the hot night air, Charlie was halfway down the block before he realized he had just walked away from a free, perfectly good double J&B. Peppy'd shit bricks if he heard about that, he thought, laughing.

Yep, a younger Charlie would have gone after the real story. And that's just what he was going to do.

Book II

June 18–27

Chapter 9

Sunday, 7:10 P.M.

The security man who'd been opening the wrought-iron gates in Hancock Park Estates for the last twenty years recognized Rena's car, waved, and let her through. She drove a block past the mayor's mansion until she came to her father's estate, a large seventy-five-year-old home made of brick. As she turned up the pebbled driveway, she stopped to let an armed security man, who was employed by her father, open the electric gate. She smiled, asked about his family, then continued up the driveway and parked next to the four-car garage. Through the rearview mirror she could see cameras mounted every fifteen feet following every move she made. She no longer paid any attention, but she remembered how violated she felt when they were first installed. As a child she used to lie in bed under the covers with the drapes drawn hiding from the cameras. She imagined having the ability to peer through walls, watching her in the bathroom, leering at her nakedness like dirty old men. Sometimes she thought that they could even see into her head, unveiling all her secrets, laughing at her fantasies. She feared that whoever was operating these cameras was writing her thoughts down and planned to expose everything to her family and schoolmates. She never told her father how she hated them because she knew they were needed to protect the priceless French Impressionist paintings in the house, one of the largest privately owned collections in the world.

Anna, her father's housekeeper, came out of the house and hugged Rena to her breast.

"Where you been, child?" the old black woman said, half

scolding, in her clipped West Indies accent. "Your daughter's been stickin' her nose out the door looking for you every two minutes."

"It's just been one of those days," Rena said, glad to see her.

"Don't you hand me none of your bull, now. Everybody's here already. The poor girl's been waiting all evening to cut the cake and open the presents."

"Is Terry here?"

"Yes, ma'am," the old woman said without bothering to hide her disapproval.

Rena was relieved. Cathy would have been heartbroken if he didn't show.

She put her arm around Anna's frail shoulders as they walked into the house. The woman had worked for the Halbrook family for almost fifty years and probably understood Rena better than anyone else. She had been her nanny when she was a baby and her confidante when she was growing up. In actuality, she was more of a mother to Rena than her real mother had been.

Elaina Halbrook was one of the few women in New York society who didn't lie about her ancestors being the first settlers to set foot on Plymouth Rock. And with those hundreds of years of social breeding came a class distinction that she firmly believed in right up to her death. One rule being: Children were to be brought up by nannies and then, when they were of school age, shipped off to finishing schools back east. That's the way it was for her and that's the way it was going to be for Rena.

As a child, on a holiday away from school, Rena once hid behind the second-floor banister and watched her parents host a black-tie dinner party for Senator John F. Kennedy a few months before he announced his candidacy for president. Elaina, who was outraged that her husband would support the son of a whiskey runner, nevertheless, when he was in her home, treated Kennedy with the same courtesy she would have given to any respectable Republican. Rena, a gangly child then, who needed braces and wore thick glasses, watched between the railings as her mother, who had movie-star beauty, gracefully moved about the house. She thought it was magnificent how Elaina, who held a champagne glass in one hand and a cigarette holder in the other, could give orders to the help while at the same time graciously listening then casually tossing out witty remarks to some of the most powerful men in the Democratic party. Looking down from the steps, Rena wished with all her might that some fairy godmother would come down and make her as beautiful and spectacular as Elaina was tonight.

Ten years later Elaina contracted stomach cancer. Rena was taken out of school and sent home to be at her side. She watched her mother's beauty shrivel away as the disease grew. At night Rena would hear her screaming and cursing in agony, saying horrible words that only the bad girls in her school used. Later Elaina would plead for the nurse to administer an extra dosage of morphine so she could die with dignity. Rena half hoped the nurse would give it to her because, for Elaina, dignity was the way one lived and died. When she did die, she was unrecognizable and weighed only sixty-eight pounds.

The day of the funeral, Rena stared at the body in the teak casket and decided she no longer wanted to be like Elaina. As protected as her life had been up to now, Rena got her first lesson in mortality: beauty and decorum were no defense against the unfeeling forces of nature. She told her father that night that she would not go back East to finish high school, that she wanted to stay here and go to a public school like other children her age. He lifted her up and hugged her and said, smiling, that she didn't need to go back there to develop character, that she had more character than all those watery-eyed, inbred wimps in that school put together.

A cheer broke out when Rena walked into the living room. Simon Halbrook moved his six-foot-five body across the room, put his arms around her, and kissed her.

"How are you, baby?" he asked.

"Fine, Dad." She saw he was still wearing his pure white mane of hair on the long side severely brushed back, intensifying his widow's peak, giving him the appearance of either a Norman Rockwell grandfather or Svengali, depending on which look suited his purposes. As he peered down at her over his glasses she wondered how many young executives must have upchucked their lunch after an intense meeting with this towering man.

"Who's that young man Cathy's with?" he asked with a twinkle in his eye.

"Who?"

"Thick glasses . . . They're in the den playing some computer game where these little things chew up people."

"Ah, Mr. Roger Harris the Third," she said, smiling.

"Anything more with that problem you had on your program?" he asked, bending his head toward her and raising his thick right eyebrow.

"No. It's been over two weeks and everything's quieted down. At least the press is off my back. I just wish the police had been more helpful," she said, frowning.

He moved his head close to her ear and said, "If you have any more problems like that, you let me know, you hear me." Norman Rockwell would never have painted the look he now had on his face. Nobody was going to play with his only girl.

Rena saw Terry across the room talking to Craig Sanders, the district attorney. They had drinks in their hands, standing next to an early van Gogh oil and laughing about something Terry had just said.

Shit! The prep's still got that look, she thought, her heart dropping a couple of inches. Tan, thin frame . . . muscular arms. He was wearing khaki pants, boat shoes, and a faded violet polo shirt. All her life she had hated preps and she ended up marrying one.

They saw Rena, grinned, and held their drinks up, motioning for her to come over. Terry took a champagne glass off a passing tray and handed it to her. Craig bent over to kiss her and she moved her head slightly, offering him her cheek. They had dated before she had met Terry and she knew he was still in love with her. Offering anything more than a cheek would be offering hope. Terry, his head cocked to the side, opened his arms wide and waited for her to embrace him. Instead, she nodded and gave him her hand.

"Glad you could make it this time, Terry," she said, pulling her hand away from his warm, tight clutch.

"You know, hon, I'd never miss Cathy's birthday if I could help it." He was all teeth, grinning at her.

"Then we must be living on different planets. Here on Earth birthdays come once a year . . . not once every decade."

"Ouch! I see you're the same razor-tongued girl I married," he said, winking at Craig.

Craig nodded sheepishly, swirling the drink in his hand and looking down at the carpet. Rena disliked it when Terry, who was aware of Craig's feelings, threw up the fact that it was he who married her and not him.

"Gosh, Rena, I may have missed a couple of birthdays but I've been busy. Don't you think it's time you let up?" he asked, embarrassed, shifting his weight from one foot to the other.

"It's hard to let up when you give me so much material to work with. You did remember to buy her a gift, I hope?"

"Of course," he said with a grin as wide as a crescent moon.

A woman in her early twenties, with long, straight red hair walked over to them, looped her arm inside Terry's, and smiled pleasantly at Rena, waiting for an introduction.

"Rena," he said bashfully, "I'd like you to meet Belinda."

There was a sticky pause as Rena tried to stop her heart from dropping further. She knew there were women in his life—there always had been even when they were married—but at least, before, he had the decency not to bring them around.

Belinda broke the deadlock by extending her hand. "My gosh, I'm such a big fan of yours," she said with a high-pitched Southern accent. "I can't believe I'm actually meeting you."

My God, she's right off the plantation. Why are you doing this to me, Terry? she thought. "Thank you. It's nice to meet you, too. What did you say your name was again?"

"Belinda," she said, dripping honey. "I love this house. It's like living in a museum. It must have been wonderful growing up here."

Aunt Jemima would be in her glory. "It was great fun roller skating down the halls trying to avoid crashing into the Monets. How did you two meet?" she asked, not really wanting to know.

Belinda didn't say anything. She looked at Terry, grinned, and gave his arm another squeeze.

"I've got some news, Rena," Terry said, turning red and looking down at his Sperry top-siders.

No, she did not want to hear it. "Tell me later, Ter. I've got to see Cathy," Rena said, trying to control her voice.

As she turned toward the den, Belinda said with a voice that could melt butter, "Isn't it awful about that little girl."

"What girl?" Craig asked.

"That girl . . . the one that was beaten up, and right over the air for goodness' sakes. Do you think she's dead?" she asked Rena, wide-eyed.

"Let's hope she isn't," Rena said. She excused herself and walked toward the den, pausing to chat briefly with some of the guests. Craig followed behind and touched her elbow to get her attention.

"You okay?" he asked, concerned.

"About what?"

"Terry and . . ."

"Scarlett? Yeah, I'm fine. Any progress on Alice?"

"Not yet. The pathologists in several counties have been notified to call my office if the body of a girl fitting your description comes in. So far, nothing. My office told me you called a few day ago and said you thought she might have red hair. What makes you think that?"

"I'm not sure," she said, not wishing to tell him about the conversation she had with Charlie Halleran. "It's just something to look out for. What about Gerald W. Jaffe?"

"I asked around. He was a New York cop who came out west about fifteen years ago and joined the L.A.P.D."

"He really had an attitude, Craig . . . as if he resented me. He wasn't interested in finding this girl at all."

"Well, he's what you'd call a sleeper. Nothing distinguishable in his career. He's just putting in the time until he retires. Nobody will be sorry to see this one go."

Rena saw Stacey and her live-in boyfriend, Ben, enter through the front door carrying a huge package. Simon walked over and introduced himself. Cathy had met Stacey a couple of months ago when she came to the station to meet Rena for dinner and they'd been buddies ever since. Stacey would talk to her on the phone, giving her advice on boys and clothing. Rena appreciated it. She didn't always have the time to do these things because of her busy schedule and, besides, getting advice from a mother wasn't the same as getting it from an older friend or big sister. When Cathy made her list for her birthday party, Stacey was the first name on it.

"What's your calendar like this week?" Craig asked.

"Are you asking me for a date?"

"That word seems to scare you. How about just dinner? Is that safe enough?"

"Sounds great."

"You know, sometimes I feel like that guy up there on the screen, the one who gets second billing and watches with a stiff upper lip as the girl he cares about pines away for the lead," he said, with a self-mocking grin.

"Craig . . ."

"I know. Give me a break."

"You got it."

Rena watched as her father poured Ben and Stacey a drink. He then put an arm around Stacey's waist and a hand on Ben's arm, steering them toward the couch. She could tell he liked them.

In the den, Cathy and Roger Harris the Third, surrounded by at least fifteen of their friends, were on the floor in front of the large screen TV engrossed in a video game. They were pushing, pulling, and tugging away on joy sticks. When the game was over, Rena sat down next to her on the floor.

"Hello, Mother. Glad you could make it," Cathy said, acting aloof for the benefit of her friends.

"Me too. And you must be Roger Harris," she said, turning to him. He was in that awkward stage, where the body couldn't make up its mind if it wanted to remain a child or grow into a man, but she could tell he'd probably turn into a fine-looking teenager.

"Yeah. How'd you know that?"

"Just a lucky guess."

Cathy was turning beet red and silently pleaded with Rena not to say anything to embarrass her.

"Want your present?"

"Sure," Cathy said. "Where is it?"

Rena took out an envelope from her pants pocket and handed it to her. Inside was a photograph, and when Cathy saw it, she let out a scream.

"A horse! It's a horse! Oh my God, she's beautiful!" she squealed, throwing her arms around Rena.

"*She* happens to be a *he*," she said, glowing inside. "He's a chestnut, a jumper, sixteen hands high."

"When can I see him?" Cathy said, trembling with excitement as she passed the picture around to her friends. "Oh m'gosh! I forgot. I'm going away with Dad for two whole months!"

"You won't be able to ride him until the fall anyway. He's still in Tennessee being broken in. He'll be waiting for you at the stables by the time you get back. You better have your dad give you plenty of lessons so you'll be ready for him."

"Does he have a name?"

"Not yet."

"I know what I want to call him. Copper Penny! Is that okay? It goes with dad's horse, Silver Dollar. Oh, Mom, I love you." She threw her arms around Rena again.

The cake-and-candles ceremony was done near the gazebo on the lawn in the back of the house. The guests ooh'ed and aah'ed as the gifts were unwrapped, especially when Cathy opened Stacey's present. It was a collection of nineteenth-century porcelain dolls. Rena knew what kind of salary Stacey was making and hoped it hadn't set her back too much. Like Cathy, Stacey was also an only child and Rena could understand how they were drawn to each other.

"Who's the woman he's with?" Simon whispered bitterly over her shoulder, staring at Terry.

Rena glanced over to Terry. Belinda still had her arm locked into his and they looked like Ken and Barbie dolls. No . . . damnit, they looked more like the two figures on top of a wedding cake, Rena thought.

"Cathy collects dolls, he collects women. Their need to surround themselves with objects is genetic, I suppose," she said, trying to hide a sigh.

"He has no business being here," Simon said with a rage that Rena had seen in him only a few times before in her life.

"He's her father and she wants him here," she said gently, touching his arm to calm him.

"He has no business bringing another woman into this house.

After the things he's done . . ." His voice trailed off as he remembered.

She could feel his muscles tightening under his summer suit. "It's only once a year . . . most times not even that. Let it be."

Terry looked her way, caught her eye, and motioned for her to come over. Rena smiled, knowing that Terry would never have the nerve to walk over with her father standing there. Terry had only been frightened of one man in his life, and that was Simon. She remembered the night when she gave birth to Cathy, the night she almost died. How outraged her father was that Terry was not there at her side. Looking up at the ferocity in his face as she lay in her own blood in the ambulance, she knew that this was the man Shakespeare had in mind when he wrote *King Lear*. The next day, when Terry finally did come to the hospital, Simon grabbed him by the arm and took him outside of her room to talk to him. Terry came back several minutes later, white-faced and breathing hard. She never learned what Simon said to him, and Terry would never tell her, but she knew that a man like Simon could never have built an empire like his without being able to have that kind of effect on another human being.

Rena excused herself and went over to Terry. As she approached him, Belinda, as if on cue, unlocked her arm from his and went over to look at the display of presents on the lawn.

"I need to talk to you, hon . . . alone," he said nervously looking around; seeing Simon staring at him, he turned his head in the other direction.

She could see he was anxious, and for Terry to have more than a "let's do lunch next week" attitude was somewhat of a rarity. "I thought we said everything that was to be said five years ago. What do you want?"

"Not here. Let's grab a bite, I'm hungry." He was pretending to be casual, smiling, but the twitch in the corner of his lip gave him away.

"Sorry, Ter, I'm busy tonight. I've got to get Cathy ready for tomorrow."

"It's important and it *has* to be tonight," he said, looking directly into her eyes, not threatening but not playing around, either.

She picked up on it. "Will this affect Cathy going away with you tomorrow if I don't?"

"Could be," he said, his eyes still on hers.

"Still the same old bastard, huh, Ter?" she said, staring right back at him.

Chapter 10

Sunday, 10:33 P.M.

She found Terry sitting at a corner table in the patio of Gresory's downing a glass of Chardonnay. He seemed jittery. He was tapping his foot on the ground and breaking the bread sticks into small pieces on the tablecloth. A Mexican busboy standing near the water tray glared at him, knowing he'd have to clean the mess up later. When Terry saw Rena, he snapped his fingers to get the waiter's attention, picked up his empty glass, and held up two fingers.

"I told Joaquin I wanted a center table," he said, annoyed, moving the table so she could sit.

"It's no big deal. Who's Joaquin?" she asked.

"The maître d' at the front door. The one with the accent, in the Italian suit . . . tells everyone he's from Paris. Lying shit. I found out he's from Montreal. Never saw Paris in his life."

"Seems real important, Terry," she said, stifling a yawn.

"Bet your sweet life it is. With all the money I've spent here over the years, you think I could at least be accommodated once in a while." He broke several more bread sticks in half.

Restaurant hopping was big in Terry's social agenda, and he would easily spend a fortune frequenting the same trendy hot spots, being friendly with the waiters, leaving big tips, and slipping the maître d' a ten each time, until finally, after a few one-hundred-and-fifty-dollar tabs, someone in the restaurant would get the chef out of the kitchen for a couple of minutes to meet Terry and acknowledge his existence. This was known as "chef fucking," a popular pastime in L.A.

"What do you want from me?" she asked, just as the wine came. The waiter handed them menus and she pushed hers to the side without opening it.

"We haven't had dinner together in a long time and I thought it—"

"Cut the crap, Terry. Why the implied threat about Cathy? I thought that stunk," she said curtly.

"I was joking, Rena, you know that. I was looking for an excuse to get you alone. It was a lousy move, you're right." He sipped his wine. "The house Chardonnay was better last month. I'm going to talk to Joaquin about it. Aren't you hungry?" he said, picking up the menu.

"No."

"The grilled tuna is marvelous."

She ordered a Caesar salad, and when she tasted the salty anchovies, found to her surprise that she *was* hungry. She ate slowly, aware that Terry, who was never known for the direct approach, would get around to telling her what he wanted when he was ready.

"Does Simon still hate me?" he asked between bites of duck covered in a bright colored sauce.

"Probably. That was a smart move bringing that mint julep into his house. It really helped matters."

"She's just a friend."

"Right, you and your millions of friends, Ter."

"I think he always disliked me, even when we were married."

"I'm sure you can understand why. I suppose he found it somewhat awkward that it was him and not you that was pacing up and down the hospital hallway the night I had Cathy, not knowing if either one of us would live or die. I believe he also felt a little strange to be the one handing out the cigars. He was under an illusion that it was supposed to be your job. Old-fashioned of him to think that, wasn't it? I had to explain to him you were in Maui putting together a business deal . . . or so you said."

"You're never going to let me live that one down, are you, Rena?" He reached across the table to touch her hand and she instinctively pulled it away.

"That's a tough one, Ter," she said, smiling. "I have to admit I was a little pissed and felt kind of dumb when I found out that Julie, my ex-best fucking friend in the whole wide fucking world was sipping zombies and listening to Don Ho under a tropical moon with you. Did she ever tell you those big tits were saltwater bags her parents gave her for her twenty-first birthday?"

Terry had a surprised look in his eyes when he heard that and Rena laughed, shaking her head.

"You guys blew your cover the day the two of you came to the hospital after Cathy was born. You both looked like two extras out of *Gidget Goes Hawaiian* with your Bain de Soleil tans. You were waving red flags in my face and everyone picked up on it . . . everyone except stupid ol' me. Some advice, Terry—next time you're married and decide to screw around on your wife, take the bimbo to Alaska. Never mind, with your luck you'd both probably come back home with frostbite."

"Ease up, okay?" he said, giving her a nonchalant laugh. A sweat stain was spreading under the armpits of his polo shirt. "This is just old stuff you're rehashing."

"Yeah, you're right, that's just what it is," she said. "Just old stuff." She touched the bottom part of her stomach under the table, the place where there was a scar from when they cut her open to get Cathy out.

How blue and still my baby looks, Rena remembered thinking through a haze of drugs as the surgeon worked feverishly to untie the umbilical cord from Cathy's neck that was draining away her life. Next to her were bags of plasma that were being pumped into her to make up for the blood she lost when she was lying unconscious on the bathroom floor of her home, hemorrhaging.

After Cathy was born, Terry's business trips became more and more frequent. Her friends from Los Angeles, with embarrassed little coughs, tried warning her when she was in town. She wouldn't listen. She believed in him then.

"I saw him in a back booth at La Scala with a young blonde," one of them said to her.

"Business," she answered.

"He made a pass at me at the Randolph's party," another one said.

"Wishful thinking," she responded jovially.

"I'm telling you, I was across the street and I saw him in Häagen-Dazs. He was with that twenty-year-old receptionist that works for my dentist. They were holding hands," someone else said.

"Pure paternalism, I'm sure," she retorted, smiling. "Er . . . which Häagen-Dazs?"

"The one on Beverly Drive."

That bothered her. The one on Beverly Drive was their secret place that no one knew about when they were in L.A. "Okay then, what flavor was he eating?"

"Chocolate, I think."

Ah-hah! It had to have been someone else. Terry was a butter-pecan man all the way.

Any illusions Rena clung to ended on New Year's Eve eight years ago. She opened the door to the guest bedroom at a friend's party thinking it was the upstairs bathroom and found Terry in the sack with Julie.

Shock . . . hurt . . . anger . . . divorce.

Terry eventually married Julie, found her in bed with Chuck, his best friend, and got a divorce.

The sum total of their lives together . . . until now.

"I guess I better come to the point," he said, sipping Remy in a large snifter. "I've got a bit of a cash-flow problem."

"What do you mean by a bit?" she asked, tensing up.

"There's a small problem at the plant, and I need greens to bail out of it. If I don't come up with the money soon, it could turn into a *real* problem," he said, looking down at his drink as he swirled it around in the glass.

"What happened? I thought catamarans and wind surfing were big business?"

"Oh, they are. The problem is the goddamn gooks are now in it, too, and they're undercutting me. The Koreans are paying their coolies fifty cents an hour with a few fish heads thrown in to build boats. I can't compete with that! Plus those strung-out surfers that work for me are now threatening to strike unless I give them a raise. The only feasible solution would be to pick up stakes and build a factory in the Far East."

"Would you have to move there?" She didn't want to hear the answer.

"I'm afraid so."

"Christ! If Cathy sees you once a year now and you live in the same state, what's the chance of her seeing you at all when you're living halfway around the world?"

"Nothing would change. She could still come and stay with me . . . twice a year if that's what she wants. Korea's a beautiful country. She'd love it."

"Korea! Damn, Terry, they shoot people in Korea!"

"It's my only chance. If I stay here I'll be bankrupt within six months."

"It's your life," she said as the busboy refilled her coffee cup.

"Now this is where the ol' cash-flow problem comes in."

The waiter brought another Remy for Terry. Rena waited for him to say something more. He didn't. He just sipped his drink.

"Why do I have this feeling that you're hitting me up for a loan?" she said finally.

"It would be a small one, hon."

"Stop calling me hon. I hated it when we were married and I hate it now. For a minute I thought the reason you wanted to see me tonight was to discuss how Cathy would react to your moving out of the country. Silly me."

"I'd probably be able to pay the whole thing back within a year." He started biting his bottom lip.

She could sense his urgency and she had to look away. "How much?"

He licked his lips and moved closer to her. "Five hundred thousand. You'll have it back, plus interest, within a year, I swear."

"Are you crazy?" she said, almost in a hiss. "Where would I get that kind of money?"

"You're worth millions."

"It's all in trusts, you know that. I wouldn't be able to touch any of it until . . ." She didn't want to say it.

"Until when? Your father dies? That's not true. I looked into it. You can borrow from it anytime you want. Look, I wouldn't be asking you if I thought there was another way." His boyish charm was turning into pure desperation.

"You have credit . . . collateral. Take a loan out from the banks," she said coldly. She was angry that he had researched her personal accounts before talking to her.

"I can't. My financial statement is a bit rocky right now, and whatever collateral I have won't cover the loan because I still owe too much money. Even if that wasn't true, there isn't enough time to liquidate my holdings. I'd be deep in Chapter Eleven by then."

"You used to have a lot of money. What happened?" she asked, amazed.

"Business has been awful," he said, closing his eyes and shaking his head. "The Japs have been coming up with new designs for faster boats and giving them to the Koreans to build. I've been sinking my own money into the business just to keep it afloat." He stared down at his hands, not saying anything for a while. "Look," he finally said, "you're the only one I can turn to."

He reached over to grab her hand again, and as she tried to move it away he held tight. The contact sent a tingling sensation through her body. He began stroking her fingers, looking at her with those boyish eyes. She relaxed her hand.

After all these years I still want that bastard, she thought.

"I know you're going to find this hard to believe when I tell you that there have been times over the last several years when I've missed you very much."

"Can it, Ter," she said, her voice quivering as he moved his hand farther up her arm. She thought back to those years of hurt, private therapy, of trying to pick up the pieces of her life again. It was a long time before she had been able to trust another man, trust him enough to go to bed with him. Terry's hands felt good, but so did the life that she now had. In fact there was no comparison.

"No, I'm not going to lend you the money, Terry. There's absolutely no reason to. You and I have been separate entities for a long time. Let's keep it that way."

His boyish eyes turned dead cold as he glared at her, and a

chill shot up her spine. She had seen many of his personality changes before but none of them had this look.

"Then you understand, if I'm forced to raise the money in other ways, I probably won't have time for Cathy this summer," he said with a cracked voice.

He always got to her with Cathy, and she wasn't going to allow it this time. "Don't threaten me. If you're not at my place tomorrow morning to pick her up, she'll be hurt but she will survive. Try to be more of a father and less of a shit, Ter. You used to be."

With that she got up and walked out of the patio and into the main restaurant. Over near the bar she saw a thin young man with long hair wearing Italian silks and went over to him.

"Are you Joaquin?" she asked.

"Yes, madam," he said with a velveteen accent. His green eyes, surrounded by long lashes, stared deeply into hers and she had to bite her lip to stop herself from laughing.

Rena took out her Visa card from her purse and gave it to him. "Put Terry Hamlin's tab on this, okay?"

"*Oui*, madam," he said, surprised.

"Next time give the man a center table, will you? The poor guy deserves it."

On Robertson, while waiting for the valet to get her car, she caught a glimpse of Terry still sitting on the patio. He was staring into space and the muscle in his jaw was throbbing. No, she had never seen him look that way before and it worried her.

On the way home, Rena turned left on Santa Monica and drove through "boys' town" in West Hollywood. It was late for L.A., and the Sunday traffic was light. The gay bars had a few stragglers, nothing like on the weekends. It was a balmy night and there were some strollers on the boulevard, mostly boys wearing shorts, walking arm in arm, stopping to peer into the men's boutiques that lined the street.

She stopped for a red light at the corner of Doheny. Across the street the township of Beverly Hills began and the changes were noticeable: streets were better paved, houses doubled in size, the foliage was beautifully manicured, and there were no sex shops and rock-and-roll bars. Rena liked the dichotomy of this intersection; it epitomized the schizoid nature of this city.

She adjusted the rearview mirror and noticed a car with one headlight about a block away also waiting for a red light near Barney's Beanery. It was the same car that had been behind her when she began driving north on Robertson.

Two miles later the car was still there. Instead of turning right on Wilshire, which was her normal route to Brentwood, she veered right on Roxbury Drive and made a quick left on Sunset. She glanced in the mirror. The car was still there.

She picked up speed and pushed down the lock on the doors. Maybe it was Terry, maybe not. No use taking chances. She wished she could see the license plate or at least the make of the vehicle, but it was too dark and the car too far away.

She made a quick left on a side street near UCLA, burning rubber on the turn as the speedometer closed in on fifty. In a few seconds she heard the same squeal of tires as the other car made the turn. It was a residential street, dark and deserted. She made a few more lefts and rights on some unfamiliar streets, hoping none of them would dead-end before she got to the safety of the bright lights and crowded boulevards of Westwood Village.

In the distance she could see Le Conte and the neon glare of Westwood. She raced past the fraternities to the main drag, looking for a cop. She soon saw one on a motorcycle in front of Tower Records and pulled up next to him. As he got off the bike and walked over to her she looked over her shoulder for the car with the one headlight. It wasn't there.

The officer, a fifteen-year veteran, nodded politely as she told him about the car following her. He told her there were a lot of goofballs out there, and that this one was probably in Hollywood by now terrorizing another unsuspecting woman. He suggested that she drive home carefully with her windows up and doors locked.

Rena drove the couple of miles from Westwood to her house with her heart pounding and her eyes never leaving the rearview mirror.

Home was a white, Spanish-style structure tucked away in the hilly terrain of Brentwood. The large trees and grounds surrounding the property secluded it from the other homes. As she drove into the garage she was grateful that it was attached to the house. She stayed in the car until the garage door closed, then rushed upstairs to check on Cathy. She was sleeping soundly, her luggage on the floor next to her bed. "Don't fuck up, tomorrow, Terry, please don't," she whispered to herself.

Rena went downstairs, checked then rechecked all the windows and locks, then turned on the alarm. In the living room, with the lights out, she opened the curtain a crack and peered outside. The street was quiet and no human shadows could be seen passing through the Malibu lights on the lawn. Relieved, Rena went upstairs, looking forward to a long hot bath.

Gerald W. Jaffe's warning light came on in his Ford Fairlane way back on Robertson. Nothing major. He had had the car long enough to know it was only a busted headlight. He'd bring it in tomorrow and have the department pay for a new one, maybe even get them to pay for a tune-up. All in the line of duty.

He sat in the car in total darkness, chewing the gum-tobacco combo, and watched the lights go off in her living room, then several seconds later go on again in the bathroom. She'd made him tonight. From now on he'd have to be more careful.

He hadn't been sleeping too well the last couple of weeks, and once again it had to do with this bitch. Ever since he'd listened to the taped phone call in the studio, he found that something was disturbing him and he couldn't pin it down.

Then the nightmares started and it was always the same. He'd find himself in a pitch black closet with the door locked. There would be a scratching noise in the corner and he'd grope his way over to the sound. His hands touched upon the long, silky hair of a child and he could hear her giggling. Her tiny hands reached up and began to play with his penis. It was a pleasant sensation. He felt her lips upon his fingers, nibbling on them, and he sighed. Her teeth were razor sharp and there were animal grunts coming from her throat. Pleasure turned into excruciating pain as she bit down . . . and, *oh, Jesus* . . . that horrible crunching sound and the feel of warm blood dripping down his naked body. He'd wake up screaming, his heart palpitating.

Then one night, right after such a dream, he remembered what he couldn't pin down. The old nightmares stopped, and a new one began.

Chapter 11

Monday, 8:10 A.M.

Rena looked at the clock on the oven and checked it against the watch on her wrist. They both said the same thing, meaning that Terry was ten minutes late. And maybe not coming.

The Beastie Boys blasted through the hallways. She could hear the toilet flushing and the door slamming in the upstairs bathroom and Cathy's voice singing along with the group. She'd been packed and ready for two days.

"Don't do this to get to me, Ter. Please," she said out loud as she tossed the unfinished coffee into the sink.

The phone rang. It's Terry, I know it. Oh, shit!

It wasn't Terry. It was Dr. Harry Steinfeld, chairman of the psychology department at USC.

"Problems?" he asked after hearing her voice.

"Terry."

"That's always a problem."

"Did you listen to the tapes?" She had sent him copies of the conversations she had had with Alice.

"Yep. Are you going to have any free time today?"

"The tone of your voice says you found something."

"Maybe."

"Is she for real?"

"Maybe."

"How about around five. After I get off the air."

"Ah, yes, I forgot. The healing hour."

"Your office?" she asked, ignoring the remark.

"Are you crazy. On a day like this? I'll be at Pepperdine shagging flies."

Hanging up, Rena could hear the *plop-plop* of the suitcases being dragged down the stairs.

"He's late," Cathy said from the hallway as she set the bags next to the front door.

"Yes, he is," Rena said, her stomach turning into knots. She turned to her daughter. "Look, sweetheart, your dad and I had a talk last night . . . an argument would be more like it, and there's a strong possibility that he may not—"

Gravel crunching in the driveway from car wheels, followed by three strong honks. Cathy looked out the window and let out a shriek. "It's Dad!"

Rena leaned against the countertop, folded her arms, and sighed in relief.

"Belinda's with him," Cathy said.

"What?" Rena went over to the window and peeked out.

Belinda was in the front seat of the 450 SL convertible, wearing shorts and a tank top without a bra. Terry was opening the trunk.

What tits, Rena thought, getting angry with herself for feeling jealous. "I didn't know she was also going to Carmel."

"I didn't know it either, but I could have predicted it," Cathy said, having trouble holding the duffel bag while trying to open the door at the same time.

"How?" She unlocked the latch for her.

"I think he's real hung up on her. Dad was talking to me yesterday about buying a ring and wanted my expertise on it. I knew it wasn't for me or you, so I guess it had to be for her."

"I never even knew she existed until last night. Where did she come from?"

"I think it was all kind of sudden. Like those Danielle Steele novels. Dad says she's an actress. Exciting, isn't it?"

"Yeah, I guess," Rena said, trying to keep down the rage. Less then twelve hours ago that prick had been putting the make on *her* at a restaurant. "I wish them all the luck in the world," she remarked, staring at Belinda's tight thighs.

Terry came up the stairs and nodded briefly to Rena while avoiding her eyes. He ruffled Cathy's hair for a second, then carried the bags down and put them in the trunk.

"Call me, sweetheart," Rena said, hugging her.

"You bet, Mom. Let me know how Copper Penny's doing, will you?"

"Who?"

"My horse," Cathy said, racing down the steps and into the car without looking back.

Two months! What a long time to be without someone you love, she thought, watching the car drive away.

Harry Steinfeld was crouched at home plate, glaring at the pitcher and holding a thirty-six-ounce bat over his shoulder. "Don't feed me junk! Throw the ball up the pipe, you fucking sissy," he yelled at the boy on the pitcher's mound. With his bald head, long gray beard, and big stomach hanging over his belt, Harry looked more like a Christmas elf then a baseball player.

The boy, looking spooked, took off his cap, wiped his brow, put the cap back on his head, and threw the pitch Harry wanted. A groan erupted on the field as the ball cleared the right-field fence. Harry threw his arms in the air, let out a yell, and ran his three-hundred-pound body around the bases doing an occasional *grand jeté* along the way as he slapped the infield players on the rump. After touching home, he turned to Rena standing near the first-base line and bowed.

"Bravo," she said, applauding. He jogged over to her with his belly shaking like aspic. "That poor boy who threw the ball looks as if he's about to cry."

"That little fucker better cry, letting me coerce him like that," he said, grabbing Rena and giving her a long, warm bear hug.

"Who are these people?"

"Mostly students in my Ph.D. program. I figure if they're going to work with patients who have phobias about dealing with life's little harassments, then they should learn firsthand what intimidation is all about by playing baseball with me. Let's go back to the locker room so I can clean up."

"Hey, you just can't quit on us," the first baseman said with his hands on his hips.

"Fucking A I can. I'm the chairman of this department and I make the rules. Besides, it's my ball." As they walked off the field to jeers, Steinfeld held up two fingers in the victory signal.

He undressed next to his open locker, unmindful of Rena,

who was standing near him. Harry loved being naked, especially in front of people. A classic story that was told about Steinfeld concerned the time one of his female students came to his office and tried to engage him in a discussion on whether or not Anna Freud was really a repressed lesbian. That was a sore point for him, given the fact that he had studied under Sigmund Freud's daughter and had worshiped her mind. Instead of biting into the argument, he took his clothes off, sat down at his desk, put his feet up, and started doing the crossword puzzle in front of the horrified student. She got the message that one didn't try and topple Harry Steinfeld's idols unless you were their equal.

"So Rena, my dear, how's the Pac-man psychology business doing?" he said, grabbing a bar of soap and a towel from the locker.

"Are you still pissed, Harry, that I traded my couch for a microphone?"

"No, not at all. It does wonders for my rigid Freudian soul to hear your voice every day—even if it is crammed between Puppy Chow products and diarrhea deterrents. I'm going to take a shower. Care to join me?"

"Don't forget to wash around the ears, Harry," she said, propping her foot up on the bench as she sat down.

"One day you're going to drop that WASPish guard of yours, rip off your clothes, and fling yourself into my arms."

"Bye, Harry," she said, waving.

"Ta-ta. I'll be out in a minute . . . then we'll talk." He tossed the towel over his shoulder and walked over to the shower room. His feet, angled out like a duck's, made slapping noises on the tile floor.

Harry was the first man she had slept with after Terry. It happened just once. She was at a low point in her life and felt that Terry had deprived her of any feelings of her own self-worth. Harry, seeing that she was troubled, invited her back to his place after class. She opened up to him and cried a lot. Afterward, they made love. She always believed it to be one of the wiser choices she had made in her life. She didn't sleep with him because he had sexually aroused her or because he looked like Warren Beatty; not with his potbelly and leprechaun grin. It was just that Harry was a rare man: he simply loved women, loved them for being who they were, and because of that they eagerly gave themselves to him. Many of the young bucks on campus were in awe of him, acknowledging that he was king when it came to the opposite sex.

Fifteen minutes later they were crossing the Pacific Coast Highway heading out toward Malibu pier. It was late in the day and the few people who were on the wharf were reeling in their lines and taking their catch, mostly rockfish, home with them.

"Hungry?" he asked, looking toward the restaurant attached to the pier.

"Not just yet." She leaned against the railing, enjoying the cool ocean breeze against her face. "Alice is real, isn't she?" she asked calmly as she watched a fishing boat slowly making its way back to shore.

"I'm afraid so. At first I thought it might be a put-on. Then, after studying her vocal patterns with an analyzer, I began to change my mind. There wasn't one false note in her voice. The machine would have shown it. Her anxiety level was quite real."

"Oh, Jesus. She *is* out there."

"There's definitely *something* out there."

"How old do you think she is—was? I really don't need this today, Harry."

"You called *me* about this, darling, remember? I'd say she is or was between five and fifteen."

"Fifteen?" she said, amazed. "I thought maybe five or six."

"Take my word for it. Your expertise is in family counseling . . . mine's in child abuse. She only *sounded* like she was five or six. In fact, I have a feeling she'd been locked away since she was a toddler, maybe at two or three."

"Run this one by me, okay, Harry?" A chill ran through her. Alice Mendoza was also around the same age when she was put in a closet.

"Okay. Take a small child . . . isolate her from the rest of society for many years. Deprive her of love, companionship, affection—do all the odious, horrifying things that were done to this girl by her father, and you're going to get a great deal of impairment. Listen to her voice real closely. It's totally monotonic—no ups, no downs. The words are slurred, sentences not completed—all classic symptoms of social retardation. That's social retardation and not brain damage. There's a difference."

"Go on," she said, pulling up the collar on her silk blouse to keep the damp wind off her neck.

"My guess is she'd been incarcerated at an early age mainly because of her choice of words, such as 'Da,' meaning Daddy. There were no past or future tenses or conjunctions, and her thoughts were compiled in no more than two or three words at a time."

"You're describing the linguistic development of an average, healthy two-to-three-year-old. What makes you think she's older than that?"

"Shit, she has to be. Your average, healthy two-to-three-year-old wouldn't have the motor skills to complete an act as complicated as dialing a phone, let alone getting the right number. A comparison would be me doing a high-wire act over the Golden Gate Bridge. It could never happen." He chuckled, slapping his big stomach.

"You're right, damnit. I should have seen it," she said, angry at herself. "The whole thought process of even communicating on the phone is much too advanced for a toddler."

"Correct. Even if the child was the brilliant illegitimate offspring of Margaret Thatcher and Albert Einstein."

They watched silently as the sun touched the water, creating an orange flair across the California horizon.

"One interesting thing, though . . . and a little perplexing," Harry said, his eyes still on the sunset.

"What's that?"

"The use of the word 'wally.' "

"You know what it means?"

"I think so. Except it doesn't make sense. Wally is a slang word for penis, like wang or dick."

"It makes sense to me. It sounds as if she was sexually abused. Remember, she used the words 'no wally.' She sounded terrified. I'm willing to bet she was badly hurt by her father, especially if he physically tried entering her at an early age."

"No, that's not what I mean. It's the word itself. I had an idea but I still checked with a friend of mine in the linguistics department to make sure. It's seems that it's an outdated East Coast expression belonging to another generation, like 'groovy' or 'hep cats.' It just isn't used anymore."

Rena turned to him, " 'Groovy' belongs to the sixties. 'Hep cats' to the forties. Where does wally fit in?" she said.

"Oh . . . somewhere in the seventies, I suppose."

"Early seventies?"

"Yes."

"Like eighteen years ago?"

"Absolutely. Why?"

She looked back at the ocean. The sun had already gone down and the sky was beginning to blend into the steel blue of the water. "You believe in ghosts, Harry?" she asked softly.

"One encounters everything sooner or later in Los Angeles."

"I think I'll take you up on that dinner," she said, folding her arms around her body to keep out the night chill.

Harry's charisma, combined with the lively atmosphere of the restaurant and the sound of the ocean hitting the beams of the pier, had a comforting effect on Rena, and she opened up. She told him about Charlie Halleran and Alice Mendoza. Being a good Freudian, Harry didn't interrupt. He just played with the wiry hairs of his beard and listened. Through the large bay windows, a thin crack of lightning lit up the black sky for a split second, exposing Catalina's hump.

"He's a reporter, you say?" he said matter-of-factly as he bit down on a piece of New York cheese cake.

"Yes."

"Interesting. Want a piece? It's quite good," he said, holding the fork up to her.

She pushed his hand away. "Come on, Harry, talk to me."

"About what? Things that go bump in the night? Give me a break, Rena! People believe what they want to believe, see what they want to see, forget what they want to forget, and so on. Life is that coherent. Except the human race is too damned arrogant to see themselves in such a simplistic light. We've got to be more fascinating than the crustaceans. After all, we've been created in the exact image of God, haven't we? You know what the differences are between a savage in a loincloth and us? One: We have three initials in front of our names . . . P, H, and D. And two: The savage gives *his* mumbo jumbo away for free, where we charge exorbitant prices for our claptrap. Now, last chance. Do you want any of this cake or can I eat the rest of it myself?"

She shook her head no. "In other words—"

"In other words, don't cloud the facts with bullshit," he said. "You have a blood-and-guts girl out there, not a friendly neighborhood poltergeist. And this Halleran fellow sounds like he was doing the Flatbush hustle on your head. What I don't like is that this girl has your home phone number. That part sounds awfully screwy. You be careful," he whispered, reaching across and holding her hand.

"I will," she said, squeezing back.

"You know what?" he said, leaning into her, grinning. "I think you should come back to my place, take your clothes off, and let me give you a deep muscle massage. You'll feel better."

Rena giggled, shaking her head. "You sound like someone out of a sixties time warp, Harry. What happened to the Jacuzzi routine?"

"I score better with the massage shtick."

She broke out laughing.

"Well, I tried," he said, shrugging his shoulders and smirking like a Grimms' brothers gremlin.

Rena bent over, grabbed his head, and kissed it. She felt fortunate to have a friend like him.

After another cup of coffee she told Harry that she wanted to be alone. She needed to think.

"I understand," he said. "The one thing our profession does best is understand."

Rena walked north on the shoulder of the highway. The air was deathly still and a thick fog hung over her like a damp spiderweb. The lightning was getting closer and the rattle of thunder, though still far away, could now be heard. It's going to be one hell of a downpour, she thought. She didn't care. In fact, it felt good. It reminded her of her childhood summers back on Cape Cod: the walks at night on the beach alone and the fresh smell of salt and sand unleashed by the humidity. The aroma was never more pungent than before a storm. It was also a time when her feelings, all different kinds, rose to the surface, creating within her an urgency to be alive. She loved those times, even though it made the sadness, which seemed to underlie her entire being, more acute.

And she felt that way now.

"Pac-man psychology," Harry called it. And it had hurt. That's because she knew he was right. For three hours, five days a week, people would call in exposing their open wounds to her, some as big as the China wall, and all she could do was try to patch them up with a small Band-Aid. In a couple of hours the Band-Aids would fall off, the skin would break open, and the sores would still be there, festering and throbbing.

It was a bad joke—on herself as well as her audience. The only people she really helped were the sponsors: they got richer. None of it was real.

Except Alice . . . *she* was real.

"You out there, Alice?" she wondered, looking up at the black sky as she stood on the rocks that jutted across the sand. "Are you still alive? Please let me help you!" The night opened up and the rain came down hard, intermingling with her tears. "Why is this happening to me?" she shouted, looking out into the nothingness. She remembered someone else saying those same words a long time ago.

It was the worst storm for the month of June in the history of Southern California. Power lines were down all over the city, streets were flooded and fatalities were running high.

Her plane from Boston had to be rerouted to Phoenix. It sat on the runway for four hours, waiting until the storm further West would ease up so it could try another landing. By the time this was deemed safe enough, it was after one in the morning.

As Rena came down the ramp at LAX, worn out and disheveled from the long hours spent on the plane, she saw Anna waiting for her.

"You look tired," Anna said, wrapping her thin arms around her.

"Where's Mommy and Daddy?" Rena asked, her inquisitive fourteen-year-old eyes scanning Anna's face.

"They couldn't make it, honey. They're at home." Her face was grim.

"Is everything okay?" Rena asked, worried.

"Everything's fine. Don't worry your head about nothing. We'll be home soon." That's all she would say. After getting the luggage, they drove back to Hancock Park in Simon's limousine.

As they rode in silence through the dark streets an occasional headlight lit up Anna's face, showing the stress in her eyes. Rena sat back, hoping the lights would stay green the rest of the way; she knew something was wrong.

As the limo pulled into the driveway Rena got out, ran toward the house, and flung open the door. She was stunned at what she saw. The downstairs was a mess, with Elaina's collection of fragile "things" broken and smashed beyond repair. Several of Simon's paintings were ripped from their frames and lay in shreds on the floor.

"My God," was all her throat would release. She turned to Anna. Anna looked away, distraught. Upstairs in the master bedroom, she could hear Elaina screaming something unintelligible. Then Simon's voice bellowing down the hallway, "Why is this happening to me?"

"Mommy! Daddy!" Rena screamed, racing up the stairs.

She threw open the door to their bedroom. Elaina, her eyes filled with rage, was punching Simon's chest. He was trying to grab her wrists. Her eyes were bloodshot and she looked as if she hadn't slept for days. When they saw Rena standing by the door, they froze. Then, suddenly, Elaina's face started to change; a softness came over it and she smiled at Rena.

"Why, what are you doing here, dear?" she asked, surprised.

Rena was in shock. She hadn't seen her parents since Easter break. "It's summer vacation. You knew I was coming today."

"I did?" Elaina tried to think, putting her hand to her forehead. "I must have forgotten, I'm sorry. This week has been an absolute mess."

Still holding Elaina's wrist, Simon looked at Rena, nodding for her to leave. "I'll be down in a second," he said gently to her.

She ran downstairs into Anna's waiting arms, crying hysterically. "What happened?" she finally managed to say. "Who did this?" Her eyes scanned the destruction in the room.

"Both of them, honey."

"How could that be, Anna? They're not like that!"

"They're human, baby. And if you try and act like a picture postcard your whole life, something's gonna snap."

"Those weren't my parents, Anna. They never said and did things like that!"

The next morning everything was back to normal, as if the rage of last night never happened. Elaina presided over a charity breakfast at the Beverly Hills Hotel, and Simon went to work. It was never discussed during Rena's summer at home, and she was too distressed by it to ever bring it up to them. Ten months later Elaina was dead.

That night had given Rena her first lesson on her way to becoming a therapist: never take a manicured, flowered garden at face value; hidden underneath the colorful surface, maggots and worms were scrambling to dig their way out.

"Alice, please help me find you!" Rena screamed into the Malibu storm.

She was answered by an even harsher rampage of rain.

Down the road, on the other side of the highway, Jaffe sat in the Kentucky Fried Chicken joint slowly sipping a container of coffee. He was watching her car in the parking lot adjacent to the restaurant. There was no need to follow her; as long as the Jag was there he knew she wasn't going anywhere far. He had a three-day growth on his face and it had been at least two days since he had a change of clothes. Jeez . . . he hadn't even been to work since the middle of last week. He'd been calling in sick with the flu, faking a cough, just like he did when he was in high school. Except he could tell by the lieutenant's voice that he wasn't buying much of it.

The nightmares had come back. This time much worse than before, and he wanted them to end. It had to do with this woman, that much he could figure out. Only he didn't know how or why. He'd been following her every move, and thanks to a friend in the Justice Department, had a tap put on her phone. He would give it one more day. If nothing significant happened, he'd have no choice but to confront her. Find out how much she knew. Make her talk . . . in any way he could. And fuck his job if he had to. These nightmares had to stop!

"Excuse me, sir," the young waitress said nervously. "We're closing."

Jaffe turned from the doorway and looked at her. Hmm, he

thought, not bad. She was about sixteen and had a creamy complexion with lots of freckles. Her red hair was spiked and worn short. He could tell she was skittish because of the way he looked. Too bad, honey. If I knew you'd be working tonight, I woulda taken better care of myself, he thought.

She had the look and the coloring he liked . . . now if only she was a few years younger. *Yum, yum.*

Chapter 12

Monday, 10:35 P.M.

Rena drove slowly, trying to avoid the rocks and mud that slid off the hillside from the storm and washed onto the coast highway. The large waves relentlessly pounded the million-dollar homes along the Malibu shore sending many of the residents scurrying to the shelter of the Beverly Wilshire Hotel for the night.

She looked in the rearview mirror. The glaring headlights of a car about one hundred yards away could just be seen through the torrential downpour hitting her back window. Even though it had stayed with her all the way to San Vicente Boulevard, she wasn't concerned. It wasn't the same car as yesterday; this one had two good lights. By the time Rena turned onto Twenty-sixth Street, the car had disappeared into the stormy night.

Gerald W. Jaffe turned south toward Wilshire, thankful that he had the new headlight put in this morning. Visibility would have been down to zero without it. There was no reason to follow her any farther. He knew she was just going home. Besides, he was too jittery from the Benzedrine to sit in a car all night on a stakeout. He took the pills to keep from sleeping. Sleep meant more dreams and he didn't want to face another night of that. If it hadn't been raining so hard, he'd have gone to Hollywood to check out the action on the streets. He was coming down from the speed and his hands were shaking at the wheel. He reached into the glove compartment, felt around until he found the vial, then popped another pill. By the time he reached Mulholland, he was flying again. He thought about maybe hitting one of the beaner bars in North Hollywood, find himself a Mex for the night. No, these pills killed his sexual appetite. Maybe he'd drive by his old house and see if he could catch a glimpse of Mary and the kids, and if he was real lucky, find the faggot schoolteacher alone and beat the shit out of him. Not a good idea; his head was all fuzzy from the pills and he didn't want to chance the drive to Northridge in the rain. *Screw it!* He'd just go back home, make himself a stiff drink, and check to see if the tap on the bitch's phone was working.

It was. His friend at the Justice Department had set up a separate phone in his apartment, and cross-connected Rena's line to it. When he was home, he could just pick up and listen without her ever knowing. And if he was out, her calls were transferred automatically to his answering machine.

He turned the machine up and poured himself three fingers of Jack Daniel's. Most of the calls he listened to were bullshit. Then he heard Charlie Halleran's voice, not once but three separate times, saying how he wanted to talk to her, how he was sorry for his behavior the last time. Halleran? What the fuck does he want with her? he thought. Then he heard a young man's voice who said his name was Fred. He sounded desperate. Said he *had* to see her. Very important.

"This is getting real interesting," he said to himself, as he finished off the drink that he hoped would calm his frayed nerves.

Rena listened to her calls on the phone machine in the bedroom as she stepped out of her clothes. There were messages from her father, her publisher, Stacey, and three from Halleran. What does he want?, she wondered. The other two were from Fred Lovell, her assistant and call screener at the radio station. She didn't like the way he sounded. His voice was cracking as he practically begged her to phone him any time tonight. He said it was urgent. Very urgent. He left the time he called and she realized that she had just missed him by only a few minutes.

She sat down on the bed and dialed Fred's number. It was busy. Well, she'd call back later. Right now she wanted to get into her robe, brew a cup of tea, and crawl into bed. Tomorrow, she was going to ask Anthony Richardson, vice-president of programming, for some time off. She needed it. And Alice . . . Rena knew there was no way she could continue working in her profession if she didn't at least make an attempt to find her.

She grabbed for her robe behind the bathroom door. It wasn't there. Miranda, her housekeeper, must have washed it and hung it in the closet.

She opened her closet, a long, L-shaped walk-in type, and saw her robe at the far end. Where's Miranda's head, putting it in such an inaccessible place? she thought. The door slammed shut as she stepped into the closet to retrieve it. She was in total darkness. "Hey, this is terrific!", she said out loud. She could smell something familiar but she wasn't sure what.

She reached up for the light chain, found it after a couple of tries, and pulled. Nothing. Holding on to the pole filled with clothes hangers, she edged her way toward the door. From somewhere in the closet she could hear scratching noises. She stopped moving and listened. They were coming from where the shoe boxes were stacked on the floor. She put on her robe. Another sound: something scurrying along the wood floor. Jesus, there's something alive in here! she realized. The scratchings were beginning to multiply, coming from different directions. Icy fear, like a cold hand touching her back, made her body jerk forward.

Suddenly a small furry thing ran across her bare foot and she let out a scream. *Rats!* She rushed blindly to where the door was, tripping over boxes and shoes, breaking her nails on the wood paneling, as she grasped blindly for the knob. It wouldn't open. *Locked!* How could that be? There is no lock on the door! Another living thing brushed past her leg and she panicked. Grabbing the handle, she banged her body against the door, screaming, trying to break the lock. It held.

The noise began to agitate the creatures, and their squeals

became louder and their movements more frantic. As she stepped back, one of them got caught under her foot and she could feel the bones snapping. Its death shriek was almost human. She shuddered, not daring to move, when she felt several of them touch her legs with their cold noses and whiskers. My God, how many were there? Dozens!

She stood still, not daring to move any part of her body, trying to ease the hysteria in her head. She knew what these vermin, when trapped in a small room like this, could do if provoked . . . or hungry.

Their horrible shrill cries were beginning to calm down. Slowly, so they wouldn't get into a frenzy again, she reached for the upper pole, the one where the dresses were hanging, and tried boosting herself up on the top shelf. Something warm touched her hand, then bit down hard. The teeth were like tiny slivers of glass. She quickly pulled her hand away, stifling a scream. *They were everywhere!*

She had to fight the terror again as her mind started comprehending the situation. No time for panic, not now. She reached for the pole and grabbed a metal hanger, brushing away one of the creatures as it tried to crawl on her arm. Carefully she pulled hard at the end piece, unwinding it from the handle. The pointed metal tip cut into her fingers, making them bleed. When it was unraveled, she groped her way back to the brass knob and jammed the tip between the frame and the latch, working feverishly to pry the door loose.

The animals were all over the floor, devouring the one she killed. One of them grabbed on to her robe and started climbing up the inside part. She could feel its hairy body on her thigh as she knocked it away. They were becoming aroused again, probably from hunger, and from smelling her blood. Their razor teeth were cutting into her feet, drawing more blood, which made them still crazier.

She kept chipping away at the wooden frame with the hanger, trying to get it firmly wedged next to the latch. It had to work! It was her only hope.

She felt the rats leaping onto her back from the top shelf. They were all over her now—on her shoulders, arms, head. She kept working frenetically, with her fingers as well as the hanger, no longer stopping to shake the animals off her body. The door would give a little, then snap back to its original position. The pain from the bites was intense. She was screaming now, not caring. All rationality disappeared. *She had to get out!*

The metal tongue from the lock cleared the broken frame and the door flew open.

At first she was blinded by the light from the bedroom as it burst into the closet. The rats leaped off her, running back into the closet or to the safety of other dark rooms.

She rushed down the stairs and out of the house into the rain. She didn't stop running until she was halfway down the street. Grabbing on to a tree, breathing hard, she realized the car keys were back in the house. There was no way she was going back in there. *Christ, no!*

As her sober self returned, so did the pain from the bites. She looked at her body and saw her blood mixing with the rain.

Across the street a light came on from a bedroom window. Her neighbors, the Finebergs. Thank God they're home!

Running over to their house, she realized what she must look like. *Hello, Mr. and Mrs. Fineberg . . . couldn't sleep. Thought maybe you'd like to play some Scrabble. I'll try not to get any blood on your Berber.*

She started laughing and crying at the same time. Rats! Her worst nightmare. At least Cathy wasn't here.

"It's the ivy. That's where they breed," Mr. Fineberg said disdainfully as he drove Rena in his canary-colored El Dorado to the UCLA Medical Center. "Beverly Hills has that problem, too. And the city won't do anything about it because they think all that greenery looks good. Nothing but politics! The sewers must have overflowed because of the rain and they probably got into your house through an air vent."

"I don't have an air vent in my closet," Rena said, shivering. She was cold and her robe was soaked. She wished she had had the presence of mind to borrow a dry one from his wife.

"You never know what you have in these old houses," he

said, adjusting his checkered golf cap over his thinning white hair. "You know the floral-pattern wallpaper we put up in the living room?"

"Yes," she said. She remembered it being pretty gaudy.

"When we took the old paper off, we found a whole other room that must have been sealed up for fifty years. You just never know."

At the hospital she received a tetanus shot and had butterfly stitches put in some of the deeper puncture wounds. Simon's chauffeur showed up an hour later with fresh clothes that Anna had given him and drove her back to the Hancock Park estate.

Anna met her in the hallway and wrapped a towel around Rena's hair. "Lord, but you're a mess. Thank goodness your father's in Switzerland. He'd have a heart attack if he saw you looking like this, girl."

"Did he say when he's coming back?"

"You never know with him."

"That's true," Rena said, a little disappointed. When she was a child, he was always away on business. She remembered all those lonely Sundays, when other children would play in the park with their fathers, and the sadness she felt.

"Your daddy's a great man. Sometimes greatness and time for family don't go together, but he did the best he could," Anna said, as if reading Rena's mind.

"I need a cup of tea."

"The water's already brewing. Go on in the kitchen."

Anna went over to the banister and took Rena's damp robe that the chauffeur had put there. "I'll dump this thing in the wash." Suddenly she stopped and looked at Rena, clutching the robe in her hands. "Where'd you get this thing?" Her voice was trembling.

Rena saw her eyes. They were glazed over, as if she were staring at something horrible within. This was not the first time she had seen her look that way. The other time was when she was a young girl.

Anna took her to this special church one Sunday when her parents were not in town. The colors of the walls were lime green, and the black parishioners were singing and dancing in the aisles to gospel music; except there was a Caribbean rhythm to it, and the language was not English but something else. Over the altar hung heads of different animals—goats, cows, and chickens. There was the salty smell of blood, and the sounds of live animals in an adjacent room. By the way people treated Anna, Rena could tell that she was important. There was this young woman who was very pregnant, and she was lying on her back next to the altar with her dress up over her thighs and her legs spread apart. Anna went up to her and touched her stomach, then put her fingers up her vagina. She then put her hand on the girl's head and slowly shook her head. The young girl screamed and it took several parishioners to hold her down. In the bus, on the way back home, Rena asked Anna what happened. At first she said nothing, a strange look on her face. Then, after many minutes, she told Rena, with a quiet voice, that the young woman's child would be born dead. When asked how she knew, Anna said she just did. Nothing was ever said about it again, and Rena never asked if the prophecy ever came true. She was never taken back to the church and, upon Anna's wishes, her parents were not told about it.

Years later, when she was in college, Rena read about a religious cult known as Santeria—a combination of tribalism and Christianity that was created in Cuba by slaves that were brought over from Africa. It also took on many converts from the Caribbean islands. Their rituals encompassed animal sacrifices, witchcraft, and even, according to the authorities from several large cities, murder. Rena suspected but never asked Anna if it was a Santeria church they had been in that Sunday.

"What's wrong, Anna?" Rena said.
"You just do what I say!"
She rushed past Rena and went into the kitchen with the robe. Rena followed and grabbed her arm as she pulled out a pair of scissors from the drawer.
"What are you doing?" she asked.
"I'm gonna destroy this thing!" Anna said.
Rena tightened her grip on her arm. "Tell me why?"
"Let go! You don't understand, girl!"
She pulled the robe away from Anna and looked at it.

"Oh, Lord," Anna wailed. "Oh, Lord! Get rid of it, please! There's gonna be trouble. Terrible trouble!"

And then Rena saw it. The robe was covered with fine long strands of red hair. And it was soft and shiny, like the hair of a young girl.

Chapter 13

Tuesday, 8:45 A.M.

Rena got out of bed slowly. Her feet were swollen and bruised from the bites, and she was groggy from the codeine the intern had given her to kill the pain. She slept in her old room last night, and it felt warm and safe, just like it used to when she was a child. The first thing she looked for was the robe she had left on the chair. It was gone.

"Anna!" she yelled down the stairs.

"Yes?" Anna said from the kitchen.

"Where's the robe?"

"In the wash."

"What?" She was stunned. "I asked you not to touch it and you agreed."

"I agreed not to destroy it. I kept my word on that."

"Goddamnit, Anna! I needed those hairs!" she said.

"Didn't I teach you not to swear! I did what is best. Meanwhile I called pest control this morning. They're fumigating your house right now."

Rena went back into the room and slammed the door. She was angry. Last night she had asked Anna about her vision. She knew it was connected with the red hairs. Anna refused to say anything more and continued to plead with her to get rid of the robe. Rena held Anna by the arms and demanded to know why. Tears welling up in her eyes, Anna touched Rena's face with both hands and said, "The child . . . the child . . . oh, that poor child!" That was all she would say. She wiped her eyes on her apron, then went over to the sink and started scouring it.

None of this made any sense. Why were there red hairs on her robe? Where did they come from? They surely weren't from her own head. Her hair was light brown.

And Anna's vision: she could see things that other people couldn't. The woman was more sensitive than others, Rena believed. Except for last night. *That poor child,* she had said. That was more than intuition. It was something that Rena's clinically trained mind couldn't comprehend.

She called Stacey.

"I need a favor," she said.

"Shoot."

"I need some clothes."

"Don't we all. Want to borrow my Saks card?"

"No, I need you to go to my place and pick up some clothes. Just don't slip on any rat shit."

"Huh?"

She told Stacey what had happened last night, and to make sure the rats were gone before she went in. Stacey was shocked and said she would be over within the hour.

Next, she tried Fred's number. It was still busy.

She then called Anthony Richardson at the station.

"I want to take some time off," she said.

"You're due. When?"

"Within a few days."

"Rena, come on," he said, choking on something.

Probably eating a sandwich, she thought. Anthony was thirty-five, had a heart problem, and weighed in at three hundred pounds. "What's that in your mouth?"

"A toothpick," he said.

"Bullshit," she said.

"How long?"

"I don't know."

"A day? A week? A month? How long?"

"I don't know."

"You can't do this to me. I need time to find a replacement."

"Dr. Harvey Waters would be more than happy to fill in for me."

"Dr. Harvey Waters is about as exciting as watching paint peel. What's so important that it has to be right away?"

"I have to go to New York."

"New York? It's summertime!"

"And the living is easy and the cotton is high . . . I still have to go."

"Okay. You understand if I can't get Waters, I'm going to have to expand Murray's time slot."

"You're a shit, Tony."

"You bet. I got a right. You're leaving me, remember?"

"Three extra hours a day of Murray Spahn on gourmet dining? The man can't even boil water, Tony."

"You can always shorten your vacation and come back."

"To what? There won't be an audience left to come back to."

They hung up.

She tried Fred again. The line was still busy.

She called the Department of City Planning.

"I need a copy of the original blueprints to my home." Rena gave the woman her name and address.

"What happened to the copy we gave you a couple of weeks ago?" the woman said after looking through her records.

"What copy?" Rena asked, confused.

"According to our records, you requested and were given a copy of the original drawings."

"How do you know?"

"I'm looking at the requisition order. You had to sign for it when you picked it up."

"What name was signed?"

"You Rena Halbrook?"

"Yes."

"Well, that's the name."

"Were you the one that issued the prints?"

"Let me see." A pause as the woman looked for the name. "Yep, it was me."

"Can you tell me what I looked like?"

"Ask your mama what you look like, honey. I'm busy here," the woman said, getting impatient.

"Sorry. Did I give you an address?"

"What would I need that for? I didn't have to mail it to you. You picked it up, remember? Are you on something, honey?"

Who was impersonating me? Rena thought.

She hung up and tried Fred again. Busy. She thought about returning Charlie's calls but decided against it. Instead she called her own home hoping the pest-control people would answer since she hadn't left her phone machine on last night. They did.

"How did they get in?" Rena asked a gravelly-voiced man on the other end.

"From the street, it looks like. The crawl space in your closet exits out to your backyard."

"I don't remember there being a crawl space in my closet."

"Sure is. It was covered over years ago by a dry wall in the closet and a cement fill on the outside. Looks like they were recently broken into. Were you doing some kind of renovation?"

"No."

"What about a robbery?"

"No."

"The reason I'm askin' is because if I was a robber, that's the way I'd do it. Nobody'd ever see you comin' or goin'. 'Cept how would they know about the crawl space? It was probably covered over before you were born. Another thing. I hope you don't mind me askin' this, but are you a peanut-butter junkie?"

"I've been known to indulge. Why?"

"Because your clothes and your shelves are covered with that stuff. If anything could attract rats, it's peanut butter. In fact, that's what we bait *our* traps with. People think they like cheese. Ain't so. They've been watching too many Tom and Jerry cartoons."

That explained the odor. How did it get there? she thought.

"Would it attract that many rats?" she asked.

"Only if they've been nesting in the crawl space. I doubt it, though. There wasn't much rat poop. Rats like to crap a lot. Strange lock you have for a closet."

"What lock?"

"The one attached to the top of your door. A swing lock."

"I don't have a lock on my closet," she said.

"Sure you do. I'm looking at it right now. In fact you had

it set so that you could open the door from the outside but not from the inside. Not a good thing, especially if you have kids."

Who's doing this to me? she thought. "When will you be through?" she asked. "Someone will be by soon to get a few things for me."

"Oh, in about twenty minutes or so. Want to know how many rats we've killed so far?"

"No, I don't."

"Maybe thirty or forty," he said, ignoring her.

"Thank you for hearing me," she said sardonically as she hung up.

Someone put those creatures in my closet, then locked me in, she thought. She dialed Miranda, her housekeeper, who came three times a week.

"*Buenos días*, Miranda."

"Miz Halbrook?"

"*Sí*. My robe . . ."

"*Que?*"

"*Mi*, er . . . *ropa*."

"What clothes?"

"Not clothes . . . *ropa* . . . *comprende?*" Rena said, wishing she had taken Spanish instead of French in school. The only time she ever used French was with the waiters at La Serre.

"*Ropa* mean clothes in Spanish."

"I'm trying to say bathrobe."

"Then say bathrobe. The word you want is *bata*," Miranda said, laughing.

"Right, *bata*. Thank you."

"It eez where I always put it. On door of bathroom. Why?"

"You didn't put it this time in the closet by mistake?" she said slowly.

"Talk right, Miz Halbrook. I cannot learn English if you try to talk like me."

"Good point." She asked again.

"No, no. Always on back of bathroom door."

"You like peanut butter?"

"*Que?* I *hate* peanut butter. That is what I live on when I walked from El Salvador to San Diego."

An hour later Stacey and Ben came over carrying several hangers of clothes and a tote bag filled with bathroom articles.

"Ben went into your house to pick out the clothes and drove your car back here. I couldn't go in, I hate rats," Stacey said, shuddering. "I hope he did a good job on matching."

"Hey, you have no qualms about letting me dress *you*," he said to Stacey, grinning, as he plopped down on the couch. Ben was supposed to be Stacey's age, except his long blond curly hair and boyish charm made him seem younger. He and Stacey were always at ease with one another, as if they'd been together for a long time. He was a sports photographer for a national magazine.

"You look like you just went ten rounds with Sugar Ray. Maybe you'd better stay off your feet today," Stacey said to Rena.

"I can't. Too much to do. Do me a favor, will you? See if you can get through to Fred. His line's been busy since yesterday. Something's wrong," she said, going upstairs to change.

"Still busy," Stacey said, when Rena, showered and dressed, came back down.

"I'd better get over there," Rena said, looking uneasy.

Ben drove them across town in his VW convertible. The heavy summer storm had cleansed the air of the ever-present orange haze, and the mountains, for once, didn't bleed into the city but stood out crisply like a backdrop on a Swiss postcard. Fred lived in an apartment on Hoover. The street was a mixture of Mexicans, druggies, and USC students.

They took the elevator covered with graffiti to the third-floor landing. The bell was broken and Rena knocked on the door. There was no answer. She put an ear up to it and listened for movement.

"Maybe he's asleep," Stacey said.

Rena turned the knob and found the door unlocked.

"Fred!" she called out as she walked in.

No answer, just the rustling of papers on the desk in the living room coming from the draft of an open window. Hundreds of books and ham-radio equipment were stuffed into the shelves that lined the walls. The lamp on the desk was lit even though the room was bathed in sunlight, and the phone was off the hook. A Brahms concerto was coming from the stereo.

"He's not in here," Ben said, sticking his head in the bedroom.

"So this is how Freddy the hermit lives," Stacey said, looking around.

Rena walked over to the desk and grabbed a slip of paper and a pen. "I'll leave a note telling him we were here."

As they began to leave, Rena heard a dripping noise coming from behind the closed bathroom door next to the bedroom. Her stomach tightened as she made her way over to it. She opened the door, looked in, and let out a short scream. Ben and Stacey rushed over to her.

"He's dead," she said, barely audible. Her knees started to give and she had to lean against the wall.

Ben pushed opened the bathroom door and peered in.

Fred was lying in the bathtub, totally submerged. His body, drained of blood, was the color of eggshells and contrasted sharply with the coral red water. His eyes were rolled back into his head and only the whites showed between the tiny slits. His sagging jaw gave him the appearance of being in a drunken stupor, and his shriveled penis bobbed up and down in the water like a submarine's periscope. On the cracked tile floor, next to the tub, was a double-edged razor coated with dried blood.

Mexican women with their babies, the unemployed, students, the drug dealers and their customers, the thieves and the drunks, all formed an arc around the apartment building and watched as two policemen carried the zipped plastic bag out the door. They talked freely, almost joyfully to each other; there was no caste system among them today. On this street, where death was a frequent neighbor, there was elation because the body was not a family member or a friend.

In Fred's apartment Rena told the police everything she knew.

"Did he ever give you any indication that he wanted to take his own life?"

"Never," she answered.

"Was he a depressed individual?"

"Yes . . . lately." That was true. In the last couple of months she had noticed a difference in his behavior, and she was just too busy to sit down and talk to him. You're one hell of a shrink! she thought bitterly about herself.

Ben had his arm gently around Stacey's shoulder as they stood by the window and silently watched paramedics load Fred's body into the ambulance three stories down.

"What a dumb thing to do, Fred," Stacey said, as she put her head on Ben's shoulder.

After the police were finished, Ben drove them to the radio station. The ride back was somber.

"Why would he kill himself?" Stacey asked, breaking the long silence. She was slouched in the backseat. "I worked on suicide hotlines . . . I should have seen the signs. He worked for you for a long time. Did he give you any indication that he was capable of doing this?"

"Sometimes the clues are not easy to decipher," Rena said, still angry with herself.

In Fred's case, the signs weren't that well hidden, and she knew that. He was sensitive, quiet . . . almost aloof. He made a good screener for her—his logical mind quickly distinguishing which calls were real and interesting. As far as she could tell, he never dated and had few friends. There were times she wanted to shake him so that his shell would crack and a feeling, smiling human being would emerge. She wondered why he wanted to be a psychologist since he gave so little of himself. Maybe he needed to see the rawness of others in order to keep himself grounded in the human race. And . . . maybe that's why he killed himself: the more he witnessed the pain of others, the more he realized how helpless he was in his own body because he could not experience it himself. Or . . . perhaps he *had* experienced it, the pain, for the first time, and couldn't live with it. Which theory applied to him? She didn't know. Perhaps he left a note somewhere explaining his actions. Maybe he told his mother about his depression; they were close. She would try to find out.

"Are you going on the air about Fred?" Ben said.

"I don't know yet. I don't see what purpose it would serve. Will you be able to handle all the calls until I find someone else?" she asked Stacey.

"Of course," Stacey said sadly. She reached over the vinyl car seat, put her arms around Ben's neck, and kissed him on the head.

They drove the rest of the way in silence, each locked in their own thoughts.

Chapter 14

Tuesday, 7:20 P.M.

Gerald W. Jaffe lay in bed naked, his body propped up on pillows as he smoked a cigarette. He watched silently as Tina Renaldo picked her clothes off the chair in the corner and started dressing.

"Slower," he whispered.

She stopped and looked at Jaffe, her eyes not bothering to hide the hate in them. But she did as he asked. Methodically she put her thin arms through the sleeves of the tank top and pulled it down over her small budding breasts, her dark nipples showing through the cheap cotton material. Next came the panties, then the French rip-off designer jeans. She kept her eyes to the wall the whole time, not saying anything. When she finished, she grabbed her purse and started to walk out of the bedroom.

"You forget something?" he said with a tone one uses on a child.

She stopped and turned toward him, the flicker of hate still in her eyes. After a moment she said sullenly, "I loved fucking you, Mr. Jaffe."

"And . . ."

"I loved when you put your cock in my mouth and in my cunt and my . . ." The tears choked off the rest and she closed her eyes tightly.

"And?"

"Please, Mr. Jaffe, please, I . . ."

He rolled over and picked up a set of handcuffs from the night table.

"And . . . I loved when you put it in my ass!" she blurted out. The tears ran down her face.

He put the handcuffs back on the table and said, grinning, "And?"

"I want to do it again real soon. I want you to teach me more tricks."

"And the most important thing?"

She looked down on the floor, took a deep breath, and said in a low voice, "I love you, Mr. Jaffe."

"I didn't hear you," he said, flicking the cigarette ashes on the carpet.

"And . . . I love you, Mr. Jaffe," she said louder, glaring at him through watery eyes.

He nodded. She was free to leave. She wiped her eyes and walked out the door, slamming it hard.

He listened to the sound of Tina's high heels rushing down the stairs, then got up and took a shower. He scrubbed hard, trying to get the smell of the Mexican girl off his body.

He had first met Tina several months ago standing outside a Latin discotheque. It was two in the morning and she was hustling a drunken kid, barely out of his teens, who was leaving the bar after last call. Jaffe walked over to them and flashed his badge. The terrified boy took off down the street, disappearing into a darkened alley. Laughing, Jaffe made Tina put her hands behind her back and cuffed her, tightening them on purpose, then pushed her into the backseat of his car. She became hysterical and told him she was in this country illegally and that she had never been arrested before. Jaffe drove slowly, stopping for all the lights, telling her about what happens to pretty things like herself in Sybil Brand Institute. By the time they reached the station, she was trembling, half out of her mind with fear and the pain from the cuffs. She told him he could do anything he wanted to her . . . anything!

And for four months, that's exactly what he did to her . . . *anything*.

Tonight was probably the last time for her, he thought, scrubbing his loins with a washcloth until they were red. She was getting too old for his tastes: she had just turned fourteen last month. Besides, he was tired of blacks and Mexicans and thought about finding some new meat. Blond, with golden curls maybe

... or fine red hair with white freckled skin. Yes, red hair! That was his favorite, but hard to come by. He'd start looking again, scouring the streets for runaways, just like he did before he was married ... or like he did back in New York.

Later, wearing a towel around his waist, he made a cold turkey sandwich, got a beer from the fridge, and called in at the station. "Yeah, the old ulcer's still acting up ... I should be in by tomorrow ... yeah ... right, see you then." He was told that it was a quiet night: one homicide and two suicides. One of them was a college kid who worked for Rena Halbrook—in fact, she was the one who found him. Jaffe tried remembering if he had met the kid. Oh yeah, the one who looked like a basset hound that swallowed a lemon, he thought to himself. Lots of things going down with this bitch.

He called Rena's number, and when she answered, he hung up. Good, she was home. He needed to talk to her in person, find out what she really knew. First, though, he wanted to make a pit stop and see an old, old friend.

"So what's your opinion? Was Marilyn Monroe killed by the CIA or what?" asked Izzy Finestein as he stood behind the counter of his grocery store adding up Charlie's bill on the back of a paper bag with a pencil stub. His sleeves were rolled up past his elbows, exposing his hairy arms, and the yarmulke on top of his head was tilted to one side and held in place by bobby pins.

"Gee, Izz, I don't think so. My guess is that she's really still alive and living in Cuba as Fidel Castro's mistress," Charlie said as he handed him a quart of Breyer's chocolate and another six-pack of Dos Equis.

"I already read that crap in that newspaper you used to work for."

"I wrote it."

"Ach! Such dreck you write."

"It's a living, Izz."

"If you have to write, be Charlie Dickens and not Charlie Shmo."

"Come on, Izzy. You expect me to write with a quill?"

"Charlie, you're a bum!" Izzy said loud enough for the other customers to hear. "You have more talent than ten writers put together. Do something with it." He put the pencil stub behind his ear as he shook his head at him.

"You know how to make a man feel good, Izzy." Charlie took his bags from the counter and walked the two blocks back to his home.

As he put his key into the lock he heard a voice coming from a Ford Fairlane parked near his house. "Hey, Charlie, my man, it's been a long time."

"Gerald W. Jaffe, as I live and breathe!" Charlie said, surprised.

"You going to invite an ex–New Yorker in or what?" Jaffe said as he got out of the car.

Neither man extended his hand. There was no love lost between them. Their relationship, which went as far back as New York, had to do with "cop-reporter" business only.

"Am I looking at a social visit?" Charlie asked as he opened the door.

"Absolutely," Jaffe said, stepping over the two bags of groceries on the ground, and walked inside without being invited. The living-room floor was covered with newspapers and magazines. "Still using the same old housekeeper, I see," he said, looking around.

Charlie put the bags on the kitchen counter, took out the two six-packs, and opened the refrigerator. "What can I do for you, Gerald W.?"

"You can start by offering me one of those beers."

Charlie tossed it over to him. Jaffe took the brown concoction out of his mouth and put it in the ashtray.

"You still chewing that shit?" Charlie asked as he opened a bottle for himself.

"Yep," Jaffe said, searching the room with his eyes. "Been using the stuff since my professional days in baseball. Calms me down."

Charlie snickered. Gerald W.'s baseball days consisted of two weeks on Pittsburgh's Double-A farm team. He was a reliever. The story he told was that his rotary cuff was destroyed when he tried throwing a ninety-five-mile-an-hour fastball. Another story, told to Charlie by a sports editor at the *Times*, was that the only thing Jaffe tried to throw was the game. Seems that he owed a bookie in town, and by giving up two or three runs the slate would be erased. The team was located in a small town in Kansas. It didn't take long before word got out about it and he was thrown out of baseball.

Jaffe was now walking around the room, touching shelves and sneaking glances in a couple of open desk drawers. Charlie picked up on it.

"What you been up to, Charlie, since they booted your ass off the *Tattler*?"

"Why? You a fan?"

"Always loved your stuff, you know that." He picked up the old newspaper clippings about Alice Mendoza that were piled on the desk and looked at them. "Ah, yeah . . . little Alice. I remember her. One of your better pieces. What are you doing with these? It's a pretty old story, isn't it?" He tried acting nonchalant but couldn't stop the quiver in his voice.

"You should know. It happened on your beat."

"Yeah. Sad story. Pretty gruesome sight, if I remember. I was just a rookie then. I must have passed that building she was locked away in maybe ten times a day. She was right under my nose and I never knew it. If I did, I would have killed that bastard."

Charlie sat on the kitchen stool and leaned his arms on the counter as he slowly sipped his beer. He wondered when Jaffe would make his move.

"Funny thing . . . I don't know if you know it, but I'm working on a case similar to this one. That radio shrink, Rena Halbrook, is involved in it."

"Oh, yeah," Charlie said, feigning surprise. "I heard about it. Think they're similar, huh?"

"Huh-huh, I do. And I think you do, too, or you wouldn't be phoning her three times a day." He pushed several magazines off the couch, sat down, and put his heel on the edge of the "Motel Six" Formica coffee table.

Without saying anything, Charlie got up, went over to the coffee table, and moved it further back, causing Jaffe's foot to hit the floor. He then sat back down on the stool.

"Sorry, my man. Didn't know it was a museum piece," Jaffe said.

"She tell you I called three times a day?"

"How else would I know?"

Charlie knew he was lying. "I don't know. Maybe you have a tap on her."

"Hey, that's illegal, man. So why you calling her?" He tried putting his foot back on the table, but Charlie had pushed it too far back, and he had to settle for crossing it over his other knee.

"I needed some advice."

"Like what?"

"I have this desire to screw my neighbor's wife who's a big-titted Hasidic Jew with six kids. I wanted to know if she thought I was a pervert. Her answer was yes."

"Come on, Charlie," he said, laughing, as he leaned back, putting his arms around the couch top. "Don't bullshit me. We've known each other almost twenty years. Christ, we're two bachelors . . . we should be putting away a few . . . hitting on a couple of broads on a Saturday night."

"Give me a break, Gerald W. You and I wouldn't know what to do with each other on a Saturday night if our lives depended on it. Besides, you and I have different tastes in women."

"What the fuck's that supposed to mean?" Jaffe asked, standing up and glaring at him. His face was tight and mean.

Charlie didn't answer him. He just stared back, wondering if Jaffe would try and get physical. Actually, he wouldn't mind if he did; he had hated the guy, even when he lived in New York, and he had fantasized more than a few times about nailing him one in the mouth. Charlie watched for any movement Jaffe made toward his left back pocket. It was well-known that Jaffe kept his black leather sap in there and would use it without hesitation.

"I said, what the fuck's that supposed to mean!" Jaffe moved closer to him, his hand shifting toward his back pocket.

He was standing next to Charlie now, and if Charlie wanted to, he could flatten the cop easily enough with a right cross. It was tempting, except the Markowitzs would hear the commotion through the two-inch walls separating them and he would wind up having to look for a new place to live. Another time, Charlie thought to himself. "It means that I like them Jewish and fat. Certainly not your type, right?" he said, his eyes never leaving Jaffe's hand.

What it really meant was that Jaffe was asked to resign from the New York Police Department because of suspected involvement with underage girls. None of the girls would testify against him because most of them were runaways or too frightened, so no charges had been filed.

Jaffe's hand moved away from his pocket and he broke out into a big grin. "Thought you were giving me some shit."

"Nah. Why would I want to do that? You about finished with your beer, Gerald W., 'cause I have things to do."

"As soon as you tell me what you wanted with that Halbrook chick. Come on, Charlie."

"Why you so interested?"

"I was there with you, remember? We both saw what that fucker did to her!"

Charlie *always* remembered. Jaffe was one of the two rookies he was with when the grizzly discovery was made. The other cop passed out, facedown on the floor, and Charlie, just as he bent over to throw up, saw Jaffe's face: it was all aglow as he stared at the remains, like a child watching his bigger brother tearing apart caterpillars.

"Okay," Charlie said, as he dumped the empty beer bottle into the trash. He decided the best way to handle Jaffe was to be semitruthful. "It's real simple. Both girls had similar names and similar situations going for them and I figured there might be a buck in it."

"Like how?" Jaffe said, tensing up.

"You know, a ghost story. The-girl-comes-back-eighteen-years-later kind of crap." He looked at the ground, trying to appear embarrassed.

It worked.

"A ghost story! Jeez, Charlie. You write the weirdest shit!" Jaffe said, shaking his head and laughing. "What did you want with Halbrook? Her approval?"

"You got it," he said, nodding and smiling and shrugging. He felt like Mortimer Snerd. He suppressed another urge to punch this asshole in the mouth.

"Okay, Charlie, it was nothing but a scam . . . figures with you," Jaffe said, relieved, as he walked toward the door. "Throw me another cold one for the road, huh?"

Charlie took a Dos Equis out of the refrigerator, shook it up pretty good under the counter where Jaffe couldn't see, and tossed it to him.

"Think up another scam, Charlie. That one's in bad taste," Jaffe said, halfway out the door, pointing the bottle at him.

Charlie watched from the window as Jaffe got in the car, started the engine, and began to drive off while twisting the top off the beer. Midway down the street, he saw the Fairlane swerve and heard Jaffe scream *"Shit!"* Charlie laughed. The sucker must be drenched to the bone.

He grabbed another beer, fighting off an urge for the bottle in the cupboard. It had been over two weeks since he had anything eighty proof to drink, and drinking beer was like drinking Sanka when you've spent most of your life on Turkish coffee. He had no choice. He had to give up the hard stuff if he was ever going to uncover why the two Alices were so alike. Heavy booze sizzled his mind, and the hangovers usually ruined a whole day.

Why was Gerald W. so interested in what I wanted with Rena Halbrook? he thought. Charlie hadn't failed to notice the look on his face when he saw the old clippings on the desk. He also saw his relief when he thought Charlie was just innocently looking for a story. What the hell does he have to do with all this? Was this a new angle? He could use one, because everywhere he turned he was finding dead ends.

He sat back, turned on the Dodger game, and waited for Rena to call him. He knew she would, especially after she saw her mail.

Rena spent most of the evening going through her clothes in the closet with Anna. The smell of peanut butter and the chemical poison, diphacinone, which was used to kill the rats, was still strong. The clothes stained with the peanut butter were piled on the floor.

Anna had insisted on coming tonight because she didn't want Rena spending the night alone. When she saw the frazzled condition Rena was in because of Fred's death, she was glad she came.

Rena checked the closet door. It closed smoothly and opened just as easily.

"How did the door close?" Anna asked. She was washing down the shelves in the closet.

"I was locked in," Rena said, looking at the shiny, new brass lock on top of the closet door.

Anna didn't say anything, but her face had a troubled look.

"You think an apparition locked the door on me?" Rena said wryly as she carried a handful of clothes on hangers into the closet and hung them up on the pole.

"I think you should leave this house. That's what I think."

"Why? The crawl space has been sealed off again, this time with cement. The rats can't get back in."

"If *she* wants them back in, they'll get back in," the old lady said with a tremor in her voice.

"*Who* wants, Anna?" Rena asked, turning to her. "Talk to me. Are you talking about the little girl that called me?"

Anna said nothing. Her lips were pressing down hard on each other as she scrubbed more forcefully.

"Or are you talking about the one who died eighteen years ago?" Rena said casually, seeing if it would get a reaction.

Anna turned sharply, her eyes filled with dread.

"Her name was Alice, too, you know," Rena said as she continued to hang up her clothing.

"You want to know too much, girl. It's not a good thing!" Anna said with a quiet ferocity as she dropped the brush into the pail.

"How much do you see, Anna?" That cold finger of terror was tickling Rena's spinal column again.

"I see nothing. I *feel*!" Anna said intensely, holding her fist to her breast. "Don't stay in this house. You go away, far away for a little while. When you come back, all this will be over." She grabbed Rena's wrist and held tightly, her twisted fingernails digging into the skin.

"All *what* will be over?"

"Just do as I say . . . *please*! You listened to me as a child, listen to me now!"

Rena had never, in all the years she had known her, seen such terror in Anna's face. The doorbell rang as she was about to tell her that she *was* leaving the house, that she was going to New York. Rena tried to get to the door but Anna held her arm in a fierce grip.

"You stay here. I'll get it," Anna said forcefully.

Rena heard mumbled voices and movement downstairs, then

the heavy door bolt being pushed aside. Anna came slowly back up on her spindly legs and handed Rena a card.

"He says he's from the police department. I made him show me his identification before I let him in. Lord, but he smells like a Louisiana hobo!" Anna said disdainfully.

More like a brewery, Rena thought, sizing him up as she came down the stairs.

"Hello, Dr. Halbrook," Jaffe said boisterously, brushing at his shirt, trying to make the beer stains disappear.

"It's somewhat late," she said coldly, looking at her watch. "Hopefully you have some information on Alice."

"Nothing current. We're hoping either a body turns up, or a neighbor or someone heard the girl and calls us. Until then, there's not much we can do," he said, looking at a crystal decanter of brandy on the side table. He could tell by her unfriendly tone that he wasn't going to be offered any. He didn't think there was much chance of being offered a seat, either. She stood near the door with her arms folded, waiting.

"I heard about the death of your assistant. It must have been a shock, huh?" he said nicely, trying to break down her defenses.

"Yes, it was. Unless, of course, you suspect that my PR firm orchestrated his demise," she said derisively. "Rest assured he's not body-surfing in Bermuda."

His pants were soaked through from the beer and irritated his crotch. He hoped she would turn around so he could scratch. "Look, I'm sorry about that—"

"—but you have to cover all your bases, yes, I know. I appreciated you trying to make me look like an opportunist to the media," she said, not bothering to hide her sarcasm.

Again, just as he had the last time, Jaffe wanted to put his hands around her lily white neck. Instead he walked past her, pulling at his crotch and looking at the furniture and the modern art on the walls. "I just had a talk with Charles Halleran. Has that loser been hustling you?"

She was surprised that he knew. "He tried."

"What did he tell you? Something about a connection between some old murder and this girl, right?"

"Yes, how did you know?"

"He's pulled garbage like this before. I suppose he showed you some newspaper articles on it."

"Yes, a few."

"Yeah, that's the way he does it," Jaffe said, nodding his head, as he paced the floor with his hands in his pockets.

He was beginning to make her nervous. His jerky movements and the continuous licking of his lips made her wonder if he was on drugs. "Is that why you're here . . . about Halleran?"

"Partially. I also wanted to know if anything else happened recently relating to this girl."

"Like what?"

He tried to sound detached. "Oh, other phone calls . . . you know, anything out of the ordinary."

She thought about telling him of the rats and her suspicions about someone being in her house last night, but decided against it. She felt it strange that Jaffe would have this much concern now when only two weeks ago he believed she concocted the whole thing. What had happened to change his mind?

She went over to the door and opened it, wanting him to leave. She was a therapist and recognized psychotic behavior. "Do you mind? It's been a rough day. If anything happens, I'll let you know."

Jaffe wanted to tell her how much he *really* minded, except he saw Anna on the top landing watching him. He'd been a cop too long to know that you don't do or say anything in front of witnesses unless they're on your side.

"I understand," he said. "Sorry that I bothered you so late." He smiled and left.

Rena watched him walk to his car, tugging at his pants and scratching himself. She decided that whatever she found out would go directly to Craig Sanders at the DA's office and not to Jaffe.

"I don't trust that one," Anna said as she slowly shuffled down the stairs.

"Neither do I," Rena agreed, still watching as Jaffe got into his car and drove away. She bolted the door and turned on the alarm.

An hour later she was in bed going through her mail. Most of it was junk that she tossed in the trash can by the side of her bed. Then she saw the legal-size envelope with Charlie's name and address on the back and opened it.

The ringing woke Charlie out of a sound sleep on the couch. He sat up, rubbed his eyes, and looked under the pillows for the phone. He figured he must have been asleep for a while because the game was over and a "Starsky and Hutch" rerun was on. He found the phone under the newspapers, clicked off the TV, and answered it.

"Is this Charles Halleran?" the voice asked.

"Yep. Is this Dr. Rena Halbrook?"

"How did you know?" she said wearily.

"You mean I'm actually right! Maybe I should try out for 'Jeopardy.' "

"Maybe you should get yourself an attorney."

"Why is that?"

"Because I'm thinking about suing you for harassment."

"Hey, come on."

"What am I supposed to do with this police report you sent me?"

"I wanted to show you that I was telling you the truth about the condition of the girl."

"According to this report, they found numerous rat bites on her body, and the body was partially devoured."

He detected a flutter in her voice. "Right. The rats had a field day on her corpse. She was pretty well torn up, mostly by the father, though." He could have gotten more descriptive in what he saw that day in the apartment: how the rats, hundreds of them, were crawling in and out of crevices in her body, eating away her face, her hands, her bowels. There was no reason to tell her. Not because she might be sensitive, but because talking about it meant conjuring it up in his mind again.

"What is it you want?" Rena asked finally.

"A story. Not a ghost story but a *real* one . . . whatever that might be. Look, I think you know something's going on here. I really need your help."

"Why?" she said.

"Because it seems you have something to do with all this, except I can't figure out what. The police aren't going to be of much help . . . not without a body. Meet with me . . . let's talk. Let's see if we can work this thing out."

"There's nothing to talk about. Nothing further has happened since that phone call two weeks ago." Again that quaver in her voice.

"I believe in listening to subtexts, doc."

"Excuse me?"

"I heard what you just said, but I also heard how you said it. They don't match."

"Good night. I hope this will be our last conversation," Rena said with finality.

"Why?" he asked, hoping she wouldn't hang up.

"Because I believe in listening to gut feelings . . . my own. And my gut feeling says not to give you an inch. Good night."

She hung up.

Damn! He slammed the phone down. He would have to go it alone then. Too bad, since she was the link in all this. But why? What does a squeaky-clean, rich psychologist have to do with the horrible tragedy of two small girls? Thinking about it made Charlie's adrenaline pump. Christ, but it had been a long time since he'd felt this way about a story!

Chapter 15

Friday, 9:45 A.M.

The nine o'clock flight to New York received clearance to take off forty-five minutes behind schedule. As the plane lifted off the runway Rena looked out the window from her first-class seat and watched the smog-covered rim of Santa Monica dissolve like cigarette smoke into the Pacific Ocean. Then the 747 made a U-turn and headed inland. She leaned back in her seat and sipped an orange juice. Next to her was a good-looking blond man with a chiseled face, wearing a light tan summer suit and reading the *New York Times*. He smiled at her politely, exposing white, even teeth and, when the flight attendant came around, ordered a Mimosa. Rena envisioned him as a retired military officer who now worked in private industry, probably defense.

She thought about Fred's funeral yesterday. It was a Spartan affair, with only a few people showing up. At the end of the ceremony, as the coffin was being lowered into the grave site overlooking the Ventura Freeway, Mrs. Lovell, Fred's mother, grabbed her arm and asked how this could have happened.

"He would never kill himself! Why would he do such a thing?" she wailed, still hanging on to her arm. Her eyes were swollen and red.

Rena didn't answer. The fact is, she thought, no one knows what really goes on inside another person, no matter how close we think we are to them. We are born alone and we die alone. But to tell this hurting old woman that would have been cruel. Instead she put her arm around her and quietly walked her back to the waiting limousine.

Craig Sanders had driven her to the airport this morning. Stacey had originally planned to take her, but Craig insisted. He kept the conversation light as the car crept along in the rush-hour traffic, mostly talking about the heat wave in New York, a new French restaurant that had opened on East Fifty-eighth, and that he had connections if she wanted good seats to *Phantom of the Opera*. They arrived at LAX early and went to the cafeteria for a cup of coffee. As he poured the Sweet 'n Low into his cup, his demeanor started to change.

"I had a look at the coroner's report on your assistant, Fred Lovell."

"And?"

"And . . . there was a ton of Valium in his bloodstream. Enough to kill him."

Rena was bewildered. She had no idea Fred had taken any kind of sedatives.

"What bothers me is how it was administered. It was done by injection. They found the needle mark on his ankle. The type of people who shoot up in the ankles are either junkies who no longer have usable veins left in their arms, or the kind that need to hide the tracks. You'd be surprised how many professionals, like doctors and lawyers, fit into that category. Since there was only one needle mark on Lovell, I could hardly call him a user. You know what's odd?" he said, filling his mouth with danish.

"What?" she said.

"The dosage was taken about fifteen or twenty minutes before he cut his wrists, and we can't find the needle or the vial it came in."

"Couldn't he have thrown them away?"

"I doubt it," he said, catching the blueberries with his tongue as they dribbled off the breakfast cake. "That much given intravenously hits like a ton of bricks in less than a second. I can't even figure out how he had the strength to climb into the tub and slice a good half inch into his wrists."

"Are you saying someone might have done it for him?" she asked in astonishment.

"I don't know," he said, shrugging. "My men are tossing the possibility around. It takes a certain amount of muscle and commitment to cut into the wrists like that, and Fred always reminded me of Pee Wee Herman, not Arnold Schwarzenegger."

He walked her past security to the gate and asked what was so important about New York in June, other than the Puerto Rican Day parade.

"You have something against parades, Craig, or Puerto Ricans?" Rena said, laughing.

"It has to do with this girl, Alice, doesn't it?" he asked, with a worried frown on his face.

She didn't answer him but was surprised and touched by his intuitiveness and hugged him tightly before she boarded. Looking over his shoulder, she caught a glimpse of a woman rushing toward the ticket counter, trying to get a boarding pass for the flight. Rena could only see the back of her head, but it was the long, straight red hair that made her stand out. The passengers who were filing past her trying to board the plane made it difficult to see, but it looked a lot like Belinda, Terry's fiancée.

When the seat-belt sign went off, Rena got up and walked into coach class. The plane was half-empty and Belinda was easy to find, her red hair acting like a beacon. She was sitting in the smoking section sipping a Bloody Mary. The two seats next to her were empty.

"Hi, remember me?" Rena asked amicably as she sat down next to her without asking.

There was no holding the petrified look on her face when she saw Rena. She opened her mouth to say something but nothing came out. The best she could do was to nod her head like a marionette and smile.

"I'm a little surprised to see you going to New York. I thought you were in Carmel," Rena said.

"Business," Belinda whispered, trying to get her voice back. She cleared her throat and said more authoritatively, "I'm doing a commercial in New York."

"Oh, yes, I heard you were an actress. I hope you don't mind me sitting here, but I saw you at the gate and I wanted to say hello before the flight attendant tells me to get back to where I belong."

"Of course not," Belinda said nervously as she brushed her hair back from her face. "My agent called me yesterday and told me I had the part." She cleared her throat again and took a large sip of her drink.

"What kind of commercial?"

"Oh, a featured dancer in a Diet Pepsi commercial. The exposure's good," she said, fidgeting with the ends of her hair.

Rena wondered what had become of the Southern accent Belinda sported at Cathy's birthday party. This is no Georgia peach, she thought. "I heard you and Terry might be getting married," she said lightly.

Belinda's head snapped toward Rena. "We're still in the talking stage. No date has been set." She lit up a cigarette and turned toward the clouds outside her window. It was obvious she didn't want to talk about it.

"How's Cathy doing? Was she much trouble?" Rena asked nicely, changing the subject.

"Oh, she's great!" Belinda replied sincerely. "We had a lot of fun riding up in the hills. We weren't too far from Clint Eastwood's ranch, you know." At the mention of Cathy, the rich, Southern twang came back.

"I'm glad to hear that. She can be hard to handle sometimes."

"We had a terrific time!" she said enthusiastically.

"And Terry? How's he?"

"Okay, I guess," Belinda said, shrugging, looking anxious again. "He seemed a little angry about something to do with money, but I don't pay much attention to his business dealings."

"Terry didn't mention where you're from, and your accent's giving me trouble."

"All over. I was an army brat."

"Interesting," Rena said pleasantly. Very interesting indeed, she thought as she stood up.

Rena said she hoped they'd meet again and made her way back to her section of the airplane. When she reached first class, she stood next to the food trays and looked through the slit in the black curtains. She watched Belinda get up, walk to the rear of the plane, and place a call on the credit-card phone. Whoever she was talking to seemed to excite her; she became agitated, her hands flying in all directions. After a while she slammed the phone down and, looking flushed, went back to her seat.

When the plane landed at Kennedy, Rena looked for her again at the baggage-claim area. She was nowhere to be seen. Rena thought it odd that the only baggage Belinda had was the tote she carried onto the plane. She didn't look like the kind of person to travel that light.

Outside, as Rena struggled with her own valise near the cab stand, she felt a strong hand take the bag from her. It was the blond, granite-faced man who sat next to her on the plane.

"Please, allow me," he said. "Porters are a dying breed in New York." He hailed a cab and put her suitcase in the trunk.

She thanked him and asked where he was going.

"The Stanhope on Eighty-first," he said.

Since her hotel, the Lowell, was not that much farther, she offered to share the cab.

He said little on the way into Manhattan. Only that his name was Robert Cameron, that he was in the electronic security business, and that he was in New York for a few days to meet with a client.

She liked the name Cameron for him; it went with his carved features. Her guess was that he was in his early forties. His eyes had deep crow's-feet that one usually gets from squinting too long into the sun. The guy would probably look just as good in camouflage gear, peering through binoculars, as he does in his khaki suit, she thought.

The cab stopped at the Lowell first, and when she tried to pay, he put his hand on her purse and held it shut. He said payment would be dinner with him tonight, and she accepted. She had originally planned on dining early by herself so she could get a decent start in the morning, but he was much too charming to pass up, she mused.

As soon as she settled into the hotel room she placed a long-distance call to Carmel, hoping Terry wouldn't pick up. She was in luck; Cathy answered.

"How are you enjoying yourself?" she asked her daughter.

Cathy, her voice going a mile a minute, gave her a complete rundown on what she'd been doing since she'd arrived. She said she was having a great time, especially when Belinda was there. "I helped Dad pick out the ring for Belinda. It's got this huge diamond with emeralds around it. I bet it cost a fortune! He said it's a surprise and I wasn't to tell her."

Rena decided not to mention that she'd met Belinda on the plane.

"She left all of a sudden. What a drag. She was really a good rider, Mom. She sure knew how to handle Daddy's horse. You know what was weird, though, Mom?"

"What?"

"They slept in separate rooms. All of Daddy's other girlfriends always stayed in the same room with him. I know I'm not supposed to be interested in these things, Mom, but don't you think it's weird?"

"I think you're right. You're not supposed to be interested in those things." Except it *was* weird. Terry was anything but a Victorian.

"That's the way it's supposed to be when you're really in love, I guess," Cathy said wistfully.

"Did she say where she was going?" Rena asked her.

"Europe. She said she got a good part in a movie, a spaghetti western she called it. She said she had to be in Italy the next day. Too bad. There's no kids my age to play with here," she said, sounding gloomy.

Since when do they drink Diet Pepsi in Italian westerns? she thought. "Where's your dad?"

"I don't know. He's been moody lately. He's always out. I never get to see him. Boy, is he pissed at you, though."

"I thought I told you to watch your language."

"Sorry."

"Do you want to come home?" she asked.

Cathy gave a long sigh, then said, "I can't, Mom. Dad says he wants me here, and I can't disappoint him."

Rena was angry. He wanted her there but didn't have any time for her. Terrific guy! "Don't worry about disappointing him. If you want to come home, just let me know. You dad has tough skin, he can take it."

"Gee, you're as pissed at him as he is at you. Oops! . . . Sorry, Mom."

After they hung up, Rena unpacked and got ready for her date. Why would Belinda lie to Cathy about where she was going? she wondered as she entered the shower stall. Perhaps she left because she and Terry had a fight and was too embarrassed to tell anyone the truth. Well, if she's not coming back, then Terry better find another finger to put that ring on.

* * *

Robert Cameron met her in the lobby at 8:30 wearing an expertly tailored navy blue suit that blended perfectly with her powder blue Anne Klein dress. They had drinks at the bar in the Post House next door, then took a cab to Lutèce.

What a perfect evening, she thought as she listened to him talk: wonderful food, a good vintage Chassagne-Montrachet, interesting conversation. The impeccable couple. Maybe too impeccable. Again she had the same feeling about him as she did in the cab: he was too detached, and his occasional hand touching and romantic looks were too much by the book. There didn't seem to be passion or expectation in any of this. He reminded her of a male escort with that charming, professional indifference: always attentive, but through vacant eyes.

He told her that he was a career soldier, a colonel in the army, before he retired to private life.

I picked that one right, she thought, smiling to herself.

She listened intently to his many stories about the Vietnam War; some were amusing, most were sad—and all were told with the expertise of a polished storyteller.

Around midnight, they both looked at their watches and nodded to each other that it was time to go. During the ride back to her hotel, he didn't try to touch her, nor did he make much conversation. Mostly he just looked out the window, staring out at the darkened stores on Fifth Avenue with his steel blue eyes.

She wondered if he would make a pass at her as he walked her up to the room, debating with herself whether on not she would turn him down.

He didn't come on or even try to kiss her. Instead he took her hand and held it warmly, asking how long she would be in New York.

"Perhaps two or three days. I'm really not sure," she said, amazed at his civility.

"Then we should get together tomorrow if you're not busy."

She told him her day was full.

"Tomorrow night, then?"

"Maybe."

In her room she got under the covers and left a wake-up call for seven. Closing her eyes, she thought about tonight and gave it only a passing grade. Cameron reminded her of one of Kurosawa's samurai warriors: a stranger who comes into a town, changes it through his physical presence, then leaves without anyone knowing anything more about him than they did before. Who was that masked man, kemosabe? She needed more than that.

No, there will be no more dates with Mr. Cameron, she thought to herself as she snuggled deeper under the covers.

Chapter 16

Saturday, 8:35 A.M.

"You know the guy who wrote this? He also lives in L.A.," Brenda said, scooting her glasses up over the bridge of her nose with her finger. She was looking over Rena's shoulder as she brushed through the news clippings on the microfilm machine.

"As a matter of fact I do know him," Rena said. She stopped turning the dial when she came across another article on Alice Mendoza by Charles Halleran. The archives, located in the cellar of the *Post* building, were deserted because of the weekend.

"He a looker?" Brenda asked.

"Why?"

"We sort of have a date when he comes to the East Coast."

Rena turned from the screen and looked up at her. She had tight kinky hair, like Nancy from the Nancy and Sluggo comic books. "Is that what he told you?" she asked.

"Yeah." She giggled.

"Did you have to do anything for him beyond the call of duty?"

"Kind of. He had me running all over the city getting him information on this dead girl."

"You did this for a blind date that may or may not materialize?"

"Hey, New York's a rough town. You take what you can get. So what do you say, you think he's cute?"

"Only if you like conger eels," Rena murmured, turning back to the machine.

Most of these articles she had seen before. Charlie had shown them to her a couple of weeks ago; just one or two written columns buried somewhere in the back pages of the paper. The front pages are reserved for the rich, she thought, amazed about how little attention this horrendous crime actually received.

She came across one small article, a commentary with Charlie's byline. It was an impassioned statement against society's indifference to child abuse. He used Alice as an example, drawing a graphic, gut-wrenching description about her existence and the appalling conditions she lived in. The piece was beautifully written and way ahead of its time. She was impressed. She didn't think the man she met who called himself Charles Halleran had this in him. In the description of the closet, he gave the dimensions to be three-and-a-half-by-five feet and the color a freshly painted deep violet. Charlie wrote:

> When I interviewed Mendoza, he said that he painted the inside of the closet violet because it was the color of Alice's favorite dress. His mind, when he told me that, was as clear as yours and mine—yet he was considered by the courts to be insane.
>
> That same evening, as I was watching the fledgling Mets being ripped apart by the Pirates in the warmth of my own home, with my daughter, Jaimie, asleep on my lap, the thought struck me: I just spent an entire day talking with a guy who brutally murdered his daughter, yet he laughed and joked like you and me, and pondered the same questions, such as why Joe Namath doesn't wear black shoes like the rest of the Jets. This man, Mendoza, could have been my next-door neighbor . . . or yours.
>
> What miniscule molecule living in his brain made him crazy? What experience in his life? What invisible bridge, separating abnormality and sanity, did he cross over? What made him different from us? Or *are* we that different?
>
> I turned off the game, tucked Jaimie into bed, and kissed her gently on the cheek good night. As I crawled into my safe, cozy bed I wondered how close to the heart of darkness we all must be.

A tinge of Joseph Conrad, but not bad. Halleran was an interesting man, more than she originally thought. She looked up some of the other articles he wrote for the paper and was shocked; most of them were on the front page, dealing with heavyweight New York politics. He even had his own column, *Charlie's Corner*, with a picture of him next to his name. Was this the same man who tried hustling her for a cheap story at the Hyatt? What happened to him? she wondered as she took the microfilm up to Brenda's desk.

"You get what you needed?" Brenda said, looking up from an Erica Jong novel.

"Most of it I've seen before."

"You're not putting me on? You really know this guy, Charlie Halleran, huh?"

"Yep."

"You think he's a real shit, though, right?" she said with a look that implied she had met enough of them before.

"What's your name?"

"Brenda."

"Let's just say he's not for you, Brenda."

"Man oh man, have I heard that one before," she said, sighing. "Want some coffee?" She leaned over the Krups and poured some into a Styrofoam cup.

"We all have heard that one before. You said you were running around for him?"

"Yeah, to the coroner's office, to the police, to the DMV, even to the hall of records . . . you name it!"

"Brenda, you just might save me some time. What are you doing for lunch?"

They sat in a corner booth in the diner across the street from the public library.

"First I had to go to the coroner's office to get an autopsy report on a girl who'd been dead for eighteen years. My God, that's when I had my first period, eighteen years ago! I'm getting old," Brenda said as she poured several large tablespoons of sugar into her iced tea.

The waitress, with bubble-gum-colored hair, shuffled over and gave Rena her Cobb salad and Brenda her tuna-fish sandwich on rye with fries.

"Why did Charlie send you to the hall of records?"

"To get a birth certificate," she said, smacking the bottom of the Heinz bottle, trying to get the ketchup out.

"Alice Mendoza's? Why?"

The ketchup poured out, covering the entire portion of fries. "I don't know. Mine is not to reason why. Mine is just to do or die . . . or however that shit saying goes."

"Did you give it to him?"

"Uh-uh. There wasn't one."

"Maybe she wasn't born in New York," Rena said, taking a bite of the soggy salad.

"Our Charlie says she was. He told me she was born at St. Vincent's and that I should go there. So naturally that's what stupid old me did. Anything for a date. They had nothing on her, either. I got depressed because I thought I failed him, do you believe it! Am I sick or what! I did okay at the DMV, though."

"What was there?"

"Well, Charlie was also looking for this *other* woman. Clara Freemont, I think her name was. He said he didn't know where she was living any longer. Vegas was the last address he had on her. He told me that I should go see this police captain he knows . . . that he'd be expecting me. Real nice guy this captain, but married with five kids. Anyway, he did a computer check with the Vegas police and found out that she had moved to Staten Island a couple of years ago. Ever been to Staten Island? What a place! Loaded with mafioso and cops. I bet their wives play mah-jongg together every Thursday," she said, smirking, as she raised an eyebrow. "I called information to try and get her phone number. It was unlisted. Next I went to the DMV to see if she had registered with them for a license."

"Did Charlie tell you who she was?" Rena said, pushing the unfinished salad aside. She had an idea that the woman was Alice's mother.

"No, and I didn't ask him. But I found her! It turned out she *did* have a license and was *still* living on Staten Island. I did great, huh? And I did all this on my own. Think I'm desperate?" she said, grinning, as she took a huge bite out of the sandwich and waited for an answer.

"I think you'll make some man one hell of a wife."

"Try and find one in New York, though. The gays are multiplying like bunnies around here." She finished off the sandwich and picked at the few french fries left on her plate.

"Do you still have her address?"

"Yeah, in my book back in the dungeon. That's what I call the archives." She ate the last fry and said, "I know Charlie's got a lot of problems, but under the circumstances I can understand why he is the way he is."

Rena had never told Brenda she was a psychologist and she wasn't about to tell her now and have to listen to "all about Charlie." She didn't have the time. She took a twenty out of her purse, picked up the bill, and handed them to the waitress.

"Sure you don't want me to pay my half?" Brenda asked.

Rena shook her head.

"His daughter was murdered by his wife. Did you know that?" Brenda said almost in a whisper as she leaned across the table.

"No I didn't," Rena said, jolted by her remark.

"She tried to kill him also, with the same knife. Almost succeeded . . . nicked the aorta." She was nose to nose with Rena now, her eyes glowing as she shared this secret.

"Did he tell you this?" Rena said, the mist over Charlie beginning to lift.

"Oh, no. In fact, when I brought it up to him, he got mad and almost hung up on me."

"Then how do you know this?"

"I looked up his name in the archives to see what else he'd written," Brenda said, looking down at the table and turning red. "Hey, what can I say? I check my potentials out. One of the things that came up on the computer was about his daughter's murder, except it was written by someone else, not Charlie. Happened only a couple of months after this other murder. People are so fucking weird," she said, shuddering.

Rena knew, without asking, that the death of his little girl must have had a devastating effect on him. She saw what kind of talent he had when his daughter was alive and when he had something to care about. Now, at least, she understood what had happened to his promising career.

Back in the archives, Rena looked at a map of the Bronx. There wasn't a street named Holmby throughout the entire borough. Did Charlie fabricate Alice's address so she would get hooked into his scheme? She looked at one of the newspaper clippings again. No, it said she had lived on Holmby.

"Maybe the street name was changed," Brenda said. She took a large dusty volume off one of the back shelves and lugged it over to the reading table. The book, containing 1969 surveyors' maps of the Bronx, was almost as big as she was.

They found Holmby in the index.

Rena and Brenda went through the volumes for each consecutive year until they found where Holmby had been changed to Martinez in 1974.

"You've been a great help," Rena said as she put the book back on the shelf. "You should have gone into police work."

"Right. The Miss Marple of Bensonhurst." She handed Rena the address of Clara Freemont and they said good-bye.

"That's gotta be One-thirty-two Martinez, lady," Rico Gonzalez said, his dark eyes quickly scanning the desolate, open area surrounding the gutted building. Normally he would never take a fare this far into the South Bronx, not after being a cabdriver for over fifteen years. This pretty señorita, however, made it pretty hard to resist, especially with the twenty-dollar bonus she stuck in the crack of his bullet-proof glass that separated the back and front seats.

"Double the meter if you wait," she said, getting out of the cab.

"I don't think so," he said, locking his doors.

"It would just be for five minutes."

"In five minutes my tires would be on a Mustang in Brooklyn."

"Triple it then, okay?"

"Up front." He opened the window a few inches and held out his hand.

She put three twenties in it. Shaking his head, grinning, he gunned the motor, screeching off to the safety of the city.

Rena coughed and brushed at her face, trying to clear away the fumes and dust that hovered in the still air. She looked around at the desolation, angry at herself for not getting the license of the cab. Most of the area surrounding the address was rubbish: the remains of buildings that were either burned to the ground or gutted. The street reminded her of old photographs she'd seen of Dresden after the bombings. Nothing moved, nothing seemed alive except, perhaps, the thick, resilient weeds that grew through the cracks in the concrete. She heard the frenzied beat of Spanish music in the distance, sounding like tribal drums warning neighboring villages that a stranger was in their midst; and much closer, she also heard the barking of dogs that sensed her presence.

A DO NOT TRESPASS sign partially obscured the address of the building. Ignoring it, she tried to open the dirt-covered metal door that hung in place by one rusted hinge. It resisted for an instant, then broke away from its rotted brace and fell to the concrete floor with a bang that echoed throughout the corridors of the building. The sounds of the dogs were louder now, coming from all directions.

Inside the cobwebbed vestibule, she realized that she didn't know the apartment where Alice had lived. The thought of checking each unit in this mausoleum made her skin crawl. In the entranceway, caked with dirt, was a list of past tenants bolted to the wall. Years of erosion made the names impossible to read—except one: MENDOZA 5C. It was a new sticker, dirt-free, put there recently. Her mind told her to get out, and fast, that she was over her head in all this. But she had come too far.

She mounted the staircase one step at a time, testing the loose metal banister to see if it would hold. Chunks of cement broken off from the walls and ceiling clogged the stairs, and she had to climb over them to get to the next landing. She had forgotten to bring a flashlight, but the holes in the crumbled walls allowed enough light in, like stage lights leading the way.

The growls of the dogs seemed louder on the third floor. Rena grabbed the railing tightly, her heart pounding, and stood perfectly still. The dogs, she realized with dread, were somewhere in the building.

Impossible! Rats, junkies, derelicts . . . yes. Dogs . . . that's crazy!

Then she remembered an article she had read several years ago in *New York* magazine—how the city was fighting a losing battle against packs of wild dogs living in deserted buildings. People had been attacked by them . . . some even killed.

She started to retreat down the steps. There was no sense in going any further. She'd already been attacked by animals once this week, and that was enough.

Then she saw them: six dogs staring up at her from the bottom landing. They were good-sized, but so thin that she could see the ribs erupting from their flimsy skin. The largest one, a mixture of Doberman and shepherd, began to snarl. With lips curled around yellowed fangs and saliva dripping from their mouths, they slowly climbed the stairs. Their legs shook from hunger.

Carefully, so as not to startle the dogs, she ascended the stairs backward, never taking her eyes off them. Down below, over the sound of the dogs, she heard heavy footsteps entering the building. Whoever was down there was now methodically climbing the stairs.

Fear took over and she bolted up the steps. Right behind, she heard the dogs take off after her, gnashing their teeth as they barked. On the fifth-floor landing she tripped over a pile of rusted beer cans and fell hard, breaking the fall with her palms. The scabs from the rat bites ripped open, causing her hands to bleed. She turned over quickly on her back to face her attackers. The dogs, no more than a few feet away, spread out and began encircling her. She could feel the heat from their panting breath and smelled their sickly odor. Not daring to take her eyes off them, she reached out to grab a piece of debris to use as a weapon. She felt the broken neck from a bottle of Gallo port and flung it at the lead dog, hitting it on the lower jaw. Whining in pain, the dog backed up, licking the blood off its face. She slowly got to her knees, knowing that the other dogs would not attack until the lead dog struck first.

The footsteps were getting louder now, and whoever was there was probably on the third-floor landing. Farther down, on the first floor, she could hear the faint sound of other footsteps. There's more than one person down there, she thought.

She looked up and saw that the next staircase led out to the roof. The door was closed, and if it was locked she'd be trapped. She couldn't chance it. Jumping up, she ran down the hallway, grabbing and twisting the knobs of the apartment doors . . . 5D . . . 5E . . . 5F. All locked!

Wrong way, damnit! 5C was in the other direction.

The first set of footsteps was moving faster, taking several stairs at a time. She thought she could hear the other person farther down but she wasn't sure.

Rena turned a corner hoping for another door, another flight of stairs.

"Oh, no!" she screamed. In front of her, several yards away, was a large hole where a wall once stood.

She was trapped.

She picked up a slat from a splintered doorframe and turned to face the animals. Something inside her wanted to give up; there was no place left to go. The dogs, as if hearing her inner voice, became more confident as they edged closer. Holding the piece of wood over her head like a club, she backed down the hallway. Behind her, the gap in the wall, resembling a shark's mouth with jagged bricks for teeth, waited patiently for her.

She froze when her foot touched nothing but empty space as she backed up. A quick glance behind showed a five-story drop to a dirty, narrow alley covered with broken bricks, glass, and a mound of old tires. Outside, she could hear the distant sound of a ghetto blaster thumping out the homogenized music of Menudo. Whoever was listening, she realized sadly, was totally unaware of her situation.

She saw how easily the world could live without her. Like Menudo, when one singer leaves, another one pops out of a mold to take his place. No one mourns. The beat goes on.

The large dog, still dripping blood from its jaw, glared at her, its growls growing more threatening; the back muscles of its legs began to tighten, getting ready to lunge. Rena braced herself, her hands gripping the sharp edges of the wall. Then, like a black missile, the animal leaped for her throat. Timing herself, she removed her arm just as the dog was in the air and let it brush past her like a bull's horns scraping against a toreador's cape. Hanging halfway out of the hole with one hand, she watched as the dog fell the five stories with the sound of screeching tires coming from its throat. It hit the courtyard, bounced up a couple of times, then stayed still.

She desperately tried swinging her body back into the hallway. As she grabbed the other side of the wall with her free hand the decayed bricks came loose and her feet slipped off the floor, causing her to dangle by one hand outside the hole. Her fingers, clutching a jutted piece of brick, were starting to slip. Looking up, she saw the dogs gnashing at her hand, just missing by hairs. Inside, two sets of footsteps were running in her direction, one of them at least a floor below.

Closing her eyes, she waited for the pursuer to find her and simply dislodge her fingers from the outer wall, sending her to a death in a place that humanity had long given up on.

Not like this! Please, God, not like this!

Then the sound of feet kicking into ribs . . . dogs yelping . . . paws scampering over the concrete floor.

Her hand was slipping now. As it broke away from the wall, another hand, big and strong, grabbed her wrist in midair and half lifted, half flung her back into the building. Her face smacked into a large, hard chest and she could feel the person grabbing her arms and holding her securely.

"Charlie, how did you . . ." was all she managed to say, before her legs turned into rubber and she crumbled to the ground, unconscious.

Chapter 17

Saturday, 3:14 P.M.

As the mist lifted from her brain she found herself sitting on the dirt floor with Charlie's hands on her shoulders and her head between her legs. She pushed his arms away and tried sitting up. A wave of nausea engulfed her, and little black specks, like shooting stars, crisscrossed in front of her eyes.

"Feeling better?" Charlie said, sitting next to her.

"I will be." She wiped the cold sweat from her brow with the back of her hand. "I *think* I owe you at least a thank-you for saving my life."

"Probably. It would have taken those mutts five minutes to make Purina out of you."

"Where are they now?" she asked apprehensively, her eyes scanning the hallway.

"Around somewhere. Watching us, probably. Don't worry. They won't attack someone my size."

"Were you following me?"

"Actually, I wasn't. I arrived in New York this morning, took the red-eye."

"To find Clara Freemont?"

"Yeah, how did you know?" He sounded genuinely surprised.

"From Brenda, your blind date."

"Jesus, what a mouth on that girl. I called her right after you left her office. She told me where you were going and I grabbed the A train uptown. Lucky for you, huh?"

"Which set of footsteps were you?" she said, holding on to Charlie's arm as she tried standing up.

165

"The second one. Lucky for you, again." He held on to her until she nodded that she would be okay.

"Did you see who it was?"

He saw the fear in her eyes. "Not really. Whoever it was heard me and ran out the door leading to the roof. I *did* get a glimpse of a leg, though, on the top stairwell."

"A man or a woman?"

"Couldn't tell. The person was wearing Adidas and black pants."

"Maybe it was a derelict," she said hopefully.

"I doubt it. The Adidas looked too new."

She sighed and drew her arms around her body. Finally she said, "I'm very frightened. I just don't know what's happening." She put her hand up to her head and started to cry. Charlie put his arms around her and held her tightly. She didn't pull away; he felt warm and comforting to her.

It had been a long time since he had held a woman while sober, and even longer since it had felt this good. Some tough lady, he thought. He touched her hair and stroked it gently, wishing the crying jag would last awhile.

She moved her head away and said, sniffling, "I need a tissue. I lost my purse somewhere in the building."

He handed her a handkerchief. "I found it on the third floor where you dropped it. I put it behind some loose bricks. You feeling better, now?"

"Yeah." She felt grateful. "I still want to see apartment 5C."

"Didn't you have enough?" he said, hoping she'd want to cry some more.

"I came three thousand miles to see it. I'm not about to quit when I'm only twenty feet away," she said stubbornly, her lips curving downward.

At the end of the hallway they came to 5C and tried the door. It was open.

She backed away. "All the other doors on this floor were locked," she said anxiously.

Charlie got in front of her and pushed the door open. Inside, they were momentarily blinded by the strong afternoon sun that beamed in through the broken windows. Shielding his eyes with his hand, he quickly looked over the foyer. The apartment was an old railroad flat: a long hallway with rooms off to the left and right.

As they walked slowly down the corridor, the only sounds that could be heard were their own footsteps. The rooms were coated with years of untouched dust, and cobwebs covered the walls like Chantilly lace. The rotted linoleum on the floor was pitted with rat shit.

"Where's the closet?" Rena whispered, trying not to awaken anything that might be alive in here.

"In the bedroom . . . the last one on the left. I remember like it was yesterday," he said uneasily.

When they reached the bedroom, Charlie motioned for Rena to stay back as he looked inside. The room was stripped bare except for moldy patches of shag carpeting that hadn't as yet been eaten by rats.

They entered cautiously. Rena, unconsciously, was holding on to Charlie's shirt. She noticed several small skeletons of rats on the floor. He nodded to Rena and looked in the direction of a closed door on the right side of the wall. She understood he was pointing out the closet and her legs felt rubberized again. He held up a hand, telling her to stop, then walked over to the closet door and put his ear next to it. Shrugging, shaking his head to say there was nothing, he pushed open the door.

"Well, well, well," Charlie said in amazement.

The walls of the closet were painted in a deep lavender, contrasting sharply with the faded, dirty walls in the other rooms.

He put his nose up to the wall and sniffed. "This was painted fairly recently," he said. "Whoever did this used an oil-based paint. You can still smell it." He lit a match to get more light.

Rena looked in and a chill touched her heart. She then remembered that the name on the mailbox was also put there recently.

Charlie, as if reading her mind, said, "Either Alice is back or we're dealing with a real sick mind here." He put his hand on her shoulder, steering her out of the room. "Let's get back to civilization."

Down the hallway he told Rena to wait and went up the staircase to the roof. The door was ajar and he opened it slowly. He stuck his head outside and looked around. There was no one there. The roof was filled with holes and he wasn't about to chance walking around. Just as he turned to go back, he saw a shiny metal object on the tar floor reflecting off the hot sun. He bent down to pick it up. It was a gold bracelet with *"Semper Fi"* engraved on the back.

"Our friend forgot something," he said, walking down the steps and handing it to Rena. " *'Semper Fi'* means 'always faithful' . . . the Marine Corps motto."

"Then it was a man," she said.

"Not necessarily. It's a women's corps, too, you know." As they walked down the stairs to the street they could hear the eerie howls of the dogs ricocheting through the building, sounding like raging ghosts that had had their resting place disturbed.

They found an off-duty taxi a few blocks away whose driver was willing to take them back to Fifty-eighth Street for an extra ten.

Rena got out first at the Lowell and Charlie continued on to his hotel on West Thirty-fifth. They were going to clean up first, then meet an hour later.

As she walked into her room she saw the red message light beeping. She phoned downstairs and was told that Cathy, her father, and Stacey had called while she was out. There were also two messages from Robert Cameron. The number the desk gave her for Simon was his New York office. He must be back from Europe, she thought.

"What are you doing in New York?" she asked as he answered the phone.

"What are *you* doing in New York?" He did not sound pleased.

"Taking in the new show at the Whitney," she said, picking up on his tone.

"Don't bullshit a bullshitter or con a conner." He loved incorporating homey sayings into his conversation. It gave him an ah-shucks charm that disarmed people, especially his adversaries. "You're here because of that girl, aren't you?"

"Yes."

"Rena, listen to me." There was a pause, then some puffing noises, and she knew he was lighting his pipe. "I spoke to Anna," he said eventually. "She told me what's taken place since I've been gone. Go home. I'll get to the bottom of all this."

"Not yet . . . maybe tomorrow or the next day." She wanted to tell him that she was going to see Alice Mendoza's mother later tonight but decided against it. He would only try to talk her out of it.

"This is not something to fool around with. Let me make a few calls and—"

"Please, Simon," she said firmly. When she got angry, she always called him by his first name. "Let me take care of myself." She knew from experience that if she allowed him to help, he would bulldoze her whole life, take over, just as if he were merging another business into his conglomerate.

"Okay, then, how about dinner tonight? Régine's? It's one of your favorite places."

"Dad, not this time around," she said with all the firmness she could muster. "I'll see you as soon as I get back to L.A. I swear." There was a long pause on the other end, and she couldn't figure out if he was hurt or thinking of another tack to use. Finally . . .

"I love you, kitten," he said softly, with a rare display of humility. "Take care of yourself, you hear? And I'll see you in Los Angeles. You've got your mother's beauty and my pigheadedness . . . some combination!"

They hung up. Next she tried Cathy but there was no answer. Then she called Stacey.

"What's up?" Rena said when Stacey answered.

"How's the big bad city?" Stacey asked.

"Big and bad."

"Having a good time?"

"Don't ask."

"Well, I suggest you get your buns home fast, love."

"Why?"

"Your fill-in, Dr. Harvey Waters, had a nervous breakdown yesterday."

"Oh, no," she groaned.

"Wait. Here's the best part—it happened while he was on the air."

"Tell me this isn't happening!"

"In your time slot. He told one caller that he had X-ray vision and that he could read minds. He said it was no big thing—that he was from Pluto and everyone on that planet had this gift. Then he read a five-page statement telling what it was like to live on Pluto. You wouldn't believe the imagination of this guy! He ended up by singing a Plutonian version of 'Feelings.' Did you know they talk just like Donald Duck?" After a long beat she said, "Hey . . . you still there?"

"Sorry . . . I was just watching my career going down the sewer. Is he hospitalized?"

"You bet. Wait, there's more. Murray is now doing his food show in your place. Tell me you're coming back soon . . . please."

"Okay, soon," Rena managed to say, just as the laughter started. Once it began it wouldn't stop. Tears ran down her cheeks. The intensity of the day . . . now this. It was too much! She laughed until her chest hurt. Finally, when it was over, she wiped her eyes on the corner of the pillowcase and said, "Sorry."

"I was that funny, huh? Listen, if you're going to stay in New York, do you want me to come out? Right now the station's got me working as Murray's assistant and I hate to tell you what that's like. Remember when I told you that I thought he only wanted me for an arm prop? Well, I was wrong. The horny bastard keeps bending over my desk trying to stick his tongue in my ear."

"Next time bite it off. No, stay in L.A. I'll be back tomorrow or the next day."

"Anything interesting to tell me?" Stacey said.

"Lots." She hung up.

While in the shower she heard the phone ring and thought it might be Cameron. She'd have to tell him that she couldn't have dinner with him. Somehow she didn't think he'd be disappointed. She wondered if anything in life ever disappointed him.

Wrapped in a towel, she called his room; there was no answer. She then called the desk and left a message. Oh, well, at least I tried, she thought to herself as she brushed her hair and blew it dry.

Charlie was waiting outside his hotel when Rena pulled up in the cab. It was a small, clean-looking place, the kind only New Yorkers knew about. He hopped into the backseat, his leg touching hers as he sat down. She didn't move it away. Somehow it felt reassuring. He looks good, she thought. He even smells nice. Not a bad-looking guy.

"One-sixty-seven Dawson Drive," Charlie said as he closed the door.

"Where's that?" Angelo Patroni said, taking the pencil from behind his ear and popping it into the dashboard.

"Staten Island." Charlie held a ten-spot up to the rearview mirror where the driver could see it.

"That won't buy a loaf of bread in this town, pal," he said, putting his beefy hand behind the seat and opening up the back door.

"What's a twenty buy?" Rena said.

"As far as the Goethals Bridge," Angelo said, closing the door again.

"Whatever happened to fares and tips?" she asked curtly.

"Nothin', we take that, too," he replied as he honked his way through the midtown rush-hour traffic.

The Verrazano Bridge was jammed up, and by the time they reached Richmond Avenue, the meter was closing in on forty dollars.

"That's One-sixty-seven Dawson Drive," Angelo said, applying the brakes in front of a neat, two-story tract home.

There were at least fifty other homes in the several-block area that had the exact floor plan and facade, and Charlie wondered, as he got out of the cab, how anyone with a few drinks in him would be able to tell which house was his.

Rena paid Angelo as Charlie walked up to the house and rang the bell. No one answered. He rang a few more times. The same thing.

"Sure you have the right address, Charlie?" she asked as she walked over.

"It's the one the DMV gave out. But that doesn't mean anything. She could have moved ten times and not have told them."

They walked around the side of the house and looked over the wire fence into the backyard. The lawn was kept trimmed and neat, and there was a patch of tomatoes growing in the corner. In the center of the slate patio was a four-foot-high plastic portable pool. All the yards in the neighborhood faced one another and all of them had the same kind of pool. The blue-collar worker's paradise, Charlie thought.

"You want something?" a middle-aged man said, wearing a tank-top undershirt, shorts, and black socks with wingtips. He was in the yard next door leaning over the fence. In his hand was a can of Bud.

"Clara Freemont still live here?" Charlie asked.

"Sure does. You people friends of hers? I never seen you before."

"We go back a long time," Charlie said, being friendly. He went over to the fence and put his arms on the top of it. "Know where she is?"

"Probably in church. That's where she is every evening about this time." He looked at the old stainless-steel watch on his wrist. "Should be back soon . . . around eight-thirty. Clara's like clockwork."

"That's a good-looking Bud you have there," Charlie said.

"Be my guest," the man said as he took a cold one out of the ice chest sitting on the redwood picnic table. "Want one, too, young lady?"

Rena shook her head no and stayed in the background watching Charlie do his number.

"Gee, you know, I haven't seen Clara in—let's see—maybe eighteen years. We used to live on the same block. She had a daughter. Alice I think her name was. Real cute—long red hair."

"She know you're coming?"

"No. Figured I'd surprise her."

"Never knew she had a daughter. I knew she had a son, though. She moved to this neighborhood about two or three years ago, and by that time the boy had already left home and was overseas in one of the services."

Rena spotted a plump woman with bright red hair going up the walkway to the front door. She put her shopping bags down, took a few deep wheezing breaths, and looked in her purse for the keys.

"Clara Freemont," Rena said to Charlie.

"Sure is. When you talk to her, tell her to give up those cigarettes or she ain't gonna be around much longer," the man said. "Hey Clara! You got a couple of old friends here," he yelled over to her. He opened his screen door and went back inside his house.

"Mrs. Freemont," Charlie said as they walked through the small passageway to the front yard.

She stopped and turned around just as she was about to enter her house. "Yes?", she said suspiciously.

"Charlie Halleran's my name, and I'm with the *New York Times*," he said, taking out his press card and obscuring the name of the *Tattler* again with his finger. "This is Marcy Shapiro, also with the *Times*."

Rena looked quizzically over at Charlie, then nodded pleasantly to the woman.

"What do you want?" she said nervously as she blocked the doorway with her large frame.

"We write for the religious section of the paper and we're doing a survey on the declining Christian values of the eighties."

"You a good Catholic?" she asked, relaxing her guard.

"Omini Domini," he said, crossing himself.

"Bullshit! You ain't no Catholic."

"Sure am. I'm just not a good one."

She tried to close the door but Charlie slid his foot inside.

"You guys don't get out of here I'll call the police." Her cheeks turned bright red as she pushed at the door again.

"You don't want to do that. They ask lots of questions, especially about the past."

She stopped pushing and, between wheezes, asked in an uncertain voice, "What kind of questions?"

"Oh, the usual. Like why an old hooker like yourself, with an arrest record, decided to move into a respectable neighborhood like this. I'd think they'd also want to know where you got the money to buy this house. The neighbors will be standing outside when they come, overhear the conversation, and before you can say three Hail Marys, the whole of Staten Island will know your past. But don't let that bother you—you just go ahead and call them."

There was a venomous look in her eyes for a brief moment, then she sighed and moved aside so they could enter.

Rena glared at Charlie as she walked past him into the living room. She didn't like the way he was strong-arming the woman.

The living room smelled heavily of sweet jasmine perfume and was filled with new, cheap furniture. Religious artifacts hung from all parts of the walls. There was even a picture of Jesus painted on black velour with eyes that blinked as they followed you across the room. On the shelf were two photographs: a blond boy around five years of age, and a girl, maybe two or three years old. The picture of the girl was older and it looked as if it had been ripped in pieces then pasted back together. She was sitting in a chair, smiling at the camera, and holding a doll in her lap. Her long hair was red, and she had on a violet-colored dress.

"Are these your children?" Rena asked sweetly.

"You got that right, honey," Clara said, putting the bags down in the kitchen and grabbing a pack of Kents from a new carton in the drawer.

The woman was bordering on obesity and her fat arms jiggled as she popped a cigarette from the pack. Her hair was an obvious dye job, more orange than red, and her lipstick, a bright scarlet, was applied at least a quarter inch past the rim of her bloated mouth. Clara took a deep drag from the cigarette, coughed heavily, then ripped a couple of sheets off the paper-towel rack and wiped the sweat off her face and arms.

"What do you people want with me? I've been straight for fifteen years now," she said, coming back into the living room. She plopped down on the couch, pushing up her dress so that she could have more room to spread her thick thighs apart. She didn't bother to offer them a seat.

"Alice was a very beautiful girl, Mrs. Freemont," Charlie said, staring at the picture of the little girl in the violet dress. He sat down on the floral-pattern love seat. Rena sat down next to him.

Her eyes darkened. "Is that what you're here for? That was a long time ago. Why can't you let that poor girl rest in peace?" she said fiercely.

"I never saw that photograph before. I wonder why?"

"Why should you have seen it?"

"I followed you to Vegas, to that motel room where you were turning tricks. I remembered asking you for a picture of Alice. You told me there weren't any."

"I must have lied. Besides, it was none of your business, was it?" she snapped. There was a glimmer of recognition growing in her face. "Hey, I remember you," she said quietly. "You were a hard one to get rid of."

"I know. I was cutting into your street time, if I remember correctly." There was a hint of anger in his voice.

It has to do with his daughter's death, Rena thought. She put a hand on his shoulder to calm him down and said to Clara, "What a horrible tragedy."

"Damn right it was," Clara said, steaming. "Everything about it was a tragedy." She looked up at the velour Christ for comfort. The eyes blinked back at her.

Rena squeezed Charlie's arm to say that she would do the talking. He moved back on the sofa. "What was it like living with your husband?"

"Carlos? Don't ask!" There was a whistle in her throat as she coughed. She leaned over to the ashtray and put out the cigarette. "He was okay at first . . . had a steady job and everything. The first couple of years were pretty good between us . . . even when Alice was first born. Why do you want to know about all this?"

"There may have been a murder similar to your daughter's back in Los Angeles," she told her honestly. "Your name won't appear in the newspaper, I promise you."

"Another child! What kind of people are out there?" Clara said, shaking her head.

"When did Carlos change?"

"When Alice was about two years old. He would come home drunk and beat her. He lost his job around that time, too."

"He was a family man before that. What happened to change him?"

"He was just plain crazy," she said, laughing then coughing. She spit up phlegm into a tissue then continued. "He was psychotic, 'cept I didn't know it when I married him. I found out later from a psychiatrist he had gone to that it was hereditary—his whole family was like that. It was rough living with that bastard, let me tell you! I took it as much as I could, found some guy, and got out. I wanted to take Alice with me," she said, her lips quivering. "But this guy didn't want any part of her. He said, 'We'll start fresh . . . make a new life in Vegas.' I believed him. He was nothing but a two-bit gambler. Took every cent I had, then left me dry. So I hit the streets again. I did okay, I guess," she said, waving her hands to show the house and furniture.

"Why didn't you call the police, try to get Alice away from him?" Charlie interjected angrily.

"I was young, okay! What the hell did I know then? I got a taste of life in the fast lane and I liked it. I wasn't about to go back." She coughed some more and spat up again. "I tried calling Carlos some years later. I wanted to see Alice again. The number was disconnected. I *did* call the police then and told them about my daughter. They said they'd send somebody over there to see if she was okay. They called me back and said that the building was condemned for the past year and nobody was living there anymore."

"How long ago was that?" Charlie said suddenly.

"What difference does it make?" She wiped the tears from her eyes with the palm of her hand.

"How long?"

"Twenty years . . . maybe more."

"Let's do it this way—what was the span between the time you first called the police up until she died?"

She closed her eyes and thought for a minute. "Maybe a year . . . maybe a little more."

Rena looked over to Charlie. He was staring up at the velour Jesus, deep in thought, and tapping his finger on his bottom lip.

"Who is this other girl?" Clara asked.

"Her name was also Alice, and what happened to your daughter also happened to this girl," Rena said to her.

"Dear sweet Jesus!" Clara moaned, wringing her hands. "What does all this have to do with my daughter?"

"Maybe nothing. We don't know yet." Rena didn't want to open up any old wounds by telling her that both girls were identical enough to pass for the same person, nor did she want to say anything about the new coat of paint in the closet that her daughter had died in. The woman had suffered long enough, mostly from the guilt of deserting Alice. Let it alone, she thought. "I think maybe we'd better be going," Rena said, getting up and looking at Charlie.

"Right," he said, coming out of his thoughts. "What's your son's name?" he asked Clara as he, too, got up.

"William," she said, tight-lipped.

"Good solid name. Where's William now?"

"In the armed forces."

"The Marines?"

"That's right," she said, getting up and going over to the front door.

"Good solid choice! That was my branch, too. *Semper fi* and all that," he said, holding up his fist. "Where's he stationed?"

"Wherever the Sixth Fleet is." She had the door open and was waiting.

"Long way from home. See him much?"

"You said you were leaving," she said coldly, holding on to the doorknob. The fatty skin hung down from her outstretched arm like sheets on a clothesline.

"You lie a lot, don't you?" Rena said to Charlie as they walked down Victory Boulevard to Richmond, where there was a cab stand. "You're not the Marine type."

"And you're not a Marcy Shapiro. What difference does it make?"

"You didn't need to tear into her like that."

"Oh, golly, gee whiz, the poor thing," Charlie said. "First she deserts her daughter, leaving her alone with that maniac, then runs off to Vegas and gets involved in the honorable profession of prostitution. What a gal!"

There was a lot of anger underlying his sarcasm, and she understood the reason for it; Charlie viewed the tragedy of Alice and his daughter, Jaimie, as one and the same. Both girls were fused in his mind. He and Clara were carrying the burden of guilt for not seeing the signs of what inevitably had to happen. Clara ran to Vegas to escape her responsibility, and Charlie buried himself in work so he wouldn't have to deal with his wife's madness. Clara was a mirror to Charlie's dark spots, and the anger he displayed toward her was actually toward himself.

They hadn't eaten all day and they grabbed a quick bite at the corner Greek diner on Richmond Avenue, then took the ferry over to the Battery in Manhattan.

It was a humid night and they stood at the front of the ferry letting the breeze from the river cool them off. Rena looked reverently up at the New York skyline, its magnificent lights reflecting off the black water.

"It was Gerald W.'s beat," Charlie said, enjoying the spray from the river on his face. "He's probably the one the precinct sent over to Mendoza's apartment to investigate the complaint."

"What?"

"Gerald W. Jaffe. The name sound familiar?" he asked, smiling. "He was a young cop, just starting out. It was his territory."

At first she was too shocked to say anything, then she nodded and said, "I see." Craig had told her that Jaffe was originally a New York cop.

"I could go down to the precinct and wade through old files to see if Jaffe *did* answer Clara's complaint. I'd stake anything on it that it was him," he said, pounding his fist on the rail.

"Why wouldn't he report a crime like that?"

"Because he's sick, that's why . . . the same as Mendoza!" he said loudly, his eyes lighting up as he began to understand the reason behind Jaffe coming to see him. "You see, Gerald W. also had a penchant for little girls. In fact, that's why he quit the force and left New York. Internal Affairs was closing in on him. I'll bet he went over there that day—to the deserted tenement—and found Alice . . . maybe chained up, who knows? He must have been in his glory when he saw she was underage. Probably dropped his pants right then and there."

"Mendoza wouldn't have allowed that," she said, not quite believing all this.

"What choice did he have? Jaffe would have exposed him if he didn't. That sick bastard must have had a field day right up until Mendoza killed her."

"It's going to be hard to prove."

"Maybe not. I want to find out if Mendoza is still alive. If he is, I want to see him. You interested?"

She saw the burning in his eyes. "Yes, I am." She folded her arms around her body to ward off the cool night air and said, "None of this makes much sense."

"You're right. And another thing that doesn't make much sense is how a five-dollar hooker could afford a home like that and have it completely furnished. If she bought it maybe twenty years ago, I'd understand—it would only have cost her thirty, forty thousand dollars. But according to her neighbor, she bought it only two years ago. That means she must have paid about two hundred thousand for it. She doesn't work, and there's no pension for streetwalkers, so where did the money come from? What bank would give someone a loan with no collateral?"

"Couldn't she have saved it?"

"I'm no mathematical genius, but at five dollars a pop she'd have to be on her back for the next two hundred years to save that kind of money."

"You're exaggerating her price."

"Not by much. We're talking over twenty years ago, and if I remember correctly, she was no knockout."

Somewhere in the night a fog horn sounded.

The ferry docked at the Battery. Outside the terminal, Charlie hailed a cab.

"Do you want to be dropped off first?" she asked.

He was wearing a shy grin as he got in next to her. "Nope. I can always walk back."

Their legs touched again, but this time she moved away, wishing that she wasn't so attracted to him. He was a loser. No, that was wrong . . . self-destructive maybe, but not a loser; that was her mother talking. He was just lost, that's all. Trying to find the connection between the two Alices was Charlie's way of putting the past asleep, a way of redeeming himself for having failed Jaimie. She hoped he'd find his way again, because he had more strength than most of the men she'd known, including Terry. *Especially* Terry.

They got out at Fifty-eighth and Lexington and walked the short distance to the Lowell.

"I'll see you tomorrow," she said, shaking his hand, letting her's linger in his longer than usual.

"I'll call you first thing in the morning." He stroked the side of her hand with his thumb and she made no movement to withdraw it. He wanted to take her in his arms but knew it would be the wrong thing to do. Not now. *Not ever!* He watched her go through the brass door and up the elevator. The smell of her perfume still lingered in the air around him. "Stick to your own kind . . . the bar women and the lonely souls of the night," he whispered to himself.

The night was still young and he wasn't tired yet. The thoughts of Alice, Jaimie, and now Rena echoed off the walls of his mind. He crossed the park and went into the Oak Room bar at the Plaza. He ordered and quickly drank a double J&B, the first hard drink he'd had in a long time. The scotch and the quiet darkness of the bar eased the pain about Jaimie and the longing for Rena. He smiled, thinking about the last time he was here and about how much it cost Bitterman. He saw they had replaced the broken mirror, and he was happy that there was a different bartender working tonight. The other one would have thrown him out.

He finished his drink and went out into the night air. A warm breeze was blowing and he decided to walk back to his hotel.

Fifth Avenue was deserted at this hour; just an occasional cab on the street. It was different when he had lived here. It was safer then, and strollers walked the avenue until all hours of the morning.

By the time he reached Forty-ninth Street, Charlie had a deep feeling that he wasn't alone, even though his footsteps were the only sounds he heard. He turned around quickly, just in time to see a shadow dart into a dark storefront.

"Jesus Christ, a mugger!" Charlie said to himself, turning the corner toward Madison. He stopped at a trash basket and grabbed a Coke bottle out of it. If this guy was determined, then Charlie would use it. He had done it before.

The shadow came around the corner toward him. Charlie crossed the street, looking over his shoulder, letting whoever it was know that he was onto him. The person also crossed the street, walking faster now. Slowing down, Charlie waited until he was only a couple of feet behind him. He didn't hear him, he could only sense him. He clutched the bottle tightly, waiting for the right time. If he was wrong about the guy . . . well, by the time the cops came, he'd be back at his hotel and asleep in bed. His gut said *now*! Charlie pivoted on his left foot, swinging the bottle. All he saw in the darkness were flecks of gray in the eyes and a head with blond hair moving lightning fast. The bottle grazed the man's left temple, and then the roof fell in on Charlie. He felt a sharp twinge in his wrist as the man grabbed it and twisted it back until the bottle dropped. A split second later, there was blinding pain in his shinbone and he fell to one knee. His eyes were tearing from the agony, but he managed to open them just as the other foot swung like a pendulum into his other shinbone. Letting out a scream, Charlie collapsed, his head hitting the cement. He tried crawling away, facedown, but the man's foot came around again, hitting him in the rib cage. This time Charlie couldn't scream because the air was sucked out of his body and he started to gasp for breath. Holding his torso for protection, he saw the foot coming at him again, heading for his face. As he picked his head up as far as he could, the foot skimmed the concrete, missing his face and nicking his chin. Charlie grabbed the leg with both hands and held on, fighting for time until he could clear his head. He opened his eyes again and the last thing he remembered seeing was the Adidas logo on a brand-new tennis shoe. The next thing he felt was a sharp ache in the back of his neck . . . then nothing.

It was still dark out when he opened his eyes. He had no idea how long he'd been unconscious. His head was facedown on the cement and his arm was dangling in the gutter; the miniature rapids of dirty water trying to drag his hand down into the sewer. He slowly got to his knees, touching himself everywhere to see if anything was broken. His parts moved but ached like hell. Looking up, he saw a young couple watching him from the window of a second-floor upscale apartment house. When they saw Charlie notice them, they slammed the window shut and turned off the lights. Upscale shits, he thought to himself as he tried standing up. He could have been dead and rotting for days before those two Volvos would have called the police.

He took his wallet out of his back pocket; it was still there—so was his money. Odd. If this clown wasn't a thief, then who was he? Maybe he just got his kicks out of beating the shit out of people. Then Charlie remembered the Adidas tennis shoe and realized it wasn't the first time they had met today.

It took a while but Charlie finally managed to drag his body back to the hotel. The night clerk pretended not to notice him when he walked in and Charlie was grateful for that.

In his room he looked at himself in the bathroom mirror. The face wasn't too bad, he thought. Lucky. Just a bloody nose and a welt near the hairline where his head hit the cement. His chest and legs were a different story: large hematomas under his rib cage and bloody purplish wounds on his shins. There was also a red mark at the back of his neck. He was going to hurt in the morning.

Who the fuck was that guy, anyway? he thought as he turned on the shower and got in. He wondered what might have happened if this creep had gotten to Rena first at the condemned building this morning. What did he want? The man's a pro, that's for sure. The hot water stung his bruises.

He stayed under the shower a long time, washing the street grime from his body. Reluctantly he got out when the pain under his chest began to throb. He put on a pair of Jockey shorts, hobbled over to his bag and got his phone book out, then looked up a number and dialed.

"Hello?" a woman's sleep-filled voice answered.

"Hey, Brenda, this is Charlie Halleran, remember me?"

"You got to be kidding. What time is it?" A pause as she looked at her clock. "Two-thirty! Jesus Christ! I don't accept dates at two-thirty in the morning." She yawned.

"Brenda, I need a favor."

"That nice woman, Rena Halbrook, says you're a schmuck, Charlie. Is it true?"

"Yeah, Brenda, there's a strong possibility. Can you still do me a favor?"

"I guess that means we're not going out, huh?"

"You like schmucks?"

"They're the only kind I know. Okay, what do you need?" she said, sighing.

"I need you to go to the Twelfth Precinct and look up the duty roster of a cop by the name of Gerald W. Jaffe. That's J-A-F-F-E."

"What's the W. stand for?"

"Who knows?"

"Is he married?"

"Forget it, Brenda."

"Only asking."

"I need to know if there were any dispatches logged under his name to One-thirty-two Holmby Street between 1968 and 1969."

"Are you fucking nuts!"

"It's all computerized. It'll only take you—"

"A couple of months!"

"One or two hours at the most. I swear."

"The Twelfth's in the South Bronx! Look, I don't mind getting laid once in a while, but you're talking gang-bang time here if some of the inhabitants happen to like Jewish girls with kinky hair."

"Take a cab. I'll pay you back. It's important, Brenda. I need the info sometime tomorrow."

"Great! Hey, Charlie, I think you and I are destined to be 'just good friends,' you know?"

"Friendship is the most solid of all foundations, Brenda."

"Screw that. I got a million friends, Charlie. I'm looking for something else that's solid, and it's not a foundation, it's between a guy's legs. Get my drift?"

"Right. See if you can get me what I need, okay?"

He hung up and called the overseas operator to connect him with the United States naval base in Naples, Italy. It would be almost nine o'clock there.

The switchboard answered.

"Personnel, please."

A staff sergeant got on the line.

"Hi, I'm special agent Martin Greenberg, and I'm with the Internal Revenue Service here in Washington. Reason I'm calling is we're looking for a Marine who's stationed with the Sixth Fleet. The name's William Freemont."

"What's he done? Not paid his taxes, sir?"

"Afraid so. Not before he joined the Marines, anyway."

"Everything you would need to know about personnel is there in Washington, sir."

"Right. Problem is it's three in the morning here and everything's closed tight till nine. I'm going to be up all night doing paperwork, and I figured I could save some time by calling you guys since the Fleet is stationed in Naples. It's a long shot, I know, and Freemont might not even be stationed there any longer—but you know the IRS, we have to go after our man, even if it *is* for a few hundred dollars. I don't have his ID number or anything to help you. Would it be too much trouble to check and see if he's still assigned to the Sixth?"

"Let me see what I can find out. You're not giving me much to work on." Five minutes later he was back on the line. "There are two William Freemonts with the Fleet. One is black . . . a first mate. The other's white and AWOL for the last two years. Do you know which one is yours, sir?"

"Yep. Do you have a photograph of the white guy?"

"Sure do. Six-foot-two, blond hair, on the thin side. If you boys pick up his scent, give us a ring. We'd also like to find him."

Charlie thanked the sergeant and hung up. He lay in bed smoking a cigarette and wondered if it had been William Freemont who messed him up tonight. He didn't think so. This guy wasn't over six feet, and he was muscular, not thin. He was pretty sure, however, the bracelet he found on the rooftop of the condemned building belonged to Freemont. If so, he'd like to return it, maybe weave it around his teeth.

Fat Clara had lied to him; she knew all along her boy was AWOL. What was he doing in that building? If it was him, that is. Someone doesn't want us to find out something, he thought, that's for sure. But what?

Charlie put out his cigarette and closed his eyes. He was exhausted and he ached all over. It's going to be a bitch of a day tomorrow, he thought as he quickly dropped off to sleep.

Chapter 18

Sunday, 8:35 A.M.

Charlie got off the phone with Maramack Psychiatric Hospital in Brooklyn, then called Rena. As he waited for the hotel to connect her he fluffed the pillows on the headboard of the bed and laid his aching body down. He was right about one thing: the pain was worse this morning, especially his shins.

"You up?" he asked when she got on the phone.

"Yes, you?"

"I have some news. I called the hospital where Mendoza was put away. He's still alive. I can't get to see him, though. Only family or someone with connections can do that."

"Let me see what I can do. A friend of mine, Harry Steinfeld, went to school with the chief psychiatrist at Maramack. Meet me at my hotel in an hour," she said.

Charlie dressed slowly, wearing baggy chinos and a loose-fitting shirt because of the bruises. He was not in a good mood—not because of the beating last night, but because of Maramack Psychiatric Hospital. Rosie was incarcerated there, in the women's section. Was she still alive? He had never found out. The last time he saw her was the night she killed . . .

Forget it! No more ghosts, goddamnit!

He lifted his foot onto the bed and slipped into his penny loafers. The fucking irony of it! He ran across the width of the country to get away from her, and if they got in to see Mendoza, he'd be right back on top of her again.

He wondered if Mendoza and Rosie had gotten to know each other at the hospital, maybe become friends during some fucking arts and crafts session. Why not? They both had a great deal in common: they had both murdered their children.

Charlie's cab pulled up next to the Lowell and he saw Rena through the glare of the door window talking to a well-dressed man in the lobby. She turned and saw Charlie, shook hands with the man, and rushed out to the cab.

"We're in luck," she said as she got in. "The hospital's letting us see Mendoza."

His stomach tightened. "Good."

"What happened to you?" she asked, seeing his face.

He told her everything, including the foot with the Adidas tennis shoe that he held on to for dear life.

She didn't say anything. She just stared straight ahead, biting down on her lower lip. When the cab reached the on ramp to the Brooklyn Bridge, she said, "Do you think it was William Freemont?"

"Could be. I wish I had gotten a better look at him. Christ, was that guy fast!"

Again, silence. Finally he asked about the man in the lobby.

"Someone I had dinner with the other night," she said. "A Mr. Robert Cameron."

"Hot and heavy?" he asked.

She laughed. "More like tepid and airy."

Charlie sat back in the seat and smiled. Their knees touched once again, not accidentally.

The traffic was light on Sunday, and fifteen minutes later they were standing outside Maramack Hospital on Atlantic Avenue.

Inside, they went through two heavy iron gates and a metal detector. Rena's purse was searched by a guard wearing a nine-millimeter Colt and Charlie had to empty his pockets. Two flights up, past more gates and guards, they were introduced to the head psychiatric nurse on Mendoza's ward.

"Hi, Dr. Eberhart told me you were coming," she said, smiling, as she shook hands with them. She was wearing a starched white uniform and holding a clipboard.

The walked down a long corridor until they came to a flight of stairs that descended into the courtyard outside.

"Mr. Mendoza is gardening right now. He's become quite

an expert during his stay with us. He's especially good with roses."

During his stay? She makes it sound like a country club, Charlie thought.

A guard unlocked the final door with a key from a large ring and they went outside.

"There he is," the nurse said.

At the rim of the concrete fence, Mendoza was down on his knees carefully twisting a large branch off a rosebush.

"They're not allowed shears or any kind of metal tools," the nurse said.

He's gotten older, Charlie thought. His close-cropped kinky hair was a steel-wool gray now, and there was a tonsure in the back like Friar Tuck.

Next to him, working their different areas of the dirt perimeter, were other inmates.

"He's expecting you," she said. She bent down and touched him on the shoulder. "Mr. Mendoza, your guests are here."

He looked up and smiled, his dark bright eyes darting from Rena to Charlie then back to her again. He stood up, wiped his dirty hands on his denim pants, and shook their hands. "It's very nice to meet you," he said with a slight trace of a Puerto Rican accent. "I never get any visitors. I hear you're a newspaperman," he said to Charlie. "Good. I like newspapermen."

"It's almost time for Mr. Mendoza's lunch. Why don't the three of you go to the dining hall together. It would be easier to talk there," the nurse suggested.

The dining hall was beginning to fill up, with each inmate going to his assigned table. Mendoza's was the one in the corner. He excused himself, picked a tray up from the pile, and stood on the food line. An orderly brought Charlie and Rena cups of coffee.

"Are they dangerous?" Charlie asked nervously, his eyes following the inmates.

"They wouldn't allow us to be here if they were," Rena said, smiling, as she patted his hand.

Mendoza came back and sat down. "The food is not so good but you get used to it," he said as he took a spoonful of the stew and ate it. "You wish to talk to me about my daughter, right?" He neatly wiped the corners of his mouth with a paper napkin.

"Yes, we would," Rena said.

"Will this be in the newspaper?" His eyes lit up. "I had many things written about me before."

"Maybe, we'll see," Charlie said.

"I kept everything that was written about me. I used to have them taped up on my walls but they made me take them down. I keep them under my bed now. If you want I could get them for you," he said excitedly.

Holding up his hands, Charlie told him it wouldn't be necessary. This guy's really nuts, he thought to himself as he saw the joy in Mendoza's face.

"Obviously you don't mind talking about this?" Rena said, smiling.

Mendoza continued to eat. "No, I don't," he said. "I loved my little girl. I just got angry with her sometimes, that's all."

"Were you also angry with Clara? Was that why you locked Alice in a closet?" Rena asked.

"Clara! She was somethin' else, I tell you!" he said disdainfully. "She was one hell of a bitch. I was a jerk to marry her. I had big ideas in my head, you know. I thought if I marry a girl who was white, then I'd be better than a fuckin' Puerto Rican. What a joke on me, heh?" He stopped to wipe the plate clean with a piece of white bread, then continued. "She was a *puta* . . . right from the day I marry her. You know what I mean . . . *puta*?"

Rena nodded.

"A fuckin' whore, that's what!" He pushed the plate away angrily and leaned back in his chair. "She get drunk on gin and fuck everybody . . . the whole neighborhood! All my friends . . . my family . . . the people who I work for. They all laugh at me. They call me a *maricón*. They say, 'Carlos, why you take that kind of shit for?' "

"Why did you?" Rena asked.

" 'Cause I loved her. That's what I tell myself," he said, winking at Rena and pointing to his head.

"I hear you slapped her around, too, Carlos," Charlie said.

"Me? . . . Maybe. I don't know," he said, shrugging. "I

forget a lot of things. She deserve more than slapping, though, know what I mean?" He winked again, this time at Charlie. "She run away with another man, you know that?"

"So I heard," Charlie said.

"Talk to me about Alice," Rena said.

"Whatever you want to know. I want to see this in the newspaper, though," Mendoza said, turning to Charlie. "It's been a long time since anybody wrote about me."

Charlie put his right hand over his heart, held up the left one, and said, "You have my word on it."

"That's good," Mendoza said, his eyes gleaming again. He took the edge of a matchbook and picked at his teeth, trying to dislodge a strand of meat.

"The anger toward your daughter started around the time Clara left you, is that right?" Rena asked.

"She was evil. You don't know how evil," he said, his eyes filled with pain.

"I'm asking about Alice, not Clara," Rena said.

"I'm talking about Alice," he snapped. "She was an evil bitch! A *puta* like her mother!"

"She was three years old," Rena said calmly.

"So what? Whores become whores the day they're born! And she was born from her mother . . . that made her a whore!"

"You said you loved her before," Charlie said contemptuously. He could feel Rena's scowling eyes on him.

"Hey, you! Don't put words in my mouth, you hear!" He moved into the table, glaring at Charlie. "Maybe I won't give you a story," he said, brooding, as he leaned back and folded his arms like a child.

Charlie knew that he'd better keep his mouth shut or he was going to blow it. He apologized to Mendoza.

Mendoza sulked for another minute, not saying anything, then in a low voice he murmured, "I loved that little redheaded cunt, man. She was real good. Know what I mean by good?" He winked at Charlie again, licking his lips.

Charlie looked away, feeling sick to his stomach.

"Did you ever meet a policeman named Gerald Jaffe? Did he ever come to your home?" Rena asked, getting to the point.

He didn't say anything at first. He was looking past her, staring at the gray wall, remembering. She knew he was thinking back twenty years. Finally . . .

"That scumbag!" he spat out. "He come to my home . . . he threaten me with what would happen if I wouldn't let him have her! He come all the time. He fuck her, then beat her! I should've killed him! I should've beat his fuckin' brains out! She was mine! He had no fuckin' right!" He was getting loud and hitting his fists on the table. A guard standing near the wall was watching him. "I am a *maricón*! I should've done somethin'!" he screamed, pulling at his hair.

Two of the guards were moving now. Charlie put his hands up, trying to say everything was under control, but they ignored him. They each grabbed Mendoza by an arm and lifted him off the seat.

"Let's go, Carlos. It's been a busy day," one of them said.

Mendoza, as if he'd had the wind knocked out of him, dropped to the ground and curled up into a ball. The guards seemed used to it, each seizing an arm and a leg and carrying him out of the dining hall.

"Damn!" Rena said, frustrated. "I wish we could have talked to him longer."

"At least we were right about Jaffe," Charlie said as he got up. "I'd love to nail him, except who'd take the word of a psychopathic killer."

Upstairs, in the main hallway, the head nurse stopped them as they were leaving.

"I heard our Mr. Mendoza was acting up again," she said. "Was he able to help you?"

"As a matter of fact, yes," Rena said. "Has he ever talked to anyone about the actual day he killed his daughter?" she asked on a long shot.

"Never." The nurse thought for a minute, then said, "No, that's not true. He was given sodium pentothal when he first arrived here, and I believe he did talk about it. That was way before my time, though."

Disappointed, Rena thanked her and started to walk away.

"It's on videotape, if you're interested," the nurse said, calling after them.

"You have it on videotape?" Charlie asked, turning around.

"The hospital has a policy of videotaping all confessions, especially when drugs are involved. It was originally shot on film, then transferred to tape. Would you care to see it?"

They absolutely did.

The nurse took them to the conference room on the third floor, where a monitor and a VCR were set up. She found Mendoza's tape listed by date and name. She fed it into the machine, told them to return it to the tape library when they were done, then left. Charlie pressed the "on" button.

A much younger Carlos Mendoza appeared on the screen. He was lying on a cot with one arm over his head, the bars in the cell casting grill-shaped shadows across his body. A doctor wearing a lab coat was injecting sodium pentothal into a vein in Mendoza's arm and talking to him in a low voice. Within seconds the drug took effect and Mendoza closed his eyes. The doctor continued to talk to him. Suddenly he opened his eyes and snarled.

DOCTOR: What do you see, Carlos? Go back.
CARLOS: No more money . . . nothin' to drink. (Pause) Where's the cunt? (His head moves from side to side, as if looking for somebody) Where the fuck you hiding, huh? Come on, quit fuckin' around. (Pause) There you are. What are you lyin' there for? Talk to me, shit face! What's the matter . . . the rats got your tongue? (Pause) You don't want to talk to me? (Getting angry) But you'll talk to wally, right? Sure you would, you fuckin' *puta.* You'll talk to wally before you'll talk to me. Like him better, huh? Okay, I'll give you wally, you cunt! Get up! Get up and clean this place up. There's shit and piss all over the fuckin' place! (Pause . . . then in a whimpering voice) Come on, baby, tell me you love me . . . come on. (Getting louder) I said come on! Say it, bitch . . . say it! (His fists flail about) Say it, you cunt! Say it!

Mendoza began pulling at the air, like he was ripping someone apart. Two orderlies held his arms down and the doctor injected him with a sedative.

The tape went to gray and white lines, then to black.

Charlie was queasy. He felt that he witnessed the actual murder.

"Do we have enough to go to the police with?" Rena asked as she got up and took the tape out of the machine.

"About Jaffe? I doubt it," he said, going over to the window and looking down at the cement yard. He watched a volleyball game in progress between the inmates. "Mendoza doesn't incriminate him on the tape. And if he tried doing it now, eighteen years later, who would believe him?"

Rena took the tape next door to the library.

While waiting for her, a lot of questions began spinning around in Charlie's head like the moons of Saturn. Yes, he was sure Jaffe was involved, but in what capacity other than having sexually molested a young girl? For obvious reasons he didn't want anyone to know; that's why he was watching them so closely back in L.A. Was he the one that beat me up last night? Charlie asked himself. Jaffe had blond hair; so did the guy wearing the Adidas. Maybe.

Except it wasn't Jaffe who made those calls to Rena or painted the closet violet. That would only bring attention to himself. What the hell are we really dealing with here?

There was also something else that was bothering him, and it had nothing to do with Jaffe. It was Rosie. Was she still alive? What was she like now? If he really wanted to know, he was only a few feet away from finding out. It was Sunday, visitors' day. Maybe it was time he found out—put away those ghosts.

When Rena came back into the room, Charlie asked if she would mind waiting, that he would be back in fifteen minutes. She told him it would be fine, that she wanted to jot down some notes about today anyway. They agreed to meet outside, near the main entrance.

Charlie asked a guard outside the conference room for the directions to the women's section. The guard took him to a window and pointed to an enclosed building surrounded by barbed wire about a hundred feet away.

As he walked through a grassy knoll to the gray stone compound his hands began to sweat and his legs felt like rubber hoses. He wasn't sure, even if she *was* there, what his reaction would be. The love he'd had for her was long gone, but what about the hate?

Or the fear. He had been frightened to death of her after she had tried to kill him. Years afterward, he'd still wake up in the middle of the night from nightmares, sweating, lying in crumpled sheets. The terror of digging his face in the dirt as tracers whizzed by inches over his head in 'Nam was nothing compared to the dread he had of Rosie.

Her laughter . . . that long knife . . . the limp, bloodied body of Jaimie. Oh, God, let the memories stop!

Charlie told the guard at the gate that he was the husband of Rose Halleran. He waited as the guard picked up the phone and talked to someone inside the compound, half expecting him to hang up and say, 'Sorry, sir, but they just told me your wife died years ago.' Instead, after a short wait, the guard put down the phone and nodded for him to go inside. Once again his stomach cramped up. *She's alive!*

A buxom, black female guard inside the visitation area showed some surprise when Charlie asked to see Rosie; even more, when he said he was her husband.

"You're the first person to see her since she's been here, and I've been here forever," she told Charlie. She then gave him directions to the ward Rosie was in.

His armpits were sweating and his face felt hot and clammy as he waited for the elevator. He wanted to leave, run away as the old fear returned, but he had come too far now.

Upstairs, he walked down a hallway until he came to a white, heavily gated door. He heard groans and screams coming from inside. His heart sank. The people in there, he knew without asking, were incurable.

Charlie was searched again before they allowed him inside. The smell of disinfectant and human feces was unbearable. He was shown to a large bare room with benches lining the walls. Sprawled out on them, in different positions, were several women. One was locked in a fetal embrace. Another, who looked catatonic, with her hands at her side, suddenly let out a piercing scream for a few seconds, then went back to being deathly still. Others were pacing the floor, talking to themselves.

"I don't see Rose Halleran," Charlie said to an orderly as he scanned the room.

"She's right there," the orderly said, pointing to a frail, older-looking woman curled up on the bench. Her knees were locked under her arms as she rocked back and forth.

There's got to be a mistake, he thought as he walked over to her. That can't be Rosie. Rosie was young and beautiful and . . .

He heard the familiar gnashing of teeth and knew there was no mistake. Her hair was now cut short with thick strands of gray in it, and her eyes, a dull black, were staring at him—no, staring through him. Whatever she was seeing, if indeed she was seeing anything, had to do with another world. The dark circles surrounding her haunted eyes made her cheekbones jut out like glacial ridges. Her mouth moved slightly, as if she were having a conversation with someone many miles away.

Charlie squatted down next to her and looked up into those sunken eyes, waiting for a flicker of life to ignite in them. There wasn't any. He opened his mouth to call her name but decided against it. What if she came out of her distant world—even for a moment? What would she say to him? *Hey, Charlie, it's been a long time, heh, heh.*

He touched her hand, the hand that at one time could send spasms through his body when it caressed him. It now lay limp in her lap and felt lukewarm and scaly, like the skin of raw fish. He sensed a muscle tighten briefly. . . but that was all.

Charlie stood up and said in his head, Good-bye, Rosie. For a moment he thought he saw the eyes move up to his face, as if she could hear his mind. He knew it was only his imagination. Rosie was dead and would always be from now on. And he was glad, because you can't hate and fear the dead . . . only the living. Charlie turned and walked out of the ward a free man.

He saw Rena waiting for him on the street. She wore a quizzical expression on her face, as if wondering where he had been. He put his hands to her face, drew it close to his own, and kissed her on the lips. At first she tried to push away but he held tight. When he did let her go, she had her eyes wide open, staring at him in wonderment.

"You want to run this one by me," she said, breathing hard, trying to catch her breath.

"I can't." And that was true. It was as if he had relinquished control of his body to someone else for that moment. Whoever it was, he wanted to say thanks, even buy him a drink.

On the way back to Manhattan, they sat at opposite ends of the car seat. Her body was leaning against the cab door, away from his. The silence between them was deafening. He wanted to tell her about Rosie, about the anger and the fear he had bottled up inside himself for all these years, that he now felt unshackled and she was the first one he saw and . . . No, that's not true. It had nothing to do with who he saw first; it had to do with Rena. She's the one he wanted. You can pick 'em, Charlie, my boy . . . Jesus!

This time he was dropped off at his hotel first.

"I've decided to take a six o'clock flight back to Los Angeles, tonight. If you find out anything more, give me a call there," she said with distance in her voice. She nodded to the driver and the cab took off uptown.

Charlie watched until it disappeared between the trucks and buses. Not once did she look back. He wanted to tell her that he could go to L.A. with her, that there was nothing keeping him here, but he didn't. What for? So they could sit like awkward bookends on an airplane for five hours, not talking, leaning in opposite directions in case their bodies "accidentally" touched. Nope, he'd find his own plane back home.

There was a message for him in the lobby saying that Brenda had called while he was out. Charlie thought about tipping the bellhop a fiver to run out and get him a pint of J&B but decided against it. Upstairs, he collapsed on the bed and dialed Brenda. While waiting for her to answer, he thought about Rena: why didn't she pull away from him when he kissed her? Forget it, Charlie. You're just reading into things.

"Hello," Brenda said with her thick Bronx accent.

"It's me, Charlie."

"Where've you been? It took me half the day but I got what you wanted. Captain Genero, that friend of yours, he's an absolute dream. He spent most of the day at the precinct helping me."

"He's married with five kids, Brenda."

"So he told me." She giggled.

"What do you have?"

"Let's see . . ." The sound of paper in the background as she turned the page of a legal pad. "On July fourteenth, 1968 . . . Hey, that's Bastille Day. Did you know that, Charlie?"

"Go on, Brenda," he said.

"At 11:38, they received a call from a woman claiming to be Clara Mendoza who suspected her ex-husband of harming her daughter, Alice Mendoza. This girl keeps popping up, huh?"

"Go on, Brenda."

"At 11:40, Gerald Wallace Jaffe, a police officer who patrols that area, was given orders to investigate at the address this woman gave on Holmby. He phoned in on a call box at 12:51 saying that the building was deserted. There was a sign on the wall stating that it was condemned by order of the Buildings and Safety Department. He said he checked the apartment from the number he found located in the lobby and saw no signs of life. That's all. Hey, wait a minute! Wasn't that the same building the girl was murdered in?"

"Yeah," Charlie said. Something was bothering him.

"Was that cop incompetent or just lying?"

"Just lying. What did you say his name was again?"

"Jaffe," she said.

"No, his whole name."

"Gerald Wallace Jaffe," she said.

"Brenda, you're the best," he said, excited.

"No, you are, Charlie. I wouldn't have met Captain Genero without you."

"You guys planning on doing it together?"

"We already did . . . in the precinct's broom closet," she said, giggling again.

"How could you?"

"Hey, any port in a storm, Charlie."

"Does that mean it's over between us?"

"Yes. I hope you don't do anything foolish, like join a monastery or become gay because of it. There are not enough straights as it is."

They hung up.

Charlie then dialed the Lowell. He was about to ask for Rena's room but changed his mind. Instead he called Kennedy Airport to find out what flight left for L.A. at six o'clock tonight. United. He then called United for reservations, hoping the plane wasn't filled. It wasn't. He booked himself onto the flight. There wasn't much time and he'd be fighting rush hour. He tossed his clothes haphazardly into his beat-up suitcase and rushed out the door. He had a lot to tell Rena and he needed to tell her in person.

Chapter 19

Sunday, 6:50 P.M.

Rena looked up from her *New Yorker* when she heard ice jiggling above her head.

"This seat taken?" Charlie asked, sitting down next to her. He was holding a plastic cup filled with Coke.

"This is first class," was all she could say when she saw Charlie.

"I know, and the flight attendant gave me just five minutes before she kicks me out, so shut up and listen." He leaned back in the thick, roomy seat. "Ahh . . . Beats the shit out of having a two-year-old kid whining on one side of you and an Irish priest trying to sell you a raffle to a church singles dance on the other."

"Why are you on this plane, Charlie?"

"I have to talk to you." He finished off the Coke, crushed the cup, and stuck it in the pouch in front of him.

"About what?" she said patiently.

"About Jaffe, mostly. We could also talk about us if you'd like."

"Let's talk about Jaffe."

"Right. That's safe enough." He turned to Rena and said, "You told me that wally was a dated East Coast expression for a man's private parts. I don't think that's what Alice was referring to when she used that word."

"What else could it have meant?"

"Gerald W.'s middle name is Wallace. The familiar form of Wallace is Wally. When Alice said, 'no more, wally,' she wasn't talking about a prick that hangs between a man's legs, she was talking about a prick named Gerald W., pure and simple."

"Come on, Charlie. Are you sure?"

"Come on where? And yes, I'm sure."

"If that's true, then we're back to both Alices being the same person again. I don't think I can handle this ghost stuff anymore."

"We'll get to that. If that shook you up, wait till you hear this one. We watched Mendoza on the videotape telling Alice to get up and talk to him. She wasn't getting up. He was getting more and more frustrated as the tape went on. Finally he went totally bonkers and ripped her apart. That much we could see."

"Yes, so what?"

"So . . . why didn't she get up when he told her to? Why didn't she talk to him? A girl treated like that would have been frightened to death of the guy and jumped when he came around."

She shuddered. She was beginning to see where he was headed. "You think she was already dead?"

"Yes, I do. I think he came into the apartment, looked for her, and found her lying somewhere, maybe hidden in one of the rooms."

The flight attendant came around with a tray filled with glasses of champagne. Charlie took one.

"What could she have died of?" Rena asked.

"Unnatural causes, maybe," he said, sipping the champagne. "Like maybe someone killed her. An autopsy was never performed or we'd know for sure."

"Only Jaffe knew she was there," she said.

"And Clara Freemont. Except my money's on Jaffe. Clara was told by the cops over a year ago that Alice had moved. There was no reason for her to come back. Besides, what reason would she have to kill her own daughter?"

The flight attendant looked his way and pointed her thumb toward coach class. "I got to go," he said to Rena, gulping the remains from the glass. "Meet me in baggage claim in about four hours. By the way, I think you should know this, you have terrific lips when you frown. The bottom one kind of droops," he said, grinning, as he got up.

She frowned at his remark.

"That's it! That's the look! Keep it up," he said as the attendant escorted him out of the cabin.

Rena dropped the *New Yorker* onto the empty seat and ordered a martini. This is all getting out of hand, she thought, sighing. Alice . . . Jaffe . . . now, Charlie. His face stayed in her head, refusing to leave. He has nice lips, too. When he kissed her, she hadn't felt an electric current pass through her like that in years. She had been aware of his moves, his touch, his smells, even the breeze he left behind when he passed by, but her mind would always push them away. Now, after that kiss, she had no choice but to admit that she was deeply attracted to him. My God, this is all wrong! she thought. He's not what I need in my life. She tried forcing him out of her mind. Except this time Charlie wouldn't go away so easily; he hung around her head throughout the rest of the flight like a pesky horsefly at a Sunday barbecue.

"Where were we?" Charlie asked, tapping her on the shoulder.

Rena had been watching the baggage carousel go around and was startled by Charlie's touch. "Ghosts, I think," she said to him.

"Ah, yes, ghosts. Let's get our bags and grab a cup of coffee."

"Let's not. I have a busy day tomorrow." Her Lark hanging bag was tossed out of the shoot and Rena grabbed it. She waited until his came around and they went out into the dry night air together.

"Still think it's a ghost, huh?" Charlie said, chewing on a stick of Dentine.

"You're the one that tried to convince me of that in the first place, remember?"

"That's true, I did try to sell you that story at one time. I was under the impression that you didn't buy it."

"I'm so confused and tired that anyone could sell me anything right now."

"Need a ride? I have my car in the C lot."

"No thanks." She gave her bag to the cabdriver at the curb and got in. She was being cold to him and she realized why: she was afraid of him. He tapped on the glass and she rolled down the window.

"You know what I think?"

"What?"

"I think our ghost is someone out there who's playing Alice, and that someone is very real and very dangerous."

"But what about the phone calls, Charlie? They were made by someone who *wasn't* playing," she said emphatically. She had too much faith in Steinfeld's expertise to doubt him. "And Jaffe . . . what are we going to do about him?"

"Find someone who's willing to listen to a story about a child murderer who's a cop and hope he doesn't mind that we don't have a shred of evidence to prove it," he said, half-kidding.

As the cab pulled away she said, "Maybe I have that person." She was thinking about Craig.

By the time the taxi got off the 405 at Westwood, Charlie was back in her mind again. She came to the conclusion that it wasn't Charlie she was afraid of, it was her own emotions; they were sprouting like weeds from her body and she was losing control. She couldn't allow that, not with him. He was all wrong. From now on she would try very hard to restrain those strange feelings.

When she arrived home, she called Craig and got his answering machine. She left a message asking him to phone her tomorrow. If Jaffe had murdered Alice Mendoza eighteen years ago, then letting him run free one more day wouldn't matter.

Gerald W. dropped his two boys off at his old house in Northridge around nine o'clock. It was a day that had started off badly for him and steadily got worse.

When he arrived around 11:30 A.M. to pick them up for the Dodger game at Chavez Ravine, Mary's lover was sitting on the lawn replacing a pipe on the sprinkler system—a system that Jaffe had paid for and put in with his own hands. Since the court restrained him from coming into the house, he normally honked his horn for his sons at the curb. But seeing that skinny faggot tinkering with his property was too much for him. First Mary, then his kids, now this. He felt like one of the characters in *Invasion of the Body Snatchers*, a duplicate of whom had come into his home and taken over his entire life. Enraged, Gerald W. jumped out of the car and ran toward him. He grabbed him by his hair, lifted him up, and flung him against the side of the house.

THE VIOLET CLOSET

"You son of a bitch!" he screamed, banging him against the stucco siding. "Get the fuck out of my life!"

Mary and the two boys rushed out of the house and tried separating them. The older boy, Pete, eleven, leaped up on Jaffe's back and locked his arms around his neck, while the younger one, Johnny, grabbed on to his belt, dug his feet into the soft turf and pulled. Mary was hitting him in the face and yelling. Jaffe fell down on top of his kids, taking his ex-wife and her boyfriend with him. She pulled at Jaffe's hair and bit him on the ear, making him let go of the schoolteacher. As he sat up holding his ear in pain Mary took her live-in by the arm, pushed him into the house, and locked the door.

"We better leave, Pop. Mom's going to call the police," Pete said, trying to catch his breath. He was still sitting on top of his father. Jaffe pushed him off hard. Getting off the ground, he grabbed little Johnny by the neck and threw him in the front seat of the car. Glaring at Pete, he told him that he'd better get his ass in the car, too. With a look of resignation, Pete put his hands in the pockets of his jeans, slowly walked over to the Fairlane, and slid in next to his brother. Jaffe drove off, and when they were a block away, he slapped Pete across the face with the back of his hand.

"I'm your father, you little shit!" he said, squeezing the boy's cheek as he drove. "You ever take that faggot's side again, I'll whip you raw." During the rest of the drive to the stadium, Jaffe fumed inside and didn't say anything more to the kids. The only sounds were Johnny's fearful whimpers.

Things didn't fare much better during the game, either. The boys sat silently up in the hot bleachers, not really watching the field. They turned down peace offerings from Jaffe of hot dogs and frozen malts, their favorite. Pete had his legs up on the seat throughout the game with his chin on his knees and an angry, faraway look on his face; his cheek was red and throbbing from where he was smacked.

Afterward, Gerald W. took them to a video arcade over on Pico in West Los Angeles. He gave them each ten dollars, then went over to the back of the room and watched the young girls clustered around the machines. Their tanned legs and young upturned breasts were giving him an erection. He wondered if they noticed how big the bulge in his pants was and if they were getting turned on by it. He'd bet those giggling little cuties were sneaking looks every chance they got. If only he could go behind a wall and relieve himself while watching them. The light-haired ones, thin and small, with little peach fuzz on their arms, were his favorites. There was no question about what he was going to do after he took his kids home; he was going to prowl tonight, hopefully catch himself a real young one, teach her things that would take her years to learn.

They grabbed a bite at Bob's Big Boy, then took in a movie in Westwood, something about a cop who was half-robot, half-human. Gerald W. wasn't paying too much attention to what was happening on the screen; he was too busy thinking about Hollywood Boulevard and what he'd find out there tonight. The "candy store," that's what he liked to call that strip between Vine and Highland. All those goodies strutting their wares, and he could have any one of them: niggers, spics, little ones, fat ones, big-titted and no-titted, the hypes and the runaways, the very young and the pulpy, overaged.

"I'll see you next Saturday, okay?" Jaffe said to his boys as he parked outside their house. They nodded and opened the car door. From the reflection of the Malibu lights on the lawn, he could see the anger that was still on Pete's face. He put his hand on the boy's neck and massaged it. "Hey, buddy, you still pissed at your dad?" Pete didn't answer, he just stared straight ahead, his lips trembling as he tried keeping in the tears. Finally he tore himself away and ran toward the house. "You guys need any extra money?" he yelled after them. They didn't respond. As soon as they reached the porch Mary opened the door and they ran inside. She glared at Gerald W. for a split second, then slammed the door shut.

"Fuckin' kids, today . . . they couldn't give a shit about their parents," he thought to himself as he turned the car around and headed for Hollywood.

By ten o'clock he was slowly cruising the "candy store." The traffic was light on the boulevard, but so were the hookers—it was Sunday, an off day for business. After the second pass, Jaffe was getting frustrated. The only ones out there were the kind that couldn't make it on a weekend night when the competition was real tough: the fat, saggy-titted types in short shorts. *Shit!* It had been a long time since he needed someone as bad as he did tonight. He couldn't call Tina Rinaldo, that little fourteen-year-old beaner. He heard she'd gotten picked up and deported.

At Vine Street he made a U-turn and started driving slowly west again. If nothing happened on this pass, he'd have to take one of the pigs. He was exploding inside and he wasn't going home alone—not tonight.

Then he saw her. She was sauntering on the north side of the street, wearing a tight miniskirt with her tote bag lazily tossed over her shoulder. Her legs were long and thin, and from his vantage point she looked to be no more than thirteen. What grabbed his attention, though, was not the body, but the hair: long and straight and as red as menstrual blood. Gerald W.'s body was tingling all over. He made another U-turn, almost smacking into an oncoming bus, and parked a few feet in front of her at the corner of Las Palmas.

"Hey, sweetie," he called after her as she turned the corner onto the dark side street. She stopped and looked his way, smiling at him with white even teeth. Her eyes were covered with big pink sunglasses, the kind Boy George had made popular. He turned the corner to where she was standing in the shadows. "You lonesome tonight?" he said to her through the open window.

She shrugged and waited, smiling teasingly now.

Jaffe scanned her body with his eyes. Her creamy skin looked flawless in the dark. "This do?" he said, holding up a twenty. He was prepared to go as high as fifty. It really didn't matter, because once they got to his special parking spot, he'd show her the gold badge and she'd do anything he wanted, when he wanted. He'd try this beauty out, and if she was as good as he had a feeling she was, he'd take her back to North Hollywood with him, whether she'd like to go or not.

She shook her head to the twenty and put up two fingers.

"You want forty?" he said, grinning at her. "You got it. Get it." As she opened the door and sat down next to him Jaffe could smell the soap on her fresh, pink-white skin. It was the kind of soap used to wash babies, and it was exciting him to the point where his groin hurt. This one was a rare flower, and he just happened to be in the right place at the right time to pluck it. He couldn't believe his luck.

She put her hand on his lap and expertly began to stroke his inner thigh. Jaffe drove several blocks south to a darkened alleyway and parked the car. He barely turned off the engine before he was on top of her, touching her full breasts and her thin solid legs; feeling the silk panties that were damp in the middle. She didn't smell like a perfumed douche, as did most of the hookers; instead she smelled of talcum powder and Vaseline. Normally he'd have his badge out by now, but shit, this was too good to stop. Her nails dug into his back as she brought his head to her face and nibbled on his ear, his lips, his neck. Jesus! She knows exactly what I like, he said to himself, with a sexual hunger he never knew could exist. Suddenly he felt his juices spring from his loins. *"No! No! No!"* he screamed.

"It's okay, baby," she said after a while in an adolescent voice as she gently stroked the back of his head. "Let's go in the back where there's more room and I'll make it nice and big again. Come on."

Jaffe let her get into the back first and then followed. He couldn't believe it. This little girl turned him on like no one else ever could. She made him lie down on the backseat as she kneeled on the floor of the car next to him. Slowly she undid his wet pants. She began stroking and nibbling on his limp penis until it started to rise again.

"Ooooh," he moaned. He wanted to take her home and lock her in a closet just like that crazy spic did to that girl in New York. Now he understood him. "Ohhhh." When you have something this good, you got to hold on to it.

"Ohhh . . . Ohhh . . . say, baby, what's your name?" he groaned with his eyes closed. He was beginning to come again. Oh, God . . . oh, God!

The ejaculation was a mixture of pulsating pleasure and excruciating pain. *Oh, God!* he screamed for the last time. He felt a deep, hot stinging sensation across the width of his neck and warm liquid started to pour out of it. His vision was blurred because the fluid was now spurting into his eyes. Just as he closed them he thought he saw a sharp, metallic instrument in the girl's hand. Instinctively his hands went toward his groin. There was nothing there, only wet, spongy skin. Like a vagina, he thought as his mind darkened. He tried screaming, except his larynx was sliced in half, and the only noise that came from his throat sounded like someone gargling with mouthwash.

Just before the warm nothingness took over, he heard the girl giggle, then say, "I'm sorry. I got so carried away that I forgot to answer your question. My name's Alice. I bet you thought I'd forgotten you, huh, Wally?"

Chapter 20

Monday, 7:35 A.M.

The doorbell rang just as Rena finished shaving her legs. She wrapped a towel around her body and peered out the bathroom window. Craig Sanders was leaning against the doorframe, yawning.

"What a night you must have had," Rena said, looking at his appearance as she opened the front door. "I hope you asked for her phone number before you left in the morning? Women are usually sensitive the day after."

"Cute," he said, rubbing the stubble on his face. His eyes were dark-circled from lack of sleep, and he was wearing jeans, running shoes, and a USC T-shirt. He picked up Rena's newspaper from the lawn and handed it to her.

"Coffee's ready," she said as he walked inside the house. "The reason I phoned you last night is because I have some information about Sergeant Gerald Jaffe that may interest you."

Craig poured himself a mug of black coffee in the kitchen. "I guess we're both on the same wavelength, then. My information about him may be more current, though."

She didn't like the sound of his voice. "Like what?"

"Open up the newspaper to the Metro section. Front page, second column."

Rena took the paper off the counter, looked at it, and let out a gasp. The heavy print read DETECTIVE FOUND MUTILATED IN ALLEY. There was a picture of Jaffe's Fairlane with the back door open and a foot hanging out.

"Don't bother reading the fine print. It isn't very pretty," Craig said, taking the section away from her.

Rena sat down on the pine kitchen chair and clutched the table, trying to regain her composure. "This is a nightmare," she hissed.

"I've been up all night with the boys from homicide and forensics, hanging out in a filthy alley in Hollywood." He stretched his arms over his head, yawned, then scratched his messy hair. "The city council's up in arms about this. He might have been a lousy cop but, nevertheless, he still *was* a cop, and they get crazy when one of their own gets murdered."

"What happened?"

"You really want the details?"

She nodded.

Craig sat up on the kitchen counter and sipped his coffee. "Ahhh, strong, the way I need it. Jaffe was found about twelve-thirty this morning by a patrol car. His throat was cut, the trachea severed. A razorlike instrument was used. He was also castrated. Forensics thinks he was emasculated first, then the throat. His mouth was slit open like a jack-o'-lantern's. We believe it was a prostitute who did it."

"Why do you think that?"

"A couple of reasons. First of all, semen was found in the back and front seat of the car and on Jaffe's pants. In the preliminary examination—there will be a much more thorough one done later on today—the semen matched Jaffe's blood type. Second of all, a prostitute working on Las Palmas Avenue saw Jaffe pick up a hooker about an hour and a half before he was found. She said she remembered the car because it was the second or third time it passed by. He was driving real slow, so she figured he was shopping."

Rena was white and slightly trembling as she asked, "Was there a description of the woman?"

"Yes, there was." He stared at Rena for a few seconds, not saying anything at first, then, "She wasn't a woman, she was a girl . . . in her early teens . . . maybe thirteen, fourteen. The witness said the girl had long red hair."

"Oh, God," she said, slamming her hand on the table.

"Listen to me. It's probably just a coincidence."

"Bullshit!"

"There are hundreds of teenage prostitutes working the streets. Jaffe, who had a reputation for liking little girls anyway, just picked on the wrong one. He might have tried something with her she didn't like . . . or maybe she was on angel dust. We don't know yet. There's also a possibility that there may have been a second party involved, like her pimp. Hopefully we'll learn more later on today."

"It has nothing to do with pimps and doped-up hookers, it has to do with Alice Mendoza," Rena said, bewildered that he couldn't see it. Sighing, she got up and poured herself a cup of coffee. No, it wasn't Craig's fault; these things weren't happening to him, just to her. If she was an innocent party looking objectively at all this, she'd probably feel the same way he did. Rena then told him about the violet closet in New York and Jaffe's middle name being Wallace. But even as she talked she realized how thin the whole thing sounded. Fresh paint and a man's name aren't proof of murder.

"Do you feel you need protection?" Craig asked.

"Be straight with me, Craig. Do you think what I just told you warrants it?"

He shook his head. "No. But I'm reasonably sure I can pull some strings with my office and get it for you."

"That kind of favoritism isn't going to help your career much. Now that Jaffe's dead I'll never be able to prove that he killed Alice Mendoza," Rena said, walking over to Craig with her arms folded. "Maybe you're right . . . maybe Jaffe was an accident waiting to happen, and this young girl with red hair was a random thing." She didn't believe that but she couldn't exploit Craig's friendship until she had more to go on.

"His hobby of collecting young chickens was bound to catch up with him sooner or later," he said, jumping off the counter and kissing Rena on the head. "I have to get a couple hours' sleep before I go to the office. Don't forget, you promised me dinner."

Rena watched Craig drive away, then locked the door. Gerald W. Jaffe was murdered and not by a random prostitute, that much she surmised. But believing wasn't enough; she needed proof. She was deeply bothered by the fact that someone saw a young girl fitting Alice's description get in the car with Jaffe, the only difference being that this girl was slightly older than Alice. The witness must have mistaken the killer's age. A thirteen-year-old couldn't have followed her to New York or have known where to go to get a blueprint of her house. This was too well planned, much too sophisticated for a teenager. Unless . . . unless this teenager wasn't alive. Her hands were shaking as she called Charlie. She let it ring for a long time but no one answered.

"Couldn't you have at least worn a suit, Charlie? This *is* a place of business," Wendell Halleran said. He was sitting behind a large mahogany desk with nothing but a gold pen and ink set engraved with his initials and two pieces of paper on it. On the shelf behind his chair was a picture of him holding his twin children on his lap, while his wife, a washed-out blonde, stood behind him, smiling, her arms around his neck.

"Wendell, you're my cousin. Since we see each other so rarely, I thought we could at least go open-neck for the occasion."

"Don't do a song and dance with me about how the same blood flows through our veins—I couldn't handle it. Just tell me what the reason is for this visit, Charlie. I hear you're out of work. I hope you're not thinking about a loan from my bank." Wendell tightened the silk Armani tie around his neck and brushed away imaginary lint from his double-breasted Valentino jacket with the back of his hand.

"What's a couple of grand to you, cuz, you handle millions every day."

"Charlie, I'm a senior officer of this bank, a vice-president. I don't handle loans. If that's what you want, then I suggest you go downstairs to that particular department and spend the next five hours filling out the proper forms. Then when the paperwork makes its slow tortuous way to my desk, I'll simply veto it. Get my drift, cuz." He moved the two pieces of paper all the way to the other side of the desk. "Anything else? I'm a busy man. Some of us have to work for a living."

"A question, Wendell: how come your secretary has this tiny little desk with paperwork stacked up like pyramids, and this aircraft carrier you're sitting behind has nothing on it but Lemon Pledge? Just joking, cuz," Charlie said, holding up his hands when he saw Wendell frown. "Actually I didn't come here for a loan, just a favor. But if you want to throw me a few thou as a bonus, that's okay with me." He was sitting in front of Wendell's desk with his feet crossed.

Wendell folded his hands and leaned into the desk. "*Me* do *you* a favor, Charlie? Are *we* serious?"

"Yes, we are. Your mother, who happened to have been my Aunt Edna, said on her deathbed that we should forgive and forget since we're the only Hallerans left."

"Let's get our facts straight, Charlie. First of all, my mother never said *anything* to *anyone* on her deathbed—being she had her larynx taken out from throat cancer five years before she died—plus she never thought much of you or your mother's side of the family. Second of all, we are not the only Hallerans left in the world. We have a cousin in Ulster who insists on blowing up English garrisons, and an uncle in Cork who is wanted by the police for selling phony deeds to properties that already belong to other people. Halleran is not exactly a name to be proud of, Charlie. Thank God Halleran is a common enough name in Ireland so that no one suspects our *real* family of being our real family. Now tell me what it is you want, so I can get on with my life."

"Let's start off with a drink first."

"The bar doesn't open until five o'clock in this office—sorry you won't be here."

"In that case how about lending me your computer for a couple of hours."

"That's it?" Wendell said, surprised.

"Kind of."

"I knew it."

"I need to tap into other banking systems in New York."

"What for? Are you taking one of those computer classes they advertise on television in the afternoon for high-school dropouts?" Wendell said, snickering.

"Nope. I just bet Trans-American Bank, this great American establishment, has a way of coming up with every home loan that was ever granted in New York or L.A. for the last five years, right?"

Wendell leaned back in his executive chair and nodded. "There are ways to get it."

"Regardless of which bank handed out the loan."

He nodded again.

"Now, I know if I gave it a name and address, it would come up with the bank who okayed the loan plus the name of the company who sold the property."

"It could. Except what you're asking for is privileged information. It's illegal for us to obtain it without the other bank's permission."

"But it can be obtained, nevertheless."

Wendell shrugged. "You need a professional hacker that can break into their system. It's all very complicated."

"And I also bet that Trans-American Bank, of which you happen to be senior vice-president, happens to have just one of those creatures right on its payroll."

"Good-bye, cousin," Wendell said, getting up.

"All I'm asking for is the use of this hacker for a few hours, what's the big deal?"

"The charge for such a person is two hundred and fifty dollars an hour to do outside work that doesn't involve this bank. You have that kind of money, Charlie?"

"I figured you'd give it to me in place of the two-thousand-dollar loan."

Wendell adjusted the crease in his silk, Perry Ellis pants, walked over to the door, and held it open. "Do I have to call security?"

"Aunt Edna would roll over in her grave if she heard you talking like that, Wendell," Charlie said, standing up and walking over to the eight-by-ten family portrait on the shelf. He picked it up. "You got two great little girls here. They must be—what?—two years old now?"

"They're boys and they're five. Let's go, Charlie," he said impatiently.

"You know what I was thinking on the way over here? I was thinking about that weekend we spent together, the time Aunt Edna died. We were starting to get close . . . like a family."

"Who remembers. You had me drunk the whole goddamn time."

Looking down at the picture, Charlie said, "It was a shame that Rhonda was in Europe at the time and wasn't able to attend the funeral. It was a beautiful affair."

"My wife's name is Barbara."

"Right, Barbara," Charlie said, snapping his fingers. "I have a thing with names, but I do remember facts. Remember what we did that weekend?"

"I told you I was drunk," Wendell said uncomfortably.

"Then let me fill in the blank parts. After we put Aunt Edna into the ground, you and I went to Peppy's on Wilshire and got blitzed. You were drinking Manhattans. I had never met anyone who drank Manhattans before—except, maybe, at wedding receptions. By the time you were on your fifth one, you had your arms around my neck and were crying your eyes out. You were babbling something about wanting to tell me a secret that you never told anyone."

"And did I?" Wendell said. There was a sheen of sweat across his forehead.

"That you did, Wendell. You told me you were into mud wrestling and that you had a thing for one of the wrestlers that worked in this bathing establishment somewhere on La Brea. You said you wanted me, your only living relative, to meet this person. What I didn't realize until we got there was that the wrestler was of the male persuasion. We went into this room, and lo and behold, a man, naked to the bone, or should I say boner, was waiting for you in a four-foot vat of mud. You handed me your wallet and told me to leave your American Express card at the front desk, that you'd sign for it later. Then you ripped off your clothes and did a half gainer into the vat. I swear, Wendell, you reminded me of the horse that dives off the pier in Atlantic City."

Wendell closed the door. He was breathing hard, glaring at Charlie. "You trying to blackmail me with this stuff, Charlie? Who are you going to tell, huh? Barbara? Go ahead, she won't give a damn. She's too busy screwing the waiters at Il Giardino and the box boys at Gelson's to give a shit. And if you think anyone at this bank will believe you . . . well, your reputation speaks for itself."

Charlie took out a folded, green American Express receipt from his pocket. He slowly opened it, pressing out the creases with his hand, and held it up, making sure Wendell could see the signature. "You should have paid cash, cuz."

Ten minutes later an employee of the bank took Charlie to the basement, past the boiler room, and down a long corridor. Next to the giant air conditioner for the entire building was a closed door. Holding her ears because of the deafening noise, she mouthed, "In there," then left him. Charlie didn't bother knocking because no one would hear over the racket. He opened the door and went in.

James Gordon sat with his feet propped up on an old wooden desk watching "Days of Our Lives" on an IBM monitor. He was twenty-three but looked like a high-schooler, with his spiked black hair and a ponytail. He wore one earring, a cross, on the left lobe. Half of a tuna sandwich and a piece of a pickle lay on the desk. The small room, probably a converted broom closet, looked like a booth at an electronics convention; it was crammed with computers, modems, a tape recorder, two printers, and enough stereo equipment to fill a stadium with sound.

"Hey, bro, you Charles Halleran?" he said when he saw Charlie.

"Yeah," Charlie nodded, squeezing past shelves filled with floppies, printouts, and other electronic gear.

"The big VP told me you were coming." He didn't bother taking his feet off the desk or getting up.

"You don't look like a hack," Charlie said.

"Hey, that's okay, you don't look like an asshole. That's not me talking, bro, that's who the big man upstairs told me to expect."

Charlie smiled and they shook hands. "Great office you got here," he said, looking around. "It's not much bigger than a coffin."

"I look at it as a trade-off. I get to sit down here in my cutoffs and T-shirt, waiting to see if the real Roman and Marlena will come back to "Days of Our Lives," while making twice the salary those jerks upstairs do in their three-piece suits and plush offices. How can I help you?"

Charlie shoved the remains of the tuna sandwich out of the way and sat down on the edge of the desk. "Someone bought a house on Staten Island, maybe two years ago. I need to know who's paying the mortgage on it and what name's on the deed."

"What do you have on this person—social-security number, driver's license . . . what?"

"Just a name and an address."

"Why don't you just run a title search on the property and go through the proper channels with attorneys who'll then write, when they get around to it, to every bank in Manhattan and wait for their reply. Of course if the loan came from an out-of-state bank or they don't want to reveal their information, being it's none of the attorneys' business in the first place, it might take a little longer. Want to bet by the time you get the answer to your question, the Cubbies will finally have won the World Series." He grabbed the pickle off the desk and popped it into his mouth.

"That's why I'm here," Charlie said, impressed.

James Gordon grinned and rubbed his hands together. "This is going to take some time, maybe three or four days, and at two-fifty an hour you're about to make me a rich man."

"You take all the time you need on this one, James. And don't worry about the expense—Wendell Halleran is footing the bill."

Rena arrived at the station earlier than usual; she needed to get today's show together and make some phone calls. The first call she placed was to Cathy to tell her she was back. No one answered. As she was dialing Charlie's number Murray Spahn walked into her office carrying a box of long-stemmed red roses.

"I see we're back," he said to her, scowling.

"Roses. My favorite. Why thank you, Murray," she said facetiously.

"They're not from me," he said stiffly as he handed them to her. "The delivery man from the florist saw me downstairs and asked if I would bring them up to you."

She had no idea who they could be from. Maybe my father or the station welcoming me back, she thought while opening the box.

"The ratings were not affected by your absence, I'd like you to know," Murray said. "In fact, I was just talking to John Handy, the new account executive. He thinks they may have been higher than usual." He punched the word "usual."

"John Handy is new and insecure, and he was just playing up to you, Murray." She had the top part of the cover off. The roses were perfectly shaped and still wet from being sprayed. It was as if every one of them had been handpicked. Tucked away inside the flowers was a smaller rectangular box with a card on the outside. She opened it up and read it: "Welcome back. I'll see you soon." There was no signature. The box had a Cartier stamp on it.

At the same moment, Bud Masterly, the owner of KROS, was giving a tour of the station to several members of the Hibitchi Corporation from Japan. Bud had just turned sixty and was contemplating retirement, and the Hibitchi people had been sending out feelers about purchasing the station from him for a long time. As they turned the corner near the elevator they heard a horrifying scream coming from Rena's office. A second later they saw Murray rushing out of her door, stopping long enough to vomit on the carpet, then continue to run down the hall knocking over two of the Japanese businessmen in the process. Outraged, Masterly hopped over Murray's mess and went into Rena's office. She was on the phone calling the police. Her face was the color of wax.

"What happened here?" he demanded. Just then he heard groans and gasps coming from the Japanese contingent and turned around. They were looking at something on the floor. Masterly followed their line of vision and saw what the problem was: Gerald W.'s organ, shriveled and white, except for the color of copper blood around the edges where it had been severed, was lying on the floor nestled in between the roses.

Chapter 21

Monday, 5:30 P.M.

After Charlie left Trans-American Bank, he went home and took his manual Smith Corona out of the closet. He tinkered around at first, outlining information on the two Alices: typing dates and places and events so they wouldn't get confused. By the time he reached today's date, his juices were flowing; there was a story here, a big one, he could feel it. He opened up his file drawer, took out the old clippings on the Mendoza murder, and looked at the date when Alice had died: June 28. Today was June 25. In three days it would be exactly eighteen years. Was there a connection or just a coincidence? No, he knew better than that; there were no coincidences where Alice was concerned. He wondered if whoever was behind this craziness was planning a big surprise party for the occasion and if Rena was the guest of honor. It was a possibility.

He dialed Rena's number and her machine picked up. He hung up without leaving a message. She was probably still at the radio station. He'd call her later.

What was she doing tonight? he wondered. Maybe they could have dinner together and he could tell her then about the eighteen-year anniversary of the murder. He then wondered if she'd let him kiss her again. Forget it, Charlie, he thought. Keep it strictly business. She made it clear she wasn't interested. As Chita Rivera had said in *West Side Story: Stick to your own kind.* Another time, earlier in his life, Rena would have been his own kind. Charlie wondered what would have happened with his future if he had met someone like her instead of Rosie. Hypothetical, Charlie . . . nothing to do with reality. Forget it!

The room became stuffy and started to close in on him. He needed to get out. Peppy's, he thought to himself. It's been a long time.

"It's been a long time, Charlie, my man," Peppy said as Charlie sat down at the bar. "What's the matter? My company ain't good enough for you anymore, or are you just broke?"

"The answer's yes to both," Charlie said. The bar was busier than usual and most of the tables and stools were taken.

Peppy stopped making margaritas for a tableful of happy-hour secretaries and poured Charlie a J&B. "This one's on me seein' I got to fight to get your business back."

"I'm sure you'll sneak this back onto my bill at the end of the evening."

Peppy laughed, showing his chipped teeth, and Charlie wondered why they looked sharper than usual. He scanned the room: lots of women here tonight; most of them straight from work, all looking around. The jukebox was playing "Sittin' on the Dock of the Bay" by Otis Redding. The bar was alive and he was feeling good. This is where I belong, he thought, not in some cab playing kneesies with a woman who wouldn't know what fun was if it hit her in the head. He quickly finished his drink and waited for his brain to kick into first. Next to him was a woman, in her early forties, sitting alone and drinking Black Velvet on the rocks. Good sign. Charlie looked her over. Not bad . . . okay breasts and firm arms, except the ass was pear-shaped and hung over the bar stool. He'd had worse.

She saw him staring at her and asked, "You come here a lot?"

Charlie cringed. How many times had he heard that dumb line before? In fact, how many times had he himself used it? "I'm a regular," he said finally. "You live around here?" Another cliché, but this one was important.

"Around the corner."

Good . . . that meant he didn't have to worry about waking up tomorrow in a different time zone. "Buy you another drink?" he asked.

She smiled and nodded. Charlie raised both glasses to Peppy. He could feel the heat of her leg on his as she moved closer to him. Now this one knows how to play kneesies, he thought. He was feeling really good, the first time in a while. She was a lock, and he could practically phone in the rest of the clichés because he knew where he was sleeping tonight.

Then he saw it. She moved her head to search through her bag for a cigarette, leaving a clear path for him to see the TV set on the shelf in the corner. It was the voice of Jerry Dunphy, the TV anchorman, but a picture of Rena covered the screen. Charlie leaped off the stool, went over to the TV, and made it louder. Most of the report was over by that time but he caught pieces about Jaffe's murder . . . something about roses . . . dismemberment.

"Hey, Charlie," Peppy said, walking over to the corner of the bar where the TV was. "Lower the fuckin' thing. It's drownin' out Otis."

Ignoring him, Charlie grabbed the phone from behind the bar and called the station. He was told that Rena had left several hours ago. "I got to go," he said to Peppy, handing him the phone.

"You goin'?" Peppy was shocked. "This is first time I ever seen you pick up on a pussy that don't have a face to match and you're leavin'. I'm disappointed, Charlie."

So was the woman with the pear-shaped ass as she watched him run out the door.

Twenty minutes later Charlie double-parked his car in front of Rena's house and got out. It was almost dark outside and the street was deserted except for a couple of telephone repairmen working in a cherry picker across the street. He walked up the path to her house and rang the bell. There was no answer. He stepped back and noticed a moving shadow in the upstairs window. The curtain parted for a brief minute and he saw a man's head staring down at him. The curtain then closed. Charlie began knocking and ringing the doorbell again, and still no one answered. "Open up!" he yelled, pulling at the door handle and banging on the stained glass.

He ran toward the back wooden fence, and when he couldn't find the latch handle, he kicked it in. Leaping over the impatiens and scratching himself on the thorns from the rosebushes, he finally reached the French doors on the patio. He banged on them, screaming, "Rena, open up!"

Again, no answer.

He searched the lawn area and picked up a loose brick from

the pathway. He stepped back and was about to throw it through one of the door panes when he was tackled hard to the ground. Strong hands were digging his face into the lawn. The pungent odor of damp grass and sod was overwhelming and he could barely breathe. Using his body like a lever, Charlie swung his elbow straight up. He felt it hit something hard, like ribs, and then heard the sound of a grunt. The man was hurt, and for that instant he was off balance. Charlie grabbed the man's hand that was holding down his head and turned sideways. The attacker easily flipped over Charlie's shoulder and landed on his back. Instantly Charlie was on top of him and had his shoulders pinned down under his knees. It was almost dark now, but Charlie could see the General Telephone logo on the man's overalls.

"I have this gut feeling you wouldn't know a telephone wire from a yo-yo string," Charlie said, breathing hard, as he looked down at the man. He had a well-groomed mustache, the kind cops wore. "You L.A.P.D. ?" he asked.

"That's correct, sir."

He *was* a cop, there was no doubt in Charlie's mind about that. L.A. police always called a suspect "sir," even before they were about to shoot him. Charlie felt something hard and cold touch the back of his head.

"I strongly suggest you get off me, sir. That's my partner in back of you and he's holding a thirty-eight S&W to your head. The reason I'm telling you this is because he's a rookie—only the second day on the force—and he spent all last night watching a *Dirty Harry* double feature. You just never know with rookies."

Charlie caught the meaning and put his hands up. The French doors opened and a plainclothesman, the shadow he had seen in the upstairs window, came running out holding a snub-nose with the hammer cocked. Within seconds Charlie's face was back in the ground again, with his hands behind his back, handcuffed. "Would you believe it if I told you that I'm really happy to see you guys?" he said, spitting out a clump of dirt.

"If you are, sir, then I'd think you're crazier than the girl who sliced off the dead sergeant's dick. Would you happen to know the person who did that, sir?"

By the time Craig Sanders arrived at KROS, the police had already finished dusting the Cartier box in Rena's office, and a forensics man using tongs was placing the severed organ in a plastic bag. He was told by one of the uniforms that Rena was upstairs in the control booth getting ready to go on the air. He raced across the hallway just as the red light went on. From the glass partition he saw Rena checking her notes. She looked pale and haggard. The taped intro with her theme music was playing. He tapped on the window and she looked up and smiled. Just as the intro ended, he silently mouthed, "I'm sorry."

He paced the floor waiting until she broke for a commercial. Ten minutes later the red light went off and he went in.

"How long before you go back on?" he said.

"Ninety seconds."

"I just wanted to let you know I feel like a jerk."

She folded her notes neatly and placed them on the corner of the desk. "Don't do that to yourself, Craig. Listening to my own dialogue with you this morning, even I found it hard to believe."

Her voice was calm, he noticed, but her hands were shaking. "Your father called me about an hour ago. He read me the riot act . . . threatened to have me fired," he said, grinning.

She laughed. "He's just letting off steam. I wouldn't worry about it."

"I would deserve it. I told him we're giving you police protection, two men for twenty-four hours a day, until this maniac is caught. He said not to bother, that he'd supply his own protection—that we were nothing but a bunch of incompetents—then hung up. We *are* keeping your house under surveillance whether he likes it or not." In the other booth Stacey motioned for him to leave. "I'll call you tonight," he said, and walked out.

The next three hours were the hardest three hours Rena had ever spent in her life. She tried keeping her show going in a calm, orderly fashion, but her insides were slowly breaking down. The horrible sight of the dismembered organ stayed in her mind like a vivid photograph. Callers would talk to her about their problems, but their words became jumbled in her head and she had to ask them to repeat themselves. Stacey had a worried look on her face, and twice the station manager came into the booth to see if Rena was all right.

Finally, when the show was over, Rena took the earphones off, threw them on the desk, and slouched down in the chair. She had been a fool to go on.

Stacey walked in and plopped down in the chair next to her. "Oh boy" was all she could say.

"I guess I thought I was superwoman today. I found out differently." Rena let out a sigh and all of a sudden she felt very tired.

"I just heard management talking among themselves. They want to know if you're going to be able to do the show tomorrow. If not, they'll put Murray back into the slot." Stacey wrinkled up her nose.

Rena put her hand up to her closed eyes and leaned her head on the back of the chair. A headache was working its way up from the back of her skull. *Management!* She realized that she wasn't a human being to them—someone who had feelings—but a statistic in their little rating wars. Steinfeld was wrong when he said she was only a catalyst for moving dog food off grocery shelves. She *was* the dog food. After a while she opened her eyes and said quietly, "Tell management to go fuck themselves."

"You better tell them that. You have a contract. If they fire you, they have to pay it off. If they fire me, I'm doing mime on the Venice speedway for spare change."

"I need to go home. I'm very tired," Rena said, getting up slowly.

"Do you want me to go with you? Ben's out of town on assignment."

She thought of Charlie and how she would give anything right now to be with him. If only she hadn't gotten frightened and turned cold on him. "I think I need to be alone tonight." She put her arms around Stacey and hugged her.

"If you need anything, just call, okay," Stacey said, squeezing her tightly.

Carrying her briefcase, Rena went outside to the parking lot. Next to her Jaguar was Simon Halbrook's black Silver Cloud Rolls-Royce.

"Good day, Miss Halbrook," a voice said from behind.

Stunned, Rena quickly turned around. The glare of the late-afternoon sun was blinding but she still could make out the sandy hair and solid body of Robert Cameron. He went around her and opened the front door.

"Please get in," he said.

"Robert, what are you doing here? This is my father's car," she said, confused.

"Yes, he asked if I would pick you up. He wants you to join him for dinner. He would have met you himself except he had to attend an unexpected meeting."

"I can't believe you know my father," she said, still amazed by his presence at the station. She got in and he shut the door. He walked around to the driver's side and entered.

"I've known your father for years," he said with his disarming smile. "We've done a lot of business together."

"Why didn't you tell me you knew him when I first met you in New York? I have to tell you I'm somewhat amazed by this."

"I don't blame you for feeling that way. I just don't think if you knew, you would have accepted my dinner offer that night. Am I right?"

"Perhaps," she said, smiling. Simon was overprotective as well as overpowering and she would not have felt comfortable dating a man he had business dealings with.

He told her Simon was waiting for her at Chasen's, his favorite restaurant in L.A. The golden light from the setting sun spilled into the windshield, causing Cameron's eyes to squint and the lines around them to deepen.

Outside the restaurant, Cameron got out of the car and opened Rena's door.

"You'll be taken back to your car afterward," he said.

"You're not joining us?" she asked, confused.

"No, I can't. I have other things that need attending to right now."

Suddenly Rena realized what bothered her most about Cameron: there was never direct eye contact; when he talked to her, he was always glancing over her head and to her left and right, as if he were looking for someone. "Perhaps we'll see each other again." She shook his hand.

"Oh, I think we will," he said confidently.

Was he that sure of himself or did he know something that she didn't? she wondered as she went past the bar and into the restaurant. Two men in khaki suits with necks like tree trunks were standing next to the maître d's station watching her as she walked by. It was early and the dining room was mostly empty. She saw Simon at a center table, with reading glasses on, holding the menu away from his body and studying it like the old men in Hollywood Park probing the racing forms.

"Dad, you've been coming here for years. I'm sure you must have some idea what's on the menu by this time," she said as she sat down.

"Hello, Rena," he said pensively.

She assumed he was upset about today's events. "Craig told me you were threatening to have him fired. Were you serious?"

"Damn right I was!" He angrily tossed the menu on the table. "You're my daughter, goddamnit, the only one I have. Some maniac's out there, harassing you, now killing people, and these incompetent bureaucrats are just sitting on their asses doing nothing."

The wine steward came over with a bottle of a '79 Meursault and proceeded to open it. Rena waited until their orders were taken, then said, "It's not Craig's fault, Simon. The police couldn't do anything until they realized I was somehow connected to all of this. I've been offered protection."

"Wonderful! Someone first had to be murdered. They needn't bother! I've already gotten you protection." He was turning red with anger.

Rena was about to say something to Simon when it dawned on her. She turned around and looked toward the bar area; the men in the tan suits were now seated at the bar, except their stools were turned around facing her way. "Are they working for you?" she said, pointing to the men.

Simon shook his head. "No, they're working for *you*." He sipped the Meursault. "Damn, but those frogs know how to make a good bottle of wine! They should, they've been doing it for a thousand years. Those Napa Valley upstarts think they have the handle on it because they charge high prices. Let them try and match this!" He held the glass next to the candle on the table and looked at the deep color of the wine.

"You're changing the subject on me."

"Naturally, you're about to give me a hard time because of what I did."

"You're right. You've done this without my permission. You should have asked me first." She was annoyed.

"And what would you have said to me? 'Please, Simon. I'm a mature adult who's quite capable of handling my own affairs.' Sound familiar? You've been telling me that since you were three." He laughed, moving his big frame across the table and kissing her on the cheek. "You're my baby and I'm going to take care of you."

She shut her eyes and slowly shook her head. Same old Simon, she thought. She was a successful professional . . . a mother . . . a sophisticated woman, and to him she would always be a child. She felt helpless about it; there was nothing she could do to change the situation.

Simon the Midas was the label given to him by his friends and enemies because he had that fine touch of buying up bankrupt companies for a song and turning them around into big money makers.

As a farm boy in Canton, Idaho, he showed nothing of the business instinct that was to make him millions later on. Painting was his passion. He dreamed about going to Paris and studying art. Secretively he collected postcards of works by the French Impressionists and hid them under his bed, afraid that his father, a stick-wielding disciplinarian, would find them. There were no art lovers in Canton, just generations of farmers. By the time he was eighteen, he had grown weary of potatoes, blights, and his father. The Japs had just bombed Pearl Harbor and he ran away to Boise to join the army. Four years later he returned from the Philippines with a six-month paycheck in his pocket and a piece of shrapnel floating around in his skull. He took a bus to New York, and on a cold January morning walked out of the Port Authority Terminal and checked into a two-dollar-a-night hotel off Tenth Avenue. The next day he registered at CCNY night school as an art major. To support himself, he took a job in the stockroom with Morgan Labs, a pharmaceutical firm with offices on Fifth Avenue.

Simon was in awe of the kind of money that was being made by the sales force, some even younger than himself. He put his studies aside—promising it would only be for a short time—and took to the road with a suitcase filled with the latest miracles of chemical science. He wasn't a slick New Yorker, the kind with a nasal twang who pushes his way into offices brandishing boxes of pills and vials of elixir; he was a country boy with a rural charm that the pharmacies and medical practitioners found refreshing. Within six months Simon had become the top salesman of the firm, and a year later became national sales manager.

He met Elaina Morgan, the chairman of the board's daughter, at the annual Christmas party. She was beautiful, charming, properly flirtatious, and unlike the farm girls he knew in Idaho, had soft white hands. Simon, wearing his finest country-boy smile, went up to her and asked her to dance. The orchestra was playing "Stardust." As she went into his arms she was amazed how gracefully this lumbering man could glide along the floor. She danced with him most of that evening until the party broke up. They then went to Ratner's on Second Avenue for cake and coffee. She was enthralled with Simon; she had never met anyone like him before. This man could actually talk about quail hunting and Monet in the same breath—and with equal fervor. She realized, listening to him talk, that this fascinating country bumpkin could do and be anything in the world he wanted. He was different, much different than the droll, spoiled rich men she had considered spending her life with.

Later, as the dawn came up on the sleeping city, they took a stroll over to the deserted financial district. At Trinity Church she let go of his arm, walked up the old steps, and slowly stroked the wooden doors. She looked so delicate up there, almost saintly, with her shawl wrapped around her shoulders, that Simon rushed up the stairs, grabbed her in his arms, and kissed her intensely. At first she gave in to him, her tongue impatiently searching for his. Then suddenly she pulled away.

"Please, Simon. We're in front of a church," she whispered.

Simon backed off, controlling his passion. He knew she was religious and respected her beliefs. "I am deeply attracted to you, Elaina," he said, breathing heavily.

"I know. Give me time, Simon. Please. When we make love, let it be right. Let's wait."

Simon waited, and three months later they were married.

The wedding gift from Elaina's father was a vice-presidency and a large share of the stock in the firm. Simon took this stock, multiplied it, and within ten years amassed enough to become the controlling shareholder. After his father-in-law died, Simon became chairman of the firm, and Wall Street watched in reverence as he combined Morgan Industries with real estate holdings to become one of the biggest mega-enterprises in the country.

"Your poached salmon looks delicious. Why aren't you eating it?" Simon said to Rena as he took a bite of his white fish.

"I suppose I'm not very hungry," she replied. From the corner of her eye she saw Murry Spahn with a brunette at least a head taller than he being seated at a table next to the kitchen. He was arguing with the maître d', demanding a better table. The maître d' shrugged, put his hands up in the air, and walked away.

"How long have you known Robert Cameron?" she asked.

"Oh, for several years. A nice man, isn't he?" He poured himself another glass of the Meursault.

"He said he does business with you."

"Did he?" he said as he finished off the last of the fish.

"Yes, he did. Be honest with me. Does he do business *with* you or does he work *for* you?"

Simon laughed. "You're a bright woman, Rena. I wish to God you had come to work for me instead of becoming a therapist. What L.A. doesn't need is another shrink."

She pushed her plate away and looked up at Simon, amazed. "Are you telling me that he was being paid to go out with me?" She was angry and her voice got loud.

Simon put his finger to his lips, telling her to hush. "He was paid to keep you alive."

"Alive! Did you know that I actually contemplated sleeping with him?"

"That's your prerogative. You're a big girl."

"Am I? I wonder. Big girls have a voice in their destiny. They choose who they go out with and *if* they need protection. Obviously you don't give me that kind of credit. I feel like a damn marionette with you pulling the strings!"

"I'm trying to protect you, goddamnit . . . mostly from your own stubbornness. What the hell were you doing in that condemned building in the South Bronx? You could have gotten yourself killed." He raised his thick eyebrows and peered down at her.

"How did you know that—wait a minute! There was another person in that building. It was Robert Cameron, wasn't it?" Rena said furiously.

"Yes, and lucky for you it was." She tried to say something, but before she could speak he held up his huge palm. "One other thing," he said sternly. "I want you to keep away from that reporter Halleran. If you knew anything about him, then you'd know he's no damn good!"

There was a distinct hush at the tables around them as the diners picked at their food while trying to listen in on their conversation. Everyone knew who Simon Halbrook was and it would make a great story to repeat after a few gin and tonics at the lounge of the L.A. Country Club this weekend.

Rena leaned away from Simon, crossed her arms, and stared at him incredulously. "Is there anything you don't know about my personal life?" Her voice was trembling.

"Not much. I figured after that fiasco with that idiot Terry, somebody had to watch out for you."

"You had Charles Halleran beaten up by Cameron, didn't you?" she said, glaring at him.

"I didn't have anyone beaten up. Robert Cameron is one of the finest security men in the business. All that electronic gear in my house is his brainchild. He's protected some of the biggest names in the world, including heads of state. I respect his professionalism, and as far as I'm concerned he has a free hand in doing his job in the manner he thinks best. And if he thinks slapping that deadbeat newspaperman around a little bit will keep him away from you, then it's all right with me." His eyes softened after a moment and he smiled. "I think we've created quite a stir, don't you?" he said, looking around. "Let's forget all this for now. You're safe and that's what matters. Would you like coffee here or would you prefer to go somewhere else?"

For a while Rena couldn't say anything; she could only stare at her father and shake her head. After a minute she said bitterly, "You're some piece of work, Simon. Your Monets and Degas have nothing on you. You create and destroy with one stroke of the hand—except you're not going to do it with me." She pushed her chair aside and stood up. "What I do and who I see is my business—not yours!" She now had her hands on the table, leaning into him, glaring. "And if you don't get those two cretins sitting at the bar off my back, I'm going to call the police and have them do it!"

Simon looked up at her, smiling innocently, and said, "They won't listen to you, my dear. They already know about them and approve. You see, the police are quite shorthanded and can use all the help they can get."

"Goddamn you, Simon!" she hissed. She then turned to walk out of the restaurant. As she passed Murray's table he held a glass of Merlot to his lips and smirked at her. Rena swerved against him, hitting his elbow, causing the deep red wine to spill onto his chin and down his white linen suit. She was out the door before he could utter the first obscenity.

She walked for over an hour, trying to shake off the fury within her. The man was a genius at control, she thought. He knew every move there was to make—even the ones that hadn't been invented yet—and had a plan to counter all of them. There was no such thing as free will in Simon's universe. His world was like an ant farm and he was the jovial child peering in.

She took a cab back to the station, got into her own car, and went home. As she pulled into her driveway she saw Stacey's car parked at the curb. Next to the garage, on the lawn, she was speaking to three men, two of them linesmen in coveralls, the third in a suit. They stopped talking when Rena approached.

"These gentlemen are police officers," Stacey said caustically to Rena. "They're under the impression that they've captured a big-time perpetrator as he tried to enter your home. They even think he might know something about Sergeant Jaffe's death."

"Who are we talking about?" Rena asked.

"Charles Halleran, Esquire. He's been calling the station from the L.A. county jail for the last couple of hours asking for you. Finally the switchboard gave him over to me and I came here looking for you," Stacey said.

The big policeman with the mustache said, "He was acting very suspicious, Miss Halbrook. We didn't believe you knew him."

"Well, now that you *do* know it, why don't you just release him?" Rena said irritably.

"We can't. He's also been arrested for assaulting an officer," the one in the suit said.

"I called the jail. They want five hundred dollars cash for his bail. Do you have that kind of cash on you at this hour of the night?" Stacey crossed her arms and grinned at Rena.

From across the street she could see two men in khaki suits leaning against a car, watching.

Damn! Life has gotten complicated in the last few weeks, she thought.

Chapter 22

Monday, 9:35 P.M.

"Yo, Halleran, up and at 'em!" the bailiff said as he unlocked the barred door of the holding area. He was a big, fat man, with a gut that hung well over his belt.

Charlie glanced up. He was lying on the floor, with his head propped up against the shoulder of a wino, and was just about to doze off. Rubbing the sleep from his eyes, he got up slowly from the cold cement floor and brushed the dirt from his torn pants. He hopped over the bodies of the other prisoners as he made his way to the cell door.

"You done made bail, chump," the guard said, hardly looking at him.

He was led out to the bail room where he saw Rena and Stacey leaning over a small window with bars. Rena was counting out loud to herself from a small stack of twenties she was holding in her hand. When the total reached five hundred dollars, she passed the bills through the bars to the cashier on the other side.

"Hey, Charlie," she said, when she looked up and saw him. "My, but you do look a mess." A smile broke out on her face.

Charlie didn't smile back. He found nothing about tonight amusing.

He signed the release form and left with the two women.

"I'll have to owe you the money," he said to Rena with some embarrassment as he got into the backseat of her Jaguar.

Stacey sat in the front seat of the car. After clipping on her safety belt, she turned to him and said, "Oh, by the way, I'm Stacey Miller." She extended her hand to him. "Rena's right.

231

You do look a mess, Charlie." There was an amused look in her eyes.

Rena started to giggle.

"It seems I get told that at least twice a day. Thanks for making my quota," he said, with an edge in his voice. He sat back and folded his arms. "Where's my car?" he asked.

"Impounded until tomorrow," Rena said.

Charlie moaned.

Rena drove back to her house. Stacey jumped out of the car, grabbed her nylon knapsack, yawned, and said that she was going home. Charlie opened the car door and watched Stacey's long-legged body race across the lawn to her parked VW.

"Try to keep my employees out of your lascivious thoughts, Charlie, okay?" Rena said, grinning. Across the street she saw the General Telephone truck parked at the curb with the shadows of two men inside. As she opened the door, she wondered where Cameron's men were. They were around somewhere watching her, she knew that much.

"Those are my new friends over there," Charlie said to her, waving to the two cops in the telephone truck.

Inside the house Charlie glanced around the room. "Where's the bar?" he asked.

She pointed to an English pine cabinet by the wall. "In there."

He went over to the cabinet and jiggled the knob, trying to open it.

"Be careful with that," she said as she bent down to help him. "It's an antique."

Charlie pushed the liquor bottles aside until he found a bottle of twelve-year-old Ballantine's. He opened the top part of the cabinet, took out a glass, and poured himself three fingers. "Thanks, I needed it."

"Nothing personal, Charlie, but you smell like my gardener. What were you doing . . . rolling around in grass?"

"Something like that," he said.

"Would you like to take a shower? Oh, please say yes."

"Yes."

"Good. Use the one in the upstairs hallway. It's Cathy's bathroom."

He followed her upstairs. She grabbed a large bath towel, soap, a tube of shampoo and handed them to him.

"Am I staying the night?" he asked.

"You might as well. It would be easier that way. I could take you to your car tomorrow. You can use the guest room or Cathy's, depending on whether or not you like waking up to an eight-by-ten-foot poster of the Beastie Boys."

Charlie made a face. "I'll take the guest room. The day the music died for me was when Jim Morrison's skin popped the big H." He went into the bathroom and started to remove his torn, grass-stained shirt.

Rena looked away and said, "What's your waist size? I might be able to find a couple of things of my ex-husband's."

"Thirty-two," he said, unbuckling his pants and slipping them off.

She glanced back in and saw him turning the water on. He was nude. Good body for a guy who doesn't exercise, she thought. "You're certainly not shy, are you?" she said, closing the door.

"Nope. You like the shy ones, huh?" he shouted, through the noise of the running water.

"Nope," she said, leaning against the wall with her arms folded. "Oh, I forgot to tell you, the knob that's marked 'hot'—"

Charlie screamed.

"—is really the cold one. I keep meaning to get them changed around."

"Gotcha," he said, with a pained voice.

She went into her bedroom and looked through the closet until she found an old Polo shirt of Terry's and a pair of chino pants. She dropped them outside the bathroom door.

Charlie came downstairs into the kitchen wearing Terry's clothes. They were much too big on him. "You ever wonder who this little guy is on the horse playing polo?" he said, pointing to the logo on the shirt.

Rena was opening the freezer, and when she looked up and saw him, a strange feeling, almost like guilt, came over her. She remembered those clothes well; Terry used to wear them around the house all the time. Now another man had them on. She felt as if she were betraying Terry. She shook the feeling off. Our minds do such crazy things to us, she thought. However, something else popped up into her head: she wondered if *she* had ever left anything behind when she separated from Terry and if he had given her clothes to another woman to wear. How would she feel about it? Hurt and angry? . . . Probably. There was no rational reason for those feelings. But when did logic ever go hand in hand with sentiment? she thought.

"Cathy's away and I don't have much in the fridge. Will Lean Cuisine lasagna be okay?"

"Sure." He went into the living room and fixed himself another scotch.

Rena looked at the clock; it was 11:30. Too late to call Cathy. She hadn't spoken to her in more than two days, and she hoped everything was all right. There had been an unhappiness in her voice the last time they talked. Terry was out most nights and not spending much time with her. Nothing unusual about that; he had done the same thing to Rena when they were married. Rena decided to call her first thing in the morning before she went riding.

They sat in the dining room. She had a glass of wine and watched Charlie as he wolfed down the last piece of lasagna.

"Was that enough to eat?" she asked.

"I guess it's enough if you weigh thirty-five pounds and have a stomach the size of a tennis ball."

"I suppose I should tell you this."

"Tell me what?" he asked.

"The man who beat you up in New York . . . he works for my father. His name is Robert Cameron."

"The guy I saw you with outside the hotel?"

"I only found out about it tonight. I have to apologize. My father was just trying to protect me."

"You wouldn't happen to have his address lying around somewhere?" he said bitterly.

"You wouldn't want it. He would probably kill you, and his upper lip wouldn't even break out into a sweat." She walked over to the phonograph, put Mozart's Concerto Number 21 in C Minor on the turntable, then went to the garden door and stared out into the blackness.

Charlie didn't argue the point about Cameron; he knew she was right. He looked at her thin frame leaning against the French doors and felt a burning in his loins. Even the scotch couldn't dull the feeling. There was a chill coming in from the garden and small goose bumps started forming on the back of her arms. He wanted to run his hands over those bumps, touch the small of her back, the nape of her neck, put his lips on the white skin under her jawbone—but he didn't; he remembered her reaction in New York when he kissed her. No, you don't find them like that at Peppy's, he thought.

They didn't say anything for a while. The music of Mozart hung gently over them. She continued staring out the door with her arms folded, rubbing them with her hands to keep out the chill. She looked deep in thought, and Charlie wondered what was going through her head. Finally he said quietly, "I think she means to kill you. I think she means to try it within the next couple of days. These are just my feelings. I have nothing concrete to go on."

She shivered slightly and hugged her body tight. Rena trusted his feelings. "What makes you think that?"

"Things have been heating up, almost as if this is all building up to some kind of a conclusion. It started with simple phone calls placed to you in the middle of the night by a little girl a couple of weeks ago. Whatever is really happening has now grown to include Jaffe's murder and possibly even another murder, your assistant, Fred Lovell. It will be exactly eighteen years on the twenty-eighth of this month when Alice Mendoza was killed. That's only two days away. My feelings say if there's going to be a culmination to all of this, then that's the cutoff date."

Rena nodded and exhaled a slow sigh. She looked like a little girl standing there, alone and scared, and Charlie ached for her. Again, there was a long stillness between them.

Aw, the hell with it!

He got up and went over to her. Putting his hands on her shoulders, he gently turned her head toward him. As he cupped his hands to her face he could see the fear and uncertainty in her eyes, but there was a craving there also.

"Don't, please, Charlie," she whispered, trying to turn away.

He didn't let her go. He touched those goose bumps on the back of her arms, the warm nape of her neck, the white flesh near her chin. She's like a candy store, he thought.

"No, Charlie." There was a huskiness in her voice, but this time she didn't move away.

He held her head gently, moving his face down to hers, searching for her lips. She tried backing off but he wouldn't let go. After a while she stopped fighting and put her arms around his neck, kissing him hard, passionately. When they separated, finally, she put her head on his chest and held him tight. "I'm scared, Charlie. First all this craziness that's been happening . . . now you."

Stroking her hair, he said, "It's just a kiss. That's nothing to be afraid of. Kissing you has been a fantasy of mine since I met you, lady."

"Do you have any others?" she asked softly.

"With you? Lots."

She moved her lips up to his neck and kissed it. "Tell me about them."

"That might take a while," he said, short of breath.

"Not too long, I hope. I only have a couple of days to live, remember?"

Charlie rolled off of her and onto the damp sheets, exhausted. Outside, he could hear the engine of the *L.A. Times* truck and the *plop* of the morning paper as it was thrown against the side of the house. He looked at the clock radio on the nightstand; it was nearing four in the morning. Turning to Rena, he propped his hand against his head and looked at her. With his other hand he removed the wet hair from her face.

"Are you ready to go at it again?" she said, smiling. She grabbed his hand from her face, brought it to her mouth, and kissed his fingers. She had never felt this uninhibited with a man before.

"I don't know if there's anything left," he said, laughing. "I hope you're not one of those black widows who drain the juice from those poor, horny, male spiders and then do them in."

"Ten dollars says you can do it one more time." She brought his face to hers and began to trace the outside of his lips with her tongue.

"I think you whittled my privates down to a stub."

"Come on, Charlie, ten bucks," she said as she wrapped her leg around him. Her hand lazily drew small circles at the bottom of his back. "My, oh my," she whispered in his ear after a few seconds.

"I think that stub just turned into a battleship," he said, climbing back on top of her.

As she opened her legs for him so he could enter her, the phone rang. Sighing, she picked up. It could be Cathy. "Yes," she said.

Static.

"Hello," she said again. A cold fear gripped her stomach.

More static, then: "Help me, Rena. Please, oh pretty please." The voice began to giggle.

She pushed Charlie off her and sat up. "Alice? My God!"

Laughter. Loud, shrieking laughter. Laughter that a child would make running free in a field while being chased by other children.

"Stop it! Who are you?" Rena shrieked into the phone.

The laughter continued for a second longer, then the line went dead.

Charlie took the phone from her. "What did she say?" he asked.

She wrapped her arms around her knees, as if to protect her body. "I think you're right, Charlie. She *does* want to kill me." Her eyes glazed over with fear.

Chapter 23

Tuesday, 6:05 A.M.

"Did I wake you, Harry?"

"As a matter of fact you did," the psychiatrist's raspy voice answered back on the phone.

"Gee, that's too bad. You're slipping, you know that, Harry?"

"Oh? In what way?" Harry Steinfeld coughed, clearing the sleep from his throat.

Rena was sitting behind the desk in her study, wearing old jeans and a T-shirt and sipping a cup of black coffee. There were dark circles around her eyes from no sleep. She put one bare foot up on the desk and said, "Alice called again last night . . . if that's really her name. She was taunting me. I think your machines lied about her veracity, Harry. I doubt very much that she was locked up in a closet like you thought. This girl is sick . . . she's already killed one man, maybe another, and I think she's going to come after me."

"Hmm . . . interesting."

"Interesting? I haven't slept in two days, my nerves are being held together by spit, I have the police and my father's private army watching me day and night—and all you can say is 'interesting.' I need something more substantial than that, Harry. I trusted you to know what you were doing. Could this girl be a lot older than we originally assumed?"

"Could be."

"Please, Harry, stay with me on this."

"I'm here, Rena. I'm just thinking, that's all. No, my machine didn't lie. That girl *was* telling the truth. Maybe I was taking her too literally . . . assuming the obvious."

She heard the floor creak upstairs. Charlie was awake. "What do you mean?" she asked him.

"Given all the components—her voice, her age, and her situation—I took it for granted that what she was experiencing was happening at the precise moment she called you."

"Wasn't it?" she said.

"Maybe not."

Rena was beginning to see a vague light in the darkness and it frightened her. "Are you saying that all this actually may have happened to her but at another time in her life?"

"Yes, and I should have foreseen that possibility, but didn't. My machines aren't at fault . . . *I* am. Traumatic experiences can be emotionally recalled years later but the machines don't know that. They're only capable of telling whether the voice patterns were legitimate, not if the person was actually going through the trauma at that particular time."

"Harry, Alice Mendoza has been dead for eighteen years. The authorities found the body in the apartment, exactly where her father said it would be. Are you telling me differently?" Her fingers were white and hurting from squeezing the receiver.

"No, I'm just expanding my earlier concept. The girl was telling you the truth, only the mistreatment that was inflicted upon her happened at an earlier date than I originally thought."

"You're talking about post-traumatic stress syndrome, aren't you?"

"Sounds like it."

"But why the similarities in the two Alices?"

"I don't know. You said there was a body, right?"

"Yes."

"Then start there."

After hanging up on Harry, she went into her study and took down several books from the library shelves dealing with child abuse. She soon found what she was looking for in a chapter dealing with post-traumatic stress syndrome in children.

Many people had become familiar with this malady when it started showing up in Vietnam veterans. It had been around a long time before that, however, and prominent in children who were sexually or physically victimized. Part of the disorder was the flashbacks—the reliving of the horrors they'd experienced. The visions were capable of being so real that the sufferer actually believed that he or she was back there again. That explained how Harry's machines could be fooled into thinking that the girl was presently being violated.

Rena read further, but it was another chapter that really caught her attention. The author wrote about how post-traumatic stress sufferers are especially affected on the anniversary of the tragedy. On that day some children will act out the experience with dolls or even with friends; others become more depressed or withdrawn than usual. Could Charlie's instincts be right? Rena thought. He told her last night, without knowing the medical terms, that everything seemed to be heading toward a climax on the anniversary of Alice's death. Except this brought up a whole new question: why would a victim of child abuse be reliving someone else's life—someone who'd been dead for eighteen years? Reading further, Rena could find nothing that substantiated this type of behavior. Yet that's precisely what seemed to be happening. She had hoped that reading about post-traumatic stress syndrome would help clarify what was going on; instead it clouded everything even further.

Putting the books away, she went upstairs, where she found Charlie in the shower. She slipped out of her clothes and went into the stall.

"Fancy meeting you here," Charlie said, kissing her on the lips.

"I need a body, Charlie." She put her arms around his waist. His tight skin, wet and slippery from the soap, felt good.

"What do you think you're holding on to, chopped liver?"

"No, I'm talking about a different body—one that's dead and three thousand miles away."

"That's a little kinky, isn't it?" He turned her around and began washing her back.

"I'm serious, Charlie." She told him everything she knew about post-traumatic stress syndrome, including the fact that he just might be right about the importance of the date of Alice's death.

"But why have her grave reopened?"

"Because it doesn't make sense that a post-traumatic stress sufferer is having flashbacks about someone else's experiences. I have to know who or what is in that casket."

"It's a little vampirish, but I'll see what I can do." He turned her around again and began to wash her front.

She felt something hard pressing against her pelvic bone and looked down. "I see we're not at half-mast this morning," she said, grinning.

"That's because the fleet's in, again." As he bent down to kiss her she put her arms on his shoulders, hoisting herself up, and wrapped her legs around his waist. He gently eased her down onto the tile floor, the water hitting his back like a tropical downpour.

Ever since Rosie, sex had been by the numbers for him; nothing memorable. Then last night happened and it was different; he felt like a fifteen-year-old kid again, doing it for the first time. All the textures and smells felt new: the sensation of touching velvet when he ran his hand over her thighs, the hot feel when he was inside her, the silkiness of her small firm breasts, the hard muscles of her buttocks. Where had he been all these years? It was as if a plate-glass window had been put between him and those other women, preventing him from touching and feeling anything, even if those anythings were nothing more than temporary lust and eventual disgust.

"Charlie," she moaned.

He propelled himself harder into her, trying to break that thick glass plate forever, shattering it into a million slivers so he could mesh his body with hers.

Charlie sat at the edge of the bed watching her sleep. Gently, trying not to disturb her, he pushed her hair away from her eyes and covered her with the sheet. He got up and looked out the window; the telephone truck was still parked across the street. A car pulled up next to it and two thick-necked men got out with a tray of coffee containers and danishes and gave half of them to the cops in the truck. He figured them for Cameron's people. Nice how they all get along with each other. He dressed quietly and went downstairs, carrying his loafers.

He found some instant coffee in the kitchen, tossed a couple of teaspoons in a cup, and filled it with hot water from the sink. The clock on the wall said 8:30 . . . that's 11:30 New York time. Almost lunch hour there and a good time to call Genero. He's probably sitting at his desk wondering which restaurant to fleece for a free meal. He picked up the phone from the counter and dialed the precinct.

"Charlie Halleran, what the hell are you doing up so early?" Genero said when he heard Charlie's voice.

"I figured I'd catch you in before you hit Little Italy for a freebie. How are the kids and the little woman doing?"

"Everybody's terrific."

"Glad to hear that. And Brenda?"

"Brenda who?"

"Brenda. You know, the one you've been sticking it to in the broom closet."

"Who told you about that?" he said uneasily.

"Brenda. She's been screaming it to the world. You must have some schlong, Genero."

"Knock it off, Charlie. You never know when those fuckers from internal affairs are listening in."

"Hey, old buddy, just congratulating you, that's all."

"Let's put it this way, Charlie. I have a wife of twenty-five years who hasn't bought a new dress since Chuck Berry played the Brooklyn Paramount. Get the picture?"

"Got it."

"Good. Now tell me what I can do for you. The only time you call me long distance and not collect is when you want something."

"Just a small favor."

"Yeah, sure. Does it have anything to do with that Mendoza case again?"

"Yep. What's my chances of getting the girl's body exhumed?"

"What? Are you fuckin' nuts! You need a court order to dig up a body. And you can't get that unless you have a damn good reason for it—like maybe someone buried the wrong person by mistake."

"There you go, Genero. You're thinking. Use that excuse if you have to."

"What the fuck! Are you serious?"

"Could be."

"You saw the body, Charlie. You saw them scrape her off the wall."

"I saw *a* body. We don't know if it was Alice Mendoza's."

"Aw, come on, goddamnit! Don't do the tarantella on my face. You know damn well it was her!"

"Okay, maybe it was, maybe it wasn't . . . maybe we'll never know. But it wasn't Mendoza who killed her."

Genero sighed. "Okay, Charlie, who did?"

"Gerald W. Jaffe. At least I think he did."

"Enough, Charlie, enough! I've known you for twenty years and this is going to be the first time I ever hung up on you. I promise you this day will be implanted in my memory."

"Gerald W.'s dead. Murdered by a girl who fits Alice Mendoza's description." Charlie heard a deep silence on the other end and knew Genero was at least nibbling if not biting on the hook.

"That scumbag Jaffe is dead?" he said finally.

He had him. Now it was time to reel in the line carefully. One wrong move and Genero would be gone. He told him everything, starting from the phone calls to Rena and the violet closet on Holmby Street right up to Jaffe's penis in the box of roses. He went into great detail about the last part, mainly because Genero had been Jaffe's partner eighteen years ago and hated him.

When Charlie was done talking, there was a long silence on the line, then: "I'll get a court order to get the body exhumed," Genero said. "I know a judge who owes me. If I'm made to look like an ass in all of this, Charlie, I swear to God I'm going to shoot you. Capisce?"

"I capisce, pal. And if I'm wrong, I'll pull the trigger myself. You won't even have to get your hands dirty."

They hung up. Charlie grabbed a banana off the top of the fridge, ate half of it in one bite, then on a long shot called Trans-American Bank. The receptionist couldn't find a line for James Gordon. That was because the bank wouldn't admit they had a hacker on their payroll, Charlie realized. He asked for Wendell's secretary instead. She got on the line and told him that Gordon had been trying to get hold of him and had left a message that he'd be catching rays this morning on the beach at Driftwood.

Charlie put on his shoes and peered out the window between the slats of the blinds. Cameron's boys were leaning against the truck listening to the young cop who had held the gun to Charlie's head last night. The other guy, the one who tackled him, was probably watching the back. The voice of the young cop was loud and his hands were flailing about. Suddenly the three broke into laughter. The clown was telling a joke—probably about fags or spades, Charlie thought. He closed the blinds before they looked up and saw him. He couldn't leave through the front door because one of those jokers would follow him. He went to the door at the side of the house and looked out through the frosted-glass pane. The door opened onto a small pathway leading both to the front and back of the house. Directly ahead of the door was a seven-foot ivy-covered fence that led to the neighbor's property. Charlie thought about his options and went with the fence. First he checked his cash situation. Ten dollars—not enough to get him to the beach by cab.

He went back upstairs, found Rena's purse, and took forty dollars. She was still asleep. He wrote her a note saying he'd talk to her later and placed it on the pillow next to her.

Leaving through the side door, he scaled the ivy fence and dropped down into the neighbor's yard. He darted across the lawn, climbed over the back concrete wall, and found himself in a tree-covered cul-de-sac. Several blocks away, on San Vicente, he hailed a cab.

Driftwood was a street on the Marina peninsula that dead-ended onto a "singles" beach. Charlie paid the cabdriver and walked past the expensive wooden condos where sidewalk and sand merged. He took his loafers off, rolled up Terry's chino pants, and scanned the small beach. It was still early, and the Driftwood crowd, mostly garment salesmen and secretaries, hadn't started filling the beach yet. Except for a smattering of topless sunbathers, it was fairly deserted right now, and he had no trouble finding James Gordon. He was sitting close to the water on a beach chair holding a reflector to his pink-white face. A joint dangled lazily from his mouth.

"Some banking hours you keep, James," Charlie said as he walked up to him and sat on his blanket.

Without looking up, James offered his hand. The sun reflected off his blue sunglasses. "Gotta take care of the ol' body, Charles. You can get all kind of diseases hanging out in boiler rooms all day." He handed Charlie the joint.

Charlie took a deep drag, held it in for a few seconds, and slowly let it out. "Hear you been looking for me," he said, handing the weed back. James took it with the right hand and Charlie saw a tattoo on his forearm: Sid Vicious Lives.

"That I have. I thought it would take a couple of days to get the info on this old broad. I was wrong."

Charlie leaned closer to him. "Talk to me, James."

"Nothing to talk about. There's nothing on her."

"You dragged me out here to tell me that?" Charlie said, getting pissed.

James grinned, still looking toward the sun. "I'm real disappointed, Charlie. I thought you were on my brain level. My not finding anything on her says a lot. You just have to read between the lines."

"Okay, so tell me nothing then." Next to the blanket was an ice chest. Charlie looked in.

"Bud or Perrier—take your pick," James said, taking the last toke from the joint, then flipping it into the ocean.

Charlie took the Bud, opened it, and wrapped a paper napkin around the can so the lifeguards wouldn't come swooping down.

"This is what I have," James said. "The development on Dawson Drive where Clara Freemont lives is fairly new—only a couple of years old." He bent down to get a beer.

"That's it?"

"That's all I could find out. She doesn't have a job, she has no trust fund—Christ, she doesn't even have a social-security number. Yet every six months for the last fifteen years she's been depositing twenty thousand dollars into a savings account under her name at a Staten Island bank. Now let me tell you what I don't know. I don't know how she paid for the house, since there's no record of any money passing hands. No loan was issued to her for the house from any bank in this known universe."

"There has to be a deed to the property. Whose name is on it?"

"Clara Freemont," James said, turning his chair slightly, following the sun's path. "However, it was quitclaimed to her."

Charlie was getting real interested. "There has to be a prior owner's name on it."

"There sure is. Belle Construction."

"Is that Bell like in Adano?" Charlie said, feeling his pockets, wishing he had brought something to write on.

No, it's Belle like in Starr. The authorized signature on the deed is a Thomas Beardsly. Turns out he's legal council for the construction firm."

"Why the hell would a construction company give her a house?" Charlie wondered aloud.

"They could do whatever the fuck they wanted with it. They're the ones who built the tract houses and were selling them. The house, by the way, was valued at that time at two hundred and ten thousand dollars. She was a call girl, right? Maybe she was balling the president of Belle Construction."

"Uh-uh. Clara's a three-hundred-pound version of Shelley Winters. Construction companies don't put up their own money. Some bank had to finance them."

"You're right. It was Glendale Trust." James peered over his sunglasses and grinned.

Charlie looked amazed. "You're putting me on! Glendale Trust is a California bank. Why would they get involved in a project on the other side of the country?"

"See, now you're doing it, too. That's an 'I don't know' question you just asked. Now it's my turn. I don't know why they gave a prime piece of real estate to fat Clara. And I don't know why Glendale Trust doesn't mention the transition of the property in their annual statement for that year. That's not very up-and-up. In fact it's downright fucking illegal."

"It's also collusion. Belle Construction couldn't have given away a house without Glendale Trust knowing about it. Why would two reputable firms risk their necks for a second-rate hooker?"

"The first rule of business, bro: Firms don't get to be firms by staying reputable. If you want to be reputable, then open up a fruit stand. You want to pass me my Hawaiian Tropic. It's under the beer."

Charlie did. "Thomas Beardsly, huh? What's the firm he's with in New York?"

"Beardsly, Harriman and Dean. And they're not in New York—they're right here on Miracle Mile. That's another 'I don't know,' right? Why would a New York–based construction company use a California law firm? You're going to have a lot of reading between the lines to do, Charlie." The suntan oil glistened off James's pink skin as he rubbed it on himself.

"James, I have a feeling you're not going to leave this beach until you've contracted skin cancer, so how about lending me your car for a couple of hours?" Charlie said as he squashed the empty beer can between his hands.

"Can I trust you?"

"I'm Wendell's cousin."

"That's no testimonial." Without turning his head away from the sun, he took the keys from the pocket of his shorts and handed them to him.

"Where's the car?" Charlie asked, looking around.

James pointed his thumb in back of him to a white Porsche Carrera parked on Driftwood.

Charlie sighed. "It doesn't go with the boiler-room image, James."

"These are trying times to be oneself, my friend," he said, dipping his hand inside the ice chest and taking out a bottle of Perrier.

Charlie drove east to Roxbury and Wilshire in Beverly Hills and parked the car in the underground garage of the office building of Beardsly, Harriman and Dean. He took the elevator up to the lobby and called Rena on a pay phone.

"You up?" Charlie asked.

"Sort of," she replied, yawning. "Where are you?"

"In Beverly Hills."

"You're not the Gucci type. Come back to bed, Charlie."

"Later."

"Why are you there and not here with me?"

"I'm about ready to march into the law firm of Beardsly, Harriman and Dean."

"Oh, God, Tom Beardsly. Is he still alive?" she groaned.

"You know him?"

"Sure do. He's an old friend of the family. Must be in his seventies by now. You know the kind . . . pinches children's cheeks until they turn red and puffy and calls it affection. What do you want with him?"

Charlie told her everything, including the relationship between Glendale Trust and the New York firm of Belle Construction.

"Is that Bell as in ding-dong bell?"

"No, it's Belle as in *voulez-vous couchez avec moi, ma belle?*"

"That's going to be tough to do if you're in Beverly Hills and I'm here. But that's interesting, though," she said, yawning again.

"What is?"

"Belle is my middle name."

He walked into an oak-paneled waiting room on the penthouse floor. The receptionist was at the other end and he had to wade through a sea of plush brown carpeting and green leather chairs to get to her.

"May I help you?" she said in a friendly voice.

"I hope so. I need to see Thomas Beardsly." In back of her, on an oak table, were three bronze busts of staunch-looking men.

"Did you have an appointment?" she asked. "Because he's with someone right now."

"No, I don't."

She dialed Beardsly's secretary. "What is your name, sir?"

"It's not important. Just tell him I'm from Glendale Trust and Belle Construction. I'm sure he'll find room for me on his busy agenda."

After a minute the receptionist hung up and told Charlie that Beardsly would see him.

While waiting, Charlie asked, "Who are those guys? Manny, Moe, and Jack?"

"Who?"

"The three guys behind you."

She giggled, pushing her long blond hair behind her back. "No, that's Mr. Beardsly, Mr. Harriman, and Mr. Dean," she said, touching each bust on the nose.

An older woman, Beardsly's secretary, entered the reception room, looked at Charlie's clothes with obvious distaste, and told him to come in. He followed her as she walked quickly through a maze of hallways until she got to the thick oak door with Thomas Beardsly's name on it.

"You may go in," she said with a plastic smile.

Thomas Beardsly sat behind his huge desk and glared up at Charlie. He was a small man with a thin frame and close-cropped, white hair. He didn't get up, smile, or attempt to shake Charlie's hand. "What can I do for you Mister . . . ?"

"My name's Halleran . . . Charles Halleran." Charlie thought he could see a hint of recognition in his watery blue eyes. There was a strong odor of cheap perfume in the air. Jasmine, he thought. Where had he smelled it before? As he sat down he could feel that the seat was still warm, as if someone had been sitting in it seconds before he came in. He didn't see anyone leave, even though the receptionist said Beardsly was with someone, and there was no back door—only the bathroom.

"What is it you want, Mr. Halleran?"

"I'm a reporter, Mr. Beardsly."

"You're an out-of-work reporter," Beardsly said with contempt. "Get to the point."

How did he know that? "Okay, what does a New York construction company, a Los Angeles bank, and an ex-hooker have in common?" For a second Charlie could see surprise in Beardsly's eyes. "Is that to the point enough?"

"I don't know what you're talking about."

"Then let's really get to the point and stop kicking around the shit, all right? It's not important to me whether your signature's on a quitclaim giving a house to Clara Freemont. I'm not looking for a story. What *is* important is keeping Rena Halbrook alive. Somebody is going to try to kill her in a couple of days and I think that someone is smart enough to get away with it. If stopping this maniac means getting to know what those two companies and Clara have in common, then I think you'd better tell me or I'm going to the police."

Beardsly's eyes darted around the room for a split second then back to Charlie. He took his glasses off, sighed, and wiped them with a handkerchief. "Between us?"

"Absolutely between us." Charlie folded his legs and put his hand to his chin.

"This much I'll tell you. It's rather very simple—just a little awkward for the person involved, that's all. Let's just say someone high up in Belle Construction bought a house for Miss Clara Freemont. It was a gift for services rendered many years ago." Beardsly winked at Charlie.

"What did he pay off Glendale Trust with? No money changed hands."

Beardsly's eyes became small and they burned like lasers into Charlie. "Who told you that?" he said after a beat.

"It doesn't matter. I know, that's all. I thought you're supposed to be straight with me."

"That's all I'm prepared to tell you," Beardsly said, his voice hardening.

The smell of jasmine still permeated the air.

"I'll bet you old Clara got more than a house from this gentleman caller. I'll bet you he's been paying her close to twenty thousand dollars every six months for a number of years." He looked into Beardsly's ashen face. "Am I right?" Charlie said.

"I think you'd better leave," Beardsly said threateningly.

"Something really bothers me. Why would a bank invest in a real estate deal three thousand miles away?" Charlie felt his head was like a magnet, drawing scattered pieces of colored metal to it, forming a picture. Then he saw it. "Unless the bank and the construction company are owned by one corporation!"

Interesting, though . . . Belle is my middle name, Rena had said to him.

"And that corporation is Morgan Industries." Charlie's heart was pumping faster. "It's Simon Halbrook who's been paying off Clara, isn't it? And it's you, as an old and trusted friend of the family, who's been doling out the money. Why?"

More jasmine. And Charlie remembered.

He got up, went to the bathroom door and knocked. "Mrs. Freemont, you on the potty? Why don't you come in from the cold and join us."

Beardsly stood up and scowled. "How dare you!"

Charlie heard the click of the bathroom latch. The door opened and Clara Freemont stepped into the office. She was holding a thick legal-size manila envelope in her hand and twisting the corners of it with her pudgy fingers. She'd been crying, and the tears traced a path of black mascara down her bloated cheeks.

"Nice to see you again, Clara." Charlie pointed to the envelope. "I wonder what that can be? Can't be your W-two forms, you don't have a social-security card. Hmm . . . I know! I bet it's twenty thousand dollars in hush money, right? Tell me, Clara. It's out of the bag now," Charlie said, folding his arms and leaning against the wall. "What's Halbrook paying you for?"

"Clara . . ." Beardsly said in a warning voice.

She waved him off with her hand. Blubbering, she said to Charlie, "Why the hell don't you ask *him*!"

Chapter 24

Tuesday, 12:35 P.M.

Rabbi Markowitz, with his black knee-length coat draped over his arm, watched the white Porsche pull up to the garage of the duplex and stop. He walked over to the car and circled around it, touching the shiny white lacquer finish. "You win this on the 'Wheel of Fortune,' Mr. Halleran? I mean, how else would you be able to pay for such a nice clean Nazi machine when you haven't paid your rent yet?"

"Gee, I could swear I left a check with Mrs. Markowitz. I forgot? I tell you, with all the business deals that I'm trying to put together, it's a wonder how I remember to dress myself in the morning," Charlie said, getting out and slamming the car door.

"I can understand that, Mr. Halleran," the rabbi said, looking at the way Terry's clothes hung on Charlie like a half-empty sack of potatoes. "I'm sure you're a very busy man with all your big-shot deals, so I won't keep you any longer. Where's my money?" He held his hand out, palm side up.

Charlie patted his pockets in the front and back. "Gosh darn it! I must have left my checkbook in the other car. I'll bring it by tonight."

"Uh-huh," the rabbi said, nodding. "You're some peach, Charlie. You're never on time with the rent, you try to kill yourself in my garage, and you eye my wife with enough lust to make even that *nafkeh* Delilah blush. And yet I like you," he said, shaking his head and shrugging. "I was born in this country and I still must have the ghetto mentality of a Lodz native. Go figure it out." He sighed, walking back to his house. As he opened the screen door he said, holding one finger in the air without turning around, "The rent, Charlie, tonight!"

"Absolutely, rabbi." Charlie went inside his own apartment, wondering how Markowitz knew he lusted after his wife. Was he that flagrant about it? He had always thought that frail little man in the black coat and baggy pants was oblivious to everything except the Torah. The rabbi saw more than he let on and had never, until today, said anything. Charlie thought of the rabbi's words to him as he opened his door. Go figure it out.

He grabbed a beer from the fridge and thought about how to get to Simon Halbrook. It wasn't going to be easy. As a reporter, Charlie knew that the bigger they were, the more insulated they became. He could ask Rena to clear a path for him, but then he'd be opening up a whole new can of worms. Simon was her father and he didn't think she'd take too kindly to the questions he'd be asking him. No, it was best not to involve her. From here on, it was going to get sticky and he wondered how their new relationship would hold up under it. Not too well, he imagined. Simon had broken the law and compromised two of his companies for the sake of fat Clara. Why? It was becoming a murky river, and if he dug any deeper, who knows what rattling skeletons would float to the top? He could always forget it, let the police handle it. Sure, he thought, and he could always stop being a reporter and buy into a McDonald's franchise. He'd have to go ahead with it, there was no other way.

He felt tired and lay down on the couch, propping his feet up on the armrest and putting the cold beer can to his forehead. It felt good, soothing. He closed his eyes. Thoughts and images floated through the horizonless landscape of his mind: Simon . . . Clara . . . Rena . . . Alice—all woven together in the brilliant abstract colors of a Miró canvas. Stacks of bills, twenty thousand dollars' worth every six months, grew in his head like computer graphics. That's forty thousand a year. Let's see, in fifteen years that's—Charlie had to think on this one—that's six hundred thousand big ones! With no end in sight! Simon, Charlie heard, was like unporous granite when it came to giving away money. Whatever Clara had on him had to be big. Without opening his eyes, Charlie reached across the coffee table and took the phone off the hook. He'd figured out how to get to Simon and he wanted to be well rested before he crossed swords with the big man.

Rena tried Cathy one more time before leaving for the station. Still no one picked up, nor was the answering machine on. She was worried. If she didn't hear from Cathy by early evening she was going to call the authorities in Carmel. She tried phoning Charlie but all she got was a busy signal. Damn! she thought. Just when I needed him.

There was a knock on the door. Rena looked out and saw her father's men waiting to take her to work. Charlie, where the hell are you? she thought as she opened the door.

Charlie woke up three hours later with a bad taste of stale beer in his mouth. Almost four o'clock. He was angry at himself for sleeping that long. He quickly got up, brushed his teeth, showered, and shaved. As he slipped on a pair of underpants the phone rang. He picked it up hoping it was Rena. It wasn't.

"Where the fuck you been, Charlie? I've been trying to call you all afternoon."

"Genero, I didn't expect to hear from you so soon." He sensed a controlled excitement in Genero's voice.

"Well, we dug up the body."

"That fast. What happened to all the red tape that New York is famous for?"

"You want to know what we found or you just want to fuck around?"

"You really found something?" He was beginning to feel anxious.

"Other than bones? Yeah, we did."

"Whose bones are they, Genero? Can you tell?"

"A young girl, Caucasian, with red hair. *That* we always knew. That's not the problem. We took the remains back to our lab to do some tests on the bone marrow. We found traces of a drug called Liathane in it."

"Go on."

"It's a drug used by doctors during code-blue situations in hospitals for heart attacks."

"And?"

"What it does is open up the arteries for a while, giving the medical team time to operate. Except if there is no blockage, it does the opposite. It closes the arteries in a healthy person, causing cardiac arrest and instant death."

"Go on."

"This is where it gets tricky. Liathane had been approved by the FDA and available for medical use for only twelve years. Alice Mendoza had it in her body for eighteen years. At first I thought, Hey, this is crazy. Did someone switch bodies on us?"

"Did they?" Charlie's stomach was flipping around inside him.

"No. The lab says the girl had been dead for eighteen years." Genero sighed nervously. "The next step was to check into the drug itself. It may have been approved twelve years ago, but it was developed seven years earlier than that. The lab that developed it had to put it through an experimental stage before the FDA would okay it."

"Who's the lab?" Charlie asked. He already knew the answer.

Again Genero sighed nervously. "The original pharmaceutical company that made the drug was called Beta Labs. But they were in financial trouble and bought up by Morgan Labs."

"How long ago was that?"

"Guess."

"Eighteen years."

"Close. That drug was highly secretive then, and was stored in a six-inch steel safe in the laboratory. Whoever gave Liathane to Alice had to have been high up on the company's totem pole to know the combination of the safe and to slip it out of the building without being checked." After a slight pause, Genero said, "I'm not quite sure what to do with all of this, Charlie."

Charlie let out a deep breath as he thought of Rena and uttered, "Oh, shit, just when it was getting good between us, too."

Chapter 25

Tuesday, 6:30 P.M.

The Santa Ana Freeway was clogged with trucks and cars resembling an unending, multicolored snake winding its way through a rust-tinted fog. At this hour nothing moved faster than a flower closing its petals in the descending sun. Horns honked and riders swore, punching their steering wheels and fantasizing beating up their children, wives, and bosses, but it didn't help; their world was on hold for the next hour.

Charlie dug his nails deep into the leather steering wheel of the Porsche, inching his way to Garden Grove. He had hoped to get to the stadium before the game and confront Simon, but it seemed unlikely now.

The stadium was the one place where Charlie knew Simon would be. He was no different than the Steinbrenners or Turners of this world: men who amassed a fortune but didn't feel complete until the child in them got what it wanted—a sports franchise. Two years ago, when Simon had purchased the California Blues, a floundering baseball team from Texas, he relocated the team midway between Orange County and Los Angeles. The problem with the Blues, other than finishing in last place for the past eight years, was that neither county really needed another baseball team; L.A. had the Dodgers and Anaheim the Angels. Simon believed otherwise. Always the visionary, he bought up hundreds of acres of land in the South Bay and northern part of Orange County and erected pricey tract communities and strip centers. A year later the aerospace and computer industries chose Simon's land to build their factories on. They saw it as *the* California dream, with its white beaches and golden orange groves.

Thousands of professionals, with their high salaries and expensive tastes, poured into the region, causing the land to skyrocket in value and adding millions more to Simon's coffers. The only thing missing, however, according to Simon, was a baseball franchise bordering both counties. He believed the population now living in that area, totaling in the millions, could absorb it. It was one of the few times in his life when he misread human nature. To his consternation, he discovered that wives, houses, and jobs may change hands in a lifetime, but team loyalty doesn't; especially when their alternative is a club with a losing record. The stadium he built for the Blues, Halbrook Arena, at the cost to the taxpayers of 120 million dollars, was working its way out of the red, not because of the team, but because of the rock concerts and weekly swap meets held there. It was Simon's one failure. He tried everything to make the team a success, even firing the manager and taking over the position himself until the baseball commissioner put a stop to it. Sportswriters dubbed it "Simon's Folly." His financial advisers suggested he sell the team, even at a loss. He refused, stubbornly holding on to it like a child who clings to a model airplane with a broken wing. It was a cold world out there and the Blues were his *Rosebud*.

An hour later Charlie turned off the freeway and parked outside the arena. With all the spaces available, he figured there couldn't be more than ten thousand people in the stadium tonight, even though the team was playing the first-place Cardinals.

He flashed his press card at the gate and the guard let him pass. The National Anthem was just winding down as he went through the turnstile. He took the elevator up to the press box on the third tier, borrowed binoculars from one of the reporters, and scanned the arena, looking for Simon's personal seats. He thought perhaps they'd be located between first and home but he was wrong. He brought the binoculars up to the third deck and checked the glass-covered box seats next to the radio booths.

Charlie saw him. He was in his private box with several well-dressed people, eating dinner. Probably friends or business associates.

Charlie made his way over to the other side of the stadium. He heard the sparse crowd roar in disbelief as Tony Peña hit a two-run homer into the center-field bleachers. Simon's going to be in a great mood after that, Charlie thought.

Standing next to the glass-covered booth, he could see Simon clearly. Tables were set up next to him and his friends, and they were eating fried chicken and potato salad. A full bar was in the corner and most of his guests were taking full advantage of it. A middle-aged woman in a peach suit, with blond hair pulled straight back like Maureen Dean, was pouring a Glenlivet on the rocks.

He was deciding if he should just walk into the booth and say, "Hey, Mr. Halbrook, can you spare a few minutes of your time?" when Simon looked over to the side and saw him. There was a mild look of surprise on his face and nothing more. Simon tossed the chicken leg he was about to eat back onto the plate, excused himself, and walked out of the booth.

"Obviously you need to talk with me, Mr. Halleran," he said pleasantly. As if reading Charlie's mind, he then said, "Yes, I know who you are. I even know you spent the night with my daughter." He brushed his thick white mane away from his forehead, took Charlie by the shoulder, and pointed to a door marked PRIVATE. A security cop stood by the entrance. "I have an office inside. Why don't we go in there?" Charlie nodded. As they entered, the officer touched the brim of his hat, acknowledging Simon. Walking down the cement corridor, Simon put his hand on Charlie's back and said sincerely, "I want to tell you that I appreciate what you've done for my daughter. Terrible thing what's been going on, isn't it?"

Charlie tried to control the anger that was welling up inside him. This man, so believable and charming now, was the same one who paid Cameron to sweep Fifth Avenue clean with his face. It was more than that; he was also the man who had administered the deadly drug Liathane to Alice. He was the only person in Morgan Labs powerful enough to take the experimental drug from the vault and leave the security plant without being searched. Charlie pushed down the anger; it would only worsen the situation. Time was running out and he needed to know what connection Simon had with the Mendozas and why he killed Alice.

They turned left into an oak-paneled room with a couch and coffee table. Simon went to the door at the end, took out a key, and entered. It was a conference room with a fifteen-foot marble desk surrounded by oak chairs. Charlie wondered how many free agents sat here negotiating their contracts with Simon. He also wondered how many actually got what they wanted. Very few, he thought.

Then Charlie saw it and froze.

The answer to Simon's connection with Alice was staring down on him. Up on the wall, overlooking the head of the conference table, was an early portrait of Simon. He was wearing a gray flannel double-breasted suit, looking proud, dedicated, faithful. He couldn't have been more than twenty-five when the painting was done. He must have been prematurely gray, because even then you could see patches of white in his hair. But it wasn't the white patches that Charlie saw; it was the rest of his hair. Simon Halbrook had been a redhead, the same as Alice!

He turned his face away from the canvas and looked at Simon. There was nothing charming about his face now; there was only hard anger in it. Simon had just realized he had made two mistakes in his life: the first was when he bought the Blues, and the second was when he let Charlie into this room. The painting had been there for so many years that he had forgotten about it.

Charlie didn't say anything at first; he just sat down, staring back into Simon's cold black eyes.

Charlie knew he was on Simon's turf and in dangerous territory, but he had to say it, he had come too far: "Alice Mendoza was your daughter, wasn't she, Mr. Halbrook?"

The harshness in Simon's face softened after a moment. He leaned back in his chair and took out his pipe, banged the bowl on his hand to get out the charred bits of tobacco, refilled it from his pouch, then lit it. Charlie waited. "Yes," Simon said, nodding. "She *was* my daughter. I had a few illicit encounters with the girl's mother many years ago and she got pregnant. What about it? Do you really think the public would be interested in this? Popes and kings had illegitimate children—it means nothing . . . especially in today's market." He puffed slowly on his pipe.

In today's market! We're not talking about commodities and margins, we're talking about a small child . . . a human being, Charlie wanted to scream at him. But he didn't. Instead he said calmly, "No, there's no story in that, Mr. Halbrook, nor was I looking for one there. Of course if it means nothing like you say, then why have you paid Clara all that money, plus the house? You don't seem to be the type that gets sentimental over a few, as you said, illicit encounters. No, what really interests me is the drug Liathane."

Simon kept puffing on the pipe, not missing a beat, but the tomcat look was back again. "What about it?" he said.

"I'll give it to you straight. Alice's body . . . your *daughter*," he said disdainfully, "was exhumed back in New York this morning. The authorities found Liathane in the remains. It was Morgan Labs who made the drug and it was you who had access to it at the time." He felt edgy and stood up, wishing for a drink. "The world thinks, including Mendoza, that he was the one who killed Alice. Well, they're wrong and *he's* wrong! She was already dead when he went crazy that morning and tore her to pieces. With the amount of Liathane found in her bone marrow, her heart had to have stopped the second it was given to her. It was probably administered by injection. I think it's a good bet that it was you who gave it to her."

The light in Simon's eyes blew out like a snuffed candle. He took the pipe out of his mouth and rubbed his forehead. He looked old and tired. "What is it you want?" he said finally. "Is it money? A job? Those things can be arranged. If you write about this, it would kill Rena, you know that, don't you?"

Charlie nodded. Yes, he had thought about it . . . he had thought about it a lot. "Why did you kill her?"

Simon knocked the residue from the pipe into an onyx ashtray on the table. "You have to understand, Charles, that I loved and adored my wife more than anything in this world. She was perfection—like a Matisse or a Monet. Except . . . except our love life . . ." His voice faded. He took a few deep breaths, trying to compose himself, then continued. "Let's just say there wasn't any, all right? Especially after Rena was born. Oh, I'd have a fling here and there—mostly when I was out of town on business. They didn't amount to a hill of beans." He let out a long sigh and said, "Then I met Clara."

"Where?"

He sneered. "On a street corner, not far from my office. I had never used a prostitute before. I suppose I thought it would be a new form of eroticism—something I hadn't known too much of in my life. She was more than I'd ever hoped for. I had never met a woman like that—so free and eager. We met twice a month in different hotel rooms for a year."

"Did she know who you were?"

"No. Not until the last time we were together. She saw my picture on the cover of *Time*. She was in a rage. She said the only reason she charged me so little each time we were together was because she thought I was just a poor slob. There was no question in my mind that she would have blackmailed me if she knew who I was. I gave her ten thousand dollars in cash to calm her down. That was a lot of money to her sort. I left the hotel and never called her again. It was over."

"But she *did* blackmail you."

"Yes. Years later, after I moved my family to Los Angeles. I was at a convention in Las Vegas, where she was working as a prostitute. She saw me outside the Sahara getting into my limousine and approached me. She said that she needed to talk with me. She told me that she had my child—a girl. I got angry and told that whore to try her con games on someone else. She showed me a picture of her. I ripped it up and tossed it into the gutter. Then she told me about her husband and the things he was doing with the girl."

"What made you give in?"

"At that time the chairmanship of Morgan Industries was about to pass to me. Anytime there's a change in management, shares in the company become very volatile. A scandal at that time would have destroyed the firm."

"I don't understand," Charlie said, frustrated. "If you were paying Clara off, then why kill Alice?"

"Because one day this girl would grow up and do more than just question who her father was, she would also want to meet him and then I'd have to pay her off, too. I have only *one* daughter and I was not about to hurt her because of a few illicit meetings many years ago."

Charlie wanted to buy it. It would make great copy, but he couldn't. It made sense what Simon had told him, but when the parts were put together, the picture was too rough and hazy. The little he knew of Simon said that he would never stand still for blackmail, especially from a simple person like Clara. Why not kill her? With his power he could have had it done a thousand different ways without implicating himself. There had to be another reason he was paying that kind of money. Also, many men can murder, some not think twice about it—but infanticide, that takes a special breed. And after meeting Simon, Charlie didn't think he was that kind. In fact, he had this intrinsic feeling that Simon had been bullshitting him all night.

And Charlie was just about to tell him that when he heard the door open. Before he could turn around, he felt a sharp pain in the soft part of his shoulders next to the neck and heard a thump as his knees hit the Berber carpet. He tried turning around but the person in back of him pressed down again. Charlie let out a scream and wanted to stand up, but his legs wouldn't move. His head was being expertly shoved toward the floor. He managed to bring his hands up onto his shoulders and felt the stubble of hair and knuckles of the other man before those thick, strong fingers exerted more pressure, causing him to cry out.

"I'll make a deal with you, Halleran," the voice behind him said. "Stay right where you are and I won't hurt you. Move and you'll feel pain like only the victims of the Inquisition would understand. Deal?"

"Deal," Charlie said, tasting the carpet in his mouth.

The man released his grip on Charlie's shoulders. Charlie decided he'd wait a few seconds before trying anything, hoping to catch the man off guard. He saw Simon's foot, then his body, as he bent down on one knee next to him.

"What am I going to do with you, Mr. Halleran? I don't think I want to go to jail for the rest of my life because an overanxious loser wants to make a name for himself."

Charlie's neck was beginning to hurt in this position. "I don't believe you killed your daughter, Mr. Halbrook, if that's any consolation."

"I'm afraid it isn't."

"Are you Cameron?" Charlie said to the guy in back of him.

"What of it?"

"You dropped something on the roof of Mendoza's apartment building. It's in my left pocket."

"Stay where you are," Cameron ordered Charlie as he put his hand in his pocket and brought out the Marine bracelet. "Not mine," he said arrogantly. "I was in navy intelligence."

Charlie figured the time was now. He pushed up on his knees and turned around, hoping to throw a left hook. Cameron was ready for it and bobbed his head, causing Charlie to miss by a couple of inches. Charlie saw the blond hair and the gray flecks in Cameron's eyes and wished he had connected, because a second later he was screaming in agony as the ex-naval officer pushed his fingers up into his thyroid gland.

Chapter 26

Tuesday, 8:40 P.M.

There still was no answer at Terry's after the third try.

Rena then called the Carmel police and asked if they would send someone over to his house in the Highlands. They called back thirty minutes later and said they had knocked and rang the bell for five minutes but no one answered, and the house was dark except for a porch light. They talked to the next-door neighbor and were told that Terry mentioned to him that he was going to take Cathy to San Francisco for a couple of days. The officer didn't seem concerned and suggested that Rena talk to her ex-husband about letting her know whenever he intended to go away with Cathy. Relieved, Rena thanked him and hung up.

Earlier that afternoon Stacey had asked if she could spend the night at Rena's house; Ben was still out of town and she was a bit lonely. Rena agreed; she could use the company herself. Besides, she hadn't heard from Charlie since this morning and she wasn't about to walk on eggshells waiting for him to call. She still had an hour before Stacey was coming, which meant she could do some work on her neglected book. She brewed a cup of decaf, took it with her into the study, and brought out the manuscript from her desk. Before turning on her word processor, she glanced out the window to see if the now familiar yellow van was out there. It was. She leaned back in her chair sipping the coffee, enjoying its soothing warmth. She knew this feeling she was experiencing was only a facade, like those two-dimensional towns in westerns, but for the first time in over two weeks she felt safe.

* * *

Charlie regained consciousness and found himself sprawled on the Berber carpet in Simon's office. A blindfold covered his eyes and his hands were cuffed to something metal, probably the leg of the conference table. The pain in his throat where Cameron had applied pressure was easing a little, but it still ached when he swallowed and he wished he had some water to drink.

Just before he blacked out, he had felt someone taping cotton wads over his eyes, then a door opening and a woman with a West Indies accent saying something in an angry tone.

He tried twisting around on his stomach, hoping to slip the cuffs under the leg, but the table was too heavy, causing the metal edges of the cuffs to bite into his wrists. He turned over again and waited. Waited for what? What were Simon and Cameron planning to do with him? Could they afford to let him walk around free knowing what he knew? A few minutes later he heard the door open, footsteps coming toward him, then the touch of a bony hand on his brow.

"You Charlie Halleran, ain't you?" The voice belonged to the old woman he had heard before he blacked out, the one with the West Indies accent.

Anna! Charlie waited until his heartbeat slowed before answering. "Yes. And you're Anna, right?"

"That's right. Ol' Rena been saying some nasty things about me?" She pulled the tape away from his eyes.

"Only good things," he said, grateful that he could see. He looked up into her wrinkled face. "You think you might know where the key is to these cuffs?"

"Maybe, but that don't mean I'm going to use it." She took a set of small keys out of her apron pocket and held them in her gnarled hand.

"I'd sure be grateful."

"I work for Mr. Halbrook, and I know *he* wouldn't be grateful. Why'd that blond-haired devil do this to you?"

"Who?"

"Cameron."

"He *also* works for Mr. Halbrook." Talking was making his throat hurt again. "Do you think I could have some water?"

She hobbled into the bathroom, came back with a glass, and held it up to his lips. There was a sadness in her eyes.

"Rena told me you see things," Charlie said.

"No, man, I *feel*, that's all. That's what I tell her."

"I bet you hear a lot, too, working for Halbrook."

Anna stared at him in amazement, then smiled and nodded. "Mostly I do that."

"Did you ever hear about a girl named Alice?"

"You let that one be, you hear!" she barked at him, her face close to his.

"The New York police suspect Simon might know something about her death. What do you think? Are they right?" Charlie was gambling now. If he was wrong and Simon had killed her, then Anna would never let him go.

She got up slowly and placed the glass on the table. "They're wrong," she said finally.

"Who did then, Anna?"

She squeezed her arthritic, twisted hands together and said in an unstable voice, "Mr. Halbrook is a proud man . . . a good one. He would never kill a poor little girl. He just had to protect the one he loved, that's all."

"Had to protect? Had to protect who?"

"What difference does it make now?"

"What does that—" Suddenly he understood what she meant. "My God! It was Elaina Halbrook who killed her." Anna didn't say anything and Charlie knew he was right. It was for her that he was paying the blackmail money and not for himself. "Why, Anna?"

"Does it matter? It happened so long ago. She's dead . . . the girl's dead—why can't you let it be!"

"It isn't me that won't let it be—it's someone else. And that someone else is killing people and is after Rena. Whatever you know might help to prevent it."

"And what about Mr. Halbrook?"

"I don't know how much can be kept quiet, Anna. It's like a flood. I don't know if there are enough sandbags to keep it back. It's Rena I'm concerned about. She's innocent in all this."

Anna sighed, then bent over him to undo the cuffs. Charlie didn't say thanks or anything. He just rubbed the red marks on his wrists and waited.

"Mr. Halbrook was seeing this other woman. You know that?"

"Yes. Clara Freemont or Mendoza. I don't know which name she used then."

"Elaina Halbrook was a good woman, but a religious one, and sometimes things go wrong with that. Instead of just giving her soul to the Lord, she also give her body . . . and that leave Simon with nothing. The problem with people who give nothing is that they demand even more back from the other person. And she was no different. She was jealous of everyone, especially women . . . even of Rena. When she found out that Simon had sex with a woman and had a child by her, the craziness inside her make her do an awful thing."

"How did she find out?"

"When Mr. Halbrook went out of town for business and not take her, she was always hiring a private detective to watch him so she could catch him doing something. He never knew about it until later. When Mr. Halbrook saw that woman in Las Vegas, the detective followed her back to a motel and found out her name. He listened in on Mr. Halbrook's calls when she phoned him, trying to get money, and discovered that she had his child. He then went and told Mrs. Halbrook about it and told her that the little girl was living somewhere in New York. She asked the detective to find out the address. He called back a few days later with it. She went out and came back later that night with a small black case."

The Liathane, Charlie thought. She had gone to Morgan Labs that night and taken the experimental drug. She probably knew the combination of the safe—after all, it was originally her father's company. And what guard would have the nerve to stop the chairman of the board's wife at the gate?

"She took a plane to New York that very morning," Anna continued. "When she returned the next day, she got all crazy and started breaking up everything in the house. Mr. Halbrook was out. She went into his study and called the woman in Las Vegas. I was in the living room and heard everything. She told her that her . . ." She stopped.

"Told her what, Anna?"

"She told her that her daughter—her bastard child—was dead, that she had killed her Alice. Then she hung up."

Charlie was astonished. "A woman with her breeding went into the South Bronx alone?"

"You never met anyone like Elaina Halbrook. The world revolved around her. When she want something she went and got it, never thinking about what might happen to her."

Yes, he had met someone with the same spunk. Rena. "What happened then, Anna?"

"Mr. Halbrook returned and asked why she didn't come home last night, she tell him what she did. They started to fight something awful. It was the same night Rena came home for the summer holidays. I went and got her at the airport. There was a terrible storm that night and her plane was delayed. Thank God for that. If she had gotten there on time she would have heard everything. Mrs. Halbrook was out of her mind and she didn't care who was listening. Lord, I could still see the poor child's face when she first walked in the house and saw what it looked like." Anna shook her head. "I worked for rich people all my life but I never could understand them. The day after she killed the girl, Mrs. Halbrook gave a party for charity at some fancy hotel. It's like nothing ever happened."

Charlie felt sick. The vision of his own daughter came back again. Jaimie's bloody body loomed in his head clearer than it ever had. A clammy sweat hung on his brow and his hands shook. "Is that all?" he said weakly.

"That's all. Instead of going to the police, that terrible woman, the girl's mother, came to Los Angeles, and she told Simon that she knew his wife had killed her daughter . . . *their* daughter. He's been paying her ever since to keep her quiet."

"She comes here every six months for her money. Where does she stay?"

"At the Beverly Hills Hotel. She says she likes the swans floating in the pond there," Anna said mockingly.

Charlie wondered if Clara was still at the hotel. "Where's Cameron?"

"In the outer office," Anna said scornfully. "He won't bother you none. He asked me to make him a cup of coffee, which I did. I also put in something else he didn't ask for."

"What?"

"A special sedative of my island. We use it to put goats to sleep before we chop off their heads. It think it works very good on Mr. Cameron."

Charlie felt his pockets. His wallet and the keys to the Porsche were gone. "Is there a car that I could borrow?" He thought about his own, impounded by the police, and about the Porsche in the parking lot of the stadium. He wondered if James had gotten his tan while waiting for him to return it.

Anna took him down the stadium's private elevator and gave him the keys to Simon's Mercedes 500 SEL. His luck in cars was getting better by the hour.

As he drove through the gate Charlie heard ten thousand fans groan in the stadium. The Blues are eating it again, he thought.

He took the Santa Monica Freeway back to L.A., got off at Robinson, and headed for Beverly Hills, stopping only for a quick hot dog at Pinks.

Today was Tuesday; Thursday would be the twenty-eighth, the day when Alice had been killed. He had one day left to find this crazy. He thought about Clara: what kind of woman would try to collect money off her dead child? Yet she claims to be a good Catholic now . . . goes to church. Elaina was a good Catholic, too, he remembered.

He turned off Beverly Drive and up the winding hill to the hotel. Be there, Charlie said to himself as he handed the keys to the valet and went up the steps.

Charlie saw her in the lounge sitting alone, sipping a Stinger. Her huge ass hung over the bar stool like ice cream slithering down a cone on a hot day.

"Hey, Clara, is that you?" he said as he sat down next to her. She turned and looked at him through red, droopy eyes. She'd been drinking for some time; the sweet smell of creme de menthe emanated from her pores. "I'll tell you—you talk about coincidences . . . in a city of millions, we bump into each other twice in one day. What do you think the odds are of that happening, huh?"

"What the fuck you want?" she slurred.

The bartender looked at him, and Charlie ordered a club soda—the first one in his life. She was a hostile drunk and he would have to handle her with a stamp marked "fragile." "You think we could go to your room and talk?"

"I don't allow men to come to my room anymore. I'm a fucking respectable woman."

"Right. I could tell. And the reason you're respectable is because good old Simon is footing the bill. Now, all that's about to blow up in your face unless you answer a few of my questions. You see, once it becomes public that Elaina Halbrook killed your daughter, there'll be no reason for Simon to pay the forty big ones each year." Those red eyes opened wide and Charlie believed he'd gotten to her. "Where's your room, kiddo?"

But then she smiled. "You don't know shit, *kiddo*. I'm too smart for all of you. You want to talk, we'll talk. Follow me." She swayed as she got off the stool. She signed her bill and held on to Charlie's arm to keep from falling. The bartender gave him a look that said, You can do better than that. Charlie shrugged back at him.

She opened the door to a suite overlooking a courtyard of palm trees and California shrubbery. Charlie whistled and said, "Simon did okay by you, huh?"

"He should . . . knocking me up like that." She dropped her purse on the couch, kicked off her high heels, and sat down on the sofa. "Want a drink? His fuckin' majesty is paying for it." She opened the cabinet over the wet bar.

Charlie grabbed her hand. She was drunk enough. "Drink later. We'll just talk for now."

"What do you want?" She leaned back in the couch, her knees several inches apart because of those huge thighs.

"How about the truth? What were you doing in Beardsly's office this morning? I can't believe we just happened to meet on your semi-annual blackmail junket to L.A."

"Maybe Jesus wanted us to meet," she said, grinning.

Her red lipstick was bleeding onto her teeth and Charlie had to look away. "Don't shit with me, Clara, or I'll blow your scam," he said. Her smile didn't fade, and Charlie wondered if she was more on top of it than he gave her credit for. "Were you hitting him up for more money?"

"Nope," she said coyly.

"No shit, Clara, remember? That was a pretty thick envelope you were holding. Lot of money in it, right? What was that all about?"

Her breath got short and she began to wheeze. "I need a drink," she said as she grabbed her purse and took out a cigarette.

"Fuck the drink. Answer me!"

She shook her head no.

Charlie walked over to the phone and picked it up; it was his last shot. "I hope you put your money in T Bills, darlin', because that's the last envelope you'll see from Simon. Oh, by the way, the deed to your house is illegal. I guess you'll be giving that up, too." *That* got to her. Into the phone he said, "Operator, the number of the *L.A. Times*, please."

At first she started whimpering, then the tears came. "Put the phone down. I'll tell you what you want to know, you bastard!" Charlie did. She took a tissue from her purse and wiped her eyes. When she calmed down, she said, "That fuckin' high and mighty Halbrook and his God-fearing, frigid wife! They thought they were such hot shit! I was just a nothing and I pulled the wool over his eyes for all these years." She snickered.

"How?"

"I really could use a drink."

"Forget it, Clara."

"Bastard," she muttered.

"How?"

"Twenty years ago, when I was livin' in Vegas, I called the cops in New York to find out about my daughter."

"I know. You told me that in Staten Island."

Ignoring him, she said, "Those shits lied to me. They said the building was condemned and that nobody was livin' there anymore. I had to find my daughter and I knew those cops weren't going to bust their asses tryin'. So I took a bus to New York and went to the building where we used to live. I saw Carlos leaving and I hid behind trash cans in the alley until he was out of sight. I went upstairs. The door wasn't even locked." Her voice started to tremble. "The kid was tied up in a closet. She didn't even know who I was. When I bent down to hold her, she bit me." Clara touched a slight scar on her neck. "God knows how long it had been since she'd seen another person other than that son of a bitch! I found some bottled water in the kitchen and cleaned her off as best I could. Jesus, did that place stink! Rats were running around all over the place. She was bitten from head to foot. I got her out of there quick before he came back. I was on another bus that night, back to Vegas, with her on it. I wanted to get as far away as possible from that crazy bastard."

Charlie sat down next to her and squeezed her hands tightly. "Are you telling me she's still alive?" he said, astonished.

Clara nodded.

"Then who was the girl they found in the apartment?"

"Who knows. Maybe some kid who happened to wander away when her mother turned her back. Maybe a runaway."

That made sense. Carlos must have gone crazy when he came back and found Alice missing. He most likely prowled the streets day after day looking for her. No, he thought, it had to be Jaffe who found her! It would have been easier for him; he was the one with the badge. He probably flashed it in front of some scared kid who looked like Alice and took her back to Mendoza's place. He could keep her there and no one would find out. He and Carlos were like partners. Carlos never implicated Jaffe at the trial, and even if he had, who would have believed him?

"Those first couple of years were terrible," Clara said. "She was undernourished, sick . . . had all these nightmares. I couldn't take her to a doctor because they'd take her away from me. I did everything myself. I had a son from this pimp I used to know. Little Billy Boy—that's what Alice called him. He was a few years younger than Alice and he'd help me take care of her. They were close . . . too close," she said bitterly. "She was a bright kid and it didn't take her long to bounce back. Except she wasn't like other girls her age. She was different." She sighed. Mucus oozed from her nose and she wiped it with a Kleenex. "She was angry . . . mean like. She would hurt other children. One time she tied a child up in a closet of a deserted house and he wasn't found for over ten hours. Parents told me to keep her away from their kids. Another time I gave her a puppy, a cocker spaniel it was, for Christmas. I found it a few months later in the garbage. Its throat was cut. She said that she had nothing to do with it, but I know it was her who done it." She cried again and wiped her nose. "I should have gone for help but I was too scared."

"Do you remember what time of the year she did these things?"

"Why?"

"Killing the dog and locking the child in the closet. Do you remember if it was summer or winter?"

"Summer, I think," Clara said, eyeing the liquor cabinet

again. "It had to be summer. I remember it being hotter than shit that day the kid was reported missing. Maybe one hundred and ten in the shade. Everybody in the neighborhood was outside searching for her."

"What about the dog?"

"The summer, too, I guess, but not in the same year. It happened around a year later. What does that have to do with anything?"

Maybe plenty, Charlie thought. He was thinking about what Rena had told him concerning post-traumatic stress syndrome: reliving past experiences on the anniversary. "Did she show any other signs of bizarre behavior over the years?"

"A few," Clara said, looking up at the ceiling as she thought about it. "Once I found her masturbating with a tire iron, screaming dirty words at the top of her lungs. Blood was dripping down her legs, but she didn't seem to care. Oh, yeah, another time . . ." Her voice trailed off as she started remembering. "Oh, Jesus I should have gotten her help! She stole dozens of rats from her high-school science class, starved them for days, then let them loose in her bedroom. When I walked into her room, she was lying on the floor, and the rats were taking bites from her body. The worst part was that she was just staring into space, like she was a million miles away. There was a smile on her face. Come to think of it, these things happened in the summer, too."

Probably on or near June 28, Charlie thought. Something began to bother him just as it had Rena: if anniversaries of personal traumas are important in this form of mental abnormality, then why is the death of another girl causing this kind of reaction in Alice? She wasn't the one that died.

"But that was the last time she did weird things," Clara continued. "She was pretty normal for the next couple of years."

Most likely her psychosis had progressed, and she did things, bigger things that she didn't want known. Charlie thought about calling the Las Vegas police to see what crimes, perhaps even murders, had been committed every year at the end of June. "Where is she now?"

"I don't know. She left home a few years ago and I ain't heard from her since."

"By herself?"

"No. She had one good friend other than her brother, William. This girl—I don't remember her name. She was leaving for Los Angeles because she was going to go to college there. Alice went with her."

"How do I find this girl?"

"I don't know."

"What's the name of the school?"

"Who knows? William was heartbroken when Alice left. Right after that, William joined the Marines. I was alone and I figured it was time to get out of Vegas. I couldn't stand those hot summers anymore, so I hit Simon up for a house. My thinkin' was he could afford it. I was the one that cleaned the shit off Alice—not him!"

"You said William and Alice were close. Where's he?"

She looked away from him. "I told you, in the Marines."

"No bullshit, Clara. I know he went AWOL a couple of years back. Look, I don't care about that. I just want to know where he is. I think he knows where Alice is hiding."

"Why does she have to be hiding?" Clara said defensively.

"Because we both know it was Alice who killed Jaffe, and she's going to do it again."

"Don't you say things like that!" she snapped, the fat on her neck jiggling.

"Come on, Clara, Alice is sick and angry. She murdered a detective who'd raped her eighteen years ago and now she's going after her half-sister. Why, I don't know yet. Maybe she's angry because Rena had everything and she didn't. After all, she was also Simon's daughter."

"I don't want her to go to jail," she wailed, holding her head in her hands.

"She's sick, Clara," Charlie said, pulling her hands away from her face. She took another tissue from her purse, wiped her puffy cheeks dry, then nodded. "When did Simon find out that she was alive?"

"Today . . . *after* I got the money from Beardsly. Hell, with Alice runnin' around, it was only a matter of time before he'd find out anyway. I was riding the gravy train as long as he thought Alice was dead and buried. But with another girl in the grave . . . well, he'd be free and clear. There was no proof that he was connected. So you don't have to threaten me, buddy," she said to Charlie. "I knew my well was about to run dry. But first I told Beardsley I needed the twenty thousand dollars a couple of months earlier, that I was having some financial problems. The old geezer didn't want to do it at first—said he had to talk to Simon about it—but I finally convinced him. I said that all the years I've been collecting, that this is the first time I ever asked for the money early." She tapped her temple with her finger. "These hotshots ain't always as bright as they think they are."

Oh, aren't they? Charlie thought. He suddenly had a small insight into the enigma of Simon Halbrook. Trying to get a handle on him was like trying to comprehend the endless layers of rocks and fossils that formed the Grand Canyon.

Clara may have thought she was blackmailing him, but to Simon, it was nothing more than restitution. He believed his wife had killed Clara's daughter and she deserved compensation; it was no different than an airline paying out money to the family of the victims after a fatal crash.

Perhaps there was even something stronger than restitution: A moral committment? Paternal feelings? Possibly. Alice *was* his daughter. Maybe the lost innocence of that Idaho country boy still breathed beneath Simon's tempered-steel heart.

Whatever the reason, Charlie believed it was Simon who really controlled the situation, and not Clara.

"What about the girl who drove down to L.A. with Alice? How do we find her, Clara?" Charlie asked.

Clara furrowed her brows, thinking. "Her name's in my address book back home. I guess I could call Jeeter."

"Who?"

"Jeeter is my next-door neighbor. He's a widower. He watches my house when I'm gone."

Charlie remembered: the old guy wearing shorts, black socks, and wing-tip shoes standing in the backyard next to her house. "You think it's too late?" he asked.

"Not for Jeeter," she said, dialing. "He's a night owl. Sometimes he and I stay up watching TV all night."

After a few rings Jeeter picked up. Charlie could tell by the conversation that they did more than just watch old movies together. When she hung up, she turned to Charlie and said, "He's got to go to my house and find it. It'll probably take a while. Can I get a drink now?"

"Yeah, you deserve it," Charlie said. He watched Clara open up the cabinet. What the hell . . . he needed one, too, after what he just heard. "While you're at it, grab the J&B. It's right next to the Beefeater's."

Stacey had just walked in the door carrying a yellow knapsack when the telephone rang. She was wearing jeans and a denim shirt. "Want me to get it?" she said to Rena, dropping the bag on the floor of the living room.

"It's okay," Rena said, picking up the phone in the kitchen.

"Is this Mrs. Halbrook?" a somber voice said.

"Yes."

"I'm Sergeant Wayne Loman with the Carmel Police Department. I spoke to you earlier."

"Right."

"We were called back to your husband's house in the Highlands."

"What for?" Rena asked, frightened.

"The neighbor who lives on the other side of your husband's house—not the first one we talked to—said there's been a smell coming from a dry well up the hill and it's been getting worse. I'm sorry to have to tell you this, Mrs. Halbrook, but we found your husband in that well. He's been murdered."

"My God!" she groaned. "Cathy! Where is she?"

"We don't know. We're searching the house and the grounds right now. So far we've turned up nothing."

"You've got to find her!" Rena screamed.

Stacey ran into the kitchen and put her hands on Rena's shoulders.

"The police departments of Monterey and Carmel are being mobilized," the sergeant said. "We've also notified San Francisco. Right now we need your help."

Rena clutched Stacey's hand, trying to regain control. "How?"

"Is there anyone you suspect who might have done this?"

"How was he murdered?" she said weakly.

She heard him suck in a deep breath, then he said, "It's not a pretty sight."

"How?"

"His throat was cut, and his mouth was sliced apart—"

"—Like a jack-o'-lantern," she interrupted.

"Yes, how did you know?"

She fought back the fear that was engulfing her and said, "Get in contact with the Los Angeles Police Department immediately. She's killed here, too!"

"She?"

"Yes, a she!"

Within seconds after she hung up, the phone rang again. Stacey made a move to get it but Rena picked it up first.

"Yes?"

Static.

"Oh, no," she moaned.

Then: "Please . . . get me . . . so dark . . . cold." It was Cathy's voice.

"Cathy!" she screamed. "Cathy! Where are you?"

A pause, whispering in the background, then: "The Mill House, Mommy. I'm supposed to tell you to come alone, Mommy, I'm so scared!" she screamed. Then the line went dead.

"That was Cathy!" Rena said to Stacey, half-crazed. "She has Cathy!"

Stacey grabbed her shoulders. "What did she say? Where is she?"

"The Mill House."

"What's that?"

"It's my family's summer home in the Malibu hills. How did she know about it? We haven't used it in years. She wants me to come alone. Oh, Christ! She's got Cathy!"

Stacey looked out the window. The two police officers were leaving the yellow van and coming toward the house. Cameron's men joined up with them.

"Cops are coming. They were listening." Stacey looked up at Rena. "What do you want to do?"

"She said alone." Rena grabbed her keys and went to the back door.

"I'm going with you," Stacey said.

"She said—"

"I know. I'll be lying down in the backseat. She won't know I'm there."

The police knocked on the door just as Rena and Stacey got

into the Jaguar. Rena pulled out quickly, hitting the plastic trash cans, and sped down the path into the street. As she turned the corner she saw the two thick-necked bodyguards racing for their car. She wasn't worried about them catching her; the Jag's twelve cylinders would easily lose them.

Fifteen minutes later Rena turned off Highway One and onto Malibu Canyon. The ride was agonizing; it felt like it was taking forever, and every time she came to a stoplight she'd hit the steering wheel in frustration. "It's only a few more miles. Maybe you'd better get down," she said to Stacey.

"Right," Stacey said, as she climbed over the seat and crouched down on the floor. She put her hand on Rena's arm and gave it a supportive squeeze.

Los Cabrillos was a winding, one-lane dirt road that was rarely used anymore. Rena drove carefully, avoiding the sagebrush and branches from the overhanging trees. After a while the foliage gave way to an open field, with the ocean three hundred feet down a jagged cliff to her left. Darkness was all around; there was no moon tonight, and the stars were nullified by a thick layer of fog. Mill House appeared to her right like a formless shadow even blacker than the night. There was a small flickering light coming from a window on the second floor.

It has to be a candle, the electricity was turned off years ago, Rena thought as she reached into the glove compartment for the flashlight. Her heart was pounding through her chest. Perhaps she had made a mistake by not telling the police. No, it was Cathy's life that was at stake. Maybe she could talk this sick girl into letting her go. That was the only chance she had.

"Do you want me to stay here or go in with you?" Stacey whispered, hidden from view in the back of the car.

"Stay here," Rena said, checking to see if the flashlight worked. "Give me a few minutes to see if I can get Cathy out. If I'm not out by then, or if you hear anything . . . get to the house down the hill and call the police."

Trying to control her trembling, she climbed the stone steps up to the front porch and tried the door. It was open. Inside was an endless black hole. "Cathy!" she screamed into the darkness. There was no answer, but she thought she could hear the floor creaking upstairs. She turned the flashlight on, pointed it into the house, and moved the beam across the room. The furniture in the living room was still covered with white sheets, as it had been for years, but she could sense that someone had been living here. Things seemed out of place; it was not as she remembered it as a child. She could also smell the aroma of cooked beef.

"Cathy, it's me!" she yelled again, aiming the light up the winding staircase. She heard footsteps descending the pine-plank stairs. Holding the light steady with both hands, she waited to see who it was. She saw the feet of a man entering the circle of light wearing old Levi's and work boots. Just as she was about to bring the beam up to see his face she heard a child scream, "Mommy, Mommy!"

It was coming from downstairs, in the basement. Rena turned the light toward the cellar door. "Cathy, I hear you! I'm coming!" She pulled at the doorknob but it was locked.

"Rena," a voice said, coming from behind her.

She turned around and saw the silhouette of a woman, her face obscured by the dark, standing by the door. Her head was haloed by the night fog.

Laughter.

Rena stepped back. She had heard that laugh before . . . from the girl on the phone. "What is it you want from me, Alice?" she said, bringing the flashlight up to her face.

Clara downed half her drink, mumbling, "Come on, Jeeter, it's just a fuckin' little book." Smacking her rubbery lips together after taking a long sip of her drink, she said to Charlie, "My biggest mistake was telling her who her real father was when she started pressing me. She was fifteen, and she was gettin' real curious why I was going to Los Angeles twice a year. I figured maybe it was time she knew. She wanted to call him. I told her if she did that, I'd break her neck! We were livin' too good for her to blow it. Then she started goin' to the library and collecting everything there was on him. Her walls in her room were filled with pictures of him and his daughter. What's her name?"

"Rena."

"Yeah, that's right. Rena. At first she'd talk to the pictures like it was her real family. Then that craziness would come out. She'd curse them and tell them how they betrayed her by leaving her. I remember one time when she brought home two pumpkins and carved out faces on them. One she named Simon and the other Rena. She stayed up all night talkin' to them. In the morning, when I went into her room to wake her up, I saw what she had done. She chopped them up and poured blood all over it from a dead cat she killed. I was sick to my stomach and beat the crap out of her."

Wait a minute! When did she find out that another girl was murdered in her place?" he said, standing up and going over to her.

Clara smiled. "She always knew about it. I made sure of that. Right from the time she was a little kid. That's the only way I could keep her in line. Every time she got testy I'd tell her how another little girl, innocent as all hell, died for her sins in that closet. That usually cut her down to size."

"You really should have taken her to see a doctor, Clara," Charlie said softly. He was not a psychologist but he now had an inkling of why Alice became psychotic over another person's tragic experience around June 28. Alice was never allowed to forget that another girl had died in her place, someone who was the same age and had her same features. The guilt that she carried over it must have been severe, especially since abused children, according to Rena, have weak egos. In Alice's fevered mind the two girls became one. She not only experienced flashbacks of her own abuse, but also visualized the abuse of the other girl—including her murder and dismemberment. That must have been a lot of anger for one little girl to carry within herself for all those years. It eventually had to come out. Clara, in trying to control a deeply disturbed child, unknowingly created a psychopath.

The phone rang and Clara picked it up. "Yeah?" she said. "Yeah, that's the book, Jeeter. Read me off the names in it, okay? I know there's a lot of them, just read them to me. No, that's not the girl . . . no . . . no . . . no." After several pages of *no*s, she said enthusiastically, "Yes, that's it. Thanks, Jeeter, you're a sweetie."

"What's the name?" Charlie said.

"No wonder I forgot. It's such a forgettable name."

"What is it?"

"Stacey Miller."

His eyes narrowed. "What does she look like, do you remember?"

"A real homely girl, heavy, with short legs. The opposite of Alice. She hung out at our house all the time after her parents died in a car crash. She didn't have any other family."

"Oh, Jesus," he groaned. "That's not the Stacey I know."

"The real reason I think she became friends with Alice was so she could get close to the boys. Alice was good at that. She was the prettiest thing you ever saw. Now, I remember!" she snapped. "Stacey was going to study psychology at a college here."

As he grabbed the phone to call Rena he was willing to lay odds that the real Stacey never made it to L.A., that she was lying in a shallow grave somewhere between Vegas and the City of Angels.

Chapter 27

Tuesday, 12:10 A.M.

A gravelly-voiced man answered the phone.

"Is this Rena Halbrook's house?" Charlie asked.

"Yes it is. Who's calling, sir?"

That "sir" again. He wondered which cop it was. "Charlie Halleran."

"One minute."

Muffled sounds, then another voice got on the line. "Hello, my name is Craig Sanders."

"The DA?"

"Yes. We're trying to find Rena. Maybe you can help us."

A warning sign shot up. "She's not there?"

"No." There was a pause before he answered and Charlie caught it.

"Maybe it's time we started trading information," Charlie said.

Craig agreed. When Charlie finally got off the phone, he was shaken. He was one day off; none of this was supposed to happen until Thursday. How did he figure wrong? Alice died on the 28th. Or did she? he thought.

"You okay? You ain't going to have a heart attack on me, are you?" Clara asked, walking over to him with her hand to her mouth.

"Do you remember the date when Elaina Halbrook called you?"

"The end of June sometime. Why?"

"She called you at night, right?"

"Yeah. That's what I told you before."

"Damn!" Charlie said as he punched the wall. Why hadn't he caught it before? Elaina called Clara at night and told her she had just killed Alice. Carlos Mendoza walked into the police station in the morning and said he had murdered her only a couple of hours before. It was the following morning! Alice had died on the 27th! He remembered that video tape he'd seen at Maramack Psychiatric Hospital and Carlos saying, *Nothin' to drink . . . no more money.* He must have been out all night on a drunk and come home the next morning and found her. The police and even Charlie believed she was killed that day. Since Mendoza had already confessed, there was no reason to do an autopsy. Death was—or so they thought— from trauma; besides, they believed she was just another dead Puerto Rican, and nobody really cared. The girl hadn't died on the 28th, she died on the 27th!

Sanders had said the Mill House. Where the hell was that? Charlie picked up the phone to call Anna. Maybe she knew.

After several rings, she answered.

"Anna . . . Charlie Halleran."

"She's already called here." There was a deep resignation in her voice.

"Who?" He already knew.

"Alice. He left right after the call. I saw him taking his gun."

"Did he say where?"

"No."

"Do you know a place called Mill House?"

"It's a house in Malibu the family used before Mrs. Halbrook died. Is that where he went?"

Charlie grabbed a pencil and ripped off the cover from the *What's Going On in L.A.* magazine to write on. "Give me the address."

"Take Malibu Canyon road and turn right on Los Cabrillos . . . maybe three or four miles up. It's the only house up there. It's on a cliff overlooking the ocean."

"Did you call the police?"

"Lord, no. Mr. Halbrook said not to. He said little Cathy's up there, too. Then he said it's time he faced it. That he's been running from it too long."

Charlie was tempted to call Sanders after he hung up on her, but he knew better than that. Cathy was being used as bait. Alice would kill her if the cops came. She'd have nothing to lose.

"Where's my daughter?" Clara said, grabbing Charlie's arm.

"You should have asked that question a long time ago," he said as he took her hand off of him. He took the Marine insignia bracelet from his pocket and tossed it on the table. "I think this belongs to your son." He left and raced down through the lobby and out the door. In the front he handed the valet ten bucks to get his car to him within thirty seconds.

As he sped down Sunset heading west at seventy miles an hour a thought occurred to him: if the real Stacey Miller had disappeared sometime other than the end of June of last year, then Alice now had to be out of control. That notion made him push the accelerator to the floor, and he prayed there weren't any speed traps with bored cops behind bushes. Hopefully he'd get there before Alice carved out another set of pumpkins.

"Stacey?" Rena said, shining the light on her face. What she saw in the doorway was hatred so total that it terrified her. As the woman slowly walked over to her the light picked up the madness in her eyes.

"You're here. I was getting worried," said the man's voice from the staircase.

Rena turned around, putting the light on his face. "Ben!" she said, astonished. He was leaning against the banister, smiling at her, with his thumbs hooked into the belt loops of his jeans. She quickly turned around again and looked at the girl she knew as Stacey, the flashlight picking up the huge emerald ring surrounded by diamonds on her finger. It fit the description of the ring that Terry had supposedly bought for Belinda. Rena suddenly felt sick and leaned against the wall. "My God," she whispered.

Charlie drove four miles past Los Cabrillos road before he realized he missed the turnoff. Cursing, he swung around, cracking the taillight on a eucalyptus tree jutting out into the road. He drove slowly until he found Los Cabrillos; the name on the sign was obscured by vegetation. Ten minutes later he came upon the clearing and saw Rena's car parked outside the house. He turned off the road and into the field about a hundred yards away and killed the engine.

There was a deadly quiet about the house and he prayed he wasn't too late. He visualized Jaimie's dead body suspended in his arms. He was too late to save her. Would it be the same way again? Not again! he prayed. Please God! Not again!

As he opened the trunk of the car and grabbed a hammer from the Mercedes tool bag for a weapon he heard another car speeding down the dirt road heading toward the house. Charlie crouched down next to the front fender. In the darkness he could make out the silhouette of a large sedan—probably Simon's limo—stopping abruptly in front of the house. A well-built man jumped out of the car. He took something out of the side pocket of his jacket and inched his way around the side of the house. Sound traveled fast in the night air and Charlie could hear the distinct click of an automatic being cocked. It was Cameron.

In the backseat of the limo, Charlie saw the figure of another man who was sitting and waiting. It had to be Simon.

Charlie thought, the family's finally being reunited.

Ben held Rena's chin between his two fingers and said, "Hey, for sisters, you two don't even look alike." He was holding a candle in the other hand.

Rena wanted to push him away but dared not. She couldn't take her eyes off of the angry, twisted face of the person she once knew as Stacey. Oh, Christ, not her! she thought. "I want to see Cathy," she said in a shaky voice.

"Why?" Alice said, cocking her head to the side.

"What do you mean why? She's my daughter."

"And she's *my* niece. I have visitation rights, too, you know."

"Your niece?" Rena said, shocked. Alice ran the back of her ring hand down the side of Rena's face and she could feel the sharp diamond breaking the skin.

"Look, Billy, she does resemble me. Around the nose and the eyes. I really am a Halbrook, you see."

Billy! His name's Ben! Rena's mind shrieked to herself. He was supposed to be out of town on a photographic assignment. Billy . . . William. My God, they're brother and sister—not lovers like they made me believe. Or were they that, too!

"Mommy!" Cathy cried hysterically from down in the basement.

Rena pushed Alice away and grabbed the door handle, tugging at it. "Open this door, goddamm it!" she screamed. Alice smacked her in the face with the back of the ring hand and she fell stunned to the floor.

"You touch me again and I'll kill you, you cunt!" Alice said as she bent over her.

William also crouched down. "Better listen to her. She's got a good track record when it comes to backing up her threats."

"Ben," Rena moaned, touching her face. Alice's ring had sliced open her cheek and it was bleeding.

"Call me Billy," he said, smiling at her.

Rena looked up. "What do you have to do with this?"

"Alice and I are like one person. We've always been like that," he said playfully, bouncing on his knees.

"Why are you doing this?" she said, turning to Alice.

"Ask your daddy." Alice sneered. "He's the bastard that brought me into this world. And you're the one who had everything while growing up, didn't you? A big house . . . summers in Europe . . . good schools. You know how I spent my formative years? In a fucking closet being ripped apart by two hairy animals. They took me any way they could—through the ass, the mouth—however they wanted. I was too small and scared to do anything about it . . . until now. Occasionally Carlos would throw me some canned food so I wouldn't starve to death. Then again, what would you know about cold Chef Boyardee? You were too busy breaking out the Wedgewood every night."

"She's a pesto pasta girl from way back. You can tell," William said, leaning his arm against Alice's shoulder and provocatively stroking her neck.

The candlelight cast deep flickering shadows on Alice's face, which reminded Rena of a Javanese death mask. Rena tried sitting up but Alice pushed her back down again. Terror was clouding up her thought processes and she tried to fight it. The main objective was to get to Cathy. Make her talk, she thought. Talking would help release the pent-up hatred within her, almost like lancing a boil. "Why do you think I'm your sister, Alice?"

"Because your daddy fucked my mommy, that's why. He's known about my existence for years—been paying my mom through the ass for that little secret . . . and more. Except the bastard took away who I was—Alice Halbrook! He even used his influence to have my birth certificate destroyed."

Rena remembered Brenda saying that she couldn't find a birth certificate at city hall or the hospital. Was this true? Was Simon her father?

"It'll all be over soon, sis."

Make her talk. "Why do you want to hurt us? What do you think I did to you? What did Cathy do to you? My God, she's only a child! We didn't even know you existed."

"Exactly! No one knew I existed." Alice put her face next to Rena's. "Not even my fucking family knew I existed! When the Halbrooks don't want to see something, they sweep it under the carpet and it becomes invisible. Whammo! You're now nonexistent!" she said, snapping her fingers. "But you wouldn't know anything about that. You've never had to live your life as an untouchable."

Make her talk! "Was it money? If it was, all you had to do was claim your right as my father's heir. There are blood tests."

"Fuck the money! It's not the money. At the beginning it was . . . but not anymore."

"The beginning?"

"That's right! You and that jerk Charlie . . . even the cops couldn't figure it out." Alice sat down next to Rena and crossed her legs as if she were confiding to her best friend. "You see, I'm real bright and verbal, but I never did well in school. I had few options, except maybe working in the casinos like the other girls I graduated high school with or becoming a whore like Mama. And I would rather commit suicide than do that. I didn't have many friends either, except one . . . fatso Stacey Miller." She laughed at the shock in Rena's face. "The real Stacey is buzzard meat as we say in the state of Nevada. I had no regrets about that one. She was a real pain, wasn't she, Billy?"

"Yes, sir, sis." The smile was still on his face as he stared down at Rena. He took another candle from his pocket and lit it, placing it on the floor.

"The thing the fat slob had was an acceptance letter from UCLA, twenty thousand in insurance money from her parents' death, and no one who knew her in California. It was too good to pass up," Alice said. "I moved down here six months ago, dyed my hair black, and became Stacey Miller. Then the luck started coming my way. I met Freddy in school. He was a TA in one of my classes. When he told me he worked for you, I couldn't believe it! I thought, this is more than luck—this is a miracle! Maybe someone really did hear my cries and prayers in that closet eighteen years ago. Whatever it was, it was just too good to pass up. Freddy and I became close . . . *real* close."

"Did you . . . ?"

"Did I what? Kill him? Sure. What choice did I have? You see, Freddy loved my ass. He'd do anything for me. In fact, he's the one who got me the interview with you, remember?"

Rena did remember. She remembered how Fred practically begged her to hire the girl.

"The poor guy was falling madder and madder in love with me. And you know the funny thing about it?" Alice said, slapping Rena's leg like a pal. "I got everything I needed from him without ever having to fuck him. What a jerk, huh? Except I felt real bad about that, considering all he did for me, so before I killed him I did a 'quickie' with him. Freddy might have been a brain but he wasn't exactly the world's greatest lover."

"Why?" Rena asked. Her mouth was parched from the terror.

"Shit! To think I outfoxed you, with all your education. I love it!" Alice clapped her hands together. "Don't you get it, dummy! Freddy was an electronics freak. Don't you remember all that crap he had in his room when we went there and found his body? He was able to intercept the telephone signals and hook in a tape of me doing me as a little girl while you were on the air. Listen!" She cupped her hands together as if she were praying, looked up to the ceiling, and said, "Help me . . . so cold . . . no more wally."

It was as if Rena were hearing Alice's voice on the phone again. "But why?"

"You and your fucking *why*s. To let you know that I was coming, that's why. To let you know what fear was. I know what it is. And I think sisters should share feelings, don't you? The most fun I had was when I made the phone calls to you at home. I was pretty convincing, huh? You'd call me right after and I'd be Stacey again, playing the concerned friend."

William laughed.

"Freddy thought I did the tape bit to play a joke on you. When he saw it was more than that, he got angry . . . pouted . . . said I used him. It was just a matter of time before he'd let you know what I did, or tell the authorities." She shrugged. "As I said before, what choice did I have? Actually that part was pretty simple. After we fucked, I made him a cup of his favorite herb tea spiked with fifty milligrams of Valium. By the time I got him into the bathtub he was almost gone. I shot him up with another fifty to make sure he stayed that way, then . . . *chung, chung.*" She made slitting motions near her wrist.

Rena could hear Cathy whimpering and moaning downstairs. "How did you get Jaffe in on this?"

"This was a coup, wasn't it?" Alice said, glowing. "I had targeted that scumbag even before I met Freddy. I knew his address and where he worked while I was still living in Vegas. My first plan was to lure him into a deserted spot, like the Sepulveda Basin, and cut his throat. I know, not too original, right? But when I found out that he was the cop you talked to when little Alice was calling you at home, it was too good to pass up. Remember, it was *me* who called the police after Freddy put my tape over the air. I requested Sergeant Jaffe since you had already talked to him that morning. That asshole was easy. I didn't even have to tighten the cord around his neck. You and Charlie took care of that by digging up his past. He was scared out of his mind. By the time I picked him up on Hollywood Boulevard, dressed like a teenage prostitute with a red wig, he was nothing but a soggy mess. He just lay back, exposing his little peepee, and all I had to do was *chung, chung.*" Again she made a hand movement as if she were holding a razor. "Now Terry baby, that's something else."

"What?" Rena said. She was beginning to feel sick.

"Terry. Your husband, idiot. Remember him?" Alice snarled.

"Yes. What about him?"

"That was some jerk."

"Terry?"

"That's the one, sweetie. Boy, you're really out to lunch today, aren't you? Wake up, huh!" She smacked Rena in the face. "Let me tell you how that one came about. I met Terry about two months ago at Spago. I guess you can call it a planned meet. Actually I followed him and his date to the restaurant on a Saturday night. I was dressed to the hilt . . . made sure I outshined all those Hollywood tit jobs there. I walked in and sat at the bar. Terry and his date, who looked about eighteen, were sitting at the other end waiting for a table. He had his arm around her shoulder, slobbering in her ear, doing a snow job on her to get her into bed. When he looked up and saw me, it was all over. He couldn't move his eyes away. He just sat there smiling and nodding, and I smiled and nodded back. When the girl went off to the bathroom, he came over to me and did his bullshit dance: said he was with the daughter of a client . . . had-to-show-her-the-town kind of shit. He asked me for my number. I said I understood and gave it to him. The creep called me the next morning wanting to know if I'd meet him for Sunday brunch at the Westwood Marquee. Jesus! Why the hell would anyone want to get together and eat ten pounds of food at ten o'clock in the morning on the first date. What a class act *he* was! We did a little bit of talking over bagels and lox and I told him I was working for you. Surprise! Surprise! We did the 'oh what a coincidence' routine, and by noon we were upstairs in a suite humping our brains out. Not a bad lay either, huh, sis?'' she said, winking at Rena. "Two weeks later he asked me to marry him. I hemmed and hawed, did the 'it's too soon' bit, that we should wait until we're sure. I said, 'Alas! Rena's my friend. How could I do this to her?' He ate it up! I had the guy eating out of my hand. He told me about his financial troubles, and that it wasn't right that you had all this money in trusts just sitting there and rotting away. Boy, did that guy have a hard-on for you! That's when I knew it was safe to tell him my real name. One weekend up in Carmel, before Cathy came, we concocted this idea. Are you ready for this, sis?'' She patted Rena's face, wiping the blood off on her blouse. "If you should happen to die, the trust, which would be in the area of twenty million dollars, would automatically go to Cathy. And Terry, being the father, would not only get custody of her, but he'd also get a healthy chunk of money each month for being the executor.''

"That wouldn't have been enough money for Terry. Besides, my father controls the trust,'' Rena said, sitting up. This time Alice didn't push her down.

"*Our* father, dearie. You're right. It certainly wouldn't have been enough money for that greedy bastard. But if good old Dad also happened to die . . . then we're talking immediate *muchos dolares.* Of course Simon would live, say for another eight or twelve months before he met with an accident. Wouldn't want anyone getting suspicious, would we?"

"I thought Terry was supposed to marry Belinda?"

"Miss Honeysuckle Rose? She's only an out-of-work actress who Terry hired to throw suspicion off our relationship. He even had Cathy go with him to buy a ring thinking it was for her. Actually it was for me." She held up her hand to show Rena the ring. "Pretty, isn't it? Emeralds and diamonds. Now I can really play the Encino bitch."

"I don't understand why you killed Terry," Rena said, inching her body up further. "If it went your way, you could have had millions."

"You don't hear right, do you? I told you it's not just the money. It's you, Daddy, and your little girl that I really wanted! Terry was in total agreement about you and Pops, but would never consent to Cathy. Besides, I didn't want that slobbering, pretentious jerk around me all the time."

"Try to listen when she talks to you," William said.

"Killing you guys off and marrying Terry is something out of an Alfred Hitchcock magazine. It would have taken the cops exactly three seconds to figure that one out. There was a better way that I could have my cake and eat it. Of course it meant giving up twenty million for one million, but when you're talking millions, who's counting?"

"And the apartment in New York," Rena said. "Who painted the closet?"

"My brainstorm," William said, raising his hand proudly. "Alice told me you were going back there, so I beat you to it. Too bad I couldn't see your face when you saw it." He giggled.

The sound of a car pulling up outside the house. William leaped up and ran to the window.

"Daddy?" Alice said.

"Yes." William flattened his body against the wall as he looked out. "There's something wrong!"

"What is it?" Alice said, rising to her knees.

"He's supposed to come alone, except he's sitting in the back of the stretch. Someone else drove. I don't see him."

Rena thought of Cameron and her heart soared with hope. It

was dark where William was standing, but she could still see him take out a gun from the back of his pants.

"He came with someone else!" he whispered nervously.

"That bastard! Find him," Alice hissed.

William jumped into the darkness and ran up the stairs. From outside, the sound of a car door closing, footsteps, the door handle turning. Alice stood up, waiting. The door opened and Simon entered, his huge frame blocking out the night sky. He had a Mark Cross flight bag slung over his shoulder. Rena got up and rushed over to him. He saw the blood and the cut on her cheek and his face turned red with anger. "Get in the car," he told her. He was in a rage. "I had no idea you were the one!" he growled at Alice, glaring.

"Surprise, huh? Sorry, Daddy, she stays here with us. Like one big happy family," Alice said, glaring back at him.

"Mommy, please come get me!" Cathy screamed from downstairs.

"I've got to get to her," Rena said, rushing over to the basement door. "Cathy, it's me, Mommy. I hear you!"

Simon removed the bag from his shoulder and tossed it at Alice's feet. "One million dollars. That was the agreement. Now give me my granddaughter."

"You skipped a generation, didn't you? I have more of your blood inside me than she does!" Alice flared, pointing to the basement door.

"There's nothing of me inside you! You're a sick animal!"

"Please, I beg you, give me the key," Rena cried out to Alice.

"You're dead! You're all dead!" Alice said, flailing her fists in the air like a child throwing a tantrum.

The sound of a gunshot rang out from upstairs and a man screamed. Several more shots were fired. Alice turned the flashlight onto the staircase and spotlit William dragging the bloodied body of Cameron down the steps by his blond hair. Rena gasped. Simon didn't move; he turned his eyes from the body and fixed them back on Alice.

"Look what I found crawling around. You were supposed to come alone, Your Holiness," William said accusingly to Simon. He had one foot up on Cameron's back and his hand to his hip, like a hunter posing for the camera with his kill. The automatic dangled from a finger of his other hand.

Rena gaped at Cameron: his head was partially blown away. Weak from fear, she sank back against the basement door, listening helplessly to the cries of Cathy. She had just seen a man die and wondered how two siblings could take a human life with no more feeling than if they had been swatting mosquitoes. She had been told by some of the best minds in her profession that heredity played no part in psychopathology; she now wondered if they knew what they were talking about. Had those two murdered before, while living in Nevada? She had to believe the answer was yes. The real question was . . . how many times?

The shots exploded in the still night, sounding like the fireworks finale in Coney Island on July Fourth. Keeping low and holding on to the hammer, Charlie raced toward the house, cursing himself for waiting this long.

Not again! Not again!

He slipped on the wet grass, got up, and ran up the cobblestone steps to the back entrance. He could tell by the beams of the flashlights darting everywhere that people were in the front room. The back door was ajar, probably jimmied open by Cameron. Charlie went into the darkness of the house hoping the shots he heard were from Cameron's gun. Please, he prayed, don't let it be the other way around!

With his hands in front of him, he felt around the room, first touching a wooden table, then a tile counter. It was the kitchen. Directly ahead, he could hear voices in another room. He went toward it until he came to the wall. He felt from side to side until he found the door. It was the kind that swung into the dining area. Pushing it carefully so it wouldn't squeak, Charlie made his way into the other room. Fragments of moving light were bleeding in from the crack of the door at the far wall. Probably leads to the living room or den, he thought.

The voices were clear now, directly on the other side of the door. He could hear Stacey—rather Alice—screaming obscenities at Simon; something to do with betrayal. Her voice was high-pitched and came in singsong waves like a small child's; nothing she said was making any sense. She was getting crazier and crazier, working herself into a fury.

Where the hell was Cameron? he thought. It then occurred to him that if Alice was still alive, then Cameron wasn't. There was no way a man like Cameron would let it get this far. That meant it was up to him now. He clutched the stainless-steel hammer, trying to shake off the fear he felt for whatever was behind the door. He had known too many crazies in his life. *Too many!*

Crouched next to the basement door, Rena felt like a spectator watching two actors on stage; everything was a blur except for the powerful presence of Simon and Alice. Rena knew there was no sanity left in Alice; she was now the little girl who was locked in that closet so many years ago. Simon, hurting, yet refusing to bend, was Lear surrounded by his daughters Regan and Cordelia.

Rena looked over to William. He was standing next to the dining-room door, watching Alice's tirade. He looked confused, not sure what to do.

Then everything happened fast. Alice took a carpet knife from her jeans pocket and rushed Simon, letting out a horrifying yell that must have erupted from the bowels of her soul. He tried warding off the blade with his arm. The knife sunk deep into his wrist. She pulled it out and plunged the razorlike blade into his stomach. Without crying out or moving his eyes away from her, he locked his big hand around her wrist, the one holding the knife still lodged inside him. He then removed his Walther PK from his jacket pocket with his other hand and brought it up to her head. For a second his face softened and a sadness appeared in his cold eyes.

The frenzied hate drained from Alice's body, too, like air being let out of a balloon. She knew and waited calmly for what was going to happen. She smiled and silently mouthed "Daddy" just as Simon pulled the trigger. Her head jerked back, and just as she fell he grabbed her and brought her gently to the floor.

"*Nooo!*" William screamed, turning his gun toward Simon. The dining-room door burst open, hitting William in the shoulder and knocking him to the ground. Charlie flew headfirst from out of the darkness of the dining room and landed on top of him. William tried to pull free, raising his gun to Charlie's face, just as the steel hammer came down with a ferocity that split open his forehead to the bridge of his nose.

Charlie rolled off him and lay on the floor for a second. He looked over at William. He was still alive and breathing, red air bubbles oozing from his broken nose.

"Charlie, please help me. Cathy's in here," Rena said frantically. She was pulling at the door again.

Charlie stood up and tried the lock. It was a cheap one. "Stand out of the way," he said to her, raising the hammer. A couple of slams and the handle broke loose. He flung the door open. It was dark inside.

"There are stairs here," Rena said.

He grabbed the light and shone it inside. The stairs led down to the pine-walled den in the basement. Black-and-white photographs of a younger Simon with Elaina and Rena as a small girl filled the walls.

"Cathy!" Rena yelled when they reached the den.

A slight whimper came from behind another door.

Charlie aimed the light beam in the direction of the sound. It was a closet.

"Oh, no!" Rena moaned.

The door was padlocked. Within minutes Charlie pushed out the bolts with the hammer, removed the door, and shone the light inside.

Cathy was sitting in the corner shivering, her arms over her eyes to block out the blinding glare of the light. The walls were painted in light violet. Rena bent down and held her, wailing, "Cathy, Cathy."

Charlie picked up the dazed and frightened child in his arms and carried her upstairs. She felt light from lack of food and dehydration. As he put her down on the sofa he looked over at Simon. He was sitting on the floor, holding Alice's head on his lap, the carpet knife protruding from his side. The sadness was still in his face.

It'll never be the same for him, Charlie thought.

Rena sat down next to Cathy, gently wiping away the dirt and tears from her face with a handkerchief.

Outside, several police cars could be heard pulling up to the driveway: their spinning red and white lights splashing across the dark walls. Car doors slammed shut and the hollow sound of two-way radios ripped through the quietness.

Charlie looked up at Rena and let out a long sigh, realizing that nothing would ever be the same for any of them again.

Epilogue

December 24

The customs line at LAX's Bradley International Terminal was unusually long, and it took the tall man in the dust-covered khakis almost an hour before it was his turn to get his bag searched.

He put his tattered leather tote on top of the counter, opening the latch so the customs agent could sift through his things. Finding nothing but soiled underwear, a pair of jeans, and a couple of shirts, the agent flipped the lid of the bag closed and looked up into the tired face of the unkempt individual standing before him. Streaks of dirt were embedded in the wrinkles around the tall man's eyes, and his long hair and red beard were in need of a trim.

"Just one bag?" the government official asked, eyeing the man up and down.

"That's right."

"Passport, please."

The man handed him a torn, shabby passport with coppery red smudges on it. The agent noticed that the nails on his fingers were long and grimy.

"This looks like bloodstains on the passport, sir," the agent said, holding it up.

"That's correct." Fatigue emanated from his voice.

The agent flipped through the stamped pages. "What were you doing in Angola? That country is off limits to American tourists." His eyes darted over to airport security, who were standing a few feet away.

The tall man sighed as he rubbed his burnt-out eyes, then

took a leather folder from his shirt pocket, opened it, and showed his ID to the agent.

The bureaucrat's face began to soften as he looked at it. "A journalist. Why didn't you say so? I heard the civil war is pretty bloody over there, even with the so-called truce."

"You heard right."

The agent looked at the name on the ID, then handed the folder back to the man. "It must be good to be home. Looks like you could use a couple of weeks' sleep, Mr. Halleran."

Charlie smiled. "I was thinking more in the range of a couple of months."

He was grateful as he stepped outside the terminal that the sky was winter gray and there was a cool breeze in the air. He had just spent five months in an African bush where the sun constantly beat down on him. He hailed a taxi, sat his weary body down on the soft seat in the rear, and gave the cabby his address. The driver drove slowly through the holiday traffic, avoiding drunken drivers coming from office Christmas parties.

The neon lights from the hotels surrounding the airport whizzed by and Charlie, feeling dizzy, closed his eyes. It must be the culture shock, he thought. Just yesterday he was watching the South African army lining up several Angolan prisoners and executing them by firing squad. Now, only twenty-four hours later, he was looking up at a billboard with a picture of a smiling Randy Newman and the electronically captioned I LOVE L.A. blinking in pastel colors above his head.

Charlie took the blood-smeared passport out of his pocket and stuck it in his tote. He had been lucky this time—luckier than he had been in 'Nam twenty years ago: the blood belonged to a UPI photographer who's stomach had been blown away by a direct hit from a grenade launcher. There was no medical help or morphine in the bush, so Charlie held the screaming man in his arms for two hours until he died. Always visions of death clouding my brain, Charlie thought, shaking his head as he ran his fingers through his hair. Christ, he had seen so much of it in the last few months! Yes, it felt good to be home, even if home meant this congested, rootless city.

Two of Rabbi Markowitz's children were throwing a softball

around on the lawn as the cab pulled up in front of the duplex. They stopped and watched Charlie get out and pay the driver.

The older boy ran up the steps, stuck his head inside the house, and yelled, "Tata, he's back!"

Rabbi Markowitz peered out the door and saw Charlie coming up the walk carrying his bag. "Ah, Mr. Halleran," he said, rubbing his hands together as he ambled down the steps. "You've come back to our humble abode. That's good. My garage feels empty without your unconscious body sprawled across its concrete floor."

Charlie smiled and they warmly shook hands. "It's good to see you, rabbi. Where's Mrs. Markowitz?"

"At the *mikvah*, where your lecherous thoughts can't reach her, thank God."

He laughed. Charlie knew the *mikvah* was a ritual bath for orthodox women that was used on the seventh day after each menstrual period.

"I like you in a beard, Mr. Halleran."

Charlie scratched the red hairs on his face. "Thanks, rabbi. I couldn't find an outlet for my electric razor in the jungle."

"No, I mean it, keep the beard," he said with a twinkle in his eye. "Put a prayer shawl over your head and no one would ever suspect you of being a goy." They walked up the path to Charlie's apartment. As he opened the door with his key the rabbi said, "We didn't know when you would be back, so my wife took the liberty of airing out your rooms once a week."

"Thanks, I appreciate it."

The smile dropped from the rabbi's mouth, and he somberly asked, "It was bad there, wasn't it?"

Charlie nodded. "It was bad."

"*Gott!* The more we learn about the world, the more expendable we make ourselves in it. What creatures we are. Go figure it out." He sighed deeply and shrugged. "Take a shower, Mr. Halleran, you need it. Oh, and Merry Christmas, my goyishe friend." With that, he slapped Charlie on the back and left.

Charlie took that shower. He stayed in the stall for over an hour, scrubbing out months of African dirt embedded in the pores of his skin. When he finally shut the water off and got out, the bathroom was misty and he had to open up the windows. He then went over to the sink, grabbed a pair of scissors from the drawer, and carefully trimmed his beard as best as he could. Looking at himself in the mirror, he decided he liked the beard and would keep it for a while.

He spent the next couple of hours going over five months of mail, then listening to his phone messages. He half hoped that Rena would have been one of the callers. She wasn't. Charlie really didn't expect her to be. It was already over between them before the *Tribune* offered him the assignment to cover the unrest in Angola.

He pulled out a six-month-old Corona from the fridge, sat down on the living-room floor, and began sifting through weeks of old newspapers that were piled up near the door, separating the ones containing his byline. He took those to the table and lined them up side by side. Charlie sipped his beer slowly and stared at his name at the top of the columns for several minutes. A smile broke out on his face; it had been a long time since he had seen his work on the front page of a reputable newspaper. The reporting was good—damn good—and his editor hinted there might be a Pulitzer in it for him. Charlie beamed. He was getting his second chance. Jaimie would have been proud.

The only thing missing from his life was Rena. Oh, well, you can't have everything, Charlie thought. Still . . . if only . . . Forget it! It was over . . . over before it really began. That night up in the Malibu hills killed any chance they had of making it.

The weeks following the killings were trying times for Rena: the pain of discovering the truth about her mother and Simon, her ex-husband's betrayal of her and his death, the humiliation of the coroner's inquest, the grand jury investigation, plus the adverse publicity heaped upon her family. Charlie knew the worst part for Rena was dealing with the effect everything had on Cathy. With all this going on, there wasn't much room left for him in her life. She decided to move to New York with Cathy for a few months to get away from everything. Charlie understood and backed off.

During that time he received offers from several tabloids to write "kiss and tell" articles about the murders and the Halbrook family. He turned them down, including an offer of fifty thousand dollars and a promise of his old job back with the *Tattler*. Soon after, Theodore von Rosmond, owner and publisher of the *L.A. Tribune*, called and offered him the job as their correspondent in Angola. Charlie was stunned; he hadn't worked as a "real" journalist in years. Why him? This was also the first time he ever heard of the owner of a newspaper with a circulation of over one million doing the hiring. "Why me?" he asked.

"Because I never forget a good writer, no matter how long it's been, and I'm in need of one now. Besides," von Rosmond said, chuckling, "I asked around in editorial circles for the name of a reporter who's crazy enough to spend several months getting shot at in a country nobody ever heard of or gives a damn about. Your name was mentioned every time."

Charlie accepted. He thought about calling Rena to share the news but decided against it. He may have understood why there was no longer a relationship between them, but that didn't mean he didn't have the right to feel hurt over it. Talking to her would only have intensified those feelings. Perhaps when he got back—if he was still alive—he would call her.

The day before he was supposed to leave for South Africa, while waiting for a light to turn green on Doheny, he saw Simon Halbrook going into Chasen's alone. He looked pale and tired, his huge body drooped over like a windblown Joshua tree. Charlie wondered if he was alone often these days. He knew he was still making lots of money, though. He later found that out from a month-old *Newsweek* he discovered lying on the floor of a Cuban-fortified bunker in the African bush. There had supposedly been a small scandal after everything came out, and for a couple of weeks the price of Morgan Industries stock had plummeted. Then people forgot or got bored with the news, and the company became more solvent than ever.

Two months ago, while on a weekend R&R in Johannesburg, Charlie went to his news bureau and called Captain Genero in New York to help him track down Rena's private number in the city. Genero phoned back ten minutes later. It was still early in Manhattan when Charlie dialed the number. After a few rings, he heard Rena's sleepy voice say, "Yes, hello?" He was about to respond when he heard another voice, a man's, asking her who it was. Charlie hung up. If there was ever any hope, that finished it. *Let it be.*

Charlie went into the kitchen, grabbed another beer, and

thought about what he wanted to do tonight. In a few hours it would be Christmas Eve. No one knew he was coming back today except his editor at the *Tribune*. Maybe he'd go down to Peppy's and have a couple of drinks. No, the drunken crowds there would not go well with his mood.

Charlie went back into the living room, put Mozart's Concerto in C Minor on the phonograph, and let the soft music filter through his head, cleaning out the memories of the past few months.

Was she back? he wondered.

He looked at his watch: 4:35. There was still time.

He lowered the music and turned on the radio, fiddling with the knob until he heard Rena's voice.

She was back!

Her show was in its last half hour. Charlie sat back on the couch and closed his eyes, listening to her silky voice, imagining she was talking just to him.

Jesus! he thought. It's like no time has passed between us at all.

Cathy had her nose pressed against the glass booth in the radio station, shoveling a Twinkie in her mouth and grinning at her mother. The half-hour news break was on. Rena shook her finger at her, motioning for Cathy to get rid of that junk food. Defiantly Cathy shook her finger back and popped the last piece in her mouth.

Rena laughed as she put the headset back on. It was good to see Cathy's sense of humor returning. Six months ago Rena hadn't had much hope of ever seeing it again. After the horrors in Malibu, she took Cathy to New York for a total change of environment. At first it seemed to be working, and to the untrained eye Cathy seemed perfectly fine. The only change in her personality was that she became somewhat withdrawn and would often be looking off into space, only half hearing what someone was saying. Rena recognized the symptoms and immediately took her to see a specialist in child trauma. Then the night terrors began, and Cathy would start screaming in her sleep, sometimes banging her fists and head against the wall. There were periods of overwhelming depression, feelings of alienation, distrust, hate—especially for her grandfather. Ativan was suggested as a tranquilizer by Cathy's psychiatrist. Rena was against medicating unless absolutely necessary and waited to see if Cathy would work her way back with the help of therapy. Eventually she did, and her terrors began to dissipate. She started laughing again, listening to music, sleeping through the night without nightmares. There would be scars from her frightful experience—there always were in cases like this—but she would survive.

New York was also a place for Rena to heal her *own* wounds. She needed the distance to put her life back into perspective, to work things out. It was hard at first to believe the truth about her family, but finally, after the police reports and the grand jury investigation, she had to accept it: her mother had been a sick, bellicose woman who murdered a child, and her father was someone she really never knew at all.

Charlie was constantly on her mind while she lived in New York. Unfortunately, because of all that took place, her attention had to be focused on Cathy. She could not give what he needed from her, and giving anything less would have been unfair to him.

She found out that he was broke. He could have made good money writing about her and her family but chose not to. She respected him a great deal for that. Rena called von Rosmond at the *Tribune* in L.A. and asked if there was room for him on the paper. At first, von Rosmond refused, stating Charlie's reputation as the reason. He remembered him as a good reporter years ago, who had become so erratic that no reputable paper would touch him. Rena was persistent and sent the publisher copies of Charlie's political articles to freshen his memory about his talent. After reading them, von Rosmond called her back and said that he'd give him a chance. A week later Charlie was in Africa.

She met Brian soon after that. He was sitting next to her at a performance of *Hamlet* at Joe Papp's theater. The timing was right: she was alone, and he was a lawyer getting over a bad divorce. There was a need, and they became friends and occasional lovers. The future was never discussed. What they had was for the moment, and they both knew it. Months later, when she was planning to return to Los Angeles, they parted on good terms.

Anthony Richardson, KROS's station manager, glowed when Rena told him she wanted her job back. He rushed out from behind his desk and embraced her in his bearlike body.

"Thank you, thank you, thank you, God!" he wailed, looking up at the ceiling. "Our ratings have been on a downhill slalom since you left." He gave her another squeeze.

She was glad to be back in the booth; that's where she belonged. The time away gave her a new outlook on the work she'd been doing. She realized it was a form of arrogance to feel that she wasn't helping people with her show. After speaking with her about their problems, most callers at least had an awareness of how to deal with them. The ones with more serious disturbances were referred to clinics to obtain extensive help, something they'd never receive without her guidance.

Her life was beginning to have an order to it again. She even felt strong enough now to deal with the upcoming murder trial of Alice's brother, William. Old wounds would have to be reopened, but she'd handle it.

After Alice's death, the Nevada authorities, upon Rena's insistence, looked into other atrocities that occurred in Las Vegas each year at the end of June. A grizzly pattern of murder and torture began to unfold. On June 28, 1982, the suffocated body of an eight-year-old girl had been found in an abandoned refrigerator. A year later, on July 13, the partially decayed corpse of a six-year-old boy was lifted out of an old mine shaft in the desert. On the same day the next year, a jogger came upon a secluded car outside the city and discovered the remains of a teenage girl in the backseat. All the windows were locked and the cause of death was listed as asphyxiation.

Originally, these deaths were treated as accidental. Rena met with the Las Vegas police and suggested that the children may have been murdered. After hearing Rena explain the importance of anniversaries in post-traumatic stress syndrome, plus her theory that Alice may have been reenacting her own suffocating environment in the closet as a child, the police reopened the cases. William was interrogated and confessed to everything, including three other murders where the bodies were never found. He had helped Alice carry out the acts because he loved her, and besides, he told them, it was fun.

Things still remained unsettled between her and Simon. Right after the grand-jury investigation, she told him that she and Cathy would be moving to New York. He wouldn't hear of it. Pacing up and down in his mansion, his footsteps echoing off the wooden floor, he demanded that they stay here, that he needed her. Rena's face flushed with anger as she told him that Cathy needed her more, thanks to him, and the best place for her was far from the ordeal she had recently gone through. He turned away in rage and she stormed out of the house.

That was the last time they talked until today. He phoned this morning and asked to see her. His voice sounded weak, the habitual sarcasm missing from it. He has seen his own fallibility, she thought.

"Do you have any plans for Christmas Eve?" he asked.

"As a matter of fact we do. Cathy and I cooked a turkey for tonight," Rena said uncomfortably.

"Perhaps we could all have dinner together," Simon said, his voice cracking.

"Cathy's not ready for that, Dad."

"Does she still hate me that much?"

"Some things take time."

"Do you?" he said somberly.

"No, but I'd be lying if I said I'm not angry and damn disappointed."

"I love her."

"I know."

"Will you tell her that?"

"I'll try."

"I'm thinking about retiring. Did you know that?"

"Yes, I heard. But I don't believe it."

"Why the hell not? Maybe I'll move to Palm Springs. Take one of those world cruises."

"I doubt it. If you didn't like what they served for breakfast, you'd wind up buying the entire cruise line so you could change the menu."

"I would, wouldn't I?" He chuckled. "Look, tell her I love her, okay? Tell her I'm sorry."

"I will."

That was this morning.

The director gave her the sign that she'd be back on the air in ten seconds. Rena looked at the clock; twenty-seven more minutes until a long weekend. She was looking forward to it.

The theme she'd chosen for today's show was loneliness during the holidays. Ironically, the happiest of occasions—Christmas and New Year's—turned out to be the most painful for a great number of people. Suicides and mental breakdowns were at a peak during this time of the year. In the studio the phones were all lit up. Melissa, the new screener for the show, pointed to the second lit button and made a gesture with her finger on her nose, meaning it was a man. Rena pushed the button down; there were too few male callers today.

"Hello, this is Dr. Rena Halbrook."

" 'Ello, Dr. Halbrook. My name's Reggie. Do you need las' names?" The man had a Northern England working-class accent.

"That won't be necessary, Reggie. How may I help you?"

"Well, ya see, doc, I 'ad this lady I was seein' when I was livin' in Liverpool. I cared for 'er a lot. Best thing that ever came into my life, she was. I'm not talkin' jus' about the sack, you know. We was good friends, too."

"What happened?" *Something odd about the accent,* she thought.

"Wrong timin' between us, I guess. Know what I mean?"

Something very odd.

"I think, maybe, if we had met at another time things would'a been different. Anyway, it's the 'olidays . . . an' I'm alone . . . and . . ."

There was a trace of a New York accent coming through the English one. Music was playing in the background; Mozart's Concerto in C Minor. The last time she'd heard that was the night she made love to Charlie.

"Now I miss 'er terribly."

My God, it's Charlie!

" 'an' I'm wonderin' if I .. if I . . ." His voice was starting to break.

"If you should call her? I think it would be a wonderful idea, Reggie." Her voice was also starting to break. "Sometimes feelings can be there but not the timing. That doesn't mean we can't go back, at least to take another look . . . not if both of you really touched at one time."

"I don' know," he said. It came out as a long sigh.

"It's Christmas, Reggie . . . a magical time of the year. Call her. You'll be surprised what might happen."

Rena smiled. She had a feeling that there would be three for turkey dinner tonight.

ABOUT THE AUTHOR

Gary Gottesfeld was born in Brooklyn, New York. He graduated from New York University with degrees in English and Theater. After working as a chief copywriter for a major advertising firm, he left to become a journalist. Gary Gottesfeld now lives in Los Angeles with his wife, Nancy, and son, Adam.